She's Come Undone

Wally Lamb

Scribner

First published by Washington Square Press, 1992
This edition published by Scribner, 1999
An imprint of Simon & Schuster UK Ltd
A Viacom Company

7 9 10 8 6

Simon & Schuster UK Ltd
Africa House
64-78 Kingsway
London WC2B 6AH

Simon & Schuster Australia
Sydney

A CIP catalogue record for this book is available
from the British Library

ISBN 0-684-86009-0

Typeset in Sabon by SX Composing DTP, Rayleigh, Essex
Printed and bound in Great Britain by
Cox & Wyman Ltd, Reading, Berkshire.

'Chiquita Banana' by Leonard MacKenzie, Jr., William Wirges, and Garth Montgomery

'Both Sides Now' by Joni Mitchell

'Tonight's the Night (It's Gonna Be Alright)' by Rod Stewart

'Everyday People' by Sylvester Stewart

'Lover Man (Oh Where Can You Be)' by Roger J. (Ram) Ramirez, Jimmy Davis, and Jimmy Sherman

'I'm a Man' by Steve Winwood and Jeremy Miller

'Mockingbird' by Inez Foxx and Charles Foxx

'Undun' by Randy Bachman and Burton Cummings

To Christine,
who laughed and cried and lent me
to these characters.

Grateful acknowledgment is extended to the Connecticut Commission on the Arts and to the Norwich Free Academy for their generous support of this project.

Thanks to the following, whose encouragement and/or critical response helped shape the book:

Lary Bloom, Theodore Deppe, Barbara Dombrowski, Joan Joffe Hall, Jane Hill, Terese Karmel, Nancy Lagomarsino, Ken Lamothe, Linda Lamothe, Eugenia Leftwich, Ann Z. Leventhal, Pam Lewis, Ethel Mantzaris, Faith Middleton, David Morse, Nancy Potter, Wanda Rickerby, Joan Seliger Sidney, Gladys Swan, and Gordon Weaver.

I also thank John Longo, former third-floor custodian at the University of Connecticut's Homer Babbidge Library, who shared his lunch and conversation with me during the seven summers this story came together and who later taught me a lesson about courage.

I am grateful that this novel fell into the loving care of my agents and friends, Linda Chester and Laurie Fox, whose sharp eyes and warm hearts helped me to prepare the story.

And finally I extend special thanks to my editor and *paisana*, Judith Regan, who, while cradling her week-old daughter Lara in one arm and my manuscript in the other, decided to midwife this novel.

Our day will come
If we just wait awhile . . .

– Ruby and the
Romantics

Toward dawn we shared with you
your hour of desolation,
    the huge lingering passion
        of your unearthly outcry,
as you swung your blind head
    toward us and laboriously opened
        a bloodshot, glistening eye,
in which we swam with terror and recognition.

– From 'The Wellfleet Whale'
by Stanley Kunitz

PART ONE

Our Lady of Sorrow

Chapter 1

In one of my earliest memories, my mother and I are on the front porch of our rented Carter Avenue house watching two delivery men carry our brand-new television set up the steps. I'm excited because I've heard about but never seen television. The men are wearing work clothes the same color as the box they're hefting between them. Like the crabs at Fisherman's Cove, they ascend the cement stairs sideways. Here's the undependable part: my visual memory stubbornly insists that these men are President Eisenhower and Vice President Nixon.

Inside the house, the glass-fronted cube is uncrated and lifted high onto its pedestal. 'Careful, now,' my mother says, in spite of herself; she is not the type to tell other people their business, men particularly. We stand watching as the two delivery men do things to the set. Then President Eisenhower says to me, 'Okay, girlie, twist this button here.' My mother nods permission and I approach. 'Like this,' he says, and I feel, simultaneously, his calloused hand on my hand and, between my fingers, the turning plastic knob, like one of the checkers in my father's checker set. (Sometimes when my father's voice gets too loud at my mother, I go out to the parlor and put a checker in my mouth – suck it, passing my tongue over the grooved edge.) Now, I hear and feel the machine snap on. There's a hissing sound, voices inside the box. 'Dolores, look!' my mother says. A star appears at the center of the green glass face. It grows outward and becomes two women at a kitchen table, the owners of the voices. I begin to cry. Who shrank these women?

Are they alive? Real? It's 1956; I'm four years old. This isn't what I've expected. The two men and my mother smile at my fright, delight in it. Or else, they're sympathetic and consoling. My memory of that day is, like television itself, sharp and clear but unreliable.

We hadn't bought the set; it was a gift from Mrs. Masicotte, the rich widow who was my father's boss. My father and Mrs. Masicotte's relationship had started the previous spring, when she'd hired him to spray-paint several of her huge apartment houses and then wooed him into repainting his own pickup truck in her favorite color, peach, and stenciling the words 'Masicotte Properties, General Manager' on the doors. The gift of the television celebrated my father's decision.

If I reach far back, I can see my father waving to my mother and me and climbing down from his ladder, spray gun in hand, as we arrive with his lunch in our turquoise-and-white car. Daddy reaches the ground and pulls off his face mask. The noise of his chugging orange air compressor is in my throat and legs, the sudden silence when he unplugs it delicious. There are speckles of paint in his hair and ears and eyebrows, but the mask has protected the rest of his face. I look away when his clean mouth talks.

We lunch in the grass. My father eats sandwiches stuffed with smelly foods Ma and I refuse to eat: liverwurst, vinegar peppers, Limburger cheese. He drinks hot coffee right from the thermos and his Adam's apple moves up and down when he swallows. He talks about 'she' in a way that confuses me: 'she' is either this half-white house of Mrs. Masicotte's or the old woman herself.

Old. I'm almost forty, probably as close now to Mrs. Masicotte's age as I am to the age of my parents as they sat on that lawn, laughing and blowing dandelion puffs at me, smoking their shared Pall Mall cigarettes and thinking Mrs. Masicotte was the answer to their future – that that black-and-white Emerson television set was a gift free and clear of the strings that would begin our family's unraveling.

*

Television watching became my habit, my day. 'Go out back and play, Dolores. You'll burn that thing up,' my mother would warn, passing through the parlor. But my palm against the box felt warm, not hot; soothing, not dangerous like the boy across the street who threw rocks. Sometimes I turned the checker knob as far as it would go and let the volume shake my hand.

Ma always stopped her housework for our favorite program, 'Queen for a Day.' We sat together on the sofa, my leg hooked around Ma's, and listened to the women whose children were crippled by polio, whose houses had been struck by lightning and death and divorce. The one with the saddest life, the loudest applause, got to trade her troubles for a velvet cape and roses and modern appliances. I clapped along with the studio audience – longest and hardest for the women who broke down and cried in the middle of their stories. I made my hands sting for these women.

My father's duties as Mrs. Masicotte's manager, in addition to painting the outsides and insides of her properties, included answering tenants' complaints and collecting their monthly rents. The latter he did on the first Saturday of every month, driving from house to house in Mrs. Masicotte's peach-colored Cadillac. By the time I was a first grader, I was declared old enough to accompany him. My job was to ring tenants' bells. None seemed happy to see my father and most failed to notice me at all as I peeked past them into their shadowy rooms, inhaling their cooking smells, eavesdropping on their talking TVs.

Mrs. Masicotte was a beer drinker who loved to laugh and dance; the package store was one of our regular Saturday afternoon errands. 'Case o' Rheingold, bottles,' my father would tell the clerk, an old man whose name, Cookie, struck me funny. Cookie always offered me a cellophane-wrapped butterscotch candy and, by virtue of Mrs. Masicotte's order, a chance to vote for Miss Rheingold at the cardboard ballot box next to his cash register. (Time after time I voted for the same Rheingold girl, whose dark brown hair and red-lipped smile reminded me both of Gisele MacKenzie from 'Your Hit Parade' and my own mother, the best looking of the three.)

My father was proud and protective of his own dark good looks. I remember having sometimes to hop around and hold my pee until he was finished with his long grooming behind the pink bathroom door on Carter Street. When he emerged, I'd stand on the stool amidst the steam and the aroma of uncapped Old Spice, watching my face wobble and drip in the medicine cabinet mirror. Daddy lifted barbells in the cellar – barefoot, wearing his undershirt and yellow bathing suit. Sometimes he'd strut around the kitchen afterward, popping his muscle at Ma or picking up the toaster to give his reflection a kiss. 'You're not conceited, you're *convinced!*' Ma would joke. 'Convinced *you*, all right, didn't I?' he'd answer, then chase her around the kitchen, snapping the dish towel at her fanny and mine. Ma and I whooped and protested, delighted with his play.

After the television came, Daddy brought his barbells upstairs and exercised in front of his favorite programs. Quiz shows were what he liked: 'The $64,000 Question,' 'Tic Tac Dough,' 'Winner Take All.' Sometimes in the middle of his grunting and thrusting he'd call out the answers to losing players or, if they blew their chances, swear at them. 'Well,' he'd tell my mother, 'another poor bastard bites the dust, another poor slob gets to stay a working stiff like the rest of us.' He hated returning champions and rooted for their defeat. His contempt for them seemed somehow connected to his ability to lift the weights.

According to my father, *we* should have been rich. Money was, in his mind, somehow due us and would have been ours had his simple parents not sold their thirty acres on Fisherman's Cove for $3,000 to a Mr. Weiss the month before drowning in the Great Hurricane of 1938. During the Depression, when my father was coming of age, Fisherman's Cove had been just marsh grass, wild blueberry bushes, and cabins with outhouses; by the time he went to work for Mrs. Masicotte, it was the cozy residence of millionaires. These included Mr. Weiss's son, who lived two driveways down from Mrs. Masicotte and golfed for a living.

My father forgave Mrs. Masicotte her wealth because she was generous with it – 'spread it around,' as he put it. In those early years, the television was only the first in a stream of presents that included a swing set for me, kitcheny things for my mother (a set of maroon-colored juice glasses, a black ice bucket with brass claw feet), and, for my father, gifts he wore home from the big house on the cove: a houndstooth sports jacket, leather gloves lined in genuine rabbit's fur, and my favorite – a wristwatch with a Twist-O-Flex band you could bend but not break.

'That's it, Jewboy, add another couple thousand to your stash,' my father shouted at the TV one night, in the middle of his exercise routine. 'The $64,000 Question' was on; a champion with round eyeglasses and shiny cheeks had just emerged victorious from the Revlon isolation booth.

'Don't say that, Tony,' my mother protested.

His eyes jumped from the screen to her. The weights wavered above his head. 'Don't say *what*?'

Ma pointed her chin toward me. 'I don't want her hearing things like that,' she said.

'Don't say *what*?' he repeated.

'All right, nothing. Just forget it.' Ma left the room. The barbell clanged to the floor, so loudly and surprisingly that my heart heaved in my chest. He followed her into the bedroom.

Earlier that week he'd brought home from Mrs. Masicotte's a thick art tablet and a tiered box of Crayola crayons. Now I opened the clean pad to a middle page and drew the face of a beautiful woman. I gave her long curling eyelashes, red lipstick, 'burnt sienna'-colored hair, a crown. 'Hello,' the woman said to me. 'My name is Peggy. My favorite color is magenta.'

'Don't you ever – *ever!* – tell me what I can and cannot say in the privacy of my own home,' my father shouted from behind their door.

Ma kept crying and apologizing.

Later, after he'd stomped past me and driven away, Ma
soaked herself in the tub – long past my bedtime, long enough
for me to fill up half the pad with Peggy's life.

She usually shooed me out when I caught her naked, but
Daddy's anger had left her far away and careless. The ashtray
sat on the edge of the tub, filled with stubbed-out Pall Malls; the
bathroom was thick with smoke that moved when I moved.

'See my lady?' I said. I meant the drawings as a sort of
comfort, but she told me they were nice without really looking.

'Is Daddy mean?' I asked.

She took so long to answer that I thought she might not have
heard. 'Sometimes,' she said, finally.

Her breasts appeared and disappeared at the surface of the
soapy water. I'd never had the chance to study them before. Her
nipples looked like Tootsie Rolls.

'He gets mean when he feels unhappy.'

'Why does he feel unhappy?'

'Oh . . .' she said. 'You're too little to understand.'

She turned abruptly toward me and caught me watching her
shiny, wet breasts. Sloshing, she strapped her arms around
herself and became, again, my proper mother. 'Go on,
skedaddle,' she said. 'Daddy's not mean. What are you talking
about?'

Mrs. Masicotte's tenants paid their rents in cash, counting
series of twenty-dollar bills into my father's outstretched hand.
On the best Saturdays, after Mrs. Masicotte's leather zip bag
was filled with money, Daddy would turn his attention to me.
He liked the way television watching had made me a mimic.

I'm Chiquita Banana and I've come to say
Bananas have to ripen in a certain way
Drive your CHEV-rolet
Through the U-S.A.
America's the greatest land of all!

Over and over, I sang the jingles he liked best. Sometimes we played 'wild ride' on the twisting roads that led out to Fisherman's Cove. I sat in the backseat of the car, a sort of junior Mrs. Masicotte, and commanded my father to speed. 'Okay, ma'am, you ready, ma'am? Here we go!' I'd grab the peach velvet cord strapped across the rear of the front seat rests as Daddy gunned the car around corners and lurched over rises in the road. 'Feel those blue-blooded shock absorbers, Dolores? We could be sitting in our living room.' Or this, which he told me once: 'This car is *ours!* I bought this showboat from the old lady.' I could smell Mrs. Masicotte's perfumy smell embedded in the soft upholstery and knew it wasn't true, even back then when I would fall for almost anything – when I thought that, like Lucy and Ricky Ricardo, my parents' fights just meant they loved each other in a noisy way.

The Saturday errands ended each week at the top of the long driveway on Jefferson Drive, where Mrs. Masicotte's white wedding cake of a house looked down on Long Island Sound. We entered through the dark, cool cement garage, the Cadillac doors slamming louder than any before or since. We walked up the stairs and opened the door without knocking. On the other side was Mrs. Masicotte's peach-colored kitchen, which made me squint. 'Mind your manners, now,' Daddy never failed to warn me. 'Say thank you.'

It was in that kitchen where I waited for Daddy and Mrs. Masicotte to be finished with the weekly business, two rooms away. Though Mrs. Masicotte seemed as indifferent to me as her renters were, she provided richly for me while I waited. On hand were plates of bakery cookies, thick picture books with shiny pages, punch-out paper dolls. My companion during these vigils was Zahra, Mrs. Masicotte's fat tan cocker spaniel, who sat at my feet and watched, unblinking, as cookies traveled mercilessly from the plate to my mouth.

Mrs. Masicotte and my father laughed and talked loud during their meetings and sometimes played the radio. (Our radio at home was a plastic box; Mrs. Masicotte's was a piece of furniture.) 'Are we going soon?' I'd ask Daddy whenever he came out to the kitchen to check on me or get them another pair of Rheingolds. 'A few minutes,' was what he always said, no matter how much longer they were going to be.

I wanted my father to be at home laughing with Ma on Saturday afternoons, instead of with Mrs. Masicotte, who had yellowy white hair and a fat little body like Zahra's. My father called Mrs. Masicotte by her first name, LuAnn; Ma called her, simply, 'her.' 'It's her,' she'd tell Daddy whenever the telephone interrupted our dinner.

Sometimes, when the meetings dragged on unreasonably or when they laughed too loud in there, I sat and dared myself to do naughty things, then did them. One time I scribbled on all the faces in the expensive storybooks. Another Saturday I waterlogged a sponge and threw it at Zahra's face. Regularly, I tantalized the dog with the cookies I made sure stayed just out of her reach. My actions – each of which invited my father's anger – shocked and pleased me.

I had long hair the year I was in second grade. Mornings before school, my mother combed the snarls out of my ponytail and dosed me with half a teaspoon of Maalox to calm my nervous stomach. My teacher, Mrs. Nelkin, was a screamer. I spent most of the school year trying to be obedient – filling in every blank on every worksheet correctly, silently sliding oaktag word builders across my desktop, talking to no one.

'Oh, don't worry about that old biddy,' my mother advised. 'Just think about the baby coming instead.'

My baby brother or sister was due to arrive in February of 1958. When I asked my parents how the baby got inside Ma, they both laughed, and then Daddy told me they had made it with their bodies. I pictured them fully clothed, rubbing furiously against each other, like two sticks making fire.

All fall and winter long, I coaxed bottles toward the mouth of my Baby Dawn doll and scrubbed her rubber skin in lukewarm water in the bathroom sink. I wanted a girl and

Daddy wanted a boy. Ma didn't care one way or the other, so long as it was healthy. 'How will it get out?' I asked her one day near the end of the wait. 'Oh, never mind,' was all she said. I imagined her lying on a hospital bed, calm and smiling, her huge stomach splitting down the middle like pants.

At breakfast time on the morning of the school Valentine's Day party, Ma decided to rearrange the silverware drawer – a task that upset her enough to make her cry.

The valentine party turned out to be a fifteen-minute disappointment at the end of the long school day. As it drew to a close and we pulled on our boots and coats and stocking hats, Mrs. Nelkin approached me. She told me to remain at my desk when the dismissal bell rang; my father had telephoned the school to say he'd pick me up. I sat in the silence of the empty classroom with my hat and coat on and a stack of valentines in my lap. With the other kids gone, you could hear the scraping sound of the clock hands. Mr. Horvak, the janitor, muttered and swept up the crumbs our party had made and Mrs. Nelkin corrected papers without looking up.

It was Grandma Holland from Rhode Island – my mother's mother – who appeared for me finally at the classroom door. She and Mrs. Nelkin whispered together at the front of the room in a way that made me wonder if they knew each other. Then, in a sweeter voice than I was used to, Mrs. Nelkin told me I could go home.

We *didn't* go home, though. Grandma led me down the two flights of school stairs and out into a taxicab, which took us to St. Paul's Cathedral. On the way there she told me my mother had had to go to a big hospital in Hartford because of 'female trouble' and that my father had gone with her. Ma would be gone for at least two weeks and she, Grandma, would take care of me. There just wasn't any baby anymore and that was that. We were having creamed dried beef for supper.

The church's stained-glass saints had the same tortured look as the women on 'Queen for a Day.' Grandma took out her kidney-bean rosary and muttered the stations of the cross while

I followed her, spilling valentines and accidentally kicking the wooden pews, raising up echoes. The candles we lit sat in maroon cups that reminded me of our juice glasses from Mrs. Masicotte. I wasn't allowed to handle the flame. My job was to drop the coins into the metal box, two dimes for two candles, clink clink.

When Daddy came home that night, he lay in my bed with me and read my valentines. He looked up at the ceiling when he talked about Ma. Somehow, he said, she had grown a cord in her stomach along with the baby. (I pictured the backseat cord in Mrs. Masicotte's Cadillac.) Just as the baby was coming out, it wrapped the cord around its neck and strangled itself. *Himself*. A boy – Anthony Jr. As my father talked, tears dripped down the side of his face like candle wax. The sight shocked me; until that moment, I had assumed men were as incapable of crying as they were of having babies.

I didn't like having Grandma there. She slept in a cot in my room and boiled all our suppers. It was unsanitary, she said, the way Daddy drank right out of the water bottle and then put it back in the Frigidaire. It was shameful that her only granddaughter had reached the age of seven without having been taught to pray. She was sick, she said, of the same old question: when was my mother coming home? She was trying her best.

Grandma crocheted as she watched TV, frowning alternately at what was on the screen and what was in her lap. She like different programs than us. On her favorite, 'The Edge of Night,' a rich woman had secretly killed a man by sticking an ice pick in his neck, but a pretty woman from a poor family was on trial for the murder. 'Look at Mrs. High and Mighty,' Grandma said, her eyes narrowing on the murderess who sat undetected in the courtroom gallery. 'She's as guilty as sin.'

My talent for mimicry came in handy with Grandma. I memorized for her the Ten Commandments and a prayer called Hail Holy Queen, about people gnashing their teeth in a scary place called the Valley of Tears. Wide-eyed, Grandma promised she would see to it that I made my first Holy Communion so that I could wear a beautiful white dress and veil and eat the body of Christ. Every morning she dismissed my fears, arguing that little girls of my age were too young to have Maalox and then sending me off unprotected to Mrs. Nelkin.

The day before my mother was due at last to come home from the hospital, Daddy gave me permission to miss school. He and I loaded Anthony Jr.'s toys and crib and bassinet into the back of the peach pickup and drove to the dump. On the way there he told me our job was to cheer Ma up and not even mention the baby. This struck me as reasonable. It wasn't her fault the baby was dead; it was Anthony Jr.'s own stupid fault.

Daddy flung the new mint-green furniture onto a pile of old mattresses and empty paint cans and got back into the truck, breathing hard. He drove fast over the rutty dump road and I bounced against the seat and door. Seagulls flew out of our way; people stood up from their garbage to watch us. I looked back at Anthony Jr.'s unused things receding quickly from us and understood for the first time the waste of his life.

My father drove toward Fisherman's Cove.

'Oh, no, not her again,' I complained. 'How long is this going to take?'

But instead of turning in at the bottom of the long driveway on Jefferson Drive, Daddy went right past it, then took a different road.

He parked at the vacant boat launch. We walked out onto a rickety dock and stood, side by side. The cold spring breeze snapped his nylon windbreaker.

'See out there?' he said. He pointed to the ripply gray water of Long Island Sound. 'Once when I was a kid about your age, I saw a whale right out past that red buoy. It was headed south and got confused. Stuck in the shallow water.'

'What happened?'

'Nothing bad. Swam around for a couple of hours with everybody looking at it. Then, at high tide, a few of the bigger boats drove in and nudged it back to sea.'

He sat down on one of the pilings looking sick and sad and I

knew he was thinking about Ma and the baby. I wanted badly
to cheer him up but singing commercials seemed the wrong
thing to do.

'Daddy, listen,' I said. 'I am the Lord thy God, thou shalt not
have strange gods before thee . . .' He watched me uneasily as I
recited the words of Grandma's Commandments, as big and
empty as the Pledge of Allegiance Mrs. Nelkin led each day.
'. . . Thou shalt not covet thy neighbor's wife. Thou shalt not
covet thy neighbor's goods.' He waited for me to finish. Then
he told me it was too cold to be out there, to get in the
goddamned truck.

My mother arrived home, puffy-eyed, her stomach empty under
the maternity blouse. The whole house filled up with the smell
of carnations from Mrs. Masicotte. What Ma wanted most, she
said, was to be left alone.

She stayed in her pajamas past spring vacation, smiling
absentmindedly at my stories and puppet shows, my television
jingles and complaints. 'Leave her alone, now,' Grandma kept
saying. 'Stop plaguing her.' Grandma herself showed no signs
of packing.

One day at school, Howard Hancin, my seatmate, raised his
hand. Up to that moment, I'd felt neutral toward Howard, so I
was completely unprepared when Mrs. Nelkin asked him what
he wanted and he said, 'Dolores Price is chewing on her word
builders. She chews them every single day.'

The entire class turned to stare.

I was about to deny it when I looked down and realized it was
absolutely true: the cardboard letters on my desk were bent and
misshapen and several were still dark with my saliva. There
was, as well, a word builder stuck to the inside of my cheek,
even as Mrs. Nelkin approached. I was guilty as sin.

She didn't scream. She scarcely raised her voice as she
addressed Howard and, by extension, the others in the class and
me. 'I suppose she thinks this is fine and dandy. I suppose she

thinks school supplies grow on trees and that I'll just reach up and pick her a new box of them. But I won't, will I, Howard? She'll just have to make do with her shabby ones for the rest of the year. Won't she?'

Howard didn't answer. Mrs. Nelkin walked back up our row, heels clicking against the waxed wooden floor. She picked up a stick of chalk. The loose skin under her arm rocked back and forth as she wrote. I didn't breathe until I saw that the words said nothing about me.

When I got home, I heard my father shouting in my parents' bedroom and ran to the safety of the parlor. He was god-damned fed up with this sob-sister business. It was his baby, too, for Christ's sweet sake. Enough was enough. The front door slammed and Grandma's footsteps went from the kitchen to my parents' room. Ma wailed and wailed; Grandma's voice was a murmur.

The television was on; a man in a suit was talking about World War II. I flopped down on the sofa, too exhausted to change the channel.

Bombs spilled from the bottom of an airplane, soldiers waved in a parade, and then something scared me in a way I'd never quite been scared before – not even the night Daddy had thrown the barbell. On the screen, skeleton men wearing diapers were trudging up a hill. Their sunken eyes seemed to be looking at me personally, watching and beckoning me from Grandma's Valley of Tears. I wanted to turn off the TV, but was afraid even to go near it. I waited for the commercial, then locked the bathroom door and sipped Maalox out of the bottle.

That night I woke up screaming from a dream in which Mrs. Nelkin took me on a picnic, then calmly and matter-of-factly informed me the sandwiches we were eating contained the flesh of my dead baby brother.

Daddy was the first one into my room – wild-haired and stumbling, wearing his underpants right in front of Grandma. She was the second one in. Then Ma. I felt suddenly powerful and excited; I kept screaming.

Ma held me and rocked. 'Shh, now. Easy. Just tell me what it is. Just say it.'

'It's *her*,' I said. 'I hate her.'

'Hate who, honey?' Daddy asked. 'Who do you hate?' He squatted down on his haunches, the better to hear my answer.

I had meant Mrs. Nelkin, but changed my mind as I spoke. I reached past him and pointed at Grandma, standing pinch-faced in her brown corduroy robe. 'Her,' I said. 'I want her to go home.'

The next day was Saturday. I was watching morning cartoons in the parlor when Ma came out of her bedroom fully dressed and asked me what I wanted for breakfast.

'Pancakes,' I said, as if the last months had been normal ones. 'Where's Daddy?'

'He's driving Grandma back to Rhode Island.'

'She's gone?'

My mother nodded. 'She left while you were still sleeping. She said to tell you good-bye.'

I could banish Grandma Holland with my newfound power, but not Mrs. Masicotte. Instead, I went each Saturday to her house, thanked her sweetly for her presents, and kept watch.

One afternoon, Mrs. Masicotte provided me with a scissors, a Betsy McCall paper-doll book, and the usual plate of sugar cookies. I ate a few of the cookies, teased Zahra with a few more, then set to work punching Betsy away from the cardboard page. I scissored the booklet's prettiest outfit and hung it off her front. 'Look, Zahra!' I commanded the cocker spaniel.

I carried Betsy over to the stove, turned on the gas jet, and held her in the blue flame. Somehow, I knew that, of all the mischief I'd done at Mrs. Masicotte's house, this was the worst, the thing that would make my father as angry with me as he could get with Ma. 'Help me!' Betsy pleaded. Her paper clothes caught the flame, browned and buckled. 'Zahra, help me! Help me!'

My intention was to shock, or at least entertain, the bloated dog, but when I looked back, she was staring still at the cookies with such intensity that I forgot, for a second, the flame, and burned my thumb and finger.

Mine is a story of craving: an unreliable account of lusts and troubles that began, somehow, in 1956 on the day our free television was delivered. Many times each week memory makes me a child again. Just last night I was, once more, in Mrs. Masicotte's kitchen, turning from the flaming paper doll to learn from the fat dog Zahra my first lesson in the awful strength of coveting, the power of want.

'Look, Zahra! I'm dying!' I moan. 'Help me! Please!'

The dog – riveted, unblinking – sees only the sugar-crusted cookies.

Chapter 2

When I was ten and a half, my family moved to Treetop Acres, a flat, freshly paved neighborhood, good for bike riding.

Our yellow ranch house, 26 Bobolink Drive, had a garage and a bathroom shower with sliding glass doors. Outside my bedroom window, a weeping willow tree tossed and switched its branches against the shingles on windy nights. We owned, not rented, this house.

Mrs. Masicotte was part owner of Treetop Acres and had finagled us a double lot. By this time, she'd bought a new silver Cadillac and given Daddy her old peach one and a set of golf clubs and a membership to her country club. Part of my father's work now included golfing with Mrs. Masicotte on weekends.

When he wasn't with the old lady, Daddy was out in back working on his lawn – leveling and seeding it, whistling as he wheelbarrowed dirt from one end of our lot to the other. He was proud of the fact that we had twice as much yard as any of our neighbors. He worked every night until dark – until he faded from himself to a dusky silhouette, then a glowing white undershirt moving on its own will, then just whistling.

Ma pressed and hung curtains and planted a small bed of pink dahlias out back, but the flowers only made her briefly happy. The new house gave her allergies, she complained; she began squirting her nose with nasal spray several times a day. The toddlers that played unsupervised on our quiet street made her jumpy. All her nerves needed, she said, was to back that goddamned Cadillac out of the driveway some day and run over someone's small child.

Jeanette Nord, my new best friend, lived at 10 Skylark Place, eight-tenths of a mile from our house, according to the odometer on my pink Schwinn. I met Jeanette on my very first spin around the neighborhood. Spotting a girl my approximate age hula-hooping on a patio, I decided to impress her with my cycling skills, then miscalculated a curb, landing, mortified, under my still-spinning wheels. 'Guess what?' Jeanette said as she hula-hooped toward me, oblivious to my bleeding knees. 'One of my Siamese cats is going to have kittens.'

Jeanette and I marveled at the similarities between us: we were both born in October, one year apart; we were both left-handed only children with twelve letters in our names; each of us favored Dr. Kildare over Ben Casey; our favorite dessert was Whip-and-Chill; our favorite record 'Johnny Angel.' We differed significantly in only two respects: Jeanette had gotten her period and had permission to shave her legs. I was still waiting for both. That spring and summer, Jeanette and I watched soap operas, swapped 45s, and planned out a shared life. After high school, we'd get an apartment together in New York and be either secretaries or Rockettes. Then Jeanette would marry a veterinarian named Ross and I'd marry an actor named either Scott or Todd. Our five children apiece would all be best friends. We'd live in next-door mansions and be rich enough for air-conditioning and color TV.

The Nords owned both the father and mother Siamese cats, Samson and Delilah. Mr. Nord, bald and boring, sold equipment to hospitals and was gone a lot on overnight trips. Mrs. Nord wore eye shadow and headbands that matched her shell tops and Bermudas. For lunch she made us foods she'd seen in the pages of her women's magazines: baked hot dogs coated in crushed Special K; English muffin pizzas; Telstar coolers (lemonade and club soda afloat with a toothpick-speared maraschino cherry – a sort of edible satellite that jabbed your lip as you drank). Mrs. Nord knew the words to

Jeanette's and my favorite songs. She taught first herself, then us, how to do the twist. ('Look! Just put your foot forward and pretend you're crushing out a cigarette from the hips. That's right!') If you squinted while looking at her from across a room, you would swear Mrs. Nord was Jackie Kennedy. My own mother sat alone on Bobolink Drive all day, talking to her parakeet, Petey, and worrying about dead children.

Around the time of our move to Bobolink Drive, I stopped kissing my mother on the lips. It had been over four years since she'd lost the baby. Daddy had tried everything to snap her out of it: cha-cha lessons, 'head-shrinkers,' a trip to the Poconos, Petey. But something about Anthony Jr.'s life and death inside Ma had changed her in some unfixable way. She'd grown herself a big rear end and developed an unpredictable facial twitch. When we grocery shopped, I ran to get items in the aisles ahead rather than be seen with her. When PTA notices were passed out at school, I folded and folded them until they were chubby little one-inch packets, easily crammed between the school-bus seats. 'Oh, my mother works,' I told Jeanette when she suggested we go over to my house instead of hers. 'She doesn't like me having company when she's not home.' But she *was* at home, practising her series of curious domestic habits. She needed, for instance, to let the phone ring three and a half times before answering it. She needed the stove timer to be constantly ticking off seconds. (Whenever the dial reached zero and dinged, she reset it for sixty minutes, then smiled with some inner, secret relief.) Petey was Ma's weirdest need of all.

Daddy had bought her the lime-green parakeet at the suggestion of the doctor Ma went to see for her nerves; he said a distraction might help. At first Ma didn't like Petey and complained about the mess he made. Then she liked him. Then she began loving him beyond reason. She sang to him, talked to him, and rigged his cage open with a rubber band so he could flutter freely around the house whenever Daddy wasn't home. Ma was happiest when Petey was perched on her shoulder during the day. I would sit at the kitchen table eating my lunch or drawing and watch her crane her neck to the right or left, stroking Petey with the underside of her chin. She was most miserable at night after supper when she and Daddy and I sat in the living room watching TV and Petey sat out in the kitchen, his cage covered over with a bath towel. 'Jesus H. Christ, would you just sit still,' Daddy would complain as she got up to check Petey one more time. Then Ma would slump back into the sofa cushions, teary-eyed and distracted. I hated Petey – fantasized about his flying accidentally out a window or into the electric fan so that his spell over Ma would be broken. My not kissing Ma anymore was a conscious decision reached one night at bedtime with the purpose of hurting her.

'Well, you're stingy tonight,' she said when I turned my face away from her good-night kiss.

'I'm not kissing you anymore, period,' I told her. 'All day long you kiss that bird right on its filthy beak.'

'I do not.'

'You do so. Maybe *you* want to catch bird diseases, but I don't.'

'Petey's mouth is probably cleaner than my mouth and yours put together, Dolores,' was her argument.

'That's a laugh.'

'Well, it's true. I read it in my bird book.'

'Next thing you know, you'll be French-kissing it.'

'Never mind French-kissing. What do you know about that kind of stuff? You watch that mouth of yours, young lady.'

'That's exactly what I'm doing,' I said. I clamped my hand over my mouth and stuffed my whole face into the pillow.

It was Jeanette who had defined French-kissing for me, voluntarily appointing herself my mentor the day we watched her cat Samson licking his erect penis on the Nords' living-room rug.

'Love of Life' was on TV. Mrs. Nord was upstairs running her sewing machine, making static lines across the picture. Jeanette was reentering the room with two Telstar drinks on a tray. 'Oh my God,' I said.

'What?'

She followed my gaze to Samson, who lapped casually at himself.

Jeanette handed me my drink. 'Aren't boys disgusting?' She laughed. We both stared at the licking.

'Maybe you should call a vet,' I suggested.

'What for? He's just giving his hoo-hoo a hard-on.'

'What?'

She laughed again and took a long sip of her drink. 'Can I ask you a personal question?' she said.

'What?'

'How much do you know?'

'Enough,' I said. I wasn't sure, exactly, what we were talking about but sensed the vicinity.

'I don't mean how much you know in general. I mean about sex.'

'You writing a book?' I said. 'Make that chapter a mystery.'

'Okay, fine,' she said. 'Pardon me for living.'

We returned our attention back to 'Love of Life.' Vanessa Sterling was arguing with her stepdaughter, Barbara, who was secretly pregnant with Tony Vento's baby. I took a quick peek at Samson, still at it. 'I just thought,' Jeanette said, her eyes on the screen, 'that if you had any questions, I could probably answer them for you.'

'Well, I don't.'

'Well, good. Fine with me.'

After a commercial, Barbara and Tony were sitting in a park with fake-looking scenery. Neither of them knew what to do about the baby, but marriage was out of the question. Tony was only a mechanic. His mother was Barbara's family's maid.

'Do you think Tony's cute?' Jeanette asked.

'Sort of. Do you?'

'I wouldn't throw him out of bed.'

I reached into my Telstar drink and fished out the cherry,

determined not to betray a reaction.

'Can you imagine them actually *doing* it?' Jeanette said.

Samson rose and stretched, ambled out of the room.

'Who?'

'Them. Barbara and Tony. Maybe they do it in real life after the show. Maybe it's not acting.'

I felt heat in my face; I felt her watching me.

'You don't know how women get pregnant, do you?'

'I do so.' On the screen, Barbara covered her face with her hands and cried. Tony punched the trunk of one of the fake trees.

My information about sex was a mosaic of eavesdropping, process of elimination, and filling in the blanks. In third grade I'd heard the term 'sleeping together' and spent time worrying that accidental fatigue could make an unwanted child – that male and female strangers sharing a seat together on an overnight train might innocently doze off and wake up as parents. For a while I'd believed that people got pregnant by rubbing their chests together. Men used their you-know-whats to go to the bathroom, I reasoned; it was their nipples that had no other useful function. (My teacher that year, Mrs. Hatheway, was pregnant. As she talked, I'd imagine her engaged with some blank-faced husband in the required nipple friction that had put a baby inside her.) Currently I knew the basics about periods and virginity. But Samson's licking had shown both me and Jeanette the incompleteness of my knowledge.

'This show is boring today,' she said. 'Let's go for a ride.'

Our bikes ticked and whirred through Treetop Acres and Jeanette told me what happened the day she woke up with her period. First Mrs. Nord had taken Jeanette shopping and bought her a skirt and a circle pin. Then they'd gone to a restaurant and had club sandwiches and Mrs. Nord had said, 'Look at us, two women having lunch together.' Then she'd just come out with it: a man and a woman got naked and French-kissed until the man's hoo-hoo got hard. Then he put it in the woman's hoo-hoo and squirted something liquidy into her. Not pee; something that looked like White Rain shampoo, according to her mother. Then she was pregnant.

The restaurant wasn't that crowded, Jeanette said, and they were in a booth way in back. Her mother stopped talking whenever the waitress came over.

Back in her bedroom, Jeanette kept talking about sex.

'True or false,' she said. 'The woman can still get pregnant if she and the man both keep their underpants on.'

'False.'

'*True!* It happened to this girl in Dear Abby.'

Jeanette slapped her arms around herself, then turned her back to me. Her hands ran themselves through her hair, stroked her shoulders, pawed all over. 'Check this out!' she giggled. 'My husband and I are French-kissing. Oh, Ross, you make me feel so passionate.'

'You're a pig,' I said. 'I'm never letting anyone do that to me.'

'Not even Dr. Kildare?'

'*Nobody.*'

'Then how are you and your husband going to have five kids then?'

I thought hard for a second. 'We're adopting them. We're adopting crippled children.'

She bounced past me and reached for her Eight Ball. She shook it hard and tipped it upside down, her palm covering the prediction. 'Would Dolores Price let Richard Chamberlain stick his hoo-hoo inside her?'

I sucked my teeth at her. 'That's so funny I forgot to laugh.'

She lifted up her hand, smiling triumphantly at what she read.

'What? What's it say?'

'"*It is decidedly so.*"'

One night in July, Daddy turned to me at supper and asked if I thought I'd like to have an in-ground swimming pool in our backyard.

'For real?' I asked.

'Why not? We got enough yard to play with out there.'

'When?'

'Well, I got a backhoe coming in first of August. The concrete has to set first. Then it takes a while to fill. Middle of the month you'll be swimming.'

I jumped up and hugged him. 'Where are we putting it? Do we have to cut down the willow tree?'

'Nope. It's going in on the other side. Where her flowers are.'

We both looked at Ma. I could tell her nerves were bothering her.

Daddy's smile slid away. 'Now what's *that* puss for?' he said.

'Nothing,' she said. 'I just wish you had said something to me before you made all your big plans.'

'Oh, don't listen to her,' I said.

She got up from the table and moved to the sink. Daddy sighed disgustedly. 'If it's money you're pouting about, I got a bonus last week from the old lady.'

She made us wait for her response. 'What for?' she said, finally.

'Played golf Sunday with the guy who owns Cabana Pools. He's an old friend of LuAnn's. Me and him hit it off. Says he'll put it in at cost.'

'It's not the money.'

'What is it then? Your goddamned pink dahlias? You afraid someone around here might have a little fun?'

She turned and faced us, then pointed a shaking finger at the window over the sink. 'The last thing I need, Tony, is to look out into that yard one day and see somebody's two-year-old floating facedown in a swimming pool.'

Daddy's laugh was snotty. He answered her slowly, as if Ma were two years old herself. 'There's a *fence*,' he said. 'The whole thing is surrounded by chain-link *fence*.'

'Kids climb fences.'

'A two-year-old kid is going to climb a six-foot fence?'

She washed the plates hard and fast, banging them against

the dish drainer. 'I can just imagine what that bonus was for.'

Daddy looked quickly at me, then took a slow sip of his iced coffee. 'What's that supposed to mean?'

'Nothing,' she said.

'No, what? Tell me.'

She spun around and faced him, suds flying away from her hands. A dish smashed against the floor. 'It means what you think it means,' she said. 'That you're an old lady's whore.'

Daddy told me to go outside and play.

'It's too hot,' I said. 'Mosquitoes are out.'

'Go.'

I walked across the kitchen on jelly legs.

Out in the garage, I poked my finger into one of the rust spots on the Cadillac. Cancer, my father called it. Mr. and Mrs. Douville, our next-door neighbors, were sitting on lawn chairs on their front porch, a citronella candle lit on a table between them.

Inside, I heard him slapping her, kitchen chairs knocking over. 'Maybe this'll cheer you up,' he said. 'Or this. How about this? Don't you ever—'

The Douvilles blew out their candle and went inside.

'Blame her all you want to . . . puts bread and butter on the table . . . sick and tired of your goddamned moods!'

The back door banged open and Daddy was rushing into the backyard, his hands cupped in front of him. Ma was running after him.

'Tony, *don't!*' Ma begged, snatching at his hands. 'I'm sorry! Please! I'm sorry!'

He flung his hands upward and let go. The small fluttering silhouette he released was Petey, who hovered in the air for a second above my mother, then headed across the yard and into the weeping willow.

'Goddamn you!' my mother screamed. 'Goddamn you to hell!' Her voice carried across the lawns.

I got on my bike and drove, fast and recklessly. The humid air pushed thick against my face; if a child had walked in front of my path, I might have killed it. I sped past Jeanette's street and past the Treetop Acres sign and onto Route 118. I squeezed the rubber handlebar caps, squeezed the shaking out of myself. I hated both of them. The harder I pedaled – the more I risked – the better it felt.

It was after dark when I got back.

As I walked toward the back door, Daddy's disembodied voice scared me. 'I was just about to go looking for you,' he said.

'Are you all right?' Ma's voice wanted to know.

'Yes.'

Squinting, I made out both their shapes. They were sitting together on the step, sharing a cigarette.

'Did you have to go off like that?' Ma said. 'I was worried sick.' The tip of the cigarette glowed briefly and I heard her exhale.

'I was just out riding,' I said. 'I had to get out of here.'

'Did you go over to Jeanette's?' my father asked.

'No.'

'What happens in this house stays in this house. It's no one else's business.'

'I know that.'

He rose and stretched. 'I'm going to bed,' he said.

Ma and I sat, leg to leg, listening to the crickets. 'Take me inside,' she said, finally. 'Make me a cup of tea.'

The kitchen light made us squint. Ma's top lip was purple and puffy. When the tea was ready, I put it down in front of her. 'Sit down,' she said, patting the chair next to her.

Instead, I walked across the kitchen and sat on the counter. 'What's a whore?' I asked.

She told me she didn't want to talk about anything right now. 'All I can picture is some cat sneaking up behind Petey. Tomorrow I'm—'

Something about my pink shorts made her stop.

'What?' I said.

She was staring down there at me.

I saw and felt it at the same time: the dark wet blotch of blood.

'That's great, Dolores. Thanks a lot,' Ma said, her face crumpling in tears. 'That's just what I need right now.'

The backhoe rattled our whole street.

Somewhere in the middle of that week's excavating and cement mixing, Jeanette's cat Delilah retreated to the Nords' linen closet and gave birth to six kittens. All morning, Jeanette and I watched the slow, strained business of Delilah pushing babies from her rump; all afternoon we studied the tiny blind things as they cried without sound and writhed in a mound against their mother. Just before I left to go home, I asked Jeanette the question I'd been trying to ask all day long.

'Do you know what a whore is?'

'A prostitute,' she said. She watched my blank look. 'A woman who does sex with men for money. Mommy says there aren't any around here. They're only in big cities. You can tell if a woman's one when—'

'Is it always a woman?'

The question stopped Jeanette and she shrugged. 'I think so. Why?'

The pool men kept swearing and laughing and asking to use our bathroom. Ma's nerves were so bad she decided to take a bus to Rhode Island and visit Grandma. 'You can either come with me or stay with Daddy,' she said.

'Stay with Daddy.'

All that week I rode my bike to Jeanette's and held the warm kittens to my chest, two at a time. At home I watched our pool fill up with water.

On the weekend, Daddy didn't go golfing with Mrs. Masicotte but stayed home with me instead, sloshing and sunbathing and running to the house to answer the phone. His voice inside was a murmur, undetectable over the murmur of the pool filter.

On Monday morning I woke up late to the sound of his

swimming. From my bedroom window I watched him catch air and dive deep, then break the surface again in some surprise place.

'How come you're home?' I called. 'Why aren't you at work?'

'Can't a guy take a little vacation with his daughter?' he said. 'Get your suit on. Come on out with me.'

By mid-morning we were lying on towels on the pool apron, working on our tans. 'By the way,' he said, leaning on his elbow and smiling. 'I been meaning to ask you something.'

'Then ask,' I said.

'What are those things?'

He was looking at the front of my bathing suit in a way that made me blush. 'What?' I said.

He reached over and tweaked one of my bumps, then cuffed me on the chin. 'You hiding walnuts in there or something?'

'Shut up,' I said. I jumped in and swam the length of the pool, hiding my smile underwater. He was a flirt, that was all. What was wrong with that? If Mrs. Masicotte was stupid enough to buy us a pool because he flirted a little, that was her problem, not ours.

It rained on Tuesday. We went off on errands like the old days, but these tasks we performed for *us*, not the old lady. From a thick wad of bills in his pants pocket, Daddy laid down money for poolside chairs, air mattresses, my new two-piece bathing suit. We were at the hardware-store counter with our pool supplies when it suddenly occurred to him that a girl of my age should have her own house key. 'Hold everything,' he told the clerk who was ringing up our order. 'We forgot something.'

For lunch we ate at a Chinese restaurant: egg rolls and lo mein and fortune cookies. 'What's it say?' Daddy asked, when I snapped open my cookie and uncurled the strip of paper.

'"*The smile you send out returns to you*". How about yours?'

'"Idle pleasure disguises itself as permanent happiness."' He tossed his fortune into the ashtray. 'Whatever the hell that means.'

All that week, we played and swam without mentioning Petey or the fight or Ma. I began to appreciate his anger, to see how someone like my mother could drive you to it – the way she crabbed and worried all day and squirted that spray up her nose. Rising and falling gently on my air mattress during a quiet moment, I looked over at Daddy and then down at the wobbly pool water and thought that, if life had been fair, he would have met Mrs. Nord instead of my mother and married *her*. They'd be living happily together now with their pool and their two daughters, Jeanette and me.

By the end of the week, Daddy was swimming a hundred laps and I was up to sixty. We sat on the pool's edge, dangling our tan legs over the sides, our eyes pink and burning from chlorine.

'Do you remember way back,' he asked, 'when I had my own painting business? Before I went to work for LuAnn?'

'You had a green pickup truck,' I said. 'And Ma and I used to bring you your lunch.'

'That's right,' he smiled.

'Why?'

'I don't know,' he said. 'I was just thinking.'

I didn't want our time together to end. I didn't want our conversation to turn sad in any way. 'Then what do you think of this?' I said. I reached down and splashed him with cold water. He growled like a lion and chased me around and around the pool.

Daddy called Ma on Sunday night. When he got off the phone, he told me Ma wanted him to drive me to Rhode Island so I could spend a couple of days with Grandma.

'What for?' I complained.

'Because you haven't seen her since Christmas,' he said.

'Big loss. Can't I just stay here with you?'

He looked away from me. 'What'll we have for supper?' he said. 'Let's order a pizza.'

The bruise on Ma's lip had faded to a yellowy green. 'I missed you, honey,' she said. We both waited out the response I was supposed to give but didn't. 'So what's new?' she asked.

I shrugged. 'Not a thing.'

'In a whole week, nothing?'

'Jeanette's having a back-to-school slumber party next week. Me and her and six other girls.'

'How was the rest of your week? Did you and Daddy have a talk?'

'We had lots of talks. We had a blast. Not one second was boring.'

'Did he say anything?'

'About what?'

'Never mind.'

Grandma's house had a camphor smell and was cluttered with religious knickknacks. Her whole downstairs had the same ugly pink-flamingo wallpaper. A series of family pictures hung on the stairway wall, one framed photograph for each step. There was one of my mother and her girlfriend Geneva Sweet wearing white dresses and 1940s hairdos, their arms hooked around each other's waists. A high-school graduation picture of Eddie, my mother's younger brother, who'd drowned at age nineteen. Wedding portraits of both my parents and grandparents. You almost had to feel sorry for Grandma in her wedding picture, standing solemnly next to her bridegroom in her shiny gown, unaware of the deaths of her husband, and her son, and her grandson, Anthony Jr.

'Old pictures are fascinating, aren't they?' Ma said, when she caught me studying them.

'Not really,' I shrugged.

I spent the remainder of my visit staring stupidly at the TV, answering Grandma's questions in single syllables and making faces at her cooking.

On the bus back home, Ma began rambling on about what being a girl had been like for her – how if she could have changed one thing about herself, it would be her shyness. Grandma had meant well, but . . . 'So when Tony came along and started calling me on the telephone, showing me all his attention, well, I just couldn't—'

'Does any of this have a point?' I sighed.

'He was supposed to tell you. That was the purpose of the whole week. Your father wants a divorce. He's leaving us.'

The bus hummed along the interstate. My head felt too numb to think. 'That's stupid,' I said, finally. 'Why would he put in a brand-new pool if he was leaving?'

She reached over and took my hand.

'Do we have to move?' I asked.

'No. He's moving. Moved.'

'Where?'

'To New Jersey.'

'What about his job? Is Masicotte moving there, too?'

'Mrs. Masicotte? She fired him. He's been having a fling with one of her tenants and she caught them. She's furious.'

For five minutes, neither of us spoke. I stared ahead and watched the seat upholstery go blurry from my tears. 'It's funny, in a way,' Ma finally said. 'She didn't mind him having a wife and daughter. He just couldn't have another girlfriend. . . . Do you have any questions?'

'Who gets to keep the Cadillac?' I said.

'We do. You and me. Isn't that hilarious?'

'Can I still go to Jeanette's slumber party?' I asked.

I spent the week swimming laps, looking up from the water at every little noise. Whenever Jeanette called, I thought it would be Daddy.

On Friday Ma came timidly out to the pool wearing her beach robe. In her hands she held her equipment: cup of tea, cigarettes, nasal spray. She struggled with the gate, walked up to the water, and dunked her big toe. 'Cold,' she said. Then she slipped off her robe and sat stiffly on a webbed chair.

'It's nice here,' she said. 'Come out of the water and talk to me.'

I sat on the pool's edge, dripping and impatient. 'I was just about to start my routine,' I said. 'What do you want?'

'Oh, nothing. Just your company. Can I ask you a question?'

'What?'

'It's silly, really. I'm just curious. . . . If you didn't know me at all – if you just looked up and there I was, some woman on the street, a stranger – would you think I was pretty or ugly?'

Her bathing suit was the same corny two-piece she'd worn ever since she'd gotten fat: flowered top, white skirt bottom, roll of bluish white flab in the middle. 'I don't know,' I said. 'Pretty, I guess.'

She was searching my face for the truth. The truth, as I saw it, was that Daddy wouldn't have left if she hadn't always been Miss Doom and Gloom. 'Pretty?' she said. 'Really?'

'Yeah, pretty ugly.'

Her lip shook. She reached for her spray.

'God, I was only kidding,' I said. 'Can't you even take a joke?'

Daddy's letter came postmarked from New Jersey: a single page of notebook paper that promised continuing love and child-support checks but failed to explain why he'd swum with me all week without telling me the truth, how he could want some woman bad enough to give us up. I'd never bothered to notice his penmanship before: fragile, tentative strokes – nothing like Daddy himself. 'Donna really wants to meet you,' the writing said. 'Just as soon as the time is right.'

At Jeanette's slumber party, I told Kitty Coffey she smelled like a hamper and was delighted when she cried. I ate greedily, danced myself into a sweat, and laughed so loud that Mrs. Nord had to come in and speak to me. 'Keep it down, honey, will you? I can hear you all over the house,' she said. 'Shut up, you whore,' I thought of saying, but only made a face. I dared each girl there to stay awake as long as *I* could – to match my energy. When the last of them faded off to sleep, I started shaking so hard that I couldn't stop myself. Maybe he'd left because I was a bad person. Because I'd wished he'd married Mrs. Nord instead of Ma. Because I told Ma she was ugly.

By dawn, my eyes burned from no sleep. I tiptoed amongst my girlfriends in the blanketed clumps on Jeanette's floor, pretending they were all dead from some horrible explosion. Because I had stayed awake, I was the only survivor.

Birds chirped outside in the Nords' graying yard. I got dressed, walked down the hall, and pedaled barefoot back to Bobolink Drive.

Out in back, the pool filter hummed. The water was silvery and smooth. Petey was sitting on the fencepost.

I clicked my tongue and approached him, repeating his name. Then my hand descended, was over him. His beak pecked lightly at my finger. I could feel his fragile bones.

I unlocked the front door with my new shiny key.

Ma was in their bedroom, awake, naked. She was standing in front of the full-length mirror, holding her breasts – gently, lovingly, the exact way Jeanette and I held the baby kittens.

Here we are, I thought: two women. 'Look!' I said.

She reeled around, startled at my voice. I let go her bird. It fluttered around and around the room, in circles between us.

Chapter 3

I was on the brown plaid sofa, watching TV and Scotch-taping my bangs to my forehead because Jeanette said that kept them from drying frizzy. Across the room on the Barcalounger, my mother was having her nervous breakdown.

Ma sat hunched over one of our fold-out TV trays, working constantly on a religious jigsaw puzzle without making any progress. She wore her knee socks and her quilted bathrobe, despite the early summer heat. She ate nothing but cubes of Kraft caramels. For two weeks, I had been reaching over and turning up the volume, trying as best I could to ignore the private curse words she'd begun chuckling to herself, trying not to see the litter of caramel cellophane that was accumulating around her chair in a kind of half circle.

It wasn't that Ma hadn't put up a fight. In Daddy's absence, she'd repainted the downstairs hallway and exercised in front of the TV with Jack LaLanne and cried and kicked the lawn mower until it eventually started. Her efforts at going it alone led her back to Sunday Mass and through a succession of brief jobs: convalescent-home cook, bank teller, notions-department clerk at Mr. Big's discount store. When winter cold burst one of our pipes, Ma called and called until she located the random yellow-pages plumber who got out of bed to come fix it.

But we'd done nothing about maintaining the pool the previous fall. Leaves had fluttered down on to the surface, then sunk and rotted; by springtime, the pool water was brown soup.

One morning in May, Ma went downstairs and found Petey dead at the bottom of his cage. 'Why me? Why always me?' she was still sobbing when I got home from school. She hadn't gone to work that day and didn't go the next day either. At the end of the week, Mr. Big's called to say they were letting her go. By then she'd already begun living in her robe.

It was Ma's hair that finally got to me. At school I sucked breath mints and carried a small bottle of Tussy deodorant in my purse for whenever I could get my hands on the lavatory pass. Ma's unwashed hair, matted and crazy, alarmed me enough to suspend the cold war against my father and contact directory assistance in Tenafly, New Jersey.

It had been almost a year since my father's move to Tenafly, where he'd opened a flower shop with his girlfriend, Donna.

'Good afternoon, Garden of Eden,' Donna said. I had spoken to her only once before, phoning the day my parents' divorce became final to call her a whore. The two prevailing mysteries in my life were: what Donna looked like and why, exactly, my father had traded us for her.

'May I speak to Tony,' I said icily. 'This is his daughter, *Miss* Dolores Price.'

When my father got on, I cut through his nervous chitchat. 'It's Ma,' I said. 'She's acting funny.'

He coughed, paused, coughed again. 'Funny how?' he asked.

'You know. Funny peculiar.'

Neither Donna nor I wished to live under the same roof, and neither the Nords nor my father would entertain my proposal that Jeanette and I live at our house for the summer and Mrs. Nord drive over with our meals and clean laundry. It was decided I would move to my grandmother's house on Pierce Street in Easterly, Rhode Island, until Ma got right again.

On the one-hour drive to Grandma Holland's I clutched my notebook filled with addresses of girls from whom I'd forced promises to write me regularly. Daddy kept sneaking nervous peeks at me and at the rearview mirror. Behind us, the U-Haul trailer wobbled and swayed from side to side. In silence I waited impatiently for the tragic highway accident that would paralyze me but wrench both my parents back to their senses. I pictured the three of us back home on Bobolink Drive, Daddy pushing my wheelchair solemnly up the front walk, eternally grateful for my forgiveness. At the doorway, Ma would smile sadly, her hair as clean and lustrous as a Breck-shampoo girl's.

Daddy didn't say much to Grandma. He deposited my bike and suitcase and cartons in the front foyer, kissed me on the forehead, and left.

Grandma and I were cautiously polite to each other. 'Make yourself at home, Dolores,' she said hesitantly as she opened the door to what had once been my mother's bedroom. The room smelled dry and dusty. The windows were stuck closed and there were little rows of insect carcasses along the sill. When I sat down on the hard mattress, it crackled under me. I tried to picture my mother in this room as a twelve-year-old girl like me, but all I could see was Anne Frank on the cover of her paperback diary.

With each trip up or down the front staircase, I watched the portrait of Eddie, my dead uncle. His blond hair was pushed up into a spiky crew cut. His eyes peeked out from beneath two bushy brows and followed my steps with eerie cheerfulness. His smile was almost a smirk, as if he might reach out from the frame and jab me in the ribs as I passed.

For supper we ate meat loaf and creamed spinach, the two of us sitting in a silence broken only by the occasional clink of fork against plate or Grandma's clearing her throat. When she got up to make herself some tea, she addressed the stove. 'She's not cuckoo, you know,' she said. '*He's* the one with the mortal sin on his soul, not Bernice.'

That evening I thumbtacked my Dr. Kildare collage to the wall and unpacked my clothes. Grandma had placed little sachet pillows in the dresser drawers. As I yanked each drawer open, the smell of old ladies from church – with their powdered wrinkly necks and quivery singing voices – drifted up toward me. In the bottom bureau drawer I discovered a little red ink message hidden in a back corner, written right into the wood. 'I love Bernice Holland,' it said. 'Sincerely, Alan Ladd.' Twice during the night I put the light on and got out of bed to make sure it was still there.

Grandma turned her TV to thunderous volume and told me I mumbled. She was still an 'Edge of Night' fan. Sometimes I'd grab a Coke from the refrigerator and slump down on the couch with her, slurping intentionally from the bottle.

'I hope you don't sit like that in school,' she said. 'It's unladylike.'

I thumbed through the *TV Guide* and reminded her I was on summer vacation.

'When I was your age at the Bishop School, I received a medal for deportment on Class Day. A girl named Lucinda Cote thought *she* was going to get it – told me as much. She was a big piece of cheese, very stuck on herself. But no, they gave it to me. And here is my very own granddaughter who can't even sit correctly on a divan.'

'What's a divan?' I said, swigging my Coke.

'A *sofa*,' she said, exasperated.

She watched in silent horror as I stuck my thumb over the Coke bottle opening and shook, then let the foam erupt into my mouth. 'Can I turn the TV down?' I asked. 'I'm not deaf, you know.'

Evenings after the dishes, Grandma hobbled around the house with her frayed prayer book which was held together with rubber bands. Then she'd settle in front of the television to watch her westerns – 'Bonanza,' 'Rawhide' – while I sat in the kitchen signing corny get-well cards to Ma and pages of complaints to Jeanette.

In our first week together, Grandma told me it was a sin the way I wasted hot water, toilet paper, my spare time. She said she'd never heard of a girl who had reached my age without learning to crochet. I retaliated by shocking her as best I could. At breakfast, I drowned my scrambled eggs in plugs of ketchup.

Evenings, I danced wildly by myself to my 45s while she watched from the doorway. It was mostly for Grandma's benefit that I mouthed the declarations of the girl singers: *My love is like a heat wave! . . . It's my party and I'll cry if I want to!* One night Grandma wondered aloud why I didn't ever listen to singers who could carry a tune.

'Like who, for instance?' I scoffed.

'Well, like Perry Como.'

'That old dinosaur?' I snorted.

'Well, how about the Lennon Sisters then? They can't be much older than you are.'

I lied and told her one of her precious Lennon sisters – Diane, the oldest, her favorite – was having an illegitimate baby.

'Pfft,' she said, flicking away the possibility with the flap of her wrist. But her lip quivered and she left my room making the sign of the cross.

Pierce Street smelled of car exhaust and frying food. Glass shattered, people screamed, kids threw rocks. 'Jeepers Christmas,' Grandma would mumble as cars squealed by at emergency speeds. She told me she had warned her husband, my grandfather, that they should follow the doctors and lawyers and schoolteachers who had moved out of the neighborhood after the war. But Grandpa had put it off and put it off and then, in 1948, had died, leaving her with teenage children and a two-family home with a leaky roof. 'This house has been my cross to bear,' she was fond of saying. She had come to see her staying on amongst the 'riffraff' as the will of God. He had placed her here as a model of clean Catholic living. She was not obliged to speak to any of her neighbors, only to offer them a good example.

At dusk each evening, Mrs. Tingley, Grandma's third-floor tenant, clip-clopped down the side steps with her bug-eyed Chihuahua, Cutie Pie. 'Come on, Cutie Pie, go poopy,' Mrs. Tingley always said, while the dog circled nervously on his tether. In all the years Mr. and Mrs. Tingley had rented from my grandmother, Grandma had assumed *he* was the drinker, not *her*. But after Mr. Tingley's death, the package-store man had kept pulling up to the curb as usual. My bedroom ceiling was Mrs. Tingley's bedroom floor. The only sound from above was the click of dog toenails, and I pictured Mrs. Tingley up there lying in bed, sipping in silence.

Across from Grandma's was a tin-roofed store divided in two. One half was a barbershop. The barber, a thin, jowly man, sat sadly at the window most of the day, reading his own magazines and waiting for customers. The other half was the Peacock Tattoo Emporium. It was run by a skinny, older woman with dyed black hair and red toreador pants. On my second afternoon at Grandma's, she waved me over from where I was sitting on the front porch, waiting for the mailman. She introduced herself as Roberta and asked me to run to the store for a pack of Newports. When I returned, she waved away the change and proceeded to dazzle me with her exotic life story. She had once been married to a sword swallower who was now in jail where he belonged. Her second husband, the Canuck, God love him, was dead. Roberta had traveled with the Canuck to both Alaska and Hawaii and liked Alaska better. She'd dreamed President Kennedy's assassination the week before it happened. She had been a vegetarian since the day in 1959 when she opened up a can of beef stew and found a baby rat.

When Grandma came outside to sweep the porch, she spotted me through Roberta's plate-glass window and motioned me home. Back inside, she hit me on the head with a rolled-up newspaper. 'Don't you say another word to that piece of garbage,' she said, her face flushed in anger. 'Don't you listen to another word of her malarkey.'

'I have a perfect right to make my own friends!' I shouted back.

'Not with chippies like that one you don't!'

The center of activity on Pierce Street was Connie's Superette, a little market housed on the bottom floor of a large, asbestos-shingled apartment building. Connie, a fat woman with Lucille

Ball red hair, sat behind the counter on a webbed porch chair. She kept a whirring electric fan trained on herself and was careful not to risk breaking her two-inch fingernails as she grudgingly rang up people's stuff. Connie's nephew, Big Boy, was the butcher. He whistled through his teeth and wore madras shirts and an apron smeared with blood. He looked like Doug McClure on 'The Virginian.'

Grandma traded at Connie's because she had never learned to drive a car, but she held a grudge against Big Boy, who had said to her one day in front of a whole storeful of customers, 'What'll it be, tootsie?' When I moved in, she was only too happy to make me her errand girl. Daily, she folded money into my palm and sent me down the street for Tums or cornstarch or prune juice. As I headed out the door, she never failed to remind me to steer clear of both Big Boy and the dirty-magazine aisle.

The Pysyks lived in the apartment above the superette. Their twin daughters, Rosalie and Stacia, were the only two girls my age on Pierce Street. They hung out on the upstairs porch, where they danced and giggled and flicked their middle fingers back to neighborhood boys who shouted vulgar remarks up to them. They had a portable record player with a plastic polka-dot case and one scratchy record, 'Big Girls Don't Cry,' which they played nonstop at top volume. Both girls wore short shorts and frilly midriff blouses and were Q-Tip skinny, although they seemed forever to be eating and drinking something. Their whole day was like a party – a private one. I was both jealous of the twins and petrified of them. Grandma had once thrown a pitcher of water at the girls and called them 'dirty DP's' when she had caught them ringing her bell and hiding behind her catalpa tree. The Pysyk sisters took an immediate dislike to me, and my daily treks to the store became nightmares.

'Hey kid!' Rosalie shouted down to me on my very first trip to Connie's. Her sister hung over the railing, smirking and eating from a bag of potato chips. 'You stuck-up or something?

Got a broom up your ass?' Behind her, the Four Seasons wailed in their scratchy falsettos.

'Oh, hi,' I called up, smiling stiffly. 'Gee, that's a good record you're playing. I'm really enjoying it.' Already I could see the three of us walking home from school together, me lending them my 45s.

'"*That's a good record you're playing. I'm really enjoying it,*"' Rosalie mimicked back. Both girls brayed like donkeys.

'What's your name?' Stacia shouted down.

'Dolores.' It came out shaky, like a request.

'Oh,' she said. 'I thought it was Fucky Face.'

Her sister squealed in horrified delight, pulling off a candy wrapper with her teeth and spitting it over the rail at me.

Each day it happened again. 'Hi, Pukehead,' one would yell as I approached the store. 'Say hello to all them cooties for us,' the other would call as I left minutes later with Grandma's groceries. My heart raced. My grandmother's change went sweaty in my fist. I smiled Anne Frank's brave smile and checked my urge to run. Back in the house, I studied my face in the medicine-cabinet mirror for clues as to why they hated me. I accepted each of their hundred imagined apologies. One night I woke up shaky from a dream in which the twins had lured me up to their porch with offers of friendship and then attempted to hurl me headfirst over the railing.

'What *are* DP's, anyways?' I asked Grandma one night. She was at the kitchen table, mumbling her rosary while I dried the dishes.

'Displaced persons. People we took in from Europe after the war. You'd *think* they'd be grateful, wouldn't you?'

I understood why they weren't. A displaced person myself, I was not so much grateful to Grandma for her charity as disgusted by her liver spots and quiet belches, the way she could reach into her mouth and, with a gurgle, remove her top teeth. Dolores Price, DP: we even had the same initials. Still, the Pysyks gave no sign of wanting to meet me on common ground.

*

Jeanette's correspondence was spotty and filled with hurtful proof that her life was proceeding without me. Two ex-friends never wrote back at all. Every Saturday a letter arrived faithfully from my mother at the state hospital. Her thoughts were hard to follow. In one sentence she'd be telling me about all the nice people in her art class. In the next, she'd be worrying about the flatiron she was sure had been left on when we closed up our house. 'I can smell the heat from here,' she insisted. 'The house will burn to the ground before anyone recognizes the g.d. truth.'

One rainy afternoon Grandma ran out of eggs. I reluctantly agreed to get her some, reasoning that not even the cold-blooded Pysyk sisters were likely to be out in a downpour. To my relief, their upstairs porch was empty, a burning yellow light bulb the only sign of life. But in the store, rounding the corner by the ice cream freezer, I ran head-on into the twins. My stomach felt the way it does on elevators. It was the first time I had seen them up close and I studied them in horror. Rosalie was eating onion rings out of a can. Stacia was thumbing through a movie magazine. Both girls had white-blond eyebrows and lots of moles. Stacia's ear was deformed. Two tiny flaps stuck out from the left side of her head as if some powerful vacuum had sucked the rest of her ear back inside her skull.

'Oh, hi, Dolores,' Rosalie smirked. 'You look even uglier when you're wet.' I beat it to the front counter.

'Hey Connie!' Stacia shouted from the back of the store. 'Wait on her quick. She's got bugs.'

Big Boy was cleaning out his butcher case, holding a necklace of franks in one hand. He stopped and, for the first time that summer, considered my existence. Connie squinted suspiciously, her chubby fingers clicking rapidly over the register keys.

My face was hot. I felt tears coming. 'I don't have bugs,' I croaked. 'They just hate my guts.'

Connie looked at me and then to the twins in aisle one. 'Don't you girls touch them magazines if your hands are greasy,' was all she said.

Stacia and Rosalie approached the counter, giggling and scratching wildly. Stacia held up a large can of Raid. 'Help! Get her out of here!' she laughed.

'Shut up,' I said. 'You dirty DP . . . you flipper ear.'

There was some scratching and hair pulling and cans of vegetables rattled off the shelves. I can't remember which twin knocked me down. Big Boy and Connie were over us, pulling us apart. 'Goddamnit! They broke one of my good fingernails!' Connie bellowed. 'Out of the store, the three of youse!'

In the version of the incident I told Grandma, I hadn't fought back. If I didn't watch it, I reasoned, I'd end up in New Jersey having to be polite to that whore Donna.

The following afternoon while Grandma and I were watching 'Art Linkletter's House Party,' a present arrived for me from the hospital. I ripped off the brown paper wrapping and Grandma and I stared dumbly. It was one of my mother's art-therapy paintings. In a clear blue sky amongst neatly organized clouds, a woman's leg was floating. On the foot was a red high-heeled shoe and from the thigh grew parakeet-green wings, strong ones, of a size that might keep an angel airborne.

It was Grandma who first broke the spell. She sat down in her big parlor chair and folded her arms around herself. There were tears in the cracks of skin around her eyes.

'I sure love it here in Easterly,' I said. It was the only thing I could think of.

She reached up and patted my arm. 'Never mind about those foolish DP girls,' she said. 'You just stay in the house with decent people like us.' She nodded her head toward the TV to include Art Linkletter.

Up in my room I spread all of Ma's letters on the bed, trying to find some trace of sanity in her penmanship. Then I wedged the painting behind the dresser.

In August, Grandma enrolled me in the seventh-grade class at my mother's old school, St. Anthony's. I had heard horror stories about parochial schools. Jeanette Nord's cousin knew someone who'd been whacked so often in the head with her own arithmetic book that she'd suffered brain damage and permanent baldness, according to Jeanette. Still, I was itchy to meet kids my own age. Grandma said rough girls like the Pysyks attended public school. It was Ingrid Bergman who finally won me over. Her sad, brave death in *The Bells of St. Mary's* on 'Channel Ten Sunday Matinee Theatre' shot straight to my heart. We registered the next day.

On the first day of school, Grandma yanked repeatedly at the waist of my plaid uniform and handed me a thermos of grape Zarex and an egg-salad sandwich she said she hoped wouldn't go bad by noon. Walking along Pierce Street, I studied myself in the storefront windows. 'Here is a girl who is pretty in a quiet way,' I told myself. 'I bet she's had a very sad life.'

In the school yard, I leaned against the cool brick building and rigged a tight smile on my face to show everyone how perfectly happy I was not to have anyone to talk to. When a dodgeball thunked me on the shoulder, I mistook it for an invitation of friendship, but two boys half my height were waving impatiently, yelling, 'Hey, kid!' I picked up the ball, and, in mid-throw, saw something that sucked the breath out of me.

Leaning against a Cyclone fence, elbowing a small cluster of shrieky girls, were Stacia and Rosalie Pysyk, wearing plaid woolen uniforms identical to my own. Things began to move too fast. A bell blared. Nuns appeared, clapping their hands and calling orders. Neither Pysyk had spotted me. I trailed into the building a safe distance behind them.

The corridors smelled of fresh paint and had creaky floors. The dim green walls were lined with framed pictures of past graduating classes and, despite my panic, I tried to locate my mother's portrait as I passed. Up ahead, Stacia took a turn down another corridor behind the sixth-grade nun. But Rosalie, apparently the smarter of the two, ambled amidst the seventh-grade group with the lethal cool of a mountain lion.

Our classroom was on the second floor at the top of the stairs. Outside the door on a gray pedestal was a plaster statue of the Blessed Virgin, her arms extended. I tramped in behind the others, addressing an emergency prayer to the statue that she'd help me discover some clever way to dodge Rosalie Pysyk for the next 180 school days. Luckily, I was assigned the last desk in the row next to the windows. Just outside was the fire escape. If worse came to worst, I thought.

Our teacher, Miss Lilly, was new to the school like me. She was a tall, frail woman and had dry, dusty-looking hair that had been teased up in front and more or less forgotten in back. She spent a large portion of the morning opening desk drawers and slamming them shut again in little bursts of temper she quickly covered over with a brief, squinty smile. I studied Miss Lilly intensely, with shriveling confidence in her ability to keep me safe from Rosalie. The fire escape looked rusty and rickety. I imagined it pulling away from the building against my weight, Rosalie laughing at the window as I fell in an arc toward the blacktop.

By late morning, each of us had been issued a pile of mildewy-smelling textbooks: *Adventures in World History, Arithmetic for Modern Youth, Science and Health for Catholic Schoolchildren*, and a religious text illustrated with black-and-white photos of the same boy and girl participating in a variety of holy activities. They were joyous or solemn as the event demanded and both were stupidly old-fashioned looking. I wondered if, by some odd quirk, I hadn't been assigned the exact same book my mother had used. I took an immediate dislike to the boy and girl in the pictures – sunny, wholesome goody-goody types, the kind of kid Grandma favored. It was she who had gotten me into this, the old bag.

At lunchtime I followed the others down to the maze of Formica tables and metal folding chairs in the basement of the school. The Pysyk twins, reunited, lunched from a large cellophane bag of cheese popcorn. Their friends began to stretch and gawk at me and the noisy lunchroom rang with whoops of laughter aimed in my direction. 'Who?' someone yelled, rising from her seat for a better look. 'That thing?'

I sat down at a table with two overweight younger girls involved in a conversation about horses. They snuck nervous glances at me and then stopped talking. 'I'm new at this school,' I said, unscrewing the top of my thermos. 'I'm in seventh.' Both girls shoved their faces into their sandwiches and chewed uneasily.

A boy tapped me on the arm. 'She wants you,' he said, pointing to one of the old-lady cafeteria workers. But when I walked up to her, she told me to hurry on if I was just going to stand there and not buy anything. I returned to my seat. My thermos had been tipped over and grape drink was splattering onto the floor. My sandwich was a soggy, purple-stained mess.

From the corner of my eye, I could see the Pysyks and their friends bending and stretching. Stacia's face was pressed against the tabletop and she was snorting. The two girls at my table stared open-faced. 'What are *you* looking at, Fatty?' I snapped at one of them.

Miss Lilly came back from lunch smelling like cigarettes. I mouthed the magic word, cramps, and she handed me the hall pass. Outside the classroom, I lingered for a moment at the statue of Mary, intending to let her in on what Rosalie had done to me. 'Hail Mary, full of grace . . .' I whispered, then stopped. Her nose was chipped and her sky-blue eyes stared out at nothing. She was unaware of the serpent curling at her feet.

Down in the main corridor I paused at the long rows of framed pictures, St. Anthony's graduates of the last forty years. I located my mother in the bottom row of the brown-tinted portraits of the Class of 1944. Her dark, frizzy hair was parted in the middle and held tight to each side with oval barrettes. Her eyes looked slightly away from the camera and she wore an expression of quiet seriousness. I was astonished that she looked more like an old-fashioned me than she did my mother. The corridor was cool and peaceful. 'Hi,' I said aloud. The sound of my voice set my heart thumping, but I continued. 'You're divorced, you know. You have a daughter. I'm her.'

For homework, Miss Lilly had assigned us a chapter on

religion and one on Mesopotamia. My bedroom was hot, so I set up the table fan from the kitchen and aimed the breeze at my face. 'Dear Daddy,' I wrote on a fresh piece of loose-leaf paper. 'I know for a *fact* that Mommy still loves you very much. We both miss you more than I can say. I think I may be coming down with stomach cancer. I just have this feeling.' Then I gouged out the words with deep, dark pencil marks that dented several of the pages beneath it.

North of what is now the region of the Persian Gulf, a civilization nearly as advanced as Egypt's began to flower. With soil enriched by the Rivers Euphrates and Tigris . . .

I stared at the whirring fan, trying to make out the shape of the blades in the blue-gray blur. I moved a finger closer and closer, watching it shake. 'They'll find me in a pool of blood. Daddy will hate himself for the rest of his life. Rosalie Pysyk will have a nervous breakdown.'

The Sumerians flourished on the flat, fertile land made rich from the alluvium of the two rivers. Their contributions to civilization . . .

I shifted the breeze away from me and the shiny pages of my opened religion book began to turn by themselves. I watched the goody-goody girl and boy in the textbook photos. 'I hate your guts,' I told them. Suddenly, the book fluttered open to page 232. A previous user – some greasy boy with dirt-caked fingernails, no doubt – had altered the photo of the model students. In the picture, the two counterparts were walking down the steps of a school that looked something like St. Anthony's, smiling radiantly at each other. Both of the midsections had been erased white. The ideal girl was wearing an inverted triangle of loopy pubic hair and two mismatched breasts that looked like garnished cupcakes. The ideal boy's hoo-hoo was a periscope. Two makeshift cartoon bubbles floated above their heads. 'How about some sex. Intercourse. That means FUCKING!' the girl said, beaming brightly. 'Mmmm Okay!!!!' the boy replied, his enthusiasm measured in exclamation marks.

The Sumerians flourished on the flat, fertile land made rich from the alluvium of the two rivers. Their contributions . . .

In the next hour, I drank two large glasses of ice water, slid my eyes repeatedly over the same paragraph in my history book, stuck my entire face one inch away from the fan, and covered the front and back of my loose-leaf with Richard Chamberlain's name and birthday in ornate block-lettering. None of it worked. Whenever I'd turn back to page 232, reasoning I'd imagined the whole thing, there they'd still be.

The next day at school, Miss Lilly was wearing an ankle-length paisley skirt and a tight turtleneck shirt that let you see the entire outline of her bra. Her hair was yanked back tightly and crowned with a bun the size of a small hamburger patty. She looked nothing like she had the day before. I wondered if she might have a split personality like Margo on 'Search for Tomorrow' – if she might even be crazy like my mother, if the whole world wasn't crazy. All morning long, I kept turning against my better judgement to page 232, wanting over and over to verify its secret existence.

On Wednesday morning, Miss Lilly smiled mysteriously and said she had a surprise for us. 'Popsicles!' someone guessed. She ignored this and pulled at the two roll-down maps that hung over the blackboard. The entire board area was filled with Miss Lilly's beautiful penmanship. She had come to school a half hour early, she said, to copy down a poem for us, 'Ode on a Grecian Urn.' She explained she was something of an expert on this poem, having written in college a paper on it that ran to twenty-three typed pages. 'Now if you will be still and concentrate very hard, I think you'll appreciate the cadences as I read aloud. After I finish, we'll discuss its beautiful meaning.'

She began in a low, moaning voice and seemed almost immediately to fall into a trance. In her hand she held a fresh stick of chalk, which she swung back and forth as she read, like Mitch Miller.

Rosalie Pysyk looked back at the rest of us and pointed to

herself. I knew Miss Lilly was in trouble. Rosalie raised her forearm to her lips, her cheeks puffed out, and she let loose an amazing reproduction of a fart, the kind I hadn't heard since my father's move to Tenafly.

The class burst into nervous laughter. Miss Lilly stopped as if someone had doused her with ice water. Her face contorted in several odd ways and she walked to the board and began erasing away 'Ode on a Grecian Urn' with swooping strokes of defeat, going over and over the same area until I realized she was crying. Rosalie sat sideways in her chair, shaking from the laughter she was swallowing. I imagined myself drawing a gun from my desk, taking aim, and killing her without so much as a quiver.

My Mesopotamia essay was a dismal failure. With a tired sigh, Miss Lilly suggested I skip lunchtime recess and revise it, little knowing the reward she was giving me. 'When you finish, just put it on my desk and join the rest of us next door at church for seventh-grade confession. Did you remember to bring your mantilla?'

I sat listening to her sandals clack down the corridor. One of the fluorescent lights made a funny sputtering noise, which the strange silence of the empty classroom amplified. I tiptoed to the front and sat down on Miss Lilly's chair. I hadn't planned it. I looked out at the rows of empty desks and was flooded with sympathy for Miss Lilly. There was a silver thermos on her desk and several notices and reminders from Sister Margaret Frances, the principal. When I picked up the battered poetry book, it opened automatically to 'Ode on a Grecian Urn.' The print was underlined and circled and everywhere on the page were little arrows and notations, each ending in an exclamation point.

Her straw purse was behind her desk. I picked it up and reached inside. Watching the classroom door, I pulled out her car keys, a pack of Winstons, and a brown plastic vial of pills. The label read, 'Sandra Lilly. Take one at bedtime when needed. NO REFILLS.' There was a five-dollar bill in her wallet, three quarters, and some seven-cent stamps. Sandwiched inside the worn, scratchy cellophane windows were her pictures: a blond woman with a bubbletop hairdo, an elderly couple standing in front of a fancy cake, and a black-and-white shot of Miss Lilly and some man at the beach. Miss Lilly's hair was wet and stringy and her bathing suit straps were down. The man wore sunglasses and had a flabby waist.

I banished him from the picture and imagined Big Boy from the superette instead. They were in the sand, Big Boy and Miss Lilly, kissing and kissing. No one else was around. They were rubbing against each other. Then, suddenly, they were both naked.

When I looked up, I saw Rosalie's red vinyl notebook. My plan presented itself to me fully developed, like a gift from God.

I put Miss Lilly's things back in her purse. I walked over to Rosalie's desk and picked up her religion book. Back at my own desk, I made the exchange, then placed my book amongst Rosalie's things.

Miss Lilly smiled at me when I slid into the girls' pew. I smiled back, feeling strangely confident. Inside the confessional, I waited for Father Duptulski to slide open his window.

'Bless me, Father, for I have sinned. It has been three weeks since my last confession. These are my sins.'

I told him I had been disrespectful to my grandmother and had sworn under my breath on eleven different occasions. Then, in the most humble voice I could manufacture, I confessed how I had sat wickedly by while I watched my good friend Rosalie Pysyk deface her religion book with a filthy, immoral picture. I listened, somewhat amazed, to the treacherous catch in my voice. 'She's really okay, Father. I'm sure she didn't even mean to do it. . . . For these and all the sins of my past life, I am heartily sorry.'

For my penance, Father Duptulski gave me ten Hail Marys, something that struck me as a reasonable punishment for an accomplice, a mere bridesmaid in crime. I knelt and prayed – not for forgiveness but for the accuracy of my assumption: that the sanctity of the confessional applied more to murderers than kids.

Back in class, Miss Lilly was talking about apostrophes when Sister Margaret Frances appeared at the door. 'Miss Lilly?' she said in a sweet voice. 'We'll be doing a seventh-grade textbook inspection.'

Miss Lilly looked bewildered. 'Will this be next week?' she asked.

'This will be today. This will be right now.'

Outside after school, Stacia milled around impatiently. 'You seen Rosalie?' she kept asking everyone. 'You seen Rosalie?'

Rosalie Pysyk was absent on Thursday but word had gotten around about what she'd done. So had the news of her punishment, which broke all school records for its severity: every afternoon until Thanksgiving vacation, Sister Margaret Frances would make an X on the blackboard. Rosalie would stand for one-hour sessions with her nose affixed to the intersection.

I walked home from school that afternoon so free of burden that my steps felt like a preliminary to flight – as if, at any next moment, I might be airborne. Power had made me hungry and I was already eating out of the bag of potato chips as Connie rang up my sale.

Grandma watched as I poked my finger into the corners of the bag for salt and crumbs, then ate two of the tapioca puddings she'd made for supper.

'My gracious, school certainly gives you an appetite,' she observed.

'It's a free country,' I said. 'Granny babes.'

That night up in my room I pulled Ma's flying leg out from behind the dresser and saw, for the first time, that it was beautiful.

I hung it above my bed.

Chapter 4

In January the hospital gave us back a new version of Ma: a smiling, twitchy woman with plucked eyebrows. She smoked menthol cigarettes now and was thin again – thinner than ever. Bony. She told me she'd spent half her months in the hospital circling the grounds with a pedometer hooked to her leg, thinking about things and walking off her 'bucket seat'. Mileage-wise, she'd gotten three quarters of the way to California.

On her first weekend home, we sat together watching the Beatles on 'Ed Sullivan'. Ma, next to me on the sofa, tapped her foot against my foot to the beat of the music. I cried silently for Paul McCartney. Across the room, Grandma shook her head and scowled.

'What's *your* problem?' I snapped, when the camera left the group to pan the hysterical studio audience. My hatred for Grandma at that moment was as pure as my love for Paul.

Her problem, she said, was that she couldn't tell the difference between the singing and those screech owl girls in the audience. If people thought *this* was hot stuff, then she guessed she just gave up.

'Fine, give up then,' I told her. 'Be my guest.'

Ma intervened, wanting to know which Beatle was which.

'That one's George. He's the quiet one. That's Paul McCartney, the cute one . . .'

'Cute?' Grandma scoffed. 'You call that homely beatnik cute?'

Ringo Starr's face suddenly filled up the screen. 'And that's Ringo,' I said. 'By the way, Grandma, he's the one.'

'The one what?'

'The one who's the father of Diane Lennon's illegitimate baby.'

Her face registered a fleeting look of alarm before she dismissed the comment. 'Nuts to you,' she said, then rose from her chair and announced that she was disappointed in me, my mother, *and* Ed Sullivan – the three of us – and that she was so disgusted, she was going to go to bed.

'Fine with me,' I said. 'Make like a tree and leave.'

When Grandma's bedroom door slammed, I looked my mother in the eye. 'I can't stand her!' I said. 'She's so *mental!*' Ma's face twitched and I looked away, down at the rug, at my feet next to her feet. 'No offense,' I mumbled.

Each morning after breakfast, Ma sat at the kitchen table, chain-smoking and checking off want ads from the Easterly and Providence newspapers. She told me getting a job scared her, but she was determined not to shy away from risk. 'That's what life's all about, Dolores,' she said. 'Climbing out onto the airplane wing and jumping off.'

My mother's job search miffed Grandma, who had already lined up a position for her as a housekeeper at St. Anthony's rectory.

'Look,' my mother told Grandma. 'One thing they taught me out there is that you cook your own goose when you limit yourself.'

'Well what's that supposed to mean?'

Ma made us wait while she lit a fresh Salem. 'It means I don't have to clean toilets and fold men's undershorts for a living if I don't feel like it. That was my life for thirteen years and look where it got me.'

Grandma shot me a brief look of alarm, then lowered her voice. 'There's a parochial-school student in this room, in case you forgot,' she said. 'I don't see as priests' underclothes are something we need to talk about in front of certain young ladies.'

My mother sighed; smoke streamed out of both her nostrils. 'Two sixty-two Pierce Street,' she mumbled. 'The house of repression.'

Grandma picked up a dish towel and flapped at Ma's cigarette smoke. 'I hate this filthy smell. It's cheap. This whole house smells cheap.'

'Oh, for crying out loud, Ma. Just because a woman smokes, it doesn't mean—'

'I see you swear now, too, Miss High and Mighty.'

'Ma, "for crying out loud" isn't a swear. You go ask Father Duptulski.'

'Well, in my day, women knew their place.'

My mother rolled her eyes at God or the ceiling and turned her attention to me. 'You can be two things if you're a woman, Dolores. Betty Crocker or a floozy. Just remember your place – even if it kills you.'

'What makes you such an authority, I'd like to know?' Grandma huffed.

'Ma, where do you think I've been for seven months? Disneyland?'

Grandma and I looked away.

'You take poor Marilyn Monroe, for instance,' Ma continued.

Grandma's eyes widened angrily. '*You* take Marilyn Monroe!' she said. 'I certainly don't want her. For instance or otherwise.' Marilyn Monroe's death – how her wickedness had finally caught up with her – was a favorite subject of my grandmother's. To Grandma's way of thinking, Marilyn Monroe resided in the same trash bin as Roberta across the street.

'But Ma, can't you see it? The poor thing got trapped. Limited by what everyone expected from her. There was this book about her in the hospital library. Deep down she was just a scared little girl.'

Grandma clamped her lips so tightly together they turned white. She got up slowly, walked over to the plastic tray where she kept her medications, and took a blood-pressure pill. When she finally spoke, it was to the stove. 'This she says about a sexpot who made three pictures condemned by the Legion of Decency. This she says about a woman who didn't even have the modesty to kill herself with a bathrobe on.'

Ma and Grandma didn't speak to each other for the next several days. Mostly, Grandma sat scowling in front of her soap operas and westerns or trailing after my mother with a jet spray of Glade. Once, when a Salem commercial was on, Grandma stuck her tongue out and gave the TV the raspberries. If she wanted to say something to Ma, she used me as a transmitter. 'Dolores, tell the chimney stack my cousin Florence is having gallbladder problems again.' Or 'Dolores, tell Marilyn Monroe's best friend that the doctor says my blood pressure's sky-high.'

None of the places where Ma filled out job applications called her back. Each evening after supper, she put on her peacoat, wrapped her striped muffler around her neck, positioned her ear muffs, and rigged her pedometer to her sneaker.

'You want to walk with me?' she'd ask. I *didn't* want to. I was a quiet detective, collecting each small sign of weirdness: the way she now made a cup of tea with two teabags, not one; the way she said, 'Will do,' when you hadn't even requested anything. She'd be gone over an hour, then come back – red-faced, nose dripping from the cold. The back door opening, the stomping of her boots in the pantry, always surprised me. Each time she went out, I braced myself for the news that Grandma or unemployment had broken her – that she'd hiked back to the hospital to be crazy again. I couldn't walk with her. I couldn't.

Somewhere during the school year, word had circulated that my parents were both dead. I didn't bother to correct the misconception. My mother's condition and my father's girlfriend were my business, not anyone else's. At St. Anthony's, I was the third student from the top of my class, behind Liam Phipps and

Kathy Mahoney. (Miss Lilly rated all thirty-one of us on a section of the blackboard labeled 'Do Not Erase.' But whenever Miss Lilly assigned team work, Rosalie Pysyk and pimply Walther Knupp and I were the last kids the captains chose. This was the price you paid for privacy.)

One night Ma knocked at my bedroom door, ashtray in hand.

'Busy?' she asked.

'Studying vocab. Miss Lilly gives us a surprise quiz every Friday.'

'Will do,' she said. She walked over to my Dr. Kildare collage and studied it. 'This used to be my room when I was your age, you know.'

'Grandma told me,' I said. I thought of pulling open the bureau drawer and sharing her Alan Ladd graffiti with her but decided against it. 'You can ask me my words if you want.'

She took my list and stared at it. There were tears in her eyes. 'This place is so bad for my nerves,' she said. 'Grandma means well, but . . .'

'Don't ask me them in order. Mix them up.'

'All right,' she said. 'Blithe.'

'"Gay-hearted."'

'"Blackguard."'

'"Scoundrel."'

'Okay. "Panacea."'

'"Cure-all."'

She put down my notebook. 'You and I are getting a place of our own, Dolores, just as soon as I can swing it,' she said. 'That's a promise.'

'"Cure-all,"' I repeated.

'"Cure-all," right . . . It's funny, you know? I spend over half a year down below – straightening myself out, figuring out why my entire marriage was one long apology. So where do I end up? Back here where the whole problem started. Driving Old Lady Masicotte's goddamned Cadillac, no less. The thing is—'

'Are you going to ask me my words or not?'

'I'm sorry. "Paradox"?'

'"Paradox"?'

'"Paradox."'

'Skip that one,' I said. 'I'll come back to it.'

'I'm a grown woman, aren't I? I can have a cigarette if I want to, can't I? . . . I hated every second he worked for that rich bitch. But I never risked complaining. Knew my place, all right . . .'

She got up and paced, then stopped to smile at her flying-leg painting. 'You like this?'

'It's okay,' I said. 'It's pretty cool.'

She passed her fingertips over the painting's surface. 'They hung another one of my pictures up in the dining room at the hospital. A still life. But I thought this one was better. This was my favorite.'

'What's repression?' I said.

'What?' She scanned my vocab list.

'You said this was the house of repression. What's repression?'

She sat on my bed, flopped back. 'Holding everything inside. Feeling guilty about everything. Dr. Markey – this doctor I worked with – told me half my problem was being raised in an unhealthy environment. That it constipated me – emotionally. So that Tony and I . . . Those were his words for it, anyway.'

'Don't tell Grandma,' I said. 'She'd go berserk.'

She reached over and stroked my cheek with the back of her hand. Her touch felt cool. 'You know what I was afraid of all the while I was in the hospital? I was afraid that by the time I got out, you'd look different. But you don't. You're just the same.'

In her absence I'd defused the Pysyk sisters and begun to write love poems in my key-locked diary. When Grandma got to be too much, I snuck over to Roberta's tattoo shop to smoke and swear about my luck, my life. Ma didn't know, couldn't see that I had changed.

'Just don't ever let it happen to you, Dolores.'

'Let what happen?'

'Let people just shit all over you. Don't you ever become some man's personal toilet the way I did . . . All those flowers she kept sending after I lost the baby. She had crust, all right, I'll give her that much.'

'Who?'

'Old Lady Masicotte. "Aren't you going to write her a thank-you note?" he'd say. There I was, trying to hold myself together from one hour to the next, and the two of them . . .' She walked out of the room, blew her nose, and came back.

'But that's all water over the dam, now, isn't it? Where were we? "Paradox."'

'"A situation . . . A situation which . . . a situation which seems contradictory but is nevertheless true." Something like that.'

We studied each other for several seconds. I decided to risk it.

I reached over and took the cigarette from her. She watched me inhale deeply, then blow the smoke over her shoulder.

'There's these two girls,' I said. 'Rosalie and Stacia Pysyk . . .'

One afternoon in early spring, Sister Margaret Frances cut into our lessons to announce over the PA that an opinion book had been confiscated. Such things were mean-spirited and unchristian, Sister informed us, and were strictly forbidden at St. Anthony's School. Any student found circulating one would wish she hadn't.

For the next several days I watched the red spiral notebook move up and down the rows whenever Miss Lilly turned her back. Outside at recess and after lunch, girls milled shoulder to shoulder around the shrine of St. Anthony, passing the book and turning every few seconds to locate the whereabouts of the nun on playground duty. From the sidelines, I was unsure exactly what an opinion book was but guessed it had something to do with either sex or popularity.

'Dolores, do me a *giant* favor?' Kathy Mahoney begged me at the close of school on Friday. Her face was flushed; it was the first time she'd spoken my name. From the other end of the corridor, Sister Margaret approached us. *'Please?* As a friend?'

All weekend long, I leafed through the opinion book Kathy had managed to wedge into my schoolbag. At the top of each page, a classmate's name was written in Magic Marker capitals. In the space below, kids scrawled their anonymous assessments. Kathy's page, the notebook's first, was filled with glowing entries: '2 Good 2 Be 4gotten.' 'Love Me Do!' 'Friends to the end!' 'Wish I had that swing in my backyard.' The Dolores Price page was an afterthought written in plain ink on the book's inside back cover. 'Don't Know Her' was the first entry, followed by a column of DKHs and one 'Ugly Isn't the Word' in Rosalie Pysyk's handwriting.

The ballpoint felt strange in my opposite hand; my penmanship came out sufficiently wobbly and disguised. 'Quiet but Cute,' I added to the comments about me. 'Worth getting to know.'

In March Ma had a job interview: secretary for a pest control company. I sat behind her on her bed as she arranged herself in front of the mirror, frowning. 'Well, this ought to be great,' she said. 'I hate talking on the phone, I haven't typed since I was in high school, I'm scared to death of bugs, and I'm mousy-looking.'

'Your hair looks better grown out like that,' I said. 'You'll get it.'

She wasn't back by suppertime.

She's run away, I thought. Abandoned me here in the house of repression.

Grandma and I ate our supper in near silence. 'Maybe she got the job and they needed her right away,' I suggested.

Grandma said she certainly hoped she didn't. There was no telling what kinds of things Ma might carry back to the house from a place like that.

As I finished up the dishes, the idea that my mother might have committed suicide came flying at me. I pictured her up in the cold night sky, walking insanely onto an airplane wing and laughing at risk. I saw her jump.

I turned to Grandma, who was Saran-wrapping Ma's supper. I hadn't planned it. I whacked a glass casserole cover against the counter, breaking it in half. 'You shouldn't have bugged her so much,' I shouted. 'If she cracked up again, it's *your* fault.'

Grandma reeled around. 'You just mind your own p's and q's, Dolores Elizabeth,' she snapped. 'Don't you dare give me the rats!' Her shaky voice told me that she was scared, too.

But at quarter of nine, the Cadillac rumbled into Grandma's alley and Ma burst through the back door. 'Sorry I'm so late!' she announced. 'Guess what? I bought a car!'

She was wearing a brand-new orange coat. Her arms cradled crinkling bags and packages. 'Can you believe it? A 1962 Buick Skylark! It'll be ready on Tuesday. It's white. A white convertible. And the best part is, we get to trade in that goddamned Cadillac. Good riddance! It'll be ready next Tuesday. Did I already say that? I got them to lower the price by a hundred and seventy-five dollars. Did all the talking myself.'

'Did you get that job?' I asked.

'Didn't even go to the interview. Who wants to work for a bunch of bug killers? What a day I've had! Look!'

She yanked off her knit hat. Her hair was platinum blond.

'What do you think?' she asked, tossing her head from side to side.

'Is it a wig?'

'Nope. It's all me!'

Grandma appeared at the doorway. 'Well?' Ma said. Her laugh was nervous. 'Somebody say something.'

Grandma shook her head and addressed me instead of Ma. 'Next thing you know, she'll be marching across the street and having that other one give her a tattoo.'

The Peacock Tattoo Emporium's waiting area was a row of kitchen chairs, standing ashtrays, dirty magazines. You could pick the tattoo you wanted from a fat loose-leaf with plastic-covered sample illustrations.

'They're *both* crazy,' I told Roberta, looking out the plate glass to make sure my grandmother couldn't see me. 'Ma *and* Grandma. They're just crazy in different ways.'

A beaded curtain was drawn between us. On the other side, Roberta was tattooing a customer. 'Well, get used to it, hon,' she cackled back. 'The whole world's nuts. Ain't it, Leon?'

'That's right, Roby,' her customer said.

I sighed and smoked and passed the time thumbing through the dog-eared magazines. In one old *Coronet*, Lana Turner's daughter gave an interview from prison about why she'd stabbed Lana's muscleman boyfriend to death. The article had pictures of the victim, Johnny Stompanato, and Lana's mansion with an arrow pointing to the bedroom window where the murder had occurred. There was a close-up of Lana's daughter, taken in her baggy prison dress. Her eerie, squashed-in face reminded me of mine and Jeanette's faces one afternoon when we'd pulled her mother's old nylons over our heads. Maybe you inherited craziness like you did brown eyes or frizzy hair, I thought. Maybe you just went nuts and did that sort of thing if your mother got a divorce and a new boyfriend.

Roberta pulled the beads aside for Leon and reminded him about the rubbing-alcohol treatment. The week before I'd watched him get a bumblebee tattooed to his shoulder. (If it was okay with the customer, it was okay with Roberta for me to watch the above-the-waist jobs. I could force myself to look at the needles once they were in, but not while they were *going* in.) Leon paid Roberta. Then he shook her hand and left.

'What'd he get this time?'

She thumbed through her loose-leaf and showed me the cobra.

'Where?'

She patted her behind. 'Left cheek. He's coming back next week for the right one. Wants a mongoose getting ready to attack. I told him, I said, if it ain't in my catalog, I ain't guaranteein' nothin'. Freehand comes out good sometimes; sometimes it don't. Says he believes in me. "Besides," he says, "who's gonna see it except me?" He's a bachelor, see? This one today was his twenty-second tat. Like I said, the whole world's crazy.'

'Sometimes I think Grandma's worse off than my mother,' I said.

Roberta laughed and sat down beside me. She lit her cigarette with the end of mine. 'Thelma's a tough old bird, like me. It's funny, though. Her and me moved into this neighborhood about the same time – 1940, it was, before the war – but she never gave me the time of day. Lost her boy Eddie in that drowning the same year I lost my hubby. When the Canuck died, she sent over this yellow cake with chocolate frosting. Had a piece of tape stuck on the bottom of the pan with her name on it. So's I wouldn't keep it on her, I guess. Been living across from each other twenty-five years and I don't think we spoke more than twenty-five words.'

'She hates your guts,' I said. 'No offense.'

'Thing is, I'm probably a little scary to Thelma. See, she ain't seen the world like I have. Me and my first hubby used to go all over the place when we were with the carnival, got to know all kinds of different people. Me and the Canuck, too. When the Canuck and I went to Hawaii, we even climbed partway inside a volcano – a dried-up one, you know. You see, Thelma never had none of that. She's sort of like a scared little girl.'

My head felt light from the smoke and coincidence. She'd just described Grandma the way Ma's book described Marilyn Monroe. Paradox, I thought: a situation or statement that is contradictory, yet true. I'd gotten it wrong on the vocabulary test but suddenly understood.

I stubbed out my butt. 'What was my uncle like?' I asked.

'Eddie? Good-lookin' kid – and full o' piss and vinegar. Used to stand over on that porch and throw snowballs. Had the cruiser parked out front once or twice. But he was a good kid.

Used to shovel my sidewalk free of charge. Terrible thing when
he died – a regular tragedy.'

Then she laughed and told me about the time Uncle Eddie
snuck across the street with a five-dollar bill. 'Said he wanted
a tattoo. A rose if I remember right,' Roberta said. 'Had me
put it right in his armpit so's Thelma wouldn't see it. Then one
hot summer day he had his shirt off and he forgot and
stretched his arms. She marched right over here and said she
was going to call the police and have me shut down. Said it
was hard enough raising a scamp like him by herself without
me making it harder.'

'How old was he?'

'Oh, fifteen or so. Antsy, he was. Used to come over here and
complain about her just the way you do. Told me and the
Canuck he couldn't wait to leave home and join the navy.'

I wanted her to keep talking about Uncle Eddie, but she got
up and told me she felt like closing for the day. 'Yup,' she said.
'Me and the Canuck. One day he'd love me right and the next
day he'd slam me against the wall.' She smiled sadly, shaking
her head. 'And I'd let him, too. How's that for crazy?'

Shortly after we got our new car, Ma landed a job as a tollbooth
collector on the Newport Bridge, a thirty-minute commute
from Easterly. Her hair looked even blonder set against her
khaki uniform. She rode back and forth to work with the top
down. Within a week, she had her first date.

I watched her eyelid twitch when she announced the news
one morning at breakfast. 'He seems like a sweetheart,' she
said. 'Hands me a Hershey's kiss with his money every
morning. Take a chance, I told myself.'

'What does he look like?'

'Kind of cute. At least from inside his car he is.'

Grandma put down her fork. She said she was getting fed up
with all this girlish nonsense from someone who was thirty-two
years old. She wanted to remind my mother that in the eyes of
the Church she was still a married woman and said she hoped

Ma wasn't reserving herself a room in hell for the sake of one little night of whoop-de-do.

I had never thought Ma as someone capable of whoop-de-do. All that week I nervously pictured her with cleavage at some nightclub, dancing cheek to cheek with Johnny Stompanato.

On her big night, Ma rushed excitedly around her room getting ready. She squirted herself with the Tabu perfume I'd sent to the hospital the Christmas before, daubed on her lipstick, and hummed 'Blame It on the Bossa Nova.' Her date owned a store on Edson Street, she told me. He sold newspapers, tobacco, and mixed nuts. I was relieved to learn they were only going to the movies.

Grandma had taken the official position that she just plain gave up. Still, it was she who sent me into Ma's room that evening, a spy armed with a holy trinity of questions: What nationality was he? What religion was he? What was his last name?

His last name was Zito. Mario Zito. 'But all my buddies call me Iggy, Miz Holland,' he explained to Grandma, who gripped the arms of her chair and refused to look at him directly.

Iggy Zito was nothing like hoody Johnny Stompanato. He was short and had ripply red hair and freckles and wore a corduroy car coat. He was somewhere between the kind of man Jeanette and I would have ignored and the kind we would have made fun of.

'And this is my daughter, Dolores,' Ma said. I gave him a one-second acknowledgement and then concentrated on the living-room rug.

'Your mother mentioned she had a little girl. These are for you, sweetheart. Just a little something, heh, heh.' He handed me a wrinkled paper bag with a grease spot on it. I hated it when you could hear a person's saliva right in their laugh.

Ma bent over and kissed Grandma, who sat ramrod straight in her chair and didn't respond.

'Don't wait up for me, now,' Ma laughed.

'Do-on't worry,' Grandma answered, rolling her eyes at the TV.

From the unlit front room we watched them get into Iggy's black station wagon. To my relief, Ma didn't slide in next to him like a teenager but stuck close to the passenger's-side door.

'Zito. That's Eye-talian,' my grandmother said as we stood together in the semidarkness. Back in the other room I opened the bag he'd given me. Inside were two *Little Lotta* comic books, a box of Good'n'Plenty, and several handfuls of pistachio nuts.

Grandma made me throw out the nuts because they weren't packaged and who knew who had touched them, where they'd been? We spent the evening playing Crazy Eights and watching television. Grandma kept referring to Ma's date as Mario Pepperoni. 'Of course, years ago,' she told me, 'you wouldn't even play with the Eyetalians. They were dirty, my father said. One step up from the coloreds.'

At the beginning of summer vacation, Jeanette Nord sent me a letter inviting me to come and stay at her house for a week. She had enclosed a snapshot of her and the kittens, now cats. Ma said she couldn't understand why I didn't take the Nords up on their offer. I couldn't quite understand it, either; I just didn't want to. I preferred to spend my summer days watching TV or sitting out on the porch reading movie magazines and thick paperback romances with the top of my shorts unsnapped for comfort.

My afternoon ritual included walking down to Connie's at four o'clock each afternoon for an ice-cream sandwich. I was licking the melting edges off of one when Ma drove her Skylark into the alley, two hours early, and sat slumped in the car. She'd put the roof up. Her blond hair looked wilty.

'What's the matter?' I called.

'Nothing. I just left early, that's all. Felt kind of sick.'

She got out of the car and sat down next to me on the porch step.

'Lot of traffic today?'

'The usual.' She pried off her wedgies and began to knead her feet. 'I'm not sure I should tell you this,' she said. 'Guess who I saw today?'

'I don't know. Jeanette?'

'Your father.'

The two words felt like a sensitive tooth I'd bitten down hard on, forgotten to favor.

'What's he doing up here? Why isn't he in New Jersey?'

'He moved back a month ago. From the sound of things, I guess his little fling didn't pan out.'

'Is he working for Masicotte again?'

Ma shook her head. 'He's working on some remodeling job out at Newport. Part of a crew or something. I told him, I said, "You still have a daughter who might like to see you. You didn't divorce her, too."'

'I *don't* want to see him! I just want him to leave me alone.'

'Well, still. He hasn't sent money in over . . . Not that that's any concern of yours, Dolores . . . What's new with you?'

'Nothing really.'

'Nothing? All day long?'

If I talked, I might cry. Why should he pay for someone he forget even existed? 'Julie on "Guiding Light" lost her baby,' I finally said.

She sighed and chuckled. 'He was so surprised to see me, he dropped his change and had to get out of the car to pick it up.'

'What kind of car does he have?'

'I don't know. Some gray thing.'

'Old or new?'

'Old. You should have heard him apologize. How do you like that? The shit he gave me all those years and what's he sorry for? Dropping a couple of quarters.'

Daddy called the next evening during 'Hollywood Palace.' Ma and Iggy were on another date. His voice on the phone sounded tinny and far away. I pictured him flat and small but alive, a talking postage stamp.

'I'm kind of busy,' I told him, trying to keep the shaking out of my voice. 'What do you want?'

'Just called to see how it's going, honey. Can't a guy call up his daughter? How's Easterly treating you?'

'Fair,' I said.

'So do you miss me or what?'

My whole body shook. But before I could phrase an answer, he interrupted. 'Didn't even notice I was gone, right? Gee, thanks a lot.' His laugh was fake.

'So I guess your mother has that tollbooth job, eh? She tell you I saw her the other day? Jesus, I almost passed out when I pulled up to that booth. How does she like it?'

'I couldn't tell you,' I said. 'You'd have to ask her.'

He laughed again, as if I'd said something good-natured. Then he coughed and cleared his throat. 'Look, you sound kind of peeved at me, Dolores. And I can understand that. Only there's two sides to every story, you know. You just remember that.'

I thought of the way his skin looked as I swam beneath him underwater in our pool. Whitish blue, color of a dead man.

'I have a nice apartment now. In South Kingstown – place called Garden Boulevard. Maybe you could visit some weekend. We could get Chinese food, how about that? Order takeout.'

My vision blurred over with tears.

'How about if I pick you up some Friday night? Make a weekend of it?'

'I don't think so,' I said.

I heard his loss of patience. 'Things weren't all pie and cake for me, either,' he said. 'Donna and I called it quits, if that's the bug up your ass. Don't be so quick to turn your old man into a bad guy.'

'Daddy? . . .'

'I can appreciate that you wouldn't take *my* side in things, not that there's sides to take. I can understand where you feel a loyalty to your mother, especially after the hospital. But sometime you go try living with a person who . . .'

'Daddy, I have to go now. Honest to God.'

'I'm not going to bad-mouth her the way I'm sure I've been bad-mouthed for two years.'

'Really, Daddy.'

'Do you need anything? Because if you need anything you just say so. Why don't you let me give you my telephone number? Then when you want to come visit, you can just call me up. All right?'

'All right.'

'You have a pencil?'

'Yes.'

He spoke a jumble of numbers that I let go by. Then Grandma was at my side, her hand around my wrist. 'Do you want to me to take it?' she whispered. 'You want me to talk to him?'

'Your mother's been getting the money I've been sending, right? Did you know I send you something every month?'

After I hung up, Grandma told me not to worry – that if he called again, she'd say I was out. She asked if I wanted to play some more cards.

'Could you just hold me?' I asked.

The request seemed to startle her, but she obliged. Her small body felt stiff and unnatural. She placed one hand against my back, trying hard to get it right, then the other. I leaned my forehead against her shoulder.

'Don't cry, now,' she said. 'You're turning out to be a good girl. Stop that crying.' I sobbed and shook against her. Her body wouldn't relax.

My mother and Iggy Zito had two more dates before she pronounced him a square and stopped seeing him. When other men called, Ma would leap for the phone. 'Hell-ooo,' she'd purr, in a sleepy voice lower than her normal one. Her new dates mostly tooted the horn out front or met her wherever they were going. Daddy called back once more. True to her word, Grandma said I was 'over at a playmate's.'

In mid-July, Mrs. Tingley died of a stroke and Cutie Pie was driven away in a Humane Society truck. Grandma fretted about being forced to rent to beatniks or 'cuckoo heads' and wished to Betsy she could afford to just go without the rent income. She had the third-floor apartment repainted and rid of dog stink, then took an ad out in the paper.

Jack and Rita Speight, a dazzling young couple in the mid-twenties, were the very first people to inquire. They reminded Grandma of 'the quality of people who *used* to live on Pierce Street' and moved in on August first. The three of us – Grandma, my mother, and I – fell promptly and hopelessly in love.

Chapter 5

Rita Speight wore windsong perfume and blue eyeliner. She was so tiny, she needed a cushion to see over the steering wheel of her green Studebaker. Each morning she drove to Women and Infants Hospital in Providence, where she worked as a pediatrics nurse. 'Like a little china doll,' Grandma murmured admiringly, watching Rita's departure. Grandma's church friend, Mrs Mumphy, knew Rita's aunt. 'She had a miscarriage when they were living in Pennsylvania,' Grandma confided to me in a whisper. 'Of course, that's between you and me.'

Jack Speight, tall and blond, was a disc jockey at W-EAS Radio. He hosted a talk show called 'Potpourri,' told elephant jokes, and played the kind of farty music my mother listened to on her car radio. He drove a maroon MG with a license plate that said JK SP-8. He was twenty-five, three years younger than Rita.

We were in the middle of a heat wave the afternoon they moved their belongings up the side stairs. I positioned myself on the front porch with sunglasses and a paperback and checked out each exotic item as it passed by: stereo cabinet, Hawaiian tiki lamps, beanbag chair, matching love seats upholstered in orange fur. Jack took off his T-shirt midway through the job. I checked him out, too.

From inside, Grandma watched the Speights' caravan of possessions. She trusted neither sports cars nor 'hairy furniture', but within the week of their arrival, Jack won her over by climbing a borrowed aluminium ladder to the dizzying height of the sloped roof and fastening a loose antenna wire that had been plaguing our TV reception with snow. From the ground below, Grandma and Ma and I watched him, our hands visors at our foreheads. Grandma handed my mother a ten-dollar bill as Jack descended the rungs. 'Make him take this, Bernice,' she whispered.

Ma held the money up to him as he reached the ground. 'Here,' she said. 'This is for you. We insist.'

'No, really. I was really glad to do it,' he said. 'Thanks anyway.'

A laughing kind of dance followed, ending with Ma holding him by the hip and stuffing the money into his pants pocket while Grandma and I smiled hard and watched intently.

Grandma's blank second-floor ceilings were now a theater of sound, and I became a devoted student of the Speight's routines. They ate supper every night at six-thirty, talked while they did the dishes, then watched TV. Their bedroom was exactly above my bedroom and I woke up at six a.m. to their alarm clock. By quarter of seven, Rita would hurry down the steps in her crisp white uniform, and her Studebaker would rattle out of the alley. Jack stayed in bed until ten of eight. I could make out his whistling as he dressed.

Grandma cashed in six S&H green-stamp books for a portable radio and put it up on top of the refrigerator. We both abandoned our afternoon soap operas for 'Potpourri.' On Tuesdays, her day off, my mother listened, too.

'He plays such nice music,' Ma said one lunchtime as she stood frying us grilled-cheese sandwiches and humming along with the McGuire Sisters. 'He and I have the exact same taste in music.'

'That's how much you know,' I said. 'He *has* to play that corny stuff. He likes rock'n'roll.'

Grandma snorted in disbelief.

'He *does*. Yesterday when he got home from work, he played a Rolling Stones album. He was dancing all by himself. It shook my whole bedroom.'

Ma said he was probably doing jumping jacks. Grandma supposed that if he was dancing at all, he was sure it was with his wife.

'Okay, fine, *don't* believe me,' I said. 'You two love him so much, I just thought you might be interested.'

The Speights went to the same Sunday mass as us and by the second week Monsignor had nabbed Jack to pass the collection basket. He winked at me and jingled the change as it passed by my face. My heart pounded almost audibly as I watched him work the pews. One time I caught Ma following his movements, too, lip-synching to the offertory prayer rather than praying it. When she saw me watching her, she jerked her eyes back to her missal and cleared her throat, prayed louder.

Out in the parking lot one Sunday after the services, Rita appeared at the Skylark's side window and tapped against the glass with her wedding ring. Ma braked hard; Grandma practically slid off the front seat.

'Hi, you guys,' Rita said. 'Jackie and I were wondering if you'd like to come upstairs to dinner tonight. Nothing fancy – just some tacos and my world-famous chili con carne.'

I imagined Grandma lunging again at the description of the menu, but not even the threat of spicy foreign food could keep her away. 'Why, that sounds lovely,' she said. 'We'll be there, won't we, girls?'

Girls, I chuckled to myself. As if we were the Marvellettes.

Shortly before we left to go upstairs that evening, Ma made Grandma promise that she'd keep still if she saw anything she didn't like.

'*You're* telling *me* how to behave properly, Bernice?' Grandma said. 'If I were you, I'd just button up that second blouse button and worry about myself.'

We clomped up the back steps, my mother carrying a bottle of wine, Grandma armed with a package of Mylanta tablets. Rita answered the door wearing a red velvet sombrero with pom-poms. 'Olé!' she said. Ma laughed louder than necessary and pushed the wine at her.

I was in love with what they'd done to the apartment. A bookcase made out of cinder blocks and plain boards held dozens of paperback romances. The bottom shelf was bowed down with the weight of what looked like over a hundred record albums. I sank into one of the beanbag chairs and gazed up at the saddest, most striking painting I'd ever seen; a Negro girl on black velvet. She was clutching a rag doll to her chest. One glistening tear – so fat and wet it looked real – sat stopped on her cheek.

Grandma declined Jack's offer to relax on the fur recliner and requested a straight-backed kitchen chair instead. She sat down, one hand on each knee, and I saw the painting catch her eye as well. She stared at it for some time. 'Say, that's quite a picture,' she said finally to Jack. 'And I'm not overly fond of the coloreds.'

Both of the Speights doted lavishly on Grandma, in just the ways she liked. Rita inquired about Grandma's blood pressure and knew exactly the pill she was taking for it. When we were called to the kitchen, Rita reached into the oven with a polka-dot mitt and extracted a little homemade chicken pot pie. 'I thought you might prefer something a little milder, Mrs. Holland,' she said. Grandma's initials had been poked into the crust with fork holes.

'Well, you are just the cleverest thing,' Grandma cooed, patting Rita's hand. 'It's so pretty, I hate to eat it.'

Ma plunked herself right down between the Speights. I got stuck sitting next to Grandma.

Jack kept refilling my mother's glass with the wine she'd brought. With each sip, she acted more and more like Marilyn Monroe. Grandma was so taken with her special meal, she seemed hardly to notice Ma's behaviour. She even reluctantly accepted a glass of wine herself, and went so far as to wet her lips at the rim.

Passing the chili bowl, Jack suddenly turned his attention to me. 'So what does Dolores Del Rio do with herself all summer long?' he asked.

'Who's she?' I said.

'You don't know Dolores Del Rio? Latin beauty of the silver screen?'

'*I'll* tell you what she does with herself all day,' Grandma butted in. 'She sits in the kitchen and listens to a certain so-and-so on the radio. You have yourself quite an admirer.'

I could have stomped her foot. '*Me?*' I snapped. 'You should talk!'

'Dolores Del Rio is exactly who's she's named after,' Ma said. 'When I was a teenager, I saw *Journey into Fear* about fifty times.'

'You know what 'Dolores' means?' Jack asked me.

I shrugged.

'It's Latin, means sadness. Our Lady of Sorrow. Why are you so sad?'

The four of them were watching me. I looked down at the table and the room went silent. Suddenly, I *was* sad – overwhelmed with sadness. 'Who's sad?' I said.

Ma began telling a complicated joke she'd heard at work. Then she stopped and whooped, throwing her head back so far, I could see her fillings. 'Oh, no,' she said. 'I forgot the punch line!'

Jack teased her and she reached over and poked him. He poked her back. Rita laughed and passed the seconds.

The Mexican food tasted fiery and delicious. I wiped the sweat off my top lip and watched Jack drink his wine. 'You know what?' I said. 'That stuff is the exact same colour as your car.' It had come out spontaneously; I felt immediately stupid.

Jack grinned at me. 'Mrs. Holland,' he said, 'this descendant of yours is a genius. Now if only she'd quit swiping money out of the church collection basket.'

Caught off her guard, Grandma was momentarily startled before she realized the joke. Then her eyes shimmered behind her gold-rimmed glasses and she reached over and slapped Jack timidly on the arm. 'You keep telling fibs and I'll give you a licking,' she chuckled.

Jack grabbed the red sombrero and placed it squarely on Grandma's small head. It sank down, bending one of her ears forward.

I held my breath, waiting for Grandma to bring the evening to an abrupt halt. Instead, amazingly, the pompons began to rock with her laughter. It was the first time I'd ever seen her risk foolishness.

That night I lay in bed with the evening's images spinning before me. I felt energized, as if electrical current were passing through me. Sleep was impossible, I told myself, then dozed, lulled by all the answers to the question of why I was so sad.

I awoke in stages, puzzled by an unfamiliar squeaking sound. Half-asleep, I imagined it was Jeanette Nord's kittens, loose somehow in my room. Then I realized – suddenly and totally – what it was: the scritching and creaking of bedsprings up over my head. Low, murmuring voices followed – nothing like their doing-the-dishes talking. 'Please' was the only word – Rita's – that I could make out.

I knew I had no business listening – that I should be blocking them out with sober thoughts: Jesus dying on the cross, bullets ripping through President Kennedy's head, ink needles stuck into Roberta's customers. But my thigh muscles shook and my mind raced wonderfully with what, during a girls-only assembly, Sister Margaret Frances had called 'impure thoughts.' I kept imagining them up there, half-naked and feverish – like lovers on the covers of paperbacks. I drew my pillow slowly toward me, kissing it first with my mouth closed and then with it open. The tip of my tongue poked out, touching the dry fuzzy cloth. 'Please,' I whispered. 'Please.'

The following morning I slept through their preparations for work. At ten-thirty I dragged myself out of bed and downstairs, ate two bowls of Cocoa Puffs, and thumbed haphazardly through *The Nun's Story*, the book Rita had lent me the night before.

'Those clothes you were going to take off the line yesterday are still there,' Grandma said, passing through the kitchen. I picked a random chapter and began reading. She yapped on about housework, girls in her day, how fortunate it was that school was starting up again in two weeks.

After lunch, I listened to Jack's program on the radio. I half expected to hear a song dedication to Dolores Del Rio or some reference to our Mexican meal, but the closest he came was playing a record by Herb Alpert and the Tijuana Brass.

Later, Grandma stood between me and 'As the World Turns,' her hands on her hips. I was slumped sideways in one of the parlour chairs, blowing under a ball of lint in a halfhearted attempt to keep it afloat.

'Those clothes are still waiting out there, Miss Itchy Britches,' she said. 'And your breakfast and lunch dishes are still in the sink. In my day, a lazy girl got a licking.'

'Fine,' I said. 'Stick out your tongue and lick me.'

She walked over and slapped me on the arm – harder than I'd expected, hard enough for it to sting. 'And they didn't sass their elders, either!'

'What are you tickling me for?' I said.

At four o'clock, I heard Jack's MG in the alley, his footsteps up, then back down the stairs. The water pipes groaned and I knew he was out in back washing his car. On my way up the staircase, Uncle Eddie's picture smirked at me from behind glass.

From my vantage point behind the bathroom curtains, I watched him appear and disappear behind the sheets and towels that waved and fluttered on the line. Ma's and my personal stuff was out there, too: two of Ma's black bras and several pairs of my gnarled-up underpants, including the one with the rippy waist.

Jack was wearing cutoffs and a faded inside-out sweat-shirt with the sleeves cut off, no shoes or socks. He whistled and sudsed the little car. I thought of the way Rita's lip curled unattractively against her gum when she laughed. She was cute, not pretty. She should do something with that short, flat hair. As she was, she just didn't deserve him.

He squatted and scrubbed his wire wheels. His legs were muscly, more furry than I'd imagined.

At the dinner the night before, Ma had acted so .... that word kids had written in the opinion book. Leaning over and giving him those little slaps whenever he teased her. *Horny*: that was the word. Ma and her stupid risks, her black-lace bras.

The green garden hose snaked between his legs; he sloshed and sprayed and wiped down the chrome. On his way past the clothesline, he looked right at my underpants. Then he went up the stairs, inside.

Audrey Hepburn on the cover of *The Nun's Story* was staring up at me from my unmade bed. Her hair was hidden by her snow-white wimple; her big eyes looked frightened. 'What are *you* looking at?' I said. 'Fuck you.' It was the first time I'd ever said the word. I felt a brief shiver of power.

Then I sat back on the bed and sobbed. Dolores Price: Lady of Sorrow.

When Ma got home from work, I stood at the top of the stairs and eavesdropped on Grandma's complaints. 'If you didn't just let her . . . As long as she's living in *this* house . . .'

'*I'll* talk to her,' Ma said. '*I'll* take the clothes in.'

When she came upstairs and knocked, I had my defense – my punch line – ready to go. 'Why don't you stop acting like a teenager?' I'd say. 'Why don't you just grow up and stop embarrassing everyone?'

But instead of criticising, Ma sat down and put her arm around me. 'Let's you and me go to the show tomorrow,' she suggested. 'Or shopping or something.'

The top of the Skylark was up, the afternoon gray and rainy. My mother and I were on our way back from our day in Providence.

We'd left in the morning and bought breakfast, then two new school uniforms for me and mohair sweaters for both of us. We'd waited half an hour in line, as well, to see a matinee of *A Hard Day's Night*. But girls in front and back of us were screaming at the glassed-in movie posters; Ma had forgotten her medication and didn't think her nerves could take it. I pouted briefly, then settled for *Mary Poppins*.

'What's your idea of a cute guy?' I asked Ma.

'I don't know,' she said. 'Someone tall, dark, and loaded. How about Vic Damone – is he available?'

'Seriously,' I said. 'Do you think someone like, say, Jack is handsome?'

She tapped the brake for no reason I could see. Then she laughed. 'Jack who? Jack Frost? Jack Benny?'

'Our Jack. Jack from upstairs.'

'Oh, I don't know,' she said. 'I never really thought about it. He and Rita make a cute couple, don't they? She's a living doll.' She reached over and turned on the radio.

'She has an ugly mouth.'

'You're too critical sometimes. I think she's cute.'

'Do you think Jacks looks anything like your brother? That picture of him on the stairs reminds me of Jack.'

'Eddie? Not really . . . Well, now that you mention it. Eddie was darker than Jack, though. Shorter, too.'

She turned the radio off. The windshield wipers made little squeaks.

'I wish it wasn't almost September,' I said. 'I hate that school. I don't have any friends.'

'This year will be different,' she said. 'God, eighth grade – I can't believe it.'

'If I still hate it, can I switch schools?'

'You *won't* hate it,' she said. 'I'm not even answering that. Light me a cigarette, will you?'

I struck the match, sucked in, passed it to her. Then I lit one for myself. We smoked in silence, the Skylark's tires hissing through the wet streets.

'How come you and Grandma will never talk about Uncle Eddie?' I said.

'Who said I won't talk about him? What do you want to know?'

'I don't know . . . Did you cry when you found out he drowned?'

'Yeah, sure I cried.'

'Did he ever see me before he died?'

'Oh, plenty of times. You were about a year old. He used to tease me because you weren't a boy. Used to hold you and call you Fred . . . Oh, God, that funeral. It was awful. He was always so full of life.'

'Did Grandma cry?'

Ma flicked off the wipers. 'I don't know, maybe. Not in front of me.'

'She didn't even cry for her own kid?'

'She was angry about it – did a lot of slamming, I remember. Pot lids, kitchen cabinets. Eddie was kind of wild. He always took chances.'

'Risks,' I said. I hated Grandma, that cold bitch.

'Julie Andrews played a good part in that movie today, didn't she?' Ma said. 'She seems so sweet.'

'She's probably a big spoiled snot in real life.' I clicked the radio back on and twisted the knob until I found W-EAS. A song ended and Jack came on. I turned it up loud; his voice filled the car.

'The eyebrows, maybe,' Ma said.

'What?'

'He resembles Eddie a little around the eyebrows. Those blue eyes that look like they're cooking up trouble.'

When we got home, I took the radio upstairs to my bedroom rather than look at Grandma. I tried on one of the new uniforms. Even the next biggest size was snug.

Jack told an elephant joke. Then I heard the organ beginning of 'Our Day Will Come.' I'd given Jeanette the 45 for a birthday present. We used to sing it together in harmony in the Nords' backseat. Jeanette hadn't written back in months.

I got up and locked my bedroom door.

My hairbrush was a microphone. I sang to the mirror, to Jack's mischievous blue eyes.

Our day will come
If we just wait awhile . . .

My lips moving around the words of the song made me feel sexy and sad. With my free hand, I reached up under the uniform.

So what? I told myself. If Rita – Grandma's little china doll – can do it . . .

I closed my eyes and the hairbrush dropped to the floor. My hands wandered the insides of my thighs, back and forth against my wet underpants. Eddie's hands. Jack's.

Chapter 6

It was already in the eighties when I slumped into the kitchen in my itchy woolen uniform on the first day of school.

'Ta-da,' my mother said. I gave her a dirty look.

It had occurred to me that Jack and I would be starting out of the house at the same time each morning and that St. Anthony's School was on his way to work. From that, I had perfected my fantasy: I would arrive in the MG amidst the confusion of buses, sharing a private laugh with Jack, then swing the door open to my newfound popularity. My hair would have come out as sleek and straight as Marianne Faithfull's. By lunchtime, I'd be class president.

But Jack had left early that sticky morning. Grandma placed a bowl of Cream of Wheat in front of me and turned on the portable table fan. My mother said she refused to think of the end of summer vacation as a tragedy and gabbed on and on about the Powder Puffs, a ladies' bowling league she'd just joined. They both saw me off at the front door; Ma squeezed my hand and told me I was pretty. By the time I trudged the half mile to school, my hair had frizzed and my sweaty hand had stained the cover of my new blue loose-leaf.

St. Anthony's saved Sister Presentation for the eighth graders. A hard little nugget of a woman seemingly unbothered by heat or humidity, she began our year with a review of the school's code of conduct, delivering several major tenets by rapping her hooked pointer against the chalkboard. She commissioned us, the eighth-grade class, to set an impeccable example for the younger grades and hinted that horrible things might happen to the imprudent student – here she established eye contact with Rosalie Pysyk – who chose not to take her seriously.

We spent the morning filling out forms and copying Sister's classroom rules and policies into our notebooks. I ate lunch surrounded by the usual empty folding chairs.

In the afternoon our class studied 'democracy in action' by electing Kathy Mahoney class president for the third year in a row. By the end of the school day, only two of my classmates had spoken to me.

During supper, Ma repeated her same drab line: give it time. She and Grandma were both abandoning me for the evening – Grandma heading to bingo and Ma to the duckpin alleys with the Powder Puffs. Sister had assigned us science and religion, about a zillion pages.

In the mirror, I watched my mother's reflection blot lipstick on a tissue pressed between her lips. She was preparing herself for bowling in the same intense way she got ready for dates. 'Don't get upset or anything,' I said. 'But I think I may have cancer of the stomach.'

'Oh, Dolores, it's just your nerves . . . Grandma says Rita started working second shift this week. Poor thing, she hates it.'

'Stop changing the subject. You should take me to see a doctor tomorrow. It feels like there's a tumor or something growing down there.'

She bent over and began to brush her upside-down blond hair. 'Gee,' she said, 'you're not pregnant, are you?'

Through the V neck of her blouse I saw the black-lace bra, her bouncing breasts. 'Are *you*? You're the one with all the boyfriends.'

She straightened up and pointed the brush at me. 'Don't be fresh,' she said.

Grandma stood in the doorway, clutching her purse and scowling. 'I told Judy Mumphy a quarter to seven, Bernice. Last time you drove us, we got stuck way in back with those noisy fans blowing a draft on us. We were chilly all night. Poor Judy couldn't even hear the numbers.'

'Get in the car, Ma. I'll be right there.'

She leaned over and kissed me. 'Just give it time, sweetheart. I've got to run. That stomach stuff is just nerves or greasy food or something. You take my word for it, Sister Mary Potato Chips.'

'Next time you go crazy again, I'll tell *you* it's greasy food. See how *you* like it.'

Ma's face fell. She walked out of the room and down the stairs, slamming the front door on her way out.

I picked the tissue off her bureau and studied the three interlocking coral O's her lipstick prints had made. They reminded me of a Chinese ring puzzle my father had bought me once, a long time ago. For days I had sat at the picnic table out back on Carter Avenue and tried unsuccessfully to undo it. Daddy hadn't called me since the beginning of summer. When I'd asked Ma if he'd been sending my child-support money, she told me we were getting by fine – that if I needed anything, all I had to do was ask her. Grandma answered me more directly: no, he hadn't.

The tattoo parlor across the street was dark but Roberta's light was on in back. There was a motorcycle parked by the side entrance, the same one I'd seen there all week. In the quiet, I heard Roberta's laugh. The streetlamps along Pierce Street came on.

I sat down at the hallway phone table and began dialing Jeanette Nord's number, then hung up. It took me a whole minute's worth of concentrating to remember our old phone number on Bobolink Drive. I got out my homework and flopped down at the kitchen table.

'Yoo-hoo.'

His hands were cupped over his eyebrows, his outline blurred by the back screen door. 'What'd I do, Del Rio?' he laughed. 'Scare you?'

'Not really,' I said. 'I was just studying.'

'Sorry to bother you, but our stupid fan conked out and I can't find our Phillips screwdriver. Granny have one I could borrow?'

'You can look,' I said. 'Come on in.'

He had on his cutoffs and nothing else. I looked away. 'Man, this heat, huh? You could fry a steak up there on our kitchen linoleum.'

I yanked open the cabinet drawer where Grandma kept tools. 'Is it in there?'

His hands fished among the tools, held fistfuls of them. I slid my flip-flops on and off my feet as I watched him. 'Everything but,' he said.

'Oh. Well, sorry.'

'That's okay. Motor's probably shot anyway. Just thought I'd crack her open and take a look since I don't have anything better to do.'

'My mother said Rita switched shifts.'

'Yeah. Well, thanks. Oh, by the way. Let me know if you ever want a ride to school. I passed you this morning. I go right by there.'

'You did? You do? Okay, thanks.'

The screen door slapped shut again. The side stairs creaked. I went back to my science chapter.

He was up there on their tiny porch. I heard him whistling.

I washed my face in the kitchen sink, then went up to my room and changed into my pink seersucker blouse. Back downstairs I yanked the fan cord so hard, I thought for a second it was going to snap off. I coiled it around my wrist, slid on my flip-flops, and headed up to him.

He was on the porch floor, his legs dangling over the edge. The only clear thing was the burning end of his cigarette. 'You can borrow this one if you want,' I said, holding out the fan. 'I'm not really using it.'

'Oh, that's okay . . .unless you're sure?'

'Here'.

There was an unfinished pyramid of beer cans next to him.

He balanced his cigarette out over the edge of the floor and reached for the fan. 'You're a sweetheart,' he said. 'How about a Coke? Dish of ice cream?'

'No thanks.'

'You sure?'

'Well . . .' I laughed. 'Ice cream, maybe.'

He got up and went inside. I turned and watched his bare back as he moved around the kitchen.

'How's school treating you?' he called out. 'All we got is vanilla.'

'That's fine,' I said.

I hung my legs over the edge of the porch and shook off my flip-flops. They fell, without a sound, to the ground below. Across the street, Roberta's light went out. I picked up Jack's cigarette and rolled it between my thumb and finger. An inch of ash fell away.

He came out holding my ice cream in one hand and Grandma's whirring fan in the other, a new can of beer in the crook of his arm. He'd plugged the fan into an extension cord that ran back inside. I pushed over and made room for him, sitting cross-legged with the beer cans in front of me.

'How can you tell when you've got an elephant hiding in your refrigerator?' he said. He sat down next to me and took a swig of beer. His furry leg brushed my leg.

I shrugged.

'There's a set of tracks through the butter.'

My laugh wasn't my natural one. 'You crack me up,' I said. 'I love listening to your show.'

He gave me a wide smile but said nothing. He sipped more beer. The fan sounded incredibly loud.

'I'm glad somebody out there does,' he finally said. 'Station manager says my humor's too – what was his word? Fanciful. Says I've got to get a better understanding of the middle-aged New England audience.'

He took several long drinks from his beer can, then reached in front of me and added it to his pyramid. 'If he doesn't renew my contract, I'm fucked.'

The word made me flinch.

'You should be on a station that plays *decent* music,' I said. 'You too good for those old farts.'

'Now what would your grandmother say if she heard that?' he said.

'Speaking of old farts,' I said.

He let go a laugh. 'Aw, come on. She's a nice old lady.'

'That's what *you* think. My mother had this brother who died when he was nineteen? Grandma didn't even cry or anything. Her own son!'

'Maybe she cried in private. People do lots of things in private. How'd he die?'

'He drowned. It's sort of weird, really, because my grandparents – my father's mother and father – they drowned, too. In a hurricane. It was a real long time ago, way before I was born. So, I had relatives on both sides of my family who drowned.'

'Well this conversation sure is cheerful, isn't it?' Jack laughed.

I felt the heat in my face. I shut up and ate my ice cream.

Pierce Street looked different from up here – smaller, more organized. 'Well,' I said. 'I better get back to my homework.'

But it was Jack who got up. 'Don't go yet,' he said. 'You're good company. I'll be right back.'

The light went on in their bathroom. I heard him peeing. He came out with a new beer. 'I'd love to make a switch, believe me,' he said. 'There's a top-forty station up in Portsmouth, New Hampshire, that's looking at me, but Rita doesn't want to move.'

'I don't want you to, either. This house was so boring before you guys got here,' I said. 'The lady who rented your apartment before you was a drunk. And she had this retarded little dog.'

He was smiling at me, running his fingers through his chest chair. 'Oh, year?' he said.

'Yeah.'

His hand touched my arm. 'How good are you at keeping secrets?' he asked.

The fan blowing against my back caused a shiver. My spoon clinked against the ice cream dish. 'Okay,' I said. 'Fine.'

'The reason she doesn't want to move is because she's pregnant.'

'Rita? She is?'

He pulled his knee up against his chest, took a sip. 'Life stinks,' he said. 'Maybe that dead uncle of yours was one of the lucky ones . . . She's already lost two babies, you know.'

'Two?'

'Which is why we left my last job in Newark. I was up for the morning show – fifty-thousand-listener potential, perfect exposure to the New York guys . . . You bored out of your skull yet? Just tell me.'

'I'm not bored.'

'She'd go nuts if she knew I was telling you all this. "It'll be okay this time, Jackie, I promise," she says. "Even if something happens, I'll be all right." You may have noticed my opinion doesn't fit into any of these little decisions she makes. You catch that? So now here's this baby coming and Randolph says I'm too – what do you call it? – too fanciful. Says he's waiting to see what happens before he renews me. Wait'll she hears that one – she'll shit the kid right out of her other end.'

My stomach heaved a little. 'I better go,' I said. But I didn't move.

He looked over at me and smiled. 'Dolores Del Rio,' he said. 'You and me against the bad guys, right?'

I didn't answer. He reached down and touched my bare foot.

'Right?'

'Right.'

'What are you?' he said. 'Ticklish or something?'

The word 'ticklish' made me flinch. I let out a nervous laugh. 'You *are*, aren't you?' he said. 'See, I told you!' His grip tightened around my ankle. His fingertips danced along the sole of my foot.

'Come on,' I said. 'Cut it out. I could fall right off this—'

He was on top of me, his knees pressing into my sides, his fingers jumping and jabbing. 'You ticklish here? What about here?'

My head thumped back against the porch floor and I bucked and shoved, unable to breathe. I couldn't stop laughing. His hair flapped on and off his forehead as he rubbed against me, tickling and poking.

'Stop it, okay? . . . *Really!*' I squealed. But he wouldn't stop.

My head rocked back and forth and I suddenly saw how close I was to the fan. My leg shot out. The tower of beer cans flew off the porch, clattering down in the alley.

The noise made him stop. He was laughing, breathing heavily. His beer breath came out in damp, sour blasts. 'Do you *mind*?' I said. 'You're crushing me to death.'

'Phew. Just don't ever let me hear you say you're not ticklish,' he laughed. He got off me. 'Teach *you* a lesson.'

I was coughing. Then crying – hard without control.

He laughed at me. 'Hey?' he said. 'Stop it. What's the matter?'

When I could speak, I told him I was sorry.

'For what?'

'For acting so stupid.'

He reached for me but I pulled away.

'What'd I do, scare you or something? I was just trying to cheer us up. All this talk about death and bosses and shit. What'd you *think* I was doing?'

'Don't mind me,' I said. 'I'm just an idiot.'

I got myself up and started down the stairs, smearing away tears.

'I still don't get it,' he said. He was leaning over the railing. 'First you're laughing your head off, then – what's the matter with you, anyway?'

Up in my bedroom, I heard his knocking and calling down at the back door. I let the phone ring and ring, echoing up the stairwell from Grandma's front hall. All he was trying to do was cheer us up. I told myself. No wonder nobody talked to me at school. I acted so retarded.

Ma and Grandma were home. I positioned myself on the bed, my science book in my lap. Grandma went by my room, grumbling to Ma about hooligans and beer cans and decent people's property.

Ma came in. She sat down on my bed and brushed my bangs away from my forehead. 'I got a strike and two spares tonight. How are you feeling?'

I shrugged without looking up from the book. 'Do you mind?' I said. 'I'm tired and I have to get this reading finished.'

'Okay, honey. Good night. I love you.'

She waited several seconds for me to say I loved her, too. I *wanted* to say it. Risk it. It wouldn't come out.

Later, in the dark, I hugged myself and thought about Uncle Eddie. Not being able to breathe up there on that porch – having no control of it: that was what his drowning must have felt like.

My right side was sore. There was a long scratch on my arm.

I was still awake when Rita got home from work. Their voices murmured up there together. My foot wouldn't stop twitching. My mind wouldn't shut off . . . It must have been something else I had felt up there when he was on me, tickling me. His knee or his elbow or something. He and Rita were married, they were having a little *baby* together, for pity's sake. I was just being a pig and an idiot. I was pitiful.

'How good are you at keeping secrets?' he kept asking me.

'Do you take sugar or are you sweet enough?' I heard Grandma say in the cheeriest of voices as I came down the stairs the following morning. Somewhere in the night, a storm had taken away the hot, gluey air. A cool breeze was flapping the living-room shades.

In the kitchen my eyes bounced from Jack's red-striped shirt to Grandma's smile to the brown cardboard bakery box on the table. Jack was sitting in my mother's place. Ma was in mine, biting into a doughnut.

'Well, *here* she is!' Grandma announced with fake enthusiasm. She dragged the kitchen stool to the table and patted the seat. 'Sit down, Dolores, and have one of these delicious pastries Mr. Speight brought us.'

Jack raised one of our coffee cups to his lips and smiled.

The room smelled of aftershave. His red-and-white pinstripes looked so crisp and clean, I wondered for a second if I'd made up the evening before.

'Hey, Dolores,' my mother said. 'How can you tell if an elephant's been inside your refrigerator?'

There was a sprinkle of powdered sugar on her khaki blouse. Jack's smile looked more than ever like Uncle Eddie's.

'I don't know.'

'Because he's left tracks in the butter.' She and Grandma grinned in anticipation.

'Oh,' I said. 'That's a pretty good one.'

Inside the box were three doughnuts, top-heavy with whipped cream and jam. At Ma's insistence, I lifted one out and onto my plate.

'Is little Rita getting used to her new schedule?' Grandma asked.

'Well, she dragged herself in last night, nodded at me as though she remembered me from somewhere, and then pulled the covers up over her heard. She's still snoring up there.'

Ma began telling a story about when my father worked nights right after they got married. I poked at the doughnut and brought a forkful to my mouth. The whipped cream was warm and yellowy. From the corner of my eye, I saw Jack watching.

'Well,' Grandma said, refilling his coffee cup, 'you tell Rita for me to lock her car doors when she's driving back and forth after dark. All these cuckoo heads and beatniks these days. Some wild Indians dumped beer cans in the alley last night. I guess they just like the thought of decent people having to clean up their messes for them.'

The table fan was on the counter, its cord wrapped tightly around the base.

'Did you hear that thunder last night?' Jack said. 'Wasn't it something?'

I had slept through it.

'You must be exhausted this morning, Ma?' my mother teased Grandma. 'She makes the sign of the cross at every lightning bolt, Jack.'

Grandma made a face. 'Well, this house hasn't been struck yet, has it, Miss Smarty-pants?'

I pushed my plate away. 'I'm not very hungry,' I said.

'Dolores, Jack said he'd be glad to drive you to school this morning,' Ma said.

'That's okay. I don't mind walking.'

'It's no trouble at all,' Jack said. 'Really.'

At the door, Grandma brushed the sleeve of my uniform and clutched me by the wrists. 'If those nasty DP sisters give you any trouble this year, just tell the teacher. Or better yet, send them to Mr. Speight and me.'

Her newfound sassiness was all for Jack's benefit. She referred to him as Mr. Speight when talking to me. What a laugh, I thought. Which of us knew Rita was pregnant – me or her? Who did she think he told his secrets to?

Outside, birds chirped and Pierce Street was shiny from rain water. My flip-flops sat neatly, side by side, just outside the door. Had my mother placed them there? Had Jack?

'Forgot to put the top up last night,' he said. He had draped towels over the seats of the MG.

I sat down on the dampness, slammed the door, locked it, then unlocked it again. I stared away from him and out the side. When he reached over for the stick shift, I pressed my knees together.

'How come you bought us doughnuts?'

'Oh I don't know . . . guess I just like to talk to people at breakfast. Don't forget, I spend the rest of the day talking to a microphone and a bunch of sound equipment.'

I started shaking. Stopped. Starting again. There was a hole in his dashboard where a radio was supposed to be. He smiled at nothing, zipping down Pierce Street. 'Nasty DP sisters?' he said.

'Rosalie and Stacia Pysyk,' I said. 'These two girls who used to bug me last year. That's them right there!'

Like audiovisual aids, the Pysyk sisters appeared ahead, trudging up Division Street. Jack beeped the horn and waved. The two of them looked up at us, amazed, and I stared right back at them.

'Why did they bug you?'

'Who knows? They just did.'

'Jealous of your looks,' he said.

My mouth scrunched to the side. 'Yeah, right.'

'No, I mean it. You put yourself next to those scrawny things, Del Rio, and it's like Miss Universe at the dog pound. Here, look at yourself!'

He twisted the rearview mirror for me to see. My hair was blowing out behind me. I looked carefree, 75 percent pretty.

I pushed the mirror back in place. 'Yuck,' I said.

He watched the road and me, in glimpses. 'Oh, by the way, I almost forgot. About that thing last night? I didn't mean to scare you or anything. You know – the beer, the heat, whatever. It was just one of those things. We're still friends, right?'

My cuticles went white against the edge of my notebook. 'Sure.'

'I tried to call you after you went in. I knew you were upset.'

'I guess I didn't hear you. I was taking a bath.'

'No big deal. So let's just forget it, okay?'

'Fine.'

He tapped his fingers against the steering wheel. He wouldn't stop smiling. 'Not to beat a dead horse or anything,' he said, 'but did you say anything to them?'

'About Rita having a baby?'

'Yeah, that. About anything.'

I shook my head. 'Why should I?'

'Right. Exactly.'

He pulled up in front of the school. 'Well, you have a good day, now. And don't let those two mutt faces bother you. Because you're a special person.' Looking straight ahead, he reached over and took my hand, squeezing it softly. He held it for several seconds. I let him.

Two mulish boys in uniform shirts and ties ran down to the curb as Jack pulled away. 'Check it out,' one of them said.

'How fast does that roller skate of your father's go?' the other one asked me. He smiled dopily, exposing a mouthful of surfboard teeth.

'He's not my father,' I said. 'He's a close personal friend.'

'Miss Price?' Sister Presentation said, mid-morning.

I felt a pulse in my neck. I knew she'd caught me.

'Yes?'

'Can you tell us what they are? The remaining sacraments?' The others craned their necks to watch.

'Baptism, confession . . .' Sister prompted. A dozen hands flew into the air; the question was a cinch if you'd been listening.

'Holy orders?' I said.

'Eric has already said holy orders.' Hope evaporated from Sister's face; I saw her harden against me. 'Did you do your homework last night?'

'Some of it.'

'Well,' Sister said. ' "Some of it" is unacceptable. A girl who can't be bothered to do the very first homework assignment of the school year is a girl who has a poor attitude, in my book. Do you recall what my policy is on incomplete homework?'

'I'm not sure,' I said.

'Then you'd better take out your notebook and look it up. We'll wait for you.'

Panic-stricken, I flipped and flipped the pages, but couldn't find it.

'Number fourteen,' Sister said, impatiently. 'Read it aloud.'

'"A student who has not completed his homework assignment will automatically stay after school on that day."'

'That's correct,' Sister told me. 'And a girl who refuses to do her homework often enough may find herself on the sidelines instead of the graduation line come June. Isn't that right, class?'

They nodded collectively.

At noon I avoided the lunchroom and went, instead, to the school yard. Kids chattered and screamed; jump ropes slapped the asphalt. A large group of third graders were squabbling over a game of Red Light. I hated this school – would rather drown than go here.

At the periphery of the school yard, past the swings, the white plaster statue of St. Anthony stood surrounded by a semicircle of chrysanthemums. I wandered over to the shrine, drawn by the presence of a solitary girl who appeared to be praying. I studied her from the back. Her legs were long and bony – praying-mantis legs. The waist of her uniform buckled in several places beneath her belt. I approached quietly. 'Hi,' I said.

She turned abruptly, gasping, slapping her flat chest. 'Jesus, Mary, and Joseph!' she said. 'You trying to give me a heart attack?'

She was a seventh grader. That morning I'd watched her pick her nose during an assembly. 'Excuse me,' I said. I started to walk away.

'Are you new here?' she said.

'Not really. I moved here last year. From Connecticut.'

'I been there. It's stupid. What made you come to this shitty school?' Her wide black eyes were sunk deep into her face and roofed by a single bushy eyebrow. Smoke was leaking between the fingers of her cupped hand and I wondered momentarily if she was somehow on fire before it occurred to me she was having herself a cigarette, an act emphatically forbidden by the St. Anthony's School Code of Conduct. I tried to relax my facial muscles of any visible signs of shock.

'Or should I say this *prison*?' she continued. 'Any school that don't even let you wear nylons—'

She took an angry little drag off her cigarette in a way that managed somehow to be both defiant and covert. 'Homework, tests – I ain't their slave. Kenny and me got better things to do. You got a boyfriend?'

'No,' I said. 'Not exactly.'

'Me and Kenny been going out for seven and a half months. Since I was in sixth grade.'

'Wow,' I said. 'Is he someone in your class?'

She snorted. 'Don't make me bust a gut. I ain't got time for baby-sittin'. He's in high school. Except he may quit next year when he turns sixteen. On account of all his teachers are out to get him. Plus, he seen this truck deliverin' stuff to their cafeteria one morning and it had a dog-food sign right on the side. Kenny says he ain't eatin' Gravy Train for anybody – they can keep their friggin' diploma. Have you ever French-kissed a guy?'

I looked away, then back. 'I'd rather not say.'

'That's my name, French. Except I ain't.'

'What?'

'French. My name is Norma French, but I'm one-quarter Cherokee Indian. Someone told me French-kissin's a mortal sin but that's nuts. Who decided that – the Pope? I'm sure he never tried it, that skinny guinea.' She held out her cigarette to me. 'Drag?'

I glimpsed Sister Presentation's classroom windows. 'No, thanks.'

'Kenny looks like Elvis. Who do you like – Elvis or the Beatles?'

I knew she was a loser. I knew exactly the kinds of things Jeanette Nord and I would have said about her behind her back. But I was suddenly filled with the fear she'd stop talking to me.

'Oh . . . Elvis,' I said.

'Damn right.' She took another sip off her cigarette. 'King of rock'n'roll and don't you forget it.'

'Plus I like the Beatles,' I said.

The skin around her eyes stretched as she laughed. One of her front teeth was gray. 'Those friggin' weirdos?' she said. 'Cut the comedy!'

She could see I needed straightening out, she said. The Beatles were all queers; you could tell that just by looking at them. Girls who made out in the indoor show were pretty hard up. When she was two years old, she'd swallowed a nail and to this day still remembered the ambulance ride. In 1963, she shook hands at the stock-car races with Miss America, who was ugly up close, whose makeup was thicker than a phone book.

'I have a friend who's a disc jockey,' I ventured.

'Oh, yeah? I call those guys disc *jerkeys*. They should just shut their traps and play the music. Watch this!'

She put her lit cigarette in her mouth and closed it. When she opened it again, the cigarette was sticking out from beneath her tongue, still burning.

'Oh my God,' I said.

'Kenny taught me that. Me and him might get engaged this year. He's thinking about it.'

The school bell gave three short blasts. 'Aw, crap,' Norma said. 'Here!'

She handed me the wet cigarette and ambled back toward the building.

I stood frozen, holding it vertically and staring. Then I threw it on the ground and scuffed it out like Lassie.

The school day ended in church for First Wednesday confession. Most of the eighth graders were pew monitors for the younger grades and the last to confess. I was one of the six in our class who had not been selected.

Above me, a pious stained-glass angel hovered before the kneeling Blessed Virgin. The angel, as blond as Marilyn Monroe and my mother, looked heavenward. Thick white smoke billowed at her feet and I thought of the rocket launchings on TV that had made Daddy so excited. 'Someday we'll drive down to Florida and see one in person,' he had promised me. He was full of promises. He had wrecked my whole life.

Students' confessions drifted out from behind the curtain.
'Yeah, but Father, *he* started it is what I'm telling you . . .' one
boy kept insisting. Stacia Pysyk, sitting amongst the seventh
graders, kept looking back to make faces at her sister, Rosalie.
Norma French, a bit apart from the others, had apparently
forgotten her head covering. Amidst the row of mantillas and
floral hats and velvet-netted headbands, she sat with a bright
red sweater on her head, the collar button fastened under the
chin, the sleeves hanging down the sides of her face like beagle
ears. Norma represented my sole inroad at St. Anthony's, and I
cringed at my pitiful lack of progress.

In the confessional, I listed my sins for Father Duptulski:
pride, swearing, disrespect for Ma. I omitted impure thoughts
and deeds and began the act of contrition.

My detention lasted an hour. On Division Street, Jack's MG
rolled along the curb, following me. I pretended not to notice.
It was a kind of game: if I turned around and looked, I'd lose.

'Hey!' he finally called. 'Want a ride?'

'Oh, hi!' I said, faking surprise. 'All right. Sure.'

The top was down. He squealed his tires taking off.

His cigarette was burning in the ashtray. I reached over and
took a puff without asking permission. He shook his head and
smiled at me. 'Naughty naughty,' he said.

'You should get a radio for this car,' I answered back.

He smiled. 'Oh, yeah? Says who?'

'Says me. Dolores Del Rio.'

Chapter 7

Jack began showing up after school two or three times a week. In my notebook I recorded the days he came but could see no real pattern in them. He waited on the Chestnut Avenue side of the church parking lot. Each afternoon I held my breath and rounded the corner past the rectory.

His moods changed from ride to ride. One day he'd buy us ice-cream cones and tease me, calling me beautiful, reaching over to stroke my hair. The next time, he'd be sulky, mumbling complaints about Rita or his job. It was the *format* of the show that straitjacketed him, he said; that's what the station manager didn't understand. He was wasting his peak years, squandering himself – he almost *welcomed* nonrenewal. He'd be in New York right now at double – triple! – his salary. Living with Rita was like walking on eggs. He seemed to talk more to himself than to me, laughing sarcastically, or snapping his fist against the dashboard.

Whenever he got that way, I felt embarrassed and fidgety – didn't know what to say. Once I told him that in my opinion he should just try not to let things bother him so much. 'And just who in the hell do you think you are, Hot Pants?' he said, his nostrils flaring. 'Your best policy might be to just shut the fuck up.'

Some days he took different ways home. 'Mystery detours' he called them. Once we rode past his radio station. Another time we idled in the rear parking lot of an abandoned grammar school – a brick building with plywood windows and tall weeds growing through the blacktop cracks. Most of *his* teachers were probably dead by now, he said – good riddance. He told me how he'd once been benched during some long-ago basketball play-off game because he played the same position as somebody's son. 'They're out to get us, kiddo,' he said, taking my hand, studying it. 'We've got to be on our guard, you and me.'

I told Grandma I'd joined the Bulletin Board Club at school – that I stayed after with other girls to decorate classrooms and hall showcases. Jack always let me off at Connie's Superette instead of at Grandma's. Inside, Connie watched me from behind the counter, her face impassive, her arms folded under her huge breasts. Sometimes one of the Pysyk sisters was out on the porch or in front of the store, watching, trying to figure us out. Jack's rides made their staring unimportant. 'Take a picture,' I called up one time to Stacia. 'It lasts longer.'

When I got back to Grandma's – usually in the middle of 'Edge of Night' – I was always hungry. I'd stuff down cookies, potato chips, overripe bananas – urgently, without noticing the tastes. Grandma sat with the shades drawn, mesmerized by her story, oblivious to my wild, risky rides.

One afternoon when Jack didn't show up, I walked downtown with Norma French. Her boyfriend Kenny met us at Lou's Luncheonette. He called me 'Dolly' instead of Dolores and blew straw wrappers in Norma's face. I sat poker-faced, forcing myself to listen to the way he laughed from the back of his throat. Dozens of blackheads studded his oily forehead. 'Wanna see something?' he asked me. He yanked up his yellowy undershirt, exposing two passion marks Norma had given him on the stomach. I got up and left rather than sit across from them in the booth and watch them kiss.

Sister Presentation assigned us science reports, due the week after Halloween. From her list of mimeographed topics, I selected 'The Miracle of Human Birth.' For over a month, I had kept Jack's secret, waiting patiently for his and Rita's announcement. Whenever I saw Rita, I studied her face, her middle, even the way she looked and laughed, for visible signs. She gave none. She was as good at secrets as I was.

I had already appointed myself the Speights' sole babysitter and picked out names: Christopher Scott for a boy and Lisa Dolores for a girl. In a recurring vision, Rita sat up weakly in her canopied deathbed and handed me the pink infant. 'I'm sorry you have to leave school,' she whispered, barely audible. 'Take good care of them both. They need you more than I can say.'

'Cup of coffee?' Jack asked.

He had taken a detour all the way down Chestnut and pulled abruptly into a doughnut-shop parking lot.

'Okay,' I said.

I studied him through the store window. He was wearing his wheat jeans and brown plaid sweater. The waitress patted her hair and laughed at something he said. She watched him from the back as he walked out.

The coffee against my lips was too hot and I blew on it, watching the oily surface that swirled on the top. 'Guess what I have to write a report on?' I said.

'What?'

'Babies. How they grow inside their mother before they're born.'

'Oh, yeah?' he said. He took a cautious sip of coffee and looked straight ahead. 'Well, whoopee.'

'When are you and Rita going to start telling people about the baby, anyways?'

'Why?' he said, looking over at me. 'Did you say anything?'

'No. I was just wondering.'

'Oh. Well, like I told you, she's a little gun-shy after what happened before. There's no hurry.'

'Grandma will probably crochet it a whole wardrobe. When is it due?'

'April. Middle of April.'

'Really? I have a *Life* magazine here that I took out of the school library for my report. It's got pictures of what babies look like as they're developing. It's weird. You want to see them?'

'See that waitress in there? Her name is Dolores, too.' He started the car up, rolled back out onto the street. 'It's on her tag. Right over her fat tit.'

I tried not to hear it. 'So do you want to look at the article?'

'I don't have to look at that kind of thing. Rita's medical books have all that stuff in them.'

'Can I just tell my mother about the baby? She won't say anything to Grandma. Or can I at least tell Rita I know?'

I knew he was mad from the way he shifted the car. 'Look,' he snapped. 'Either I can trust you or I can't.'

'You can,' I said. 'I was just asking.' I took a large gulp of coffee. The hot bitterness of it choked me. I coughed and coughed. Coffee jumped out of the cup, spilling in my lap and on to the floor.

Jack pulled to the side of the road. He reached down with a napkin and wiped the floor. 'I'm sorry,' he said. 'It's just that I'm under a lot of pressure lately.'

'Forget it. I shouldn't bug you. I'm the one who's sorry.'

His hand touched my ankle. He slid his fingers inside my sock and moved them up and down. I pressed my foot hard against the floor so it wouldn't jump. I didn't want him to tickle me. I didn't want to make him mad. 'You and me,' he said. 'We're special people.' Then he straightened up, put the MG in gear, and drove me back to Pierce Street.

I started the report that night, lying belly down on my bed, copying facts on to index cards in the manner Sister had ordered. I counted backward from April fifteenth, then forward again to the current date. She had to be at least two months pregnant. *Limb buds are quite discernible and the primitive heart beats rapidly*, the article said. *The embryo is the size of a peanut in a shell.*

Jack walked across the floor upstairs. He was just nervous about it; all expectant fathers were like that. On 'My Three

Sons', Robbie Douglas had driven all the way to the hospital without even realizing he'd forgotten his wife. We were good friends, Jack and me. I'd help him through it.

The fetus pictures took up several whole pages. Some of them reminded me of the sea monkeys I'd once seen advertised on the back of a comic book and sent away for. I'd waited weeks and weeks for them to arrive. 'Place in a glass of ordinary tap water and watch them come to life!' the instructions said. But they remained brittle and lifeless, floating at the top for days until my mother made me flush them down the toilet.

The following day in school, Kathy Mahoney placed a small box of party invitations on top of her desk. All morning long, I watched her walk back and forth to the pencil sharpener, dropping envelopes on desktops whenever Sister Presentation wasn't looking. Just before lunch, she took her final trip, tossing the empty stationery box in Sister's wastebasket.

Norma ran up to me at the end of the day, calling my name loudly enough for others to turn and smirk.

'What are you, deaf or something? You want to walk down to Lou's?'

'Look,' I said, loudly enough for Kathy and the others to overhear. 'Stop bothering me, okay?'

She looked more curious than hurt.

'I just don't want to be friends with you anymore. That boyfriend of yours gives me the creeps.'

Norma sucked her teeth. 'Look who's jealous,' she said.

'That's a laugh and a half!' I said, with as much contempt as I could manufacture. 'Maybe if he used a vat of Clearasil, I could look at him without puking.'

Her lower lip protruded. She socked me in the stomach.

'Girl fight!' someone shouted. People rushed around us in a circle.

I swallowed vomit back down my throat. In tears, I screamed at Kathy Mahoney, at all of them. 'I'm not *your* free show!' Then I ran past the rectory and on to Chestnut Avenue, their staring and laughing following me.

'Drive fast!' I ordered Jack. 'Get me away from this fucking school!'

That night, my father called. Ma held out the receiver, exasperated. 'Then *you* tell him you don't want to see him,' she whispered. 'I'm sick of him accusing me of everything in the book.'

I snatched the phone. 'What?' I said.

I listened to more of his promises: miniature golf, restaurant food, movies.

'Do me a favor?' I said. 'Just pretend I died.'

I heard him draw a breath. Then he told me he had just about had it with my busting his agates, that it was about time I got off my high horse and realized—

I hung up on his big speech.

Jack showed up after school the next day. 'Well, well, well, if it isn't the Queen of Sheba,' he said as I climbed into the car. 'I was about to take off if her highness kept me waiting any longer.'

'What am I supposed to do?' I snapped. 'Just get up and leave early?'

He pulled away and down the street. There was a small brown liquor bottle between his legs. 'Well, it's over,' he said. 'They're shit-canning me. One more month and I'm out of there.'

'Your job? Oh, my God . . . What are you going to do?'

'Right now I'm going to take me and you on a little adventure,' he said. He lifted the bottle and took a quick, sneaky drink.

'Where? I sort of have a lot of homework tonight. I'm still working on that report.' I didn't like it when he was drinking. I didn't want him touching my feet.

'Fine. Forget I mentioned it.' His laugh was bitter.

'You'll get a job at a *better* station, Jack. W-PRO, maybe. Any station would be lucky to get you.'

He shook his head and snickered.

'I guess a ride would be okay. As long as it's not too long.'

'Forget it. Don't do me any fucking favors.'

'No, please. I want to. Really. Where should we go?'

He turned to me and smiled. 'If I told you,' he said, 'it wouldn't be an adventure.'

He drove out on Route 6 until the stores became houses, then woods. The autumn air smelled of apples and wood smoke. Nothing looked familiar. I stuck my arm out the window and let it go limp. Pockets of cold wind kept pushing it up. Canada geese made an arrowhead in the sky.

'My mother's got this thing about flying,' I said. 'In my room I've got this picture she did of a flying leg. When we lived at our other house, she used to have a parakeet who—'

'I don't want to talk about your mother,' he said. 'Just shut up. I'm not in the mood.'

'You'll get a better job. Things will be all right.'

He chuckled and sipped from his bottle. 'Want some?'

I shook my head, shocked that he'd ask.

'That's a good little pussy,' he mumbled.

'Look, I don't think that—'

'You don't think *what*?'

'Nothing,' I said. 'Just forget it.'

We rode and rode. When we were nowhere in particular, he turned his blinker on. A hand-lettered sign said 'Animal Shelter – Town of Westwick'. Then we were on a bumpy road lined with pine trees.

'I don't get it,' I said.

'I haven't been out here for a while. There's a reservoir off thataway. And a waterfall somewhere around here. Listen for it.'

The road dipped and rose and Jack swerved his way around the ruts and puddles. I thought of the wild rides with my father in Mrs. Masicotte's car. 'So why are you taking us here?' I asked.

'I was thinking about this place today while I was on the air. Thinking about you, too. You'd be surprised how many times a day I think about you. I want to show you something. This will break your heart.'

'What?'

'Don't be impatient,' he said. He had on his teasing smile.

'Has Rita ever seen it?'

He took another sip without answering me.

'Are you drunk or something?'

'Hey,' he said. 'Didn't I tell you a while back to shut up?'

'Okay, fine,' I said. 'Just remember, I have homework.'

I listened for that waterfall but heard, instead, the sound of barking dogs up in the trees. It got louder, came down to the ground. Up ahead was a cement building.

Jack slowed, pulled on to a crunchy gravel driveway, and cut the engine. 'There,' he said.

The dogs were behind chain-link pens that ran the length of one side of the building. Their angry barking filled up the air. A big white one kept lunging at us, buckling the fence with each charge.

Jack got out of the car. He tried the doorknob of the building, called hello, knocked on the metal door. 'Guy I know's the dog warden but it looks like no one's home,' he called back to me over the barking. 'Come on out and see the pups.'

I approached hesitatingly. One had a cloudy eye; another had scratched his back raw. The white dog bared his pinky-gray gums at us and bit at the wire of the cage. 'Why are they out here?' I said.

'These are the poor fuckers nobody wants. Keep them here a couple of weeks. Then they gas 'em.'

He reached out and placed his hand on the small of my back, drawing me in next to him. 'Don't they have sad eyes?' he said. 'Makes you want to sit down and cry.'

I couldn't see it. They were riled and dangerous-looking and I felt no sympathy. Their claws clicked against the concrete floor as they paced, dodging their turds and their slimy water bowls.

Jack started rubbing my back. The dogs seemed to calm. 'The

world is a lonely place, all right,' he said. 'Just look at these guys.'

'Yup. So where's this waterfall?'

'We're friends, right?' he said. 'Can I ask you for a favor?'

'I don't know. What is it?'

'You promise you won't take it the wrong way?'

'I won't,' I said.

'Could I give you a kiss – just a friendly one?'

My stomach pulled in; blood pounded in my head. 'I don't think so.'

'Some friend.'

Then he bent toward me and kissed me anyway – softly, on the mouth. His breath was smelly and sweet from the liquor. His fingers dug into my back. The dogs were barking again.

'That felt nice,' he said. 'Nicest kiss I ever had. Don't be afraid.'

He tried to do it again but I pulled away and stood by the car. 'And you said there's a reservoir?' I said. My voice was quivery.

He laughed and got back in the car, shaking his head. I got in, too. Our door slamming echoed in the trees. His hand moved to the ignition switch, then stopped.

'Can I ask you something?' he said.

'What?'

'Do you think much about sex?'

'No,' I said. 'Can we go?'

'Because I think you're very, very sexy – as if you didn't know already. Sometimes when she and I are . . .'

I wanted to be back at Grandma's, in the bathroom with the door locked, figuring everything out. 'Can we just go?' I said.

He reached in front of my knees and flopped down his glove compartment. I was surprised to see his hand shaking a little. He pulled out a rolled-up magazine.

'See this,' he said.

It took me a second to figure it out: a woman on the cover had her mouth on a man's penis. I flung it back at him.

'Here,' I said.

'Don't you want to take a look? Aren't you curious?'

I started to cry. 'No.'

'You sure?'

'Shut up.'

He chuckled. 'They're doing a great job with you over at that school. You're going to make a terrific nun.'

I didn't speak.

'Stop shaking. It's just a magazine.' He was trying to sound calm and cool, but his words came out tight and his breathing was quick and jerky. I could tell he was losing his temper. 'Sometimes I forget what a little kid you really are,' he said. 'What a little baby . . .'

I jammed my hands under my legs. 'I'm not a little kid. I just don't feel like looking at dirty pictures,' I said. 'So shoot me.'

'Maybe I will,' he laughed. 'The thing is .. . the way I look at it, anyway, is that love isn't dirty. And neither are pictures of it. But some people's minds are.'

'What's that supposed to mean?'

'Besides, it's not even mine. I borrowed it from someone for a joke. But I guess I made a big mistake . . . Either that or I was misled by a little cocktease who's probably going to run back and tell Mommy.'

'Look, I don't tell her stuff, okay? And I'm not that thing you just said, either.'

'What thing?'

'You think I'm such a baby, but I'm not.'

'Okay, okay,' he said. He reached over and began playing with my hair. 'Because we're good friends, you and me, and I hate to think I couldn't trust you.'

'Well, you can, all right? Can we just go home now?'

He rolled the magazine back up and ran the edge of it against my leg, down to my foot, over and over. 'I'll probably have this for a while. Before I have to give it back to that guy. You tell me if you ever want to look at it. We'll look at it together.'

'No thanks,' I said.

'"No thanks,"' he mimicked. He slid it under the seat.

A few of the dogs were lying down. One paced his cage.

'Dolores,' he whispered. 'Look.' His hand was between his legs. He was rubbing his lump, watching me.

I turned away and stared hard out the window, tears falling fast. 'Would you please stop that?' I said. He didn't even seem to be the same person. A sudden thought slammed into me: I might not *get* home.

'Stop what?' I could hear him still doing it.

'That!' I said, flailing my hand back at him. Then I flung the door open, was out of the car, running past the dog pens. The animals barked and leapt. None of it seemed real.

He caught me behind the building. I lost my balance and he fell down onto me. He twisted my arm back, yanking and pulling. 'Don't tickle me!' I cried. 'This isn't funny. What are you doing?'

He didn't seem to hear. 'Little Miss Innocence . . . fucking fed up with your bullshit. Give you what you been looking for.' The words spit out of him. 'Look at me when I'm talking to you!' he shouted. 'Bitch!'

His knee jabbed against my leg, pinching the skin against the ground. I looked.

'Now, say it: say "Fuck me, Jack." Tell me to fuck it into you.'

When I swung, he reached out and caught my wrist, pressing the bone against the ground. He gave my arm another painful yank. This isn't Jack, I told myself. Somebody – Daddy, the *real* Jack – will come and save me.

With his free hand, he yanked my skirt up and I heard something tear. 'If you rip this uniform, you're paying for it!' I screamed. 'Honest to God!'

'Shut up,' he whispered. Begged. 'Listen. It's nicer if you don't fight it. We're friends, you and me. Don't wreck it. I can't . . . It won't hurt if you don't fight. I promise . . .'

He kept fumbling and poking at me. I tried to pull my head up, to punch and spit, but my fists wouldn't land. The drool fell back against my chin. His elbow swung out and jabbed against my throat, gagging me.

His rubbing was rough and mean. His pants were down. 'I hate you!' I shouted. 'You pig!'

I stopped fighting, cut off by the pain of it. The sound of the barking dogs fell away so that all I could hear was his cursing and grunting, over and over, in rhythm with each thrust, each rupture. He's splitting me open, I thought. He'll break me and then I'll die.

I turned my head away and watched my fingers rake the dirt. My hand opened and closed, opened and closed. I couldn't feel myself controlling it. 'Just pretend I died,' I had told my father – and I knew no one was coming for me, that I was by myself.

Jack's anger shook us both. Then he stopped altogether, his dead weight on top of me. He was whimpering, catching his breath. When he got up, he kicked me hard on the leg and walked back out in front.

I heard him talking softly to the dogs, soothing them.

On the drive back home, he sobbed and talked. He wouldn't shut up. 'We're awful people, you and me. Don't think this was all my show. We did what we did together.'

My mind was numb; my insides burned. He seemed to drive so slowly.

He was talking about some gun. 'You don't think I'd use it. But I would. What would she want to live for, anyway, if she found out what we just did . . . You want to call my bluff and tell, you just do it . . . I'll leave a note. Think of all the questions they'd have for *you*.'

When he pulled up near Connie's, he reached over and brushed dead grass off my uniform. I was scared not to let him. 'I feel so much closer to you now,' he said. 'You and I are together in this. If you tell anyone, I'll do it. You'll probably hear the shots. Her and me will be lying up there with half our heads blown away. Two deaths, thanks to you.'

Three, I thought. The baby. I got out of the car. I looked only at my shoes, one in front of the other, getting home.

Inside, the table was set for supper. Ma's mail was waiting

for her on the counter. Potatoes were peeled and cut up in water on the stove.

The TV blared in the parlor. I walked past Grandma and up the stairs. My blouse had a dirt smudge on the sleeve. My underpants and legs were filthy with blood and him.

I looked at myself in the medicine-cabinet mirror. What had happened was going to be always on me, in me, as permanent as one of Roberta's tattoos. 'Dolores,' I said. I repeated my name over and over until it sounded warped and unreal. I was never going to be myself again.

I eased down into the bath. I'd made it hotter than I thought I could ever stand. Through the clear, steaming water I watched my skin redden, studied the swollen place on my leg where he'd kicked me. A thin streamer of blood floated on the surface near my knee. I opened my sore legs wide to the scalding water.

I was afraid to stay in my room, afraid to be alone. I could hear him up there.

Grandma looked up from her story. 'How was school today?' she asked.

'All right.'

'You say that exactly same thing every afternoon. Don't you ever have a day that's swell?'

'No.'

I wanted Ma – to see her face, hear her voice. Know she was real, know I was inside the house with her and not out there. But when she got home, I saw it wasn't enough. Her mouth talked about her supervisor, her aching feet, her bowling average. The thing that had happened ached up inside me but was invisible.

Rita miscarried on a Sunday afternoon in November, the week after she'd sat at our kitchen table and told us the good news. Grandma called me to the dining-room window and whispered in my ear about the spotting. We watched Jack walk her to the car and ease her down into the passenger's seat, then drive her away. At bedtime they still weren't back.

I awoke in the dark, drawn out of a troubled sleep where dogs chased me, cornered me, licked at my feet. I sat up and told myself to admit it: we had killed that baby, Jack and me – destroyed it with the filthy thing we did. I wasn't Little Miss Innocence. Hadn't I gotten into the car with him all those afternoons? Touched myself thinking about him that time? Baby-killer Dolores, guilty as sin.

Downstairs it was shadowy and still. Steam seeped from the radiators. The front door handle was cold. The cold sidewalk against my bare feet kept me going.

Roberta's back light was on.

'Dolores?' she said. She was in pin curlers, pajamas. My knocking had scared her. 'What's the trouble, honey? What?'

I leaned into her shoulder and sobbed.

Told.

She hugged me and rocked me against her and made me a cup of tea. The comfort of it, the warmth I swallowed, was the first thing I'd felt in weeks.

At dawn, we walked back across the street to wake up Ma.

PART TWO

Whales

Chapter 8

Mr. Pucci, my guidance counselor at Easterly High school, was a wispy man with small hands and a discreet toupee. He had been my only friend during my miserable three and a half years at the school. 'Hi, pal,' he'd call to me between classes as I slouched past his office door, eyes on the linoleum tiles, waiting hungrily for his acknowledgement. I knew his tiny, sunless cubicle almost as well as I knew my own bedroom: the frayed venetian-blind cord, the non-blooming geraniums cramped together on the windowsill, his poster – 'I'm High on High School' – which curled away from the yellow cinder-block walls. On his neat desk, he kept a picture cube with his nephews' faces on each surface. 'Uncle Fabio,' they called him. I knew that, too.

I felt both protective and possessive of Mr. Pucci and silently cursed the boys who mimicked his lispy speech as they passed by in the corridor. I hated his other counselees, who took up his time with their trivial issues while I sat fidgeting in the office with my most current personal crisis. Mr. Pucci had seen me through eight smoking suspensions, $230 worth of unreturned library books, sixty-seven days absent during senior year alone, and four years' worth of unreasonable teachers. He talked the girls' gym instructor into exempting me from communal showers. He personally called the parents of the football players who, for a joke, campaigned for my election as Spirit Week queen. When my Spanish teacher, Senorita O'Brien, insisted on seeing me as a name in her grade book instead of someone with

unique and delicate personal problems, it was Mr. Pucci who
got my foreign-language requirement waived. We *were* pals; I
had sworn at him, trusted him with minor secrets, and sobbed
into his desk blotter after each cruel remark someone hurled.
Then, in April of my senior year, he called me out of study hall
and sank an ax into my heart.

Ma's Tabu perfume filled up the office. She was wearing her
tollbooth-collector's uniform and was seated on an unfamiliar
metal folding chair that had been dragged in for the occasion.
My school records were fanned out across Mr. Pucci's desk. 'Sit
down, Dolores, sit down,' he began. His palm was extended out
toward my regular seat; his smile was unfamiliar. 'I've asked
your mother to come in today so that the three of us can talk
about your future.'

It was a setup, an ambush. 'Can we do it some other time?' I
said. 'I have an important quiz to study for. Plus, I think I may
be getting a migraine.'

Ma was snapping and unsnapping the clasp of her pocketbook. 'I've gotten off from work special, Dolores. I think we
should both hear what Mr. Pucci has to say.' I was suddenly,
blatantly, aware of secret telephone conversations between
them. The revelation made me limp. I sat.

'After careful consideration of Dolores's needs and her
capabilities, Mrs. Price, I'd like to prescribe college – despite
what's here before us in black and white.' The *real* story, he told
Ma, lay in my love of reading and the potential several of my
teachers thought they detected in me. Teachers! There were two
types: the ones who treat you like dirt and the ones who were
all over you with their Geiger counters of hope. I dropped my
face into the impassive look I'd perfected from Julie on 'The
Mod Squad.' With my knees, I buckled and unbuckled the side
of his metal desk. I had been in love with Mr. Pucci's gentleness,
our rituals. A million times during our talks I'd imagined
leaning toward him and placing my hands around his tiny
waist, feeling my fingertips touching in the back. 'I happen to
believe in Dolores's future, Mrs. Price,' he said. His frail,

anxious face was framed in geranium leaves. 'And if she decides not to go to college, you may both regret it for the rest of your lives.'

He hit the jackpot with that word: regret. It was regret that had mostly motivated my mother since the night Roberta walked me back across the street. Ma had insisted on driving me to the emergency room, though the emergency was two weeks old. On the way there, her teeth chattered out of control while I sat in stone silence. She saw me not for what I was – an accomplice in the baby's murder – but as Jack's innocent victim. I was able to drop her to her knees with demands. So I did.

Upon my insistence, Ma had withheld our terrible secret from Daddy and chosen not to press charges against Jack, letting him escape down the back stairs with his and Rita's things that next weekend while we visited Grandma's cousins in Pawtucket. 'Believe you me, I'd like nothing better than to see that filthy bastard rot behind bars,' she told the state-police detective who sat downstairs in our parlor. 'But that kid up there is thirteen years old. She just needs to pretend it never happened.'

Out of regret, Ma paid for homebound tutoring for the remainder of the school year, though she swore on a stack of Bibles that no one at St. Anthony's School could have *possibly* found out. My first tutor, Mr. McRae, kept looking at me funny. The second, Mrs. Dunkel, was a retired schoolteacher with a powdered neck and pottery bracelets that clacked against the kitchen table. Mrs. Dunkel dozed while I read her assignments. She was safe and sweet. Dr. Hancock – the psychiatrist they made me talk to – was not. Though Ma regretted doing it, she told Dr. Hancock she was terminating his weekly attempts to force me to discuss Jack Speight. This was at *my* request, she explained to him, though *I* had phrased it more in terms of a demand: if she made me go to any more of the psychiatric sessions, I would go up to Grandma's attic with a soupspoon and a can of Drano and kill myself.

The city of Easterly declared me normal enough to attend

regular high school the following year. Ma's sick notes always mentioned regret. 'I regret to inform you that Dolores has been ill with a sore throat . . . a stomach problem . . . a bad head cold' she'd write on days when I felt too depressed or keyed-up to attend. She never refused to write the excuses, though she didn't like lying; you could tell from her foreshortened, abrupt penmanship. By then, Ma's regret had ritualized itself into a weekly array of victim's consolation prizes from the grocery store. She returned each week with shopping bags full of goodies for me: packaged cookies, quarts of Pepsi (I preferred it warm), cigarettes, magazines, and fat paperbacks. I kept my treats in the labeled grocery bags on top of the twenty-one-inch color console Motorola TV Ma had bought me for my bedroom on my fifteenth birthday.

'If she decides not to go to college, you may both regret it for the rest of your lives,' Mr. Pucci told her. With my college education, he was offering a chance to avoid a life sentence of regret. Ma bit the bait. Hard.

I spent the next several weeks whining and pouting and shrieking. How, I wondered, could she be so cruel to me after all I had gone through? I couldn't stand school *now*; why should I sign on for four more years of torture?

College catalogs began arriving in the mail with address labels in my mother's handwriting. They were filled with *terrifying* photographs: students and professors sitting together on lawns holding pleasant conversations; goggled chemistry majors wielding their Bunsen burners; beaming girls brushing their teeth together at a row of dormitory sinks. I tore them up as fast as they arrived. For days I refused to come downstairs for either school or supper, holing up in my room with the goodies Ma still faithfully provided. When I wasn't giving her the silent treatment, I was pleading with Grandma to intervene for me. Colleges were full of drugs! College girls got pregnant! I began sobbing about overdoses and nervous breakdowns. When I knew Ma was listening, I'd hustle to the bathroom and stick my fingers down my throat, gagging dramatically. 'I can't even keep anything down anymore,' I'd whimper as I passed her worried face in the hallway. Then I'd go back to my room and feast on Fritos, Flings, Devil Dogs, Hostess Sno-Balls – unwrapping the cellophane as quietly as possible.

The gray circles under Ma's eyes puffed up and her fingers danced and fidgeted as she filled out applications under my hateful glare. But I could not make her give in. She was determined not to battle regret the rest of her life. I was going to college.

By the end of May, eight schools had rejected me. Ma's last hope was Merton College in Wayland, Pennsylvania, but the application was a sticky one. It required an essay on the one person in the world I'd most like to meet. Ma stewed and paced for a week and then rented a typewriter. She called in sick and started one evening after supper, hunting and pecking her way through the night. The following morning I stood at the kitchen table eating my breakfast – chocolate doughnuts and a mug of Pepsi. Ma's cheek was pressed up against the enamel tabletop and she was snoring out of distorted, pushed-together lips. Around her were dozens of wadded-up paper balls – enough false starts to decorate a float in the Rose Bowl parade. I reached over and rolled her finished product out of the typewriter.

If I could meet one person in this whole world, it would be Tricia Nixon, the President's Daughter. She is friendly and her blond hair is very pretty. She also has neatness and good manners. She makes me feel that if your ever in Washington, you could call her up and ask her to go shopping or show you the sights or just sip a soda with you. She is a friend to every girl in this great country – even little old me.

Very truely yours,
Dolores Price

Ma squinted and woke. She watched me cautiously as I put the paper down in my doughnut crumbs.

'Well?' she said.

'You spelled "truly" wrong.'

'But besides that. What do you think?'

'Do you want the truth?'

She nodded.

I swallowed a mouthful of doughnut and smiled assuredly. 'This wouldn't get me into a school for retards.'

Ma's lip poked out and I thought with satisfaction that I'd made her cry. Then, suddenly, she shoved the typewriter off the table. It banged down in front of me, inches away from my bare feet. She was pointing to the typewriter but looking at me. 'If that thing is broken, it will have been worth it,' she said. 'I am *not* . . . some piece of dog crap!'

Merton College wished to inform me that I had been accepted. All I needed to do was send them my tuition fee and have the doctor mail back the enclosed physical-examination form. That weekend, the war escalated.

'There are two things in this world I am not about to do!' I shrieked down the stairwell to my mother at the end of a Saturday-night battle that had included three broken dishes and a slapping session. 'Number one is go to any college. Number two is put my feet up in those stirrup things and have some pig doctor come walking toward me, snapping his fucking rubber gloves.'

Grandma had been in the parlor watching 'Mannix' when the fight started. I imagined her stiffening, knees pressed together bone to bone at the sound of the 'fucking.' The past four years had changed Grandma, cowered her. She knew how to handle sass, not rape. From the moment I'd returned from the emergency room that night, Grandma had treated me as a stranger, someone exotically dangerous. She spoke only once of 'that business with him,' sliding her good rosary beads on to my nightstand 'in case you need them.' Sometimes I'd catch her staring at me with something close to fear. She, too, indulged me – not as a victim, but as someone on whose good side she felt safer. She said nothing about my weight, my erratic attendance at school and Sunday Mass, or about the uniform I'd come to adopt – gray sweatshirt, fatigue jacket, bell-bottom jeans. When, during my junior year, I began to smoke openly throughout the house, Grandma placed a can of Glade on my bureau and held her tongue.

She was right to fear me. I scared myself. I had, after all, indirectly killed Rita's baby – or rather, God had killed it because of the chances I'd taken, the things I'd let myself think, do, have done. Ma didn't realize this; I was sure Grandma did.

But the mention of stirrups and rubber gloves proved to be a tactical mistake. I was seated on my bed, consoling myself with a stack of Pecan Sandies and the very same 'Mannix' episode Grandma was watching downstairs when Ma came in – red-eyed, without knocking – and walked over to my television. 'Get out of my room!' I screamed. 'Get out of my life!' Her back was to me. She pushed aside the bags of groceries and bent behind the set. 'Don't you dare touch any of my—'

The TV voices went dead in mid-sentence and Ma turned to face me. A steak knife was in one hand, the hacked-off television plug drooping from its wire in the other. There were tears in her throat as she spoke. 'I will get this fixed . . .when and if you have that physical and get that form signed. I happen to believe in your future.'

It took Grandma to locate Dr. Phinny, a tired old GP who, my grandmother had been assured by her church cronies, did little more than hold a stethoscope to you and tap your knee with a rubber mallet before signing whatever you wanted. 'None of that other monkey business,' she whispered, looking away from me. On the eve of the appointment, she suggested timidly that I might like to wear a blouse and my nice navy skirt to the doctor's but said nothing when I came down the following morning in my sweatshirt and bell-bottoms, armed with my cigarettes and a mug of Pepsi.

Ma gassed and braked through downtown Providence looking for Dr. Phinny's building. She sang along with the radio, trying to act casual. 'It's clowns' illusions I recall, I re-ally don't know clowns . . .'

'It's *clouds*' illusions.' I said it between clenched teeth.

'What?'

'It's *clouds*' illusions I recall. If you're going to sing it, sing it right.'

'I'm sorry,' she said. She pulled abruptly to the curb and jerked the brake. We both bucked forward and Pepsi lapped out onto my jeans.

'I'm sorry again,' she said. 'I'm sorry, I'm sorry, I'm sorry. This is the building.'

'The *pink-a-pink-a* of the directional signal got louder and we both waited to see what I'd do. I considered running down a side street and not calling her until I was forty years old and she was on her deathbed. But I'd already missed a crucial murder on 'Guiding Light,' not to mention Betty Jo's wedding on 'Petticoat Junction.' She hadn't bought me a new paperback in three weeks. It was like starving.

'Why don't you get out here and I'll find a place to park,' she said.

Then I was out of the car, slamming the door with a force gathered from twenty-one days' worth of abstinence.

Dr. Phinny's office building was tall and sooty with brass decorations turned aqua. Next door, the clattering plates and conversations of a coffee shop burst into the street whenever customers emerged, walking past me, stealing sneaky glimpses. A woman hurried by, pulling the arm of a little boy whose inclination was to linger and look. 'See that red car!' she said, yanking him past me. 'Here's a mailbox!'

Two stores down was an abandoned laundromat. A group of unplugged washing machines huddled in the middle. I studied myself in the plate glass. My long, straight hair was definitely my best feature. I ironed it every morning, whether I was going to school or not, reasoning that split ends were a small price to pay. I hung my head forward then flung it back, watching my hair fly, my hoop earrings sway. I *sort of* looked like Julie on

'The Mod Squad,' in a way. I liked her style, the way she seemed bored with everyone. She'd been on Merv Griffin the week before my mother cut the plug. 'I don't see it as acting,' she'd told Merv. 'It's just . . . being.'

I'd pierced my ears that February, during the week I was suspended for smoking in the equipment room when I was supposed to be taking modified gym. 'I've got better things to do than whack at Ping-Pong balls,' I'd told the vice principal and Mr. Pucci. 'I mean, what's the point?' Then I'd gone home and worked Grandma's spare sewing machine needle in and out, around and around, practicing my Julie look while I did it, as if my heart weren't racing. Later, when my ear got infected, I blamed Ma. 'What do you expect when you make me live in a house that doesn't even have any stupid peroxide?' I'd said.

Across from the laundromat was a dirty-book store. 'Sexational Reading!' a window banner proclaimed. 'We carry Luv Gel.' I wasn't taking my underwear off for *any* doctor, I didn't care if he was 103 years old and blind. I'd get a job somewhere and *buy* a TV if I had to.

Ma rounded the corner, smiling a hopeful smile. 'This won't be anything, honey,' she said, squeezing my hand.

'Oh,' I said, pulling it back. 'You can tell the future now?'

The rickety elevator smelled like urine. Though we were its only passengers, it stopped on each floor, opening its doors to no one while we waited rigidly. As it reached Dr. Phinny's floor, I turned to my mother. 'You must really hate me,' I said.

Her hand was shaking, crinkling the form the college had sent. 'I don't hate you,' she said.

'But deep down you must. Or else you wouldn't be doing this to me.'

'I love you,' she said, just loud enough for me to hear.

'Bull crap.'

We were his first patients of the day; it had been one of my stipulations. The upholstered waiting-room chairs were patched with electrical tape. There was no receptionist. Through a pane of ripply blue glass, I watched him walk back and forth behind the door that led to the inner office, like a person underwater.

Ten silent minutes after we'd arrived, he emerged, looking as old and tired as Grandma had promised. He stared at me briefly, squinted, and handed me a folded paper gown. 'She can go into that room on the left and get undressed,' he said, addressing my mother. 'She can put this thing on and get up on the table.'

I rose hesitantly and waited for Ma to do the same. 'Aren't you coming?' I hissed.

She shook her head and curled up the magazine she'd been pretending to read. 'I'll be out here. You'll be fine.'

The walls of the examining room were the color of mustard. Above a drippy sink hung a drugstore calendar: two Technicolor spaniels in a wicker basket. To the left of the examination table was a wastebasket, empty except for a single blood-stained gauze pad.

I took off my sandals and jeans and pulled the sweatshirt over my head. I was still wearing my bra and T-shirt and a pair of underpants that was going to stay on, no matter *what*. The old pervert could look at his other female patients if anyone else was stupid enough to show up. They couldn't make me go to college. They couldn't drag me there. All I wanted was to get my TV shows back.

The gown rustled and crinkled as I fumbled with the paper tabs at the back of my neck. I tried moulding the paper to myself but it fanned out stubbornly, like a giant bib. In the outer office, Ma and the doctor were mumbling. I sat up on the table and fished out a cigarette to calm my nerves. I smoked it fast, watching the ash tumble down the tunnels of the stiff gown.

He was scanning the form when he came into the room. He stood before me, reading.

'Look, I'm not taking anything else off,' I said, addressing the spaniels. When I looked back at him, he was staring directly at me.

'You're too goddamned fat,' he said.

I took a defiant drag on my cigarette and willed myself not to cry. The remark made me dizzy. For the past four years, Ma and Grandma had played by the rule: never to mention my weight. Now my jeans and sweatshirt were folded in a helpless pile beside me and there was only a thin sheet of paper between my rolls of dimply flesh and this detestable old man. My heart raced with fear and nicotine and Pepsi. My whole body shook, dripped sweat.

'Any trouble with your period?' he asked.

'No.'

'What?'

'No trouble,' I managed, louder.

He nodded in the direction of his stand-up scale. The backs of my legs made little sucking sounds as they unglued themselves from the plastic upholstery. He brought the sliding metal bar down tight against my scalp and fiddled with the cylinder in front of my face. 'Five-five and a half,' he said. 'Two hundred . . . fifty-seven.'

The tears leaking from my eyes made stains on the paper gown. I nodded or shook my head abruptly at each of his questions, coughed on command for his stethoscope, and took his pamphlets on diet, smoking, heart murmur. He signed the form.

At the door, his hand on the knob, he turned back and waited until I met his eye. 'Let me tell you something,' he said. 'My wife died four Tuesdays ago. Cancer of the colon. We were married forty-one years. Now you stop feeling sorry for yourself and lose some of that pork of yours. Pretty girl like you – you don't want to do this to yourself.'

'Eat shit,' I said.

He paused for a moment, as if considering my comment. Then he opened the door to the waiting room and announced to my mother and someone else who'd arrived that at the rate I was going, I could expect to die before I was forty years old. 'She's too fat and she smokes,' I heard him say just before the hall rang out with the sound of my slamming his office door. I was wheezing wildly by the time I reached the final landing.

On the turnpike on the way home, Ma said, 'I could stand to cut down, too, you know. It wouldn't hurt me one bit. We could go on a diet together? Do they still sell that Metrecal stuff?'

'I've been humiliated enough for one fucking decade,' I said. 'You say one more thing to me and I'll jump out of this car and smash my head under someone's wheels.'

The repairman from Eli's TV was parked in front of the house when we pulled into the alley. I waited in the parked car, watching his head move back and forth up in my bedroom window. When he finally drove away, whistling, I pounded up the stairs past Grandma and locked the door. I snapped the 'on' button and held my breath. Suddenly, 'The Newlywed Game' lit up on the big screen.

'Does your husband kiss you with his eyes opened or closed?' Bob Eubanks asked one of the new wives.

Still unable to relax, I rifled through my various bags and packages. I started with Mallomars, stuffing them whole into my mouth. That old man's voice wouldn't go away. 'You're too goddamned fat,' he kept saying.

'She'll say I keep them closed but I really keep them open,' a newlywed husband said.

'You do?' his wife said, worried.

'Eat shit,' I'd told him, and he hadn't even blinked. I slugged down a mugful of Pepsi, trying to calm myself. The week before, Ma had bought me a new product to try: Swiss cheese in a squirt can. I'd made a face when she'd shown me, but now I decorated crackers and chips with ribbons and ribbons of the stuff. I found some stale Lorna Doones and concocted little Swiss cheese and Lorna Doone sandwiches. I squirted dabs on each fingertip, like nail polish, and licked them off one by one, repeating the process until the can hissed air. Calmer, I opened a bag of M&M's. I was able to eat them in their normal sequence: red, green, yellow, yellow, brown.

*

My plan to end the impasse concerning my future was so beautifully simple, I was amazed I hadn't thought of it earlier. No high-school diploma, no college. I would simply fail my finals.

During exam week, the corridors were a wall of noise. My classmates had secured their futures, their prom dates, and had gotten an early start on their summer tans. I passed among them, invisible, like a brief shadow over their excitement.

In world-history class, I filled in the blue-book test pages with cross-hatching so intricate it looked like weaving. I ran a brand-new Bic pen dry.

'To what extent does Hamlet's dilemma mirror that of modern man?' my English teacher wanted to know. In front of me, the other kids coughed and sighed, pausing only to shake out their writing hands. I knew what she wanted: she wanted us to talk about alienation – about how it felt to be left out in the cold. She wanted me to pity Hamlet from my seat at the back of the room at a special table because I was too fat to fit at the regular desks. All year long her eyes had skidded over me as if I didn't exist. The invisible freak. Well, I *didn't* feel sorry for stupid Hamlet and his stupid indecision. I felt sorry for the *old* king, the ghost, the one who has the poison crammed up inside him and dies while everyone else gets to go on with their lives. 'Don't know – didn't read it,' I scrawled across the mimeographed test paper.

In physiology I borrowed Mr. Frechette's laminated lavatory pass and got home with it in time to catch the second half of 'Search for Tomorrow'.

'Mail, Dolores,' Grandma said when I came downstairs later that afternoon. Her voice dropped. 'Your father,' she whispered.

On the outside of the card was a chimpanzee wearing a mortarboard. When I opened it, a hundred-dollar bill fluttered to the floor. 'Wish I could be there for your big day. Use for luggage. Love, Daddy,' the note said.

I imagined the thank-you note I'd dare to write him. 'Dear Daddy, Thank you so much for wrecking my whole life. Did you know that I am now a fat elephant and am not having any big day because I flunked my exams? I'm returning your money. Tape it to a brick and shove it up your ass sideways. Love, Dolores.'

I cried my way through a bag of cheese popcorn and a can of Ma's butterscotch Metrecal. While I did, Mr. Pucci, bent still on being my pal, was at school convincing my teachers to look the other way. He drove over the next afternoon to deliver both the good news and the cap and gown I was to wear in the graduation procession. I hadn't bothered to show up for the rehearsal.

'Dolores, please!' Grandma stood over my bed, her cheeks pinkened with exasperation. The graduation gown was draped over her arm. 'That poor man has driven here specially to deliver this. He's waiting downstairs to see you. What am I supposed to say?'

I stared at the TV screen in a counterfeit trance. 'Tell that homo to mind his own business,' I said.

He waited another fifteen minutes for me to change my mind. At the window, I watched his yellow Volkswagen drive away from the curb. I pulled the wet, dusty curtain from inside my mouth, belatedly aware I'd been chewing the fabric. I placed the mortarboard on my head and walked back and forth in front of the mirror, watching the way it sat foolishly uncommitted to my skull, the way it called cruel attention to my plump cheeks, the hopeless wobble of my concentric chins.

Two nights later, Ma and Grandma stood before me in their new flower-print dresses and stiff beauty-parlor hair. 'I'm not going,' I said. 'It's a farce. I told you that already.'

'Why, I can't understand why a young lady would purposely miss her own commencement exercises,' Grandma said.

'Oh, honey, come on,' Ma goaded. 'I thought maybe we could go out to China Paradise afterwards and celebrate.'

'There's nothing *to* celebrate,' I said.

'Or someplace else. Even someplace ritzy, what the hell.'

I flopped back on my bed and clamped my eyes tight. 'For the last time,' I said, 'I am going to watch "Laugh-In." Then I am taking a bath. I am *not* going to put on that retarded hat and walk across the stage with all those hypocrites.'

'Well, Mr. Pucci will certainly be disappointed in you,' Ma tried.

My eyes sprang open. 'Speaking of hypocrites!' I said.

Grandma put her hands on her hips. 'Well, so what, Bernice?' she said. 'Miss Party Pooper can just stay here. We'll go anyway. I'll even try that chinky-Chinaman food. Who needs *her* to have a good time?'

'Great bluff, Grandma,' I said. 'Brilliant. Very convincing.'

When they actually did pull out of the driveway, I was outraged. 'Traitors,' I said aloud. In retaliation I grabbed my father's hundred-dollar bill and slammed out the front door.

I hadn't stepped inside Connie's Superette in three years. Breathlessly, I filled my cart with boxed desserts, canned potato sticks, whatever crossed my path. Wheeling past the delicatessen counter, the red center of a roast beef caught my eye. 'I'll take that,' I said.

Big Boy sucked his cigar without interest. 'Quarter pound? Half?'

'I mean I'll take the whole thing.'

His eyes widened. 'Lady,' he said, 'this piece of beef runs a good eighteen, nineteen pounds. It'll cost you about forty bucks.'

To Big Boy, I was some anonymous eccentric fat lady. I felt buoyed by my new identity. 'That's my business, isn't it?' I snapped.

He shrugged. 'Sliced or unsliced?'

'Unsliced.'

At the counter I handed Connie the hundred, ignoring the way she studied the bill front and back. The total came to $79.79. Connie counted soft, limp fives and ones onto my palm and I was instantly sorry I'd forfeited the hundred.

Back at home, I hacked the beef into several odd-sized pieces, using Grandma's most brutal knife. The deeper I cut, the more purply raw the meat became. I gagged and choked, swallowing whole the cool, rubbery hunks I couldn't manage to chew through. When my jaws ached, I wrapped the rest of the meat back up in its butcher paper and hit it in the bottom of the garbage can outside. Ma had probably written Daddy to get that card out of him. Luggage for college was probably her idea, too. She couldn't wait to get rid of me – only she wasn't going to.

Grandma kept a bottle of Mogen David wine in her night table. 'That stuff,' she called it. She used it on nights she couldn't sleep. The cork made a wet sucking sound as I extracted it. The sour, syrupy liquid dribbled down my chin as I drank. Back in my room, I filled my mouth with potato chips and pastries, crunching and chewing until my cheeks filled out with sweet, salty pulp.

The toilet swung back and forth like a pendulum. I couldn't make it stop. Then I threw up quarts of purple mush. I made the bathwater as hot as it would go – as scalding as the night he'd done it to me – and eased myself in. not that it worked. Not that it ever washed away.

I was sitting naked at the edge of my bed, ironing my wet hair, listening intently to the sizzle. I watched my fingers reach over my big belly and disappear. They stroked the insides of my legs, the tuft of hair I couldn't see. 'Just a little,' I told myself. 'What else do I have? Why not?'

My fingers became Mr. Pucci's small hands, moving lightly, in little, understanding half circles. He knew. He knew . . . Jack Speight's face interrupted briefly, threatening as always to wreck things, but the strokes empowered me and I banished Jack. Then I was lying back on the bed, my body light and freed of fat, my fingers bold and faithful to the rhythm.

My stomach pulled in. My back arched. The sensations kept lasting and lasting.

The bed shook.

The doorknob shook.

'Hi, honey,' Ma called from behind the door. 'Can I come in?'

'No!' I said, struggling for my underpants. 'I'm sleeping.'

'Graduation was nice. Kind of long. Mr. Pucci gave me your diploma. You want to see it?'

'Nope.'

'Grandma and I went to China Paradise after all. Mr. Pucci came with us. I got you a number sixteen – shrimp lo mein and spareribs. Are you hungry?'

'I'm sleepy. Put it in the refrigerator.' I was pulling on my sweatshirt, yanking covers around myself.

I woke up later – abruptly – from a leaden sleep. Outside it was dawn, raining. I thought about what my body had done for me, what I'd let it do. But sleep had stolen the power I'd felt and Jack's face was tangled up in my headache. 'You pig,' he said. 'You slutty cocktease.'

On TV, there were only religious shows and test patterns. I remembered the lo mein and tiptoed downstairs, carefully avoiding the creaky step near the bottom. If either one of them gets up now and talks to me, I thought, it will kill me. I will die.

Their curled-up graduation programs were on the kitchen counter. I located my name, then ripped them up and threw them in the garbage pail. Back in my room, a black-and-white 'My Little Margie' rerun had begun. I watched it without sound, eating strands of congealed noodles, biting into cold, sticky shrimps curled tightly into their fetal positions. When I looked out, the sky had lightened to pear gray. A wet breeze was stirring the catalpa tree.

Chapter 9

In early July a seven-page letter arrived from a girl in Edison, New Jersey, who mistakenly thought I was going to be her college roommate. It was written in pink felt pen, the *i*'s and exclamation marks circled instead of dotted. Her name was Katherine Strednicki, she wrote, but everyone called her Kippy. She liked the Cowsills and Sly and the Family Stone. Her boyfriend, Dante, had taken her to see the play *Hair* in New York but had made her look away at the naked parts. They were serious, but not pinned or anything. She wondered what clubs I'd been in in high school and if I'd like to go in halvsies on matching Indian-print curtains and bedspreads. Her mother would sew the curtains; I could pay them back in September, no sweat. Kippy was hoping to become a pharmacist, but she didn't approve of doing drugs for pleasure. She preferred to get high on life and hoped I did, too.

My mother was in her room, slipping into her khaki uniform slacks. 'I decided I like third shift after all,' she said. 'Nighttime travelers need you more than people in the day. All those paper coffee cups on the dashboard. You'd be surprised how many of them want to stay and chat.'

I handed her the letter. 'Ma,' I said. 'I just can't do it. I'm too fat. I'm too afraid.'

She sat back on the bed and we both looked at her in her bureau mirror. 'Of what? What are you afraid of?'

'Of people like her. Normal people.'

'*You're* normal!'

'That's easy for you to say,' I mumbled.

'Like hell it is! Like hell!' She sighed, free-falling backward, her head bouncing on the mattress. When she spoke, her voice was pillow-muffled. Her eyes glimmered. 'I'm afraid, too,' she said. 'Afraid the way you're going, you'll end up like me.'

She was confusing me. This was *my* tragedy. Why were we talking about her?

'I'd get there and people would stare at me,' I said. 'Look at me!'

'Look at *me!*' she shot back. She pointed accusingly at herself in the full-length mirror. Her hair looked wilty. Her bottom lip sagged. 'I'm thirty-eight years old and still living with my mother. I've wanted to get away from that woman all my life. And here it is, ten-thirty at night. I'm tired, Dolores. I just want to go to bed. But instead, I'm on my way to work, dressed up like . . . one of the goddamned Andrews sisters.'

In the mirror, we shared a smile. I wanted to reach over and rub her back, tell her I loved her. I opened my mouth to say it, but something else came out. 'What if I get so depressed down there that I slit my wrists? They could call here and say they found me in a pool of blood.'

'Oh for Christ's sweet sake!' Her hairbrush flew past me and hit the wall. She slammed into the bathroom, banging the medicine-cabinet door once, twice, three times. Tap water ran for several minutes. When she came back, her eyes were red. She bent over and picked up the brush, picked strands of hair from the bristles.

'You don't want to go to college? Don't go. I can't keep this up. I thought I could, but I can't.'

'I'll get a job,' I said. 'Maybe I'll go on a diet. I'm sorry.'

'You're sorry, I'm sorry, everybody's sorry,' she sighed. 'Write that girl a letter. Don't let her get stuck with those bedspreads.'

I stopped her as she headed for the stairs. 'Ma?' I said.

She turned and faced me and I saw, in her eyes, the dazed woman she'd been those first days when she'd returned from the mental hospital years before. 'Goddamnit, Dolores,' she said. 'You've made me so goddamned tired.' Then she was down the stairs and out the door.

That evening, having won my war, I didn't know what to do with myself. I wasn't hungry. On TV, my regular programs were preempted; the stupid moon mission was hogging all the channels. Grandma sat in her big chair, fretting that walking on the moon would cause trouble with the weather, which was bad enough as it was. I dozed and dreamed about the dog-pound dogs. A black Doberman bounded toward me, barking, but then stopped abruptly and began to speak. 'We eat secrets,' he said. He began to lick my feet . . .

Grandma poked me awake with the capped end of her knitting needle. 'Go to bed,' she said. 'You're muttering so loud, I keep dropping stitches.'

I awoke in a jumble of covers to what I first thought was Jack Speight's voice down in the parlor. 'Just a dream . . .' I advised myself, squashing my head back into the pillow.

I heard him again. Two of them.

Then Grandma's voice.

Out in the alley, radio static crackled. The catalpa tree kept blinking icy blue. The clock said 3:15. Why a police cruiser?

I tiptoed toward the stairs. It was something bad; I knew it. Grandma was slumped and shrunken on the sofa, rubbing her arm up and down, up and down. Both troopers sat leaning toward her. I gripped the railing and waited.

'. . . An out-of-state rig from Charlotte, North Carolina. Asleep at the wheel, says he woke up right while it was happening.'

Who woke up? Daddy?

Grandma began to cough and then choke. Then she stopped. We all waited.

'Why was she out of her booth?' she said.

'They're not sure, ma'am. She'd just had her break . . . probably never even realised it was happening. Probably never felt a thing.'

'That's right,' the other one said. 'That's probably true.'

A strange tingling went through me, and the troopers' heads enlarged. I heard shrieking brakes and Ma's voice: 'You've made me so goddamned tired' . . . I both saw and felt a kind of glitter. The living room rocked and swooped. My stomach dropped out between my legs . . .

Eyes closed, I wondered whose lumpy hands were beneath me.

My head throbbed. I opened my eyes a crack. I was on the hallway floor. The banister was broken, leaning diagonally against the wall, its broken-off posts as jagged as shark's teeth.

Over me, the trooper's face turned red, a forehead vein bulged. 'Jesus, Al, we gotta call in,' he grunted. 'I can't even budge her.'

There was a groan – mine – and I reached up and touched the pain in my forehead, the blood seeping out of my eyebrow.

'Hold on,' the man said. 'Here she comes. Here she is.'

The night after my mother was killed, Neil Armstrong walked on the moon. Grandma, tiny and breakable, sat at the hall telephone table calling out-of-state cousins from her address book with the pop-up metal cover, repeating over and over the funeral arrangements she'd made earlier in the day. She fed me tea and her nerve pills, tiny yellow knobs of bitterness I let melt on my tongue like Holy Communion.

I whimpered and waded through the weekend, muddled by images: my puffy sewn-together face in the mirror – a butterfly bandage stuck over my eyebrow where they'd sewn the stitches; Roberta in the doorway, her mouth moving over words I couldn't hear; Ma's clothes still out back on the clothesline; the astronauts bouncing through moondust like lighthearted robots. Someone on TV claimed the moon walk was a hoax, staged by the government to make itself look good. This felt odd: that your mother could be a covered body being loaded, over and over, into an ambulance all weekend long on the Channel Ten news. Was Ma dead if her mail still arrived? If her blouses still fluttered that way outside in the clothesline breeze?

Mr. Pucci came to the front door with a purple African violet so lush and fleshy it looked edible. He sat next to me on the sofa, squeezing my hand as he talked, his fingers as cool and smooth as beach stones.

If death meant she was just somewhere else – if heaven existed – then she could, right at that second, be reuniting with her dead baby, Anthony Jr. Rewarded, finally, for her troubles. Rid of me . . . 'You've made me so goddamned tired,' she'd said. 'I've wanted to get away from that woman all my life.' Maybe she'd done it on purpose, run *toward* that truck. To get some rest. To get away from Grandma and me. That's what I wanted to ask Mr. Pucci about – if he thought Ma could have done it on purpose, if he believed in some kind of heaven. But I didn't. We watched TV and smoked cigarettes. President Nixon telephoned outer space.

The matches in Mr. Pucci's hand shook whenever he lit our cigarettes. 'It's probably not even real to you yet,' he said. 'Does any of it seem like it's actually happening?' I didn't know how to answer. I was watching how we'd filled the room with floating smoke, how our slightest movements stirred it. I was back at our old house on Carter Avenue, the night Daddy threw the barbell and Ma soaked herself in the tub, smoking, her brown nipples half in, half out of the water.

Grandma chose a gold-colored coffin. 'Champagne mist,' the undertaker called it in his hypnotist's voice. He suggested a closed casket, smiling an odd smile – fixed and dim-witted, like a porpoise's. If I had just agreed to go to college, I thought, then she'd be alive. Things would be normal.

'*You're* normal!' she'd said. Maybe in death she finally knew; I killed babies, mothers. I deserved this pain, was owed my misery.

Grandma's friend Mrs. Mumphy had her daughter drive us to calling hours. Grandma and I sat in the back of the big, rumbly station wagon and I stared out at passing drivers and pedestrians having a regular Monday afternoon. Then, just as we pulled into the driveway of the funeral home, it occurred to me that Daddy might be there. 'You didn't call him, did you?' I asked Grandma.

She handed me another yellow nerve pill wrapped inside a yellow Kleenex. 'Dolores, please, don't plague me,' was all she said.

The funeral home had thick carpet the color of windshield frost. In the foyer was an autograph book on a lighted stand and a small stack of souvenir pictures: Jesus, His sacred heart exposed like a biology-book illustration. Ma's name was printed on the back in fancy, old-fashioned letters: Bernice Marie Price. I'd asked her once if we could go to court and have our last name changed. She'd laughed at the idea. 'What do you think we are, movie stars?'

The room smelled of carnations and candle wax. Grandma knelt before the coffin, her lip quivering in a silent prayer. On soap operas, they resurrected the dead. People disappeared in plane crashes, were gone for years, then fought off amnesia to return. 'She's not in that box,' I told myself. 'So it's not sad. That's why I'm not crying.'

On a stand above the coffin was a spray of white and yellow roses with a gold cardboard cutout some florist had stapled to a satin ribbon. 'Beloved mother,' it said. They were supposed to be from me, only they weren't. I'd never once used the word 'beloved.' It was fake, part of this death vocabulary. Everything here was fake, except for the flowers. In their own way, they were fake, too. I'd given Ma grief, not flowers, and now I'd gotten grief back. 'Get out of my life!' I'd screamed at her the night she cut the cord to my TV.

The undertaker sat Grandma in a green velvet parlor chair and me on a fancy cushioned bench with the kind of embroidery Grandma sometimes did: crewelwork.

Cruel work.

I'd spent the last months of her life making her miserable,

using horrible language, hurling four-letter words like rocks. The bench was hard despite the cushion. I attempted a deal with God: one more day with her and you can blind me, amputate a leg, put a truck in front of *my* life.

Our seats made a right angle with the coffin. We sat rigidly, waiting for mourners. Grandma said the air conditioner was too cold and buttoned her cardigan sweater to the top button. She reached for my hand, clutched it with her cold, rough fingers. It should have been *her* in that casket and Ma next to me.

The undertaker pushed open his front door. I'd imagined only strangers, tollbooth people and St. Anthony's parishioners, but the first mourner was mine – Mrs. Bronstein, my third-year English teacher at Easterly High. She wore a purple minidress I remembered from class. Her slip showed when she knelt at the coffin. I recalled odd things about Mrs. Bronstein's class: Lady Macbeth's blood-stained hands, the day a wasp flew in and interrupted some boy's oral report. 'I can't say she's easy to deal with, but there's a bright girl hiding inside there,' she'd once told Mr. Pucci in front of me. She meant inside my fat. The week before on 'Carol Burnett,' Carol and Harvey Korman wore padded costumes and played a fat couple, gnawing on ham bones, crashing into things and bouncing back off walls. After the commercial, Carol had detached her fat and come out in a slinky gown, yanking on her earlobe to tell her family everything was okay. 'Here I am at my mother's wake,' I thought, horrified, 'thinking about Carol Burnett.'

Roberta approached me and kissed my forehead, just above the stitches. 'I could love you,' I thought, accepting her wide-armed hug. I sobbed and held on to her, rocking, not wanting to let go.

The room filled slowly with old people, Grandma's lady friends and their husbands. Grandma and I were like royalty – queens for a day. Strangers offered me their limp hand and Mass cards, then sat down to murmur and stare.

A red-haired woman in a tollbooth uniform like Ma's was on her way home from work. 'We're all just sick about it, sweetheart,' she said. I nodded appreciatively. 'It should have been you,' I thought. '*Your* children should be here, not me.'

An old man kissed my cheek and pressed something into my hand: a twenty-dollar bill folded repeatedly into a tiny, hard square.

I took a cigarette break at the rear of the parlor, silencing the men's murmured conversations with my presence the same way I silenced people at school, clearing the little wood-paneled room. I ran my fingers along the empty row of coat hangers, making them swing and dance. I wrote my initials in the ashtray sand and buried the twenty-dollar bill. When I got back, Jeanette Nord and her parents were at Ma's coffin.

Jeanette had frosted her hair and grown hips like her mother's. Her father wore the same plaid sports jacket I remembered since when I used to sleep over at Jeanette's on Saturday night and go with them to their Methodist church the following morning. Jack Speight had raped me and Ma was dead and Mr. Nord still wore that coat. I wanted to rest my head against the lapel, but Mrs. Nord kept talking about Jeanette's life.

Jeanette stretched a smile across her face. She made several tries at looking at me. 'I'm really sorry,' she said. Then her mouth bent and she began to choke and laugh.

'I'm really *am* sorry,' she said. 'Nothing's funny.' She looked panicked but the laughing continued. 'I don't know what to say. It's just . . I mean, what am I *supposed* to say?' Then she turned and plowed her way toward the metal folding chairs.

'She *wanted* to come,' Mrs. Nord said. 'It was *her* idea.'

On the second night of calling hours, Father Duptulski knelt before Ma's casket and led the rosary. His being there rallied Grandma. 'Blessed art thou amongst women and blessed is the fruit of thy womb,' she repeated after Father, over and over, her voice the loudest in the room.

Daddy was there!

He stood in the foyer, waiting for the rosary to be through. He'd grown a mustache and wide sideburns – muttonchops. His eyes looked out at nothing. His hands kept making and unmaking fists. I thought of the night he'd cupped Ma's bird, Petey, in those hands – had sent him flying away from her while she begged and cried. 'You killed us both, you bastard,' I sat and thought.

Grandma's praying dropped off and I could tell she saw him, too. If Grandma's God was real, why wasn't *Daddy* my dead parent?

He walked hesitantly toward me, his eyes widening at what I looked like. 'What did you expect?' I thought. My anger was as huge as I was.

He squatted before me. 'Hi,' he whispered.

'I don't want to talk to you.'

Grandma reached for my hand. 'All right now, Dolores—' she began.

'I don't want him here, Grandma.' Only I did. I wanted him to hold me, swim with me – wanted him not to have gone away.

The mourners became a row of ghosts.

'Honey, it's all right,' Daddy said. 'I'll help you through—'

'Don't talk to me,' I said. 'Go fuck yourself. Is Old Lady Masicotte still alive? Go fuck her.'

It wasn't me. It was the fat girl. The blood drained from his face.

Grandma withdrew her hand. 'Oh, please . . .' she said.

Father Duptulski was there, pulling on the sleeve of my dress. 'Come on now, missy, let's you and me take a little walk outside,' he said.

'Why should I take a walk with you? You don't even know my name. Just tell my so-called ex-father to leave.'

'Now look,' Daddy said. A smile kept blinking on and off his face. 'Be fair, okay? This is terrible for everyone and—'

'Just leave!' I shouted.

Grandma's face was bloodless, too. Father Duptulski's

fingers dug into my fat. 'Come on,' he kept nudging. 'Come on.'

Daddy wouldn't leave. He was whispering at my face with sweet liquor breath. 'I can understand what you're going through . . . not the time or the place . . you don't know the whole . . .'

'Shut up! Shut up! Shut up!'

I was out on the sidewalk before I unclapped my hands from my ears and stopped yelling it. Father Duptulski kept patting my shoulder. A new mourner arrived, unaware. 'What do you think of those Mets, Father? You praying for those guys or something?' Father Duptulski waved him away.

A car jerked out of the parking lot, Daddy at the wheel. He drove past us, braked, backed up. He was crying. 'I'm no saint,' he called out to Father Duptulski. 'But I never, *ever* deserved—' He turned his eyes to me. 'You get yourself some help!' he screamed. 'Or I'll get it for you!'

'You stay the fuck away from me!' I screamed back. The car bucked and sped away.

An hour before the funeral the next day, I decided not to go. Grandma, horrified to silence by my behavior with Daddy, didn't push it. 'People are just hypocrites,' I told myself. From the parlor window, I watched Grandma walk out to the waiting limousine and lower herself in. I would honor my mother in ways that mattered.

The refrigerator was filled with unfamiliar pans and tins from church ladies. Meatballs, baked beans, a turkey, cream puffs. Roberta had sent over a pan of golumpkes. I took a soupspoon and someone's lemon-meringue pie and headed for my room.

On the stair landing I paused at my favorite picture of Ma. She was seventeen, standing on Grandma's front porch with her friend Geneva. Both girls wore pageboy hairstyles and white blouses with puffy sleeves, off to some important high-school function. They stood with their arms around each other's shoulders, laughing at the camera. Once I asked Ma who'd taken the picture, but she couldn't remember. Maybe Ma's death took it, I thought. Maybe it was laughing back at her, knowing everything that would happen, as she posed in happy ignorance. In Ma's young face there was no trace that Anthony Jr. would strangle himself inside her. That her husband would leave, that her daughter would become me.

For as far back as I could remember, Ma had gotten letters from Geneva. Geneva Sweet, 1515 Bayview Drive, La Jolla, California. You could tell she was rich from their Christmas cards: oversized foil Madonnas on the front, inside her and her husband's names printed in letters that rose right up off the page, letters you could feel as well as read. Geneva's husband Irving owned an imported-rug business and treated her like Princess Grace, Ma had once said. 'But he's shorter than Geneva, a little homely man. Not handsome like Daddy.'

The morning before, Grandma had called Geneva to tell her about Ma and she'd asked to speak to me. 'Bernice and I have written to each other all our lives,' she said. 'It's as if the bottom's dropped out of my life. If there's every anything . . . *anything!*'

In the picture, Ma was the prettier of the two, the one laughing the most. Next to Ma, Geneva seemed plain. What was it that had turned her into Cinderella and killed my mother? The picture kept asking me that question.

I'd ironed my funeral dress the night before and hung it from the curtain rod, expecting until that morning to go to the services. Now, at my bedroom door, I mistook the dress for a person and caught my breath.

The flatiron was facedown on the ironing board. I plugged it in and pushed the button, feeling with my fingers the transition from cool to warm to hot. The pain seemed comforting and logical. The woman at the fat-ladies' dress shop where we'd hurriedly bought the dress had disapproved of my size, had frowned at the way nothing quite fit me. I sat back down on my bed, eating spoonfuls of the lemon pie and marveling at the degree of my exhaustion . . .

*

I awakened to the sound of car doors slamming outside. I shoved the empty pie plate under my bed and checked the lock. People talked in the front hall, quiet at first, then louder. That morning, I'd helped Grandma carry the broken stairway banister out to the yard, walking backward down the steps, sure I'd fall. Plates clinked. High heels scuffed up the stairs to the bathroom. I'd forgotten to turn off the flatiron. The air above it wiggled.

Mrs. Mumphy's daughter came to my bedroom door and asked if I wanted to go downstairs and visit. I didn't mind the interruption. Sleep had made me strangely patient.

'Can I make you up a plate then?' she called in.

I smiled. 'No, thank you.'

I was involved in a contest befitting a mother killer. I licked my palm and held it to the hot iron.

'It was a beautiful ceremony,' Mrs. Mumphy's daughter called in.

The skin hissed on contact; the seeping heat made my hand shake. I held it there. My ring became a circle of deeper pain.

'Just beautiful.'

By the six-thirty news, the last of the lingerers had done the dishes and left. Grandma got into her housecoat and fell asleep in the parlor chair. The astronauts bobbed in the ocean, safe, waving to the cameras on their way into quarantine. I watched Grandma's slackened jaw, her bobbing head. In her sleep, she was uttering sounds: part speech, part gurgle. 'Take it back,' I whispered to Grandma's sad-eyed, sacred-hearted Jesus. 'Make *her* the one, not Ma.'

I went upstairs to Ma's room – the first time since she'd died. The clothes she'd worn the week before were laundered and folded in a stack on top of her mother-of-pearl hamper. Outside, rain drummed against the garbage cans. Grandma had stripped the bed.

I sat down at Ma's desk, not sure of what it was I wanted to write. A suicide letter? Who would I write it to, other than Ma?

My hands were blistery and sore from the iron, the pen painful between my fingers.

> *Dear Kippy,*
> *I can't wait to meet you. Either my parents or my boy-friend will be driving me down to school. The bedspreads sound fab. How much do I owe you? We seem to have a lot in common!!*

This was what my mother had wanted for me: a Tricia Nixon life. I'd create one for her, a gift. Maybe I'd lose weight. Or maybe Kippy was fat, too. I saw us walking to class, two jolly fat girls, sharing a joke – my mother's death successfully hidden.

I knew I'd lose my nerve if I waited until morning to mail it. I took Ma's trench coat out of her closet and put it over my shoulders. Smelling her smell. Shaking from love.

I was short of breath by the time I got to the mailbox on Terrace Avenue. It was the farthest I'd walked in months. People drove by, staring. A car of laughing boys slowed down. 'Hey, Tina, I'm a sperm whale, you want to get laid?' one of them called.

I was immune, my head filled with a clarity as sharp as pain, as hot as the face of the flatiron.

'I love you, Ma. This is for you. For you, Ma. I love you.' I chanted it over and over, like a Hail Mary. I dropped the letter in, heard the soft sound of it hitting the bottom.

That night I slept on Ma's bare mattress, her trench coat over me like a sheet, and woke up smiling from a dream I just missed remembering.

Chapter 10

By August, Grandma had locked her jaw again, relocated her sense of purpose, and begun the tissuey flipping of yellow pages.

A carpenter came to put up the new banister and, while he was there, replaced a rotting porch step. Two middle-aged women materialized to shampoo the rugs – look-alike sisters in pink rayon uniforms who giggled and called to each other over their whirring machinery.

It was as if Grandma could obliterate pain by scouring it away. As if she could wash and wax sorrow, hire strangers to suck it up a vacuum hose. In this confusion of cleaning, Grandma allowed herself the luxury of forgetting about me. I kept startling her, just by walking into whatever disinfected room she'd placed herself. She was seated at the kitchen table Brillo-ing silverware when I told her.

'I've decided to go to that college after all. Like she wanted me to.'

Grandma looked up accusingly, trying to read a joke on my face. Then she left the room.

All that day, she slammed things. She finally spoke at supper. 'If you're going away, then what was all that fuss about? Why did you have to plague her?'

Her face looked confused rather than angry. My announcement had genuinely confounded her. For the first time since Ma's death, I felt as sorry for Grandma's loss as I did for my own. But when I tried to speak, something locked in my throat. 'It was between her and me,' was all I said. 'It was personal.'

Her face darkened and she got up to leave the room. 'Well, nuts to that,' she said.

I sat paralyzed, staring at the doorway through which she had just walked. I heard again the awful crash of that rented typewriter as it hit the floor, saw Ma's flushed, warring face after she'd cut the television wire.

I rested my face against the cool tabletop. I deserved this pain – deserved more, even, than what I was feeling. It was me who deserved death, not Ma.

The next morning, Grandma handed me the bankbook in which Ma had been depositing my college money. Two fifty-dollar bills were sticking out of both ends: cash she'd never had time to deposit. The first entry was for $12, made in September of 1962, the month after daddy had left us. The end ones were for larger amounts – $75, $100 – made every fourteen days – every payday – right up through the hell I'd put her through.

I wrote Kippy a long letter, inventing a life for myself: part-time counter girl at McDonald's, treasurer of my senior class. My mother ran the hospital gift shop; my father was a pediatrician whose office was attached to our house, like Marcus Welby. By our third exchange, I had a boyfriend, Derek. I made him British for practical reasons; he could be sent back quickly to England for those 'fab' double dates and 'groovy' college weekends Kippy began referring to.

I composed the letters sitting on the stairs, a clipboard resting diagonally against my big belly. The fresh wood smell of the banister was a comfort somehow. 'Raw wood' the carpenter had called it. But Grandma was planning on a mahogany stain and varnish; she was eager for it to match. She said it was high time to rewallpaper, too, and took down the stairway photos, even the ones of my mother, *especially* those. She wrapped the pictures in newspaper and stacked them in a cardboard box, leaving rectangles of vivid pink flamingos amongst the faded ones along the staircase wall. Grandma couldn't remember how old the wallpaper was, but Grandpa had hung it, so it was before 1948. Why did I ask?

'No reason, really,' I shrugged, doing the private math that placed my mother in her senior year in high school about the time she'd locked arms with her friend Geneva and posed on the front porch in her white dress.

That afternoon I took the photograph from the upstairs closet, brought it back to my room, and held it against Ma's painting of the flying leg. What frightened me was the chasm between the two – the distance between Ma's innocent black-and-white smile and the disembodied winged leg she'd painted during her crazy days. This was what could happen to you: you could end up this far from where you thought you were going. That was what scared me about college . . . but my fear didn't matter. I brushed my lips against the cool, flat glass that covered my mother's face, brushed my fingertips against the dips and rises of the hardened paint. I told Ma that I loved her and missed her and was going to college to make her happy.

Kippy's letters were confessions on Snoopy stationery. She hated her parents sometimes, her mother in particular. She was still a virgin technically, though Dante, her boyfriend, was pressuring her. Derek was pressuring me about the same thing, I wrote back, but the last thing I wanted was to end up pregnant and living in England, having to wear old-lady hats like Queen Elizabeth – ha-ha. In my letters, I was someone Ma would have liked, the kind of person she called 'a hot ticket'. Maybe I'd somehow manage to slip into this created girl's life. Or maybe Kippy would love me for my letters, forgive the rest.

Each morning when I woke up, I knew by heart the number of days left before Freshman Orientation Week; just passing the kitchen calendar created waves of nausea. After I mailed my letters, I'd come home and throw up in the toilet, gagging quietly with the water running so that Grandma wouldn't hear.

A month before Ma's death, Grandma had put down a $25 deposit on a four-day bus trip to Amish Country with her old-lady friends, the St. Anthony's Travelettes. Now Mrs. Mumphy called Grandma daily to coax her into going, in spite of everything.

'Well, I don't *care* if Father Duptulski thinks it's a good idea for me to go or not, Judy,' Grandma argued back. 'That wallpaper hanger is coming that week. What if they serve spicy food? And besides' – here her voice became sober and throaty – 'there's the girl.'

She always referred to me as 'the girl' when talking to her friends, always with that drop in her voice, as if I were a monster kept under wraps – Mr. Rochester's crazy attic wife in *Jane Eyre*. I'd written on one of Mrs. Bronstein's essay tests once that I liked that lunatic wife better than I liked boring Jane. Mrs. Bronstein had handed the comment back circled with a string of question marks.

'Grandma, go!' I told her. The thought of three days alone in Pierce Street house excited me. Free from Grandma's attempt to clean my mother away, I would instead call up the remaining evidence of her life, poking my way through attic cartons and closets and bureau drawers until I had the whole of who she was, or as much of the whole as possible – until I'd reconstructed the steps that led her from Grandma's front porch to the highway where her life had ended. 'Take some extra Pepto-Bismol with you! And don't worry one second about me!' I insisted.

Grandma chewed her lip and scowled. 'You wouldn't let the wallpaper man in. You'd pretend no one was home and I'd get back here and find nothing done. After I've set my heart on a change.' She nodded toward the cellophane-covered rolls leaning against the telephone table. She'd chosen a pink scallop-shell pattern against a coffee-ice-cream-colored background. 'And besides, it wouldn't be right. People would criticize me for going gallivanting so soon. Or be overly nice to me. It would get too quiet. I wouldn't be able to sleep and then I'd have to sit there and think.'

'Grandma, not going would be like taking twenty-five dollars and throwing it down the sewer.'

She frowned at that. 'Judy Mumphy thinks I'm foolish not to go. What if that wallpaper man is unreliable? He sounded sleepy over the telephone.'

'He's probably overworked. Exhausted because he's so good. I can handle things.' To prove my point, I grabbed the Electrolux and started vacuuming the stairs. I was sweating and panting by the time I reached the top, in a lust for her absence. From the bottom, Grandma watched me distrustfully, her hands on her hips, searching for the catch.

Later on, dusting the living room, Grandma kept pausing absentmindedly on objects. 'What is it?' I asked her. 'What's the matter? Are you getting a dizzy spell?'

'Dizzy spell? Of course not.' She sat down in her big chair, her bony hands curving around the stuffed chair arms. 'I was just thinking,' she finally said, 'about Bernice. About how she always loved a trip. She and Eddie both, but Bernice especially. When she was a little girl, we used to have our big meal at noontime on Sunday. Then their father would take us all out in the sedan for a drive. Bernice used to close her eyes and stick her whole face out the window to catch the breeze. By the time we got to where we were going her hair would be a nest of snarls.'

I held my breath; if she took notice of me, she might stop talking, and her talking about Ma was like salve on a wound. Grandma's smile was far away.

'When Eddie was a baby, she used to follow me around like a shadow – used to *beg* me for jobs to do. 'Course, later on she got so moody. You'd ask her to do something for you and she'd put on a face like you insulted her . . .' She turned and looked at me, puzzled. 'It's peculiar, though, isn't it?' she said. 'The fact that I've lived longer than them both – that baby and that helpful little girl.'

For a quick moment, I saw Grandma as she saw herself: a decent woman whom God, for unfathomable reasons, had chosen to punish. I almost loved her for her bewilderment. I almost touched her.

'No kidding, Grandma,' I said. 'You deserve a little fun.'

'Those Amish people don't even let you take their picture,' she said. 'You have to hide somewhere and trick them. They're odd ducks.' Her eyes narrowed back to normal. 'I'll tell you one thing,' she said. 'I'm not about to use one of those bus toilets. They'll just have to stop and wait for me whether they like it or not.'

At eight a.m. on Thursday, Grandma stood waiting at the front door, armed with an ancient brown suitcase. She had written a check for the wallpaper man and hidden it in the bread box beneath the milk crackers. 'If he looks shifty, just don't let him in,' she said. 'To hell with it.' She nodded at her own curse, pleased with herself for having added it. Then the familiar honk of Mrs. Mumphy's daughter's station wagon sent her hobbling down the walk. Abruptly, I was alone.

I had intended to start investigating right then, to begin in the attic and work my way down through Ma's things, but instead, I drew the shades, flopped back on the couch, and turned on 'Morning Matinee Theatre.' The movie was black and white: *The Miracle of Marcelino*. People's lips moved separately from their translated voices, finished ahead of time. A mysterious orphan boy was found in the desert and taken to a monastery to live. After a series of events that were either miracles or coincidences, the boy was bitten by a scorpion and then touched by God, who spoke down from heaven, reclaiming him. Marcelino ascended through the monastery ceiling on a ray of bright light. 'Bullshit,' I reassured myself, switching the station, even as God's dubbed voice explained the logic of the boy's death to the dumbstruck monks.

With Grandma gone, lunch could be any time you felt like having it. In the kitchen I set the oven at 425 and read the directions on one of the Hungry Man TV dinners I'd chosen. You had to remember to peel back the foil fifteen minutes before the end if you wanted the chicken to come out crispy. Things were never as carefree as commercials led you to believe.

Mike Douglas's cohosts were the has-been Kingston Trio. I had all day to get to Ma's stuff. There was no hurry whatsoever.

The mail came: circulars, a letter from Kippy, a large manila envelope addressed to 'Miss?Price.' Kippy wrote that Dante wanted to make love as a way of sealing their future, of making sure they'd stick together. I thought of Jack's sticky slime on my legs that day. 'Should I or shouldn't I?' Kippy asked.

I ate my way down a tube of Ritz crackers without relief and imagined Kippy and her boyfriend heavy-petting, his hands poking and fumbling with the snap on her jeans. 'Playing with fire,' Dear Abby called it.

> *Met her on a mountain*
> *There I took her life*
> *Met her on a mountain*
> *Stabbed her with my knife*

As the Kingston Trio sang in their choirboy voices, it abruptly occurred to me that the wallpaper man could turn out to be Jack Speight with a different name. Or someone like him. Some man just as bad.

There were enough hazardous knives and ice picks and sharp-tipped meat thermometers for every room in the house. It took me half an hour to get them all planted. He was due at eight the following morning. If he touched me, I'd plunge first and ask questions later. I wondered how far Grandma had gotten. By now she must be in a different state.

I opened the big envelope last: 'Miss?Price,' in handwriting painstaking and oversized.

Inside was the front cardboard panel of a cereal box. On the back, Scotch-taped to the gray cardboard, was a bank check for $500 and a family photograph of people I had never seen. 'Pay to the order of Miss?Price' the check said.

When I shook the envelope, a loose-leaf-paper letter dropped out. The handwriting was the same as the outside address:

> *. . . have sold a piece of his Daddy's property on Hickory*
> *Lake . . . a little something for all your troubles . . . and if*
> *he could write I'M SORRY on every single grain of sand in*

*the ocean, it wouldn't show one tenth of his sorrow . . . has
not been able to sleep through the night since it happened
. . . am sending this picture so you can see he is a
CHRISTIAN FAMILY MAN, not some crazy alcoholiac.
Sincerely your's, Mrs. Arthur Music.*

It was one of those discount-store portraits with a fake hearth
in the background and everyone's hand resting unnaturally on
someone else's sleeve. She had written their names in ballpoint
pen on each shoulder. 'Earlene (me)' she wrote against her
turquoise sleeveless shell. The boys had wide crew-cut heads
and looked like the kind of children who got beaten.

I looked at him last. He wore heavy black glasses, white shirt,
oily Elvis hair. He was so skinny, his pants crimped up beneath
his belt buckle. I wanted to keep believing some driverless truck
had killed her, not a person with a face and a family.

By the time I could get up and walk to the kitchen, the TV-
dinner foil had blackened. The room was thick with heat, the
food ruined. I put the check in my pants pocket and walked
over to the stove.

The family browned and curled at the edges, then caught the
gas-jet fire – like the screaming paper-doll girl in Mrs.
Masicotte's kitchen. Mrs. Masicotte had paid us off, too: with
presents, a pool.

The yellow flame licked and shriveled Arthur Music's serious
smile, but I knew as I watched him go that it was no good – that
the burden of his face was mine now, like the burden of Ma's
death. Mine to carry, mine forever.

The face of my mother's killer. Jack's face.

My partner in crime.

All the dead bolts and pulled shades and hidden knives in the
world couldn't protect you from the truth. And I sat there and
closed my eyes and felt Jack again, ramming himself into me –
felt that blind, never-ending pain, over and over, on the
afternoon we'd killed Rita's baby.

When you deserved it, even the mail could rape you.

Chapter 11

'Guess who?' The wallpaper man said, holding up a basket of paint-splattered tools. He had curly, shoulder-length hair and bib overalls with no shirt underneath. One of his eyelids drooped. His smile was gap-toothed: Howdy Doody on drugs.

He kept walking in and out the door, up and down the stairs, whistling 'Lady Madonna.' Grandma was probably somewhere in a roadside coffee shop, nibbling a corn muffin and receiving bad vibrations.

'Yoo-hoo,' he called up the stairs. 'You guys got a radio or something I could listen to? I work better with tunes.'

'In the parlor,' I said, calling down the directions to Grandma's old cabinet-model radio.

'Whoa – a golden oldie,' I heard him say. 'Dig it.'

'Plug it in first. It has to warm up.'

Static crackled, stations whizzed by at top volume. He settled on a screamy song I didn't recognize, one I didn't think Grandma's radio was even capable of playing.

'Yoo-hoo again,' he called up over the music. 'I'm going to be putting up staging, so I don't want to trap you in up there.'

'There's a butcher knife waiting for your heart if you try,' I almost shouted back.

The cuffs of his overalls were frayed; the seat was embroidered with mushrooms. I watched from the doorway as he bathed the old flamingo wallpaper with a sponge, staining it with big, swooping strokes, and making little rips in it with a can opener. The hallway smelled of vinegar. I was supposed to pay him for this vandalism?

'You know how flamingos get pink?' he said as I tiptoed past. He peeled off a long shred of paper, like sunburned skin. 'Shrimp. They eat shrimp. It turns them pink.'

He smiled broadly at me. That droopy eyelid threw his whole face out of balance. If it was a joke about the shrimp, I didn't get it.

I went out to the kitchen and chain-smoked, filling the rain trap with butts the way Grandma hated – waiting for the nicotine to rev up my blood. I'd lived in this house for five years and never whistled like that.

'Pucci, F.,' the phone book said. '102B Marion Court.' He'd offered to talk any time. Leaving the house open to this hippy would horrify Grandma, I thought, with some satisfaction.

He sang along with every single song that came on. I had to wait for a commercial just to get a word in. 'Excuse me. Do you happen to know where Marion Court is?'

'Marion Court? Marion Court? Oh, yeah . . . those brick apartments off Penny Avenue. Past Burger Chef and Schiavone Chevrolet.'

'How far is it?'

'Five miles? Six?'

'Oh,' I said. 'I have an appointment there.'

I was not about to take a bus – walk down a narrow aisle while people looked up from their laps for the free show. In the yellow pages I found the number for the taxi station and stared at it until my eyesight blurred. I imagined getting in the back and not noticing until we'd sped up that the driver was Arthur Music, come back from North Carolina to beg my forgiveness. Or kill me. I saw myself throwing open the door at sixty miles an hour, leaning toward the rushing pavement as he pleaded into the rearview mirror.

''Scuse me,' he said.

I took in a sharp breath. My hands flew into the air.

'Oops, sorry. Hey, look, I gotta go pick up some more sizing on Fountain Street. You need a lift over to Marion Court? What time's your appointment?'

'Well, it's flexible,' I said. 'They're expecting me whenever.'

Someone had spray-painted '*Que pasa?*' on the passenger's-side door of his truck. The question-mark dot was a peace sign. I stepped up and in, lowering myself amongst the seat debris. Cardboard coffee cups rolled around at my feet. I wondered if he'd ever driven up to Ma's tollbooth – if coins had ever passed between them.

My weight slanted his whole truck; the ride through Easterly felt lopsided. Luckily, he played the radio at a volume that ruled out conversation. The truck rattled and creaked and reeked of gasoline.

'Here's Burger Chef,' I said. 'I'll walk from here.'

'That's okay. I'll take you the rest of the way.'

'No, thanks. I'd like to get some fresh air.'

'Suit yourself,' he shrugged. 'That one's Penny Avenue across the street there. Follow it all the way down. Marion's the first or second left.'

It was the *fourth* left – a good mile down the road – that jerk! Grandma and I would be lucky if that hippie-dippie didn't hang the wallpaper upside down. My feet burned and I was winded. Mr. Pucci would probably answer the door and there I'd be, having a heart attack. He had started this whole college thing. If I died, it was *his* fault!

There was a flower box in his window. Marigolds. 'I'm the only kid at school who's seen these,' I thought. His doorbell looked like a miniature breast. I pushed the nipple and waited.

A man as slight as Mr. Pucci answered the door. He was wearing cutoffs and a blue-and-white striped tank top and holding a spatula. He took in my size. 'Yes?' his little mouth said.

'Is Mr. Pucci home?'

Now he was looking at my sweat. He had Julius Caesar bangs. 'Uh, no, he's not.'

'When will he be back?'

He patted at his hair, the spatula waving over his head. 'Um, God, I'm not sure. He went shopping.'

'I went to some trouble to get here. Do you mind if I wait for him out on the steps? And can I have a glass of water?'

'Well, sure . . . come on in.'

The apartment had a kitchenette with swinging saloon doors. I stepped down into a sunken living room filled with plants. On the wall was a framed poster of Rudolph Nureyev frozen in midair, his body curved like a parenthesis. I sat back on the white sofa. That's when I saw the jukebox.

It glowed purple and pink across the room. Above it was a glittering poster close-up of Dorothy's powder-blue ankle socks and red ruby slippers. 'I like Mr. Pucci's jukebox,' I said.

He was lifting cookies off a cookie sheet. 'Play something,' he said. 'Can I get you a glass of wine? A Fresca or something? You're Ingrid, right?'

'No!' I said, more huffily than I'd meant to.

'Oh. I thought you were a friend of his from school.'

'I *am*.' It dawned on me who he'd mistaken me for: Miss Culp, a middle-aged history teacher at Easterly who was fat like me. Bertha Butt, the kids called her. She sometimes ate lunch with Mr. Pucci in the teacher's cafeteria. Her students were always making her cry.

'Mr. Pucci was my guidance counsel. My name is Dolores.'

He looked up, enlightened. 'Oh, right . . . right,' he said. Then he came down into the living room with iced tea and four cookies on a plate. He placed them on the coffee table next to me. 'Buddy's mentioned you,' he said. 'I'm Gary. I'm really sorry about your mother.'

'It's okay,' I shrugged. 'Is Buddy Mr. Pucci?' He'd never invited *me* to call him that. I felt our intimacy evaporating.

Gary went back up to the kitchen, leaving a trail of cologne. He had the beginning of a bald spot at the crown of his head.

'Are you a relative of his?' I asked.

He laughed nervously. 'Oh, we're roommates,' he said.

'Oh. I like your jukebox. Did I already say that?'

'Go ahead and play something. You don't need money; it's jammed. I've got to finish these while they're warm or else they'll stick. We're going to a cookout at four o'clock this aft.'

'You and Buddy?'

I pressed D-1 and the record player glided down its row of options. A dough-faced woman with three chins watched me from inside the glass. She didn't smile. She blinked when I blinked.

> *Don't know why, but I'm feeling so sad*
> *I long to try something I've never had . . .*

As the tinny, girlish voice sang through the speaker cloth, I pressed my knees against the song, hearing and feeling it both. That voice was far away and beautiful, as sad as Ma. I looked up at Mr. Pucci's friend, my face asking the question. 'Billie Holiday,' he said. 'She gets the pain right, doesn't she? Isn't she something?'

That's when I realized: they were homos together. All those snickering remarks about Mr. Pucci from kids at school . . I imagined the two of them kissing, then made myself stop imagining it. You're a perverted pig, I told the fat woman in the jukebox glass.

Mr. Pucci walked in carrying two grocery bags. He stiffened when he saw me. One of the bags slipped but he caught it.

'Dolores,' he said. 'Hi. How are you?'

'Good,' I said.

'Good,' he repeated. He looked over at Gary. 'Good. Great.'

He drove me home in Gary's car, sidestepping the fact that I wouldn't fit into his Volkswagen. Unlike the hippie van, the inside of Gary's car was uncluttered, sterile. A plastic litter bag hung from the cigarette-lighter knob, flat and empty.

'I'm so happy for you about college.' Mr. Pucci said. His voice had relaxed to normal; it was my being in his house that had given it its nervous edge. 'Your mother . . . she'd be very happy about it.'

'How long has Gary lived in your apartment?'

His foot tapped the brake for no reason. 'Oh, I don't know. A while.'

'Is he a teacher?'

'He's a travel agent.'

'Oh.'

What I was picturing was myself, living there with those two thin, safe men instead of going off to college. Doing their housework, playing that jukebox. 'Do you mind if I just come right out and say something?' I said.

'That depends,' he said. I didn't recognize his laugh.

'What?'

'What I wanted to say was, if you and Gary are homos, it's fine with me. It doesn't bother me in the least.'

His hands squeezed the steering wheel; his ear turned pink. 'God, what a thing to say to me! Sometimes you just go over the line.'

'I'm sorry. *Boyfriends* not homos. I didn't mean . . .'

'Gary's my *roommate.*'

'Well, whatever. It's no business of mine, right?'

'I mean, what an assumption!'

'I'm sorry. Are you mad at me? Pal?'

'No, I'm not *mad* at you but . . . Jesus Christ, Dolores!'

I waited past two traffic lights' worth of silence. 'I'm sorry I went to your house, okay? It's just . . . I don't think I can go to college. I know it would have made her happy, but I'm too scared.'

'Look at me,' he said. 'Within one month you'll be writing me a letter saying how happy you are – how glad you are you decided to go. How you've met this friend and that friend. I'll bet you any amount of money.'

'I won't make friends,' I said. 'Everybody hates you if you're fat.'

'No, they don't. That's an excuse you use. Don't be hypocritical.'

'Well if you ask me, *you're* the hypocrite. *Buddy!*'

'Stop it,' he snapped. 'Cut it out!'

I sat on the front step where he'd dropped me off, composing the letter of apology I'd write. I'd write both him and Gary letters – in separate envelopes with separate stamps. Maybe they *were* just roommates. What did I care? I'd remind him that pals forgave pals – that my mother's death was still messing up my head. I'd meant to tell him about that check I'd gotten from Arthur Music – that photograph of his *Watchtower* magazine family – but he'd rushed me out of there so fast. He'd tricked me all along with that word of his: pal. Some friendship! His white apartment – that sad singing – already seemed tunneled and distant, one more thing I'd lost.

Inside, the stairway wall had turned white and blank, with a network of veinlike cracks. Strips and pieces of the old paper littered the stairway and foyer, rustling like dead leaves under my feet.

The radio was off. 'Hey?' I called. 'Mister?'

I reached inside the telephone table, took out the corkscrew I'd hidden there and walked slowly toward the kitchen. If he jumped out at me from somewhere, I'd blind him.

He was sitting cross-legged like Buddha in the backyard sun. His eyes were closed; his lips moved slightly. If he was having a drug trip on our time, I'd just rip up Grandma's check and call the cops.

Keeping an eye on him, I tiptoed around the kitchen, making myself a salami sandwich, blaming the three-quarter-inch wad of meat slices on everything I'd put up with: Mr. Pucci's hypocrisy, the letter from Arthur Music, this freak in the backyard. I was on my second sandwich and a napkinful of Cheetos when he walked inside, bleary-eyed, without bothering to knock.

'Oh, hi,' he said. He looked at my sandwich, not me. 'You got any peanut butter and a couple more slices of that bread? I been out there for fifteen minutes trying to meditate with my stomach growling.'

'How come you stopped working?' I snapped. 'We're not *paying* you to meditate.'

'You're paying me by the job, not the hour,' he said, smiling. 'The plaster's got to dry before I can size it.'

I handed over the peanut-butter jar.

He ate his sandwich in the parlor, flipping the stations on Grandma's TV. Then he came back in the kitchen and asked if he could make another one. He sang while he did it. 'By the way, my name's Larry Rosenfarb in case you're interested.' A quarter of his new sandwich disappeared with the first bite. He chewed, smiled, swallowed. His hand disappeared inside the Cheeto bag. 'Tell me your name and I'll stop calling you "Yoo-hoo" and "Excuse me."'

I paused long enough for it to be uncomfortable for him. 'Dolores,' I finally said.

He stopped chewing. 'Like the mouthwash?'

'Do-*lor*-es.'

'Oh, okay. Thought you said Lavoris.' He laughed and whacked the side of his head, as if it were a broken TV.

He was irritating-weird, not psycho-weird, that much I could tell; I could pretty much see I needn't have bothered with the knives.

The noontime news was about the Woodstock festival. Rock music had closed down the interstate. A helicopter view showed people's heads, milling and clustering, like molecules in a science movie.

'Far fucking out!' Larry shouted. He flopped into Grandma's parlor chair so hard it sent cushion dust flying. He leaned toward the television as he watched. 'Me and my old lady were thinking of going up there, only our kid got an ear infection two nights ago and we missed our ride. The brakes on my truck are for shit or else I'd still try it. I could just see me rear-ending half of America – everyone under thirty walking around with one of those neck-brace things.'

The newscaster said Woodstock had been proclaimed a disaster area – that nothing quite like this had ever happened before.

'And here you and me sit in the living room in Rhode Island,' Larry said. 'It figures. Fuck a duck.'

'You and me,' he'd said – as if we were a twosome. When I answered the door that morning, my fat hadn't even shocked him.

'Is your kid a boy or a girl?' I asked.

'A girl. Tia. Tia the Terrible.'

'How old is she?'

'Year and four months. She just learned how to walk. Got into my eight-tracks the other day and yanked out about nine yards' worth of *Disraeli Gears*. Lucky for her she's cute, the little shit. Looks just like Ruthie – my wife.'

I saw his wife as Yoko Ono: floppy hat, hair in her eyes, lying in bed for peace. 'I wanted to name her Free! Check it out: F-R-E-E-exclamation mark. Like the punctuation is part of the name, right? Ruthie didn't like it, though. Said all's she could think of was like 'Free Sample.' That's not what I meant, though. I meant, you know – unencumbered. Only after she said it, all *I* could think of was free sample, too.'

He went out to the hallway to check the drying. 'Nope,' he said. Then he was back at the television, flipping channels. 'Mind if we watch "Jeopardy"?' he asked. The show was on the screen before I could answer.

He sat on the rug and shouted correct answers to the contestants. His wild hair blocked off a corner of the screen.

'You're pretty smart,' I said during a commercial.

'And you thought all I could do was hang wallpaper.' He laughed. 'You're just catching me during one of my fallow periods, that's all. One of my compost years. I'm expecting a creative leap pretty soon now.' He turned to the TV screen. 'What is a cygnet, asshole?' he shouted at a floundering contestant.

'What is a cygnet?' Art Fleming repeated.

'Can I use your phone?'

I watched him through the doorway. He paced back and forth, stretching the cord further than I thought it would go. 'Hi,' he said. 'How's the fleas?'

Grandma talked secrets into the telephone; Larry shouted. 'Okay, okay, calm down. Call the vet. We'll get the fucker dipped again and we'll spray the shit out of the house and camp down at Burlingame . . . I should be through by noon tomorrow. Then, fuck it, we'll just drive up there with our shitty brakes and see what's cooking.'

When he returned, he said, 'We've been dog-sitting for this ugly mutt named Chuck for these friends of ours who are going cross-country? So two days ago our whole apartment starts breaking out with fleas? I'm talking zillions, man – Poppy Seed City all over your feet. Ruthie's good and freaked – afraid if we spray, the grandchildren will mutate or something. You should see how ugly this dog is, man. Chuck. Old Chucker the Fucker.'

'You could stay here,' I said. 'The three of you. Sleep here overnight.' I wanted to see that little girl.

'Yeah?' he said. 'Nah.'

'I don't mind. I'd like it.'

'You sure?'

'I'll cook supper.'

He shrugged, smiling. 'We'll all cook supper,' he said. 'Have us a party.'

When he left at four to pick them up, I wondered if he'd come back. An hour went by. An hour and a half. My fat must have occurred to him belatedly, I thought. I started on a bag of crinkle-cut chips.

Then they were there in the alley, gabbing and slamming doors. Larry's curls were wet and stringy. He'd changed into bell-bottom jeans and a paisley blouse, the kind Linc wore on 'Mod Squad'. A dashiki. 'You stay here, Flea Bag,' Larry called into the truck.

His wife was short and squat with hoop earrings and brown hair woven into a fat braid. Larry was holding on to soup-pot handles with potholders. His wife was loaded down with bags, packages, the baby on her hip, and a fold-up high chair hooked to her wrist, the legs banging behind her. 'Have a kid some day and your traveling days will be over,' she said to me as she entered. Her voice was low and smooth – the kind of voice you don't question.

She dropped her belongings in the middle of Grandma's parlor and began moving knickknacks and breakables to higher ground. 'This is so nice of you,' she said. 'I've been snapping fleas and crying all day.'

I'm normal, I thought. A normal person meeting new friends.

'By the way, I'm Ruth,' she said, shaking my hand.

Tia had red-painted toenails and pierced ears. Her diaper was a calendar dish towel.

In the kitchen, cabinets opened and pans clattered. 'Aw, shit,' Larry said.

'What's the matter?' Ruth called.

'I forgot the coriander.'

'In the diaper bag,' Ruth said. She had a wide, shiny forehead and a big rear end that stuck out from her granny dress.

Tia slapped Ruth's leg and whined.

'How did you guys meet, anyway?' I asked.

'Larry and me? We were in VISTA together – assigned as partners.' Something snapped, and, suddenly, there was Ruth's whole shoulder, her fat breast. I looked away, then back again. 'Blackroot, West Virginia. "Ask not what your country can do for you," et cetera, et cetera.'

Ruth's breast, laced with veins, was dripping milk; I could tell it had a heaviness to it from the way she lifted it to Tia, who opened her mouth and latched on to the purple nipple. Ruth pressed her lips together in pain, then relaxed and smiled and kissed the top of Tia's head.

They always ran the VISTA ads on middle-of-the-night television: blond all-American types in khaki shorts, yucking it up with grateful Navajos. No one in those ads looked like Ruth or Larry.

'Did you like it there?' I asked.

'Blackroot? *Loved* it for a while. We were organizing a Head Start program for preschoolers. You know, shrink a little of the disadvantage, give them a better shot. The locals thought it was kind of silly, but they were pretty polite. We were a novelty. The women liked Larry. The men liked my boobs. I could get them to do anything for me, except look up.' She passed her fingers through Tia's curly hair, hunting for fleas.

Her eyes met mine. 'Your hair is gorgeous,' she said.

I tried not to smile. 'No it isn't. How long were you in West Virginia?'

'Eleven months. Then the bottom fell out.'

'Do you guys own a vegetable peeler?' Larry yelled in.

'It's in the metal cabinet, middle drawer,' I called back to him. 'What do you mean, the bottom fell out?'

'First I got pregnant with Tia. Then some of the local kids got drunk and beat up Larry.'

'How come?'

'Well, to begin with, he made the mistake of telling someone he was opposed to hunting. Therefore, he was queer.'

I pictured Mr. Pucci and Gary, sitting together on their white sofa.

'Then they saw how much he liked playing with the four-year-olds in our program – full-out, down-on-the-floor-with-them *enjoyed* himself. So someone got the idea he was probably molesting them – "diddling" them, they called it. He almost lost his left eye in that fight. Not to mention his idealism. It was pretty awful. We got married in a hospital in Baltimore. Kazoo music, Popsicles. Larry wore an eye patch and yellow pajamas. A male nurse sang "Chapel of Love". My parents were horrified.'

'Because you were pregnant?'

'Oh, they didn't know I was pregnant yet. They were just freaked about the ceremony. Not exactly something you'd invite the Lenox and "Oh Promise Me" crowd to, you know? Tia, hold on a second,' Ruth said, changing breasts. 'Who do you think I am – Elsie the Cow?'

Too much was happening! I wanted to watch him cook. I wanted her to keep talking.

'Plus I had dropped out of law school less than a year before. Mother and Daddy hadn't trusted VISTA from the beginning. You should have seen them both the day of the wedding: the I-told-you-so looks were flying around like spears. Poor Mother.'

'I'm going to college in three weeks,' I said. 'Maybe.'

'Why maybe?'

I shrugged. 'I don't know. I'll probably hate it.'

'Oh, go anyway. I usually learn more from the situations I hate than the ones I love, you know?'

Larry came in with a bottle of wine and three of Grandma's china cups. The wine tasted sour and exciting.

'I tell you,' Larry said, 'I've spent one day here and I've seen enough flamingos to last me a decade. How did you folks manage to live with that wallpaper so long?'

'Don't blame me. This is my grandmother's house.' I took another sip of wine. 'She's a real bitch.'

Saying it made me blush, but no one seemed to notice. Larry was making faces at Tia, coaxing giggles out of her. 'I think I'll take a stroll out to the glove compartment,' he said.

Ruth rolled her eyes. 'Don't you think you'd better ask first?'

He turned to me. 'What do you say, Dolores? Want to engage in a little predinner reefer madness? Double your pleasure, double your fun?'

'What?'

'Do a number? Get high?'

I couldn't recall Grandma's face. 'Go ahead,' I told him. 'It's fine with me.'

Larry rolled the joints in little tissue-paper squares, then lit one, taking a series of weird little drags. It popped and glowed and a spark flew to the rug. The four of us watched it die beneath Ruth's big toe.

He took the joint out of his mouth and stared at it so closely that his eyes crossed. 'This stuff is cosmic,' he said. 'Dolores?'

I shook my head. 'Maybe later,' I said. 'How about Ruth?'

'Oh, I can't,' she said. 'The breast-feeding. So how come your grandmother's a bitch?'

I took another gulp of wine. 'She just is. She's had a shitty life.'

Tia's head flopped back and her whole body went limp against Ruth. I sat there aching for Ma, wondering if she had ever breast-fed me.

'Is it just the two of you who live here?' Ruth asked.

'Yup,' I said. I reached for the joint, surprising myself. 'Maybe I *will* try this.'

'My grandmother's cool,' Ruth said. She smiled down at Tia, tracing a finger against her eyebrow. 'Eighty-three and she still runs her own farm, does all the canning, everything.'

I imitated Larry's sipping of the joint, but exhaled the sweet smoke too quickly. 'Hold it in, hold it in!' Larry coaxed. 'We got us a novice here, Ruthie.' When I got it right, he smiled and pointed a thumb at Ruth. 'Her grandmother's real Zen. It's her mother who's the bitch.'

Ruth frowned. 'She is not.'

'All those polite little notes at holiday time. All those Neiman Marcus stuffed animals for Tia. But that's okay. I forgive you.'

He leaned over and kissed her. They kissed for so long, I stopped looking away. I took another drag. Held it in. Let it out.

'I can be a bitch sometimes,' I said softly, but neither of them heard. They were still kissing.

'Are you high?' Larry asked, stirring his soup.

'No,' I said. Then the stove warped. Ruth's shiny forehead stuck me as hilarious. 'A little, maybe. I'm not sure.'

Ruth frowned. 'Larry, that isn't the zombie stuff you got from Steve, is it? I don't trust that guy.'

'Ruthie, give it a rest,' Larry smiled. 'It's Woodstock weekend.' He reached up under his dashiki and scratched himself. A fleck of ash floated from his beard into the soup.

Ruth shook her head and sighed.

Supper was a feast: honeydew melon, Ruth's molasses bread,

funeral meatballs from the freezer, Larry's creole eggplant stew. I ate slowly, letting the new tastes explode in my mouth. Somewhere in the middle of the meal, Larry got up from the table and did a flamingo imitation so funny I couldn't breathe. This is all really happening! I thought. I dunked another slice of Ruth's sweet bread into my stew.

'Look at that shit-eatin' grin,' Larry said. I looked around for it, then realized they were both staring at me, smiling in approval. 'Who, *me?*' I asked, delighted.

Then the radio was on and we were at the sink doing dishes, Ruth's big rear end swaying to the music as she washed.

> *I'm a man, yes I am*
> *And I can't help but love you so*

Larry grabbed two of Grandma's prescription vials and shook them like castanets. He was rolling his hips to the rhythm in a way I couldn't stop watching. 'You know what?' I said.

'No, what?'

'You're sexy.' Then I blushed and covered my face with a dish towel.

Ruth closed her eyes when she danced, and rocked in a private, sexy way. Then *I* was dancing! They insisted. Timid at first, I risked nothing more than a few tentative steps, a swinging of arms. Larry took my wrists, guiding me, and then the music was inside of me, coaxing my body into the dancing. I felt free – a weightless astronaut, Carol Burnett without her fat suit. My long, gorgeous hair rocked from side to side.

Larry went out somewhere for ice cream. That dog had gotten into the house, was licking spilled wine off the kitchen floor. I thought of the dog-pound dogs the day Jack had raped me. Felt his ramming. That truck ramming Ma.

'My mother got killed last month,' I said.

Ruth looked up and waited, confused.

'In an accident. There was this truck.'

She brought me to the couch and we both sat. First I talked.

Then she did. It was her touch, not her words, that mattered: her leg against my leg, her hand at the back of my head, drawing me to her. Her other hand cupped my shoulder, squeezing it at the worst of what I told.

When Larry got back, he knelt before me, rubbing my cheek while Ruth told him about Ma. 'It's all right, it's all right,' he kept saying, and his touch, too, comforted me – those warm, rough-skinned knuckles brushing away my tears, skidding gently against my fat face.

Somewhere in the middle of the night, I woke up on the parlor floor, stiff and tingly-headed. 'They've left me,' I thought.

Across the room by the window there was a sigh.

A milky shape moved up and down, folding and unfolding like a flower in a time-lapse movie. In my gathering consciousness, I stared at their marriage, their wholeness. I saw, for a second, my parents – the things Ma and Daddy must have done, the kind of wholeness *they* must have had. Then lost. Losing that was what had made Ma crazy.

'I want, I want . . .' Ruth kept saying. Then Larry's breath caught and they whimpered and clung together, their bodies rocking as one. I lay there, shaking and staring and wondering how the poison Jack Speight had let go inside of me could be what Larry let go in Ruth – what Ruth wanted.

By the time I woke up again, it was bright morning. Larry had put up the first two strips of seashell wallpaper. He was wearing cutoffs and his dashiki, black socks on his chalky legs. He mumbled measurements in his head and moved businesslike along his staging.

'Hiya,' he said.

I looked away. 'Where's Ruth?'

'She went to the store for orange juice. We wiped out your whole supply this morning. Well, Tia did. She got real curious about what the bottom of the carton looked like.'

'I don't care about that. You sure are working fast. God.'

'Yeah, well, I'm kinda hot to finish by this afternoon. We're going to try to make it up there. To the festival.'

I knew it was hopeless: the possibility of their taking me with them.

The back screen door slapped shut. 'Good morning,' Ruth said. 'How are you doing?'

'All right,' I said.

'Do you know you have mint growing in your backyard?'

'I do?'

She held a leafy bouquet to my nose. 'You picked that *here*?' I said.

'Uh-huh. I think I'll make a shampoo for Tia if it's all right with you. You want one, too?'

She half filled their soup pot and brought the water to the boil. Stalk by stalk, she dropped in the mint. The kitchen air turned moist and sharp. With Grandma's paring knife, she shaved curls of soap into the liquid.

'This is so great,' I said as Ruth massaged the sweet suds into my scalp. Tia walked over my toes with her tiny bare feet. 'How did you learn to make shampoo?'

'In the Appalachians. I learned it from the old woman whose house I was staying at. Ida Brock. You should have seen her: two brown teeth, potbelly, the same checkered dress every single day. But she had these liquid black eyes that you could hone the truth on. And long, wavy white hair. She kept it in a ponytail during the day, but first thing in the morning, it would be down and flowing – like yours. It was beautiful hair.'

'How come you left law school? Did you flunk out.'

'Oh, God, no. I was doing fine academically – studied my head off, knew just how to play the game. The faculty loved me. Especially my advisor, who I made the mistake of sleeping with. "We have great things in store for you, Ruth," he kept whispering. Never had the nerve to ask who "we" was. Just kept chalking up those A's because I knew that's what he liked. He and my parents, both. Good little obedient Ruthie.'

The lather was cool and fragrant. Her fingers massaging my scalp felt wonderful.

'One afternoon, we were in bed together at his house – his wife was away – and he goes to the closet and pulls out a suitcase. All that was in it was this pornographic joke magazine – these close-up pictures of genitals – male and female – all fixed up to look like faces. Pubic-hair Afros, penis noses, vagina mouths: pages and pages of this stuff. "Look at this one", he kept saying. I mean, this guy publishes in the *Yale Law Review,* for Christ's sake. So, right there, I just got so tired of the whole thing. Angry, too. He was sitting up in the bed, naked, and I reached over and took hold of his limp little prick. "And look at *this* tiny little garden slug," I said. "This one's the biggest joke of all." I withdrew the next morning . . . I mean, it was more than just that one thing, my leaving, but that's the one that sticks in my mind: him sitting there getting off on pictures of genitals fixed up like Mr. Potato Head.'

'All men are pigs,' I said.

Her hands stopped the shampooing. 'No they're not. Larry's not.'

I thought of their flowering the night before.

'Well, anyway, I'm probably not even going to go to college,' I said. 'It's what my mother wanted, not me.'

'Oh, go!' she said. 'Try it at least. Think of it as an adventure.'

She rinsed my hair with warm water and toweled it dry, then wrapped it in a turban. 'What if I don't like adventure?' I said.

Ruth dragged over a kitchen chair and sat down facing me. 'Then cultivate a taste for it. Take a chance. That's how you grow.'

'Look at me,' I said.

'I'm looking. What?'

'My size.'

'What about your size?'

'Growth isn't exactly something I need.'

She didn't laugh or look away. 'If I didn't go into VISTA,' she said, 'I never would have met Larry. Tia wouldn't exist.'

Tia had the cabinet open and was crawling in with Grandma's pots and pans. Larry's singing carried in to us from the stairwell. Ruth's gaze made me shiver.

Then the pans clattered to the floor and she was out of her chair and running to stop the damage.

When they were ready to leave, I handed Larry his check. 'Here you go,' I said. 'Have fun at Woodstock. Drive carefully.'

'Have fun at school,' Ruth said.

The dog was barking. Everyone was hugging and thanking everyone. From the truck window, Ruth held up Tia's hand and made it blow kisses. Larry honked all the way down Pierce Street.

I might have made them up, I thought, only they'd left evidence: the new wallpaper, a flea on my leg, dried orange juice sticking to my sneaker bottoms when I crossed the kitchen floor.

Grandma got home late in the afternoon, hours after I'd gotten back from the bank where I'd cashed in Arthur Music's check for a thick stack of twenty-dollar bills. 'The new wallpaper looks pretty,' she called out to me. The back-door screen made a veil for her face. 'What are you doing out there by the ash can?'

'Nothing,' I told her. Bees were in the grass and the afternoon sun warmed my face and arms. I had just found the mint.

Chapter 12

On the second page of the Merton College catalog was a photograph of Hooten Hall, its parking lot full of gaping trunks and smiling freshmen, cars clogging the lawns, fathers hefting footlockers. Here, in person, was the same parking lot, the same crisscrossed white birch trees – only deserted and still. I put down my suitcases and Ma's wrapped-up painting on the front step and tried the door-knob again. A car drove by, so singular that it roared. I walked from window to window, listening to the clack of my own Dr. Scholl's.

It was just as well. Things had gone sharply downhill from the Port Authority bus terminal in New York when a hunchbacked old man had hobbled down the entire aisle, coming to rest with a sigh on the back seat next to me. From New York to Philadelphia, I sat yanking Ma's trench coat around me as he blew and blew his nose and nibbled food from an oil-spotted paper bag. I spent three hours on the same chapter of *Valley of the Dolls*, worrying that his garlic breath would seep into the fabric of Ma's coat – that Kippy would smell his smell and think it was me.

One of two things was happening. Either Merton College had folded over the summer and been too cheap to spend a stamp to tell me, or the other girls had seen me struggling up the long flight of steps and locked the door. I imagined them huddling on all fours beneath the windowsill, giggling like Munchkins. Either way, I reasoned, I'd given college a fair chance and was now free to trudge back to the station and purchase another streamer of those purple tickets that would land me back in Easterly, my obligation to Ma fulfilled.

What if you don't even like adventure?

Then you cultivate a taste for it.

Easy for Ruth to say. She didn't have to be standing there, looking at herself mirrored back in locked glass doors. She didn't have to suffer sore hands from suitcase handles and bruises from those heavy bags banging against *her* legs. She apparently didn't even have to answer their fucking phone, no matter how many millions of times I'd let it ring that last week. I wouldn't hang up for fifteen or twenty minutes. The sound of the ringing put me in a kind of trance – became a kind of companion, even – so that once I got mixed up and thought I was calling my mother, was scared someone would pick up and it would be Ma.

I took a quarter out of the trenchcoat pocket and tapped it against the glass. 'Hey?' I said, barely louder then a speaking voice. 'Excuse me?'

To my horror, someone appeared.

A fat woman, lumbering behind the double doors. She stopped, squinted out, then walked toward me with a jumble of keys. My breath caught. Locks unsnapped. The door yawned open. This would end badly, I knew.

'What?' she said.

'I'm new,' I answered. 'A new freshman.'

'Yeah?'

Her eyes were pale blue, her hair a black bowl cut.

'Dolores Price? This is my dorm. Are you the house mother or something?'

She let go a snort of laughter. 'I'm the "or something." You're a little early, ain't you?'

'I got this letter that said we should arrive somewhere between ten and four. It's ten after four . . .'

'Between ten and four *next* Thursday.'

'I'm *sure* I have the right date.' I hadn't gotten the dry heaves over September 7 for nothing. I was surer of that date than anything else in my whole life.

'You can come in and put your stuff down for a minute, but you ain't supposed to be here until next week. I got my orders. There's no linens or nothing. Buildings and Grounds ain't even sent over my new mattresses yet.'

'Look, I *have* the right day. I can prove it.'

'You do that then,' she said. 'But hurry up. I got work to do.'

Once you left Easterly, you saw the world was full of these people: ticket sellers, snack-bar clerks. They assumed they were better than you just because they knew their own routines.

She led me into a shabby lounge area that smelled of dead cigarettes and something else – something sickening sweet, like rotting fruit or spilled drinks. She clicked a pole-lamp switch and four ruby-coloured megaphones lit us in watery red.

On the long bus trip down, I'd hunched my shoulders to the gawkers and counseled myself on the dignity of remaining a private person. Now here I was, sweat-drenched, heart thumping, displaying the entire contents of my opened suitcases, forced to prove that I was right and they were wrong. I made little hills of underpants on the threadbare sofa. She looked over my shoulder. I imagined her smirking, but when she spoke, her attention was somewhere else.

'Look at this,' she said, pointing to a circular brown stain on the top of an end table. 'Burning-hot popcorn popper on knotty pine and varnish. This is how smart you college girls are.'

'I'm *sure* I've got that letter here,' I insisted. A handful of bras dangled from my fist.

The Merton college literature was in a side pocket, curled around a can of malted-milk balls and held in place with an elastic band. Though the date on the page kept jumping, kept blurring from my tears, I saw that she was right. For a month and a half, I'd mistakenly fixed every fucking stomachache on the wrong date – on the date the late-tuition charge began. I was supposed to be safe at home in Easterly.

'Oh, this is just great!' I said. I stared up hard at the ceiling, tears dripping behind my ears. 'I'm such a stupid asshole. Now what am I supposed to do?'

'Go home,' she said. 'Come back in a week.'

'Where do you suppose I live – down the street?'

The pole lamp flickered.

'You paid too much for this.'

She was holding a jar of Tang. 'Down at the Big Bunny this week they got the large size on special for seventy-nine.'

My eyes met hers. That smug look was gone.

'Ordinarily I'd say call campus security and see what he says, but he's on vacation this week. Gone fishin' in the Smokies, him and his wife. Somebody could break in here at night and take every single stick of furniture. But that's between you and me and the lamppost.' She nodded at the pole lamp.

'Oh terrific,' I said. 'I've just been on a bus for ten hours. Now I have to turn around and go back. *If* I'm lucky. *If* they even have a bus going back to Rhode Island tonight.'

'Is that where you're from – Rhode Island? A fatty like you in that little bitty state?'

'Fuck you!' I said. She wouldn't have fit into that bus seat much better than I did.

The Tang clunked back into my suitcase.

'Like I said, I got work. I'm lockin' up at five-thirty.' She thumped down the hall, eyes to the floor.

For half an hour I sat in the lounge, trying unsuccessfully to think of ways to kill myself in Wayland, Pennsylvania. You couldn't just ring some stranger's doorbell and ask to borrow their car keys and their garage. I considered capitalizing on my heart murmur – going outside and galloping around the dormitory until my heart burst. But the long bus ride had exhausted me. I couldn't even manage to get off the sofa.

When she came back, she was wearing a white nylon windbreaker with 'Dahlia' embroidered on the pocket. She was carrying a flashlight.

'I been thinkin', she said. 'For the time being, just for tonight because it's gettin' late and hoozy-whatsis is up in the Smokies someplace, I guess I could let you stay here. Just don't put any lights on. Use this instead.' She handed me the flashlight. 'I looked you up. Dolores, right? You're in two-fourteen. There's mattresses there, but there ain't any sheets. If the town cops see lights, they'll stop and look. I don't want any trouble.'

I wasn't crazy about this idea, but it seemed less complicated than suicide. All I'd have to do was sit in the dark and breathe.

'Is there a TV or anything?'

'No watching TV! They'd be up here in about two seconds.'

'Okay,' I said. 'I guess that's what I'll do. Thanks.'

I pictured Ma's row of pink dahlias that had grown briefly out back on Bobolink Drive. The weekend before the men had come to install our pool, Ma had transplanted them to the shady side of the house. They'd dropped and shriveled – hadn't survived the move.

'I'd let you stay at my house,' she said, 'but my shithead brother's home this weekend. Here.' She wrote her telephone number on my Merton letter. 'Pay phone's around the corner across from the john. If you have any trouble, you can call me. I ain't goin' out tonight.'

'Dahlia?' I said.

She looked puzzled, then held a finger up to the embroidered name. 'This was somebody else's.' she said. 'Someone who used to live here. Left half her stuff here when she graduated. My loss, her gain. I'm Dottie. So, if you want to give me a ring, I'll be there. Just call. Okay?'

'Okay.'

'Okay then. See you tomorrow. I don't have to come in on Saturday, but I will.'

She locked the door from inside, walked out, and tested it. Then she trudged down the stairs without looking back. I stood there, watching the fat wobble on her big ass.

The maze of corridors grew logical on my third walk through the building. The rooms were opened, anonymous except for personalized vandalism: a strip of missing ceiling tiles in room 107, a peace sign painted on the door of 202. My room was at the end of the second floor.

At first, Kippy's and my beds looked identical. Graciously, I chose the side with the chipped bureau top and the stained mattress.

'Kippy! Finally!' I said to the mirror. 'Kippy, it's me!'

My chin rested in a beard of fat. My eyes were small and piggy-looking. 'I'm sorry I look like this, Kippy. I've had a bad life and—'

I switched bureaus, picked up my suitcases and slammed them down on the other side of the room. I flopped down on the unstained mattress. Hadn't *she* ever told a lie to anyone? What made *her* so infallible?

Just outside my room was a battered filing cabinet with old tests and term papers. 'Rebirth Symbolism in Shakespeare's Major Tragedies . . . Trace the effects of New Deal legislation from its inception through present times . . . If Tom, who had one blue-eyed blond grandparent and three brown-eyed, brown-haired grandparents, married Barbara, a brown-eyed blond whose grandmothers . . .'

I slammed the drawer shut; the ringing metal sound shot down the long corridor and I wondered if it had alerted the town police. Back in my room, I peeled the brown paper wrapping off of my mother's flying-leg painting. 'Are you happy now?' I shouted. 'I'm here, aren't I?'

At dusk I took the flashlight and explored the basement floor. There was a laundry room with washers, dryers, an ironing board and a soda machine. In the next room, a cabinet-model television sat on top of an enamel kitchen table. Metal folding chairs were grouped around it in a semicircle. It looked like a kind of altar. A heavy chain was wrapped around the legs of the set and fastened to a thick iron staple embedded in the wall. I gave that staple several good yanks, then grabbed it tight and leaned back with all my weight. Kippy could disown me, a flood could happen, they could drop the bomb, and still that thing would hold.

Back in the lounge I ate supper by flashlight. Two Sprites from the machine and a jumbo-sized jar of macadamias. For dessert I had the malted-milk balls and a roll of Oreos. I ate them the way I did back in Easterly: popped off the roof first, then raked two threads through the frosting with my front teeth. Then I filled my mouth with soda and felt the cookie collapse in on itself. The ritual both soothed and disappointed me. You were the same person, no matter what state you happened to be stuck breathing in.

Friday night. I imagined Grandma sitting alone in the parlor watching 'Ironside,' her new scallop-shell wallpaper rising up behind her, the TV screen lighting her face in silver. Even watching TV, Grandma was at attention, scowling her scowl, ready for the worst. From Pennsylvania, Grandma seemed fragile. Mortal. I wondered if she missed me – if she was sitting up in Easterly, worrying. I saw her fretful face like Auntie Em's inside the witch's crystal ball. Poor Grandma. Her daughter was boxed in the ground, not in heaven, no matter how many rosaries she sat and mumbled. I thought of dialing her on the pay phone to tell her I was all right. Except I *wasn't* all right . . . Auntie Em would have praised God and accepted the charges. I wasn't so sure about Grandma.

I licked my finger and stuck it into the empty nut jar, poking at the salt on the bottom. So far, college wasn't *that* bad, if you thought about it. Maybe a fantastic coincidence would occur and each girl at Hooten Hall would independently decide to withdraw, leaving me this entire private dormitory. I wondered where the old smelly hunchback man from the bus ride was now and what his life had been before we traveled together at the back of that burping Greyhound bus. That foreign newspaper he was reading looked Jewish. Maybe he was Anne Frank's father – the family's only survivor – and I'd missed an important opportunity because of garlic breath. There was no logic in life whatsoever, that much I saw. Anne Frank had had a loving, protective father and died anyway. I had Daddy, who was dead to me.

Somewhere after dark, I followed my swooping flashlight ray back up to my room. I thought I heard noises. Rats? Jack

Speight? The door locked with a heavy, reassuring thunk.

My mattress felt like an English muffin. The cinder-block walls glowed in the moonlight. 'I'll never sleep,' I thought. Then, without warning, I was in a dream on the beach, talking to a flatfish.

He had washed ashore on purpose and come looking for me, flip-flopping himself past other sunbathers until he got to my blanket. Sand covered him like Shake'n'Bake, but his eyes were clear and purposeful. 'Follow me,' he said. The water I jumped into became the pool water back on Bobolink Drive. I followed the fish into chilly depths I hadn't known existed in our pool. Drowning seemed irrelevant. Bells were ringing and I knew it was Ma, calling me, somehow, underwater.

I sat up. It was this empty dormitory in Pennsylvania again. Down the corridor, the pay phone was ringing off the wall.

I fumbled with the door lock. The flashlight ray wobbled ahead of me. Too slow, too slow! Maybe Larry and Ruth had gotten my number. Maybe they'd hang up if I didn't–

'Hi, it's me,' the woman said. Someone I couldn't quite recall. 'Ruth?'

'Who's Ruth? Who'd you let in?'

'Nobody. I was just dozing.'

'This is Dottie. I just called to check. And to tell you I'll be in at eight o'clock tomorrow morning. You like cream cake?'

'Cream cake? What time is it?'

'Right now? Quarter of eleven. There's this bakery on Hazel Street that had day-old stuff at one-third off. I'll bring you some breakfast tomorrow morning. At eight. Don't smoke any cigarettes near your mattress, now. I don't want to have any explaining to do. All right?'

'All right.'

'You were lucky I didn't have any plans for tonight. Or else I couldn't have called you like this. I'm doing you a big favour. By rights, I should have sent you home.'

I hung up the phone and hugged myself to stop from shaking.

Back in my room I located *Valley of the Dolls* and read. I had an inch and a half of pages left to go. I didn't know what I'd do if I finished.

Somewhere in the middle of the night, I made my way down to the basement and sat. The dull chill of the linoleum floor numbed my ass, but the soda machine's hum soothed me. I read and read by its glow, one hand on the paperback, the other clutching that iron staple. When I looked up from the print, it was morning – the first pink stingy light.

'You see, everyone thinks they're too good for day-old pastry, like one-third off is charity or something. The world is full of snobs. Snobs and slobs. I ought to write a book.'

The room smelled faintly of her sweat. Everything about her repulsed me. I smiled sweetly and finished my second slice of cake.

'If people want to be snobs, let 'em. Their loss, my gain.'

We were probably within twenty pounds of each other, but I wouldn't have been caught dead in the shorts she was wearing. 'This is really nice of you,' I said.

'What is?'

'Bringing me breakfast on your day off. I mean, God.'

She waved me away. 'Have some more – that's what it's here for.'

I reached for the wedge she'd cut me, cupping my other hand beneath to catch the crumbs.

'Look at that! See?'

'See what?'

'Fat slob this, fat slob that. You hear that all the time. You're like me: a *clean* fat. I could tell that right off. Why do you think I let you stay here? . . . I see it all the time. The dirtiest, sloppiest girls are the *skinny* ones. Year after year, same thing. You can tell who the pigs are going to be just by looking at them. You take Jackie Kennedy. Or Jackie whatever her name is now. I bet in private she's a very sloppy person. I bet you any amount of money.'

She looked pleased for having let me know. We both took

sips from the Cokes I'd bought us downstairs. Dottie leaned back on Kippy's mattress and pointed her soda bottle at me.

'Let me tell you something, see? If you'd come here yesterday with those suitcases and been some skinny little ninety-pounder, I would have turned you right around and sent you back where you came from. But you were a fatty, see, so I knew I could trust you.'

This was new. For four years I'd been hated or ignored because of my weight. With Dottie, it was an advantage.

She hooked her foot around the chair leg and scraped it toward her, then hefted up her legs. Marbled with squiggly blue veins, they looked like huge blue cheeses.

'What's that supposed to be, anyway?' she said. She was making a face. My eyes followed hers to Ma's flying-leg painting, leaning against the wall.

'Just a picture,' I said, blushing.

'A leg with wings on it? What's it supposed to *mean?*'

I didn't want this moron even looking at it. 'I'm not really sure,' I shrugged. 'Tell me about Hooten.'

Maybe I'd ship Ma's painting back to Grandma's, I thought. Come to think of it, I didn't want Kippy staring at it, either.

'. . . And there's this girl Rochelle that's dorm president this year. Got the rest of them fooled, but I bet you'll see right through her. Miss Tiny Twat. Lays out there sunbathing on the lawn so everyone coming and going to class can get a good look. One time I caught her spitting a hawker right into the drinking fountain. "Excuse me," I say to her, "but the other girls might like to drink out of that."'

' "I haven't got the slightest idea what you're talking about," she says. And there's her fucking phlegm in the bubbler. Conceited bitch . . . Last year her and this other girl started this petition thing to get me fired. Stare at them in the shower, ha! Who's got time to stare at them when I'm cleaning up all their messes for them? First she parks herself out there in a bathing suit. Then she accuses *me* of staring.' There were tears in her eyes; her hands were fists. '"Just go about your business," my foreman says. "You're a good worker. Just keep your nose clean."'

She scared me. Still, she had declared me an ally, a 'clean fat.' There was a kind of authority in those dozens of keys on her ring. And she'd let me stay, had brought me food like Ma always had. She was here. She was somebody.

'You want a cigarette?' I asked her.

When I lit hers, I noticed strands of gray in her blunt black hair. 'How old are you?' I asked.

'Me? Twenty-nine. Hey, you know what? I got three aquariums at my house. One in the kitchen, one in the parlor, and one in my bedroom. I got piranhas. You feed 'em canned shrimp and they attack it. The angelfish are the ones in my bedroom. They're my special cuties. Hey, maybe someday you could come see them. My fish. You could come over for supper.'

She reached for the remaining rectangle of cream cake. 'Here, let's split this,' she said, breaking me a handful. 'Open your mouth.'

Twenty-nine: she was too old to be my friend, too young to be my mother. 'So tell me about you,' she said.

'About me?' I laughed. I told her the plot of *Valley of the Dolls* instead, rambling on about the three main characters, how their bad choices had wrecked their lives.

She was smiling at me without listening.

'What?' I said. 'What's the matter?'

She leaned toward me. With her finger, she wiped a fleck of frosting off my chin, brought it back to her own mouth, and licked.

Then her gaze was over my shoulder. 'A leg with wings,' she said, shaking her head at Ma's painting. 'That's wild!'

Chapter 13

The Strednickis tried the lock three times before they got the door open. I listened to the click of metal on metal, relieved that the shades were down, grateful for every extra second Kippy wouldn't see me. She was the first to enter. I watched her hand pat the wall until she located the light switch. 'Something stinks in here,' she said. Then she saw me.

Her parents stared, light-dazed. No one spoke.

I'd been ready for her earlier – had braced myself all morning long as strange voices faded in and out of rooms, up and down corridors on the other side of my locked door. I'd skipped both breakfast and lunch, hoping it might make me look more reasonable. But by three o'clock I'd had enough and taken out the day-old unsold birthday cake Dottie had bought for our party the day before. 'Happy Birthday to—'. No one had wanted it but Dottie and me.

'Hi,' I said. 'What do I owe you for the bedspreads?'

Kippy was wearing a turned-down sailor cap with autographs written on it. 'Just a second,' she began. 'They told me downstairs that two-fourteen is mine and my roommate's room.'

'I'm her.'

Part of me enjoyed the panic overtaking her facial muscles. Parents, a boyfriend, a peppy little life: she was overdue some-one like me.

'Don't forget to figure in the tax on those curtains and bedspreads,' I told the three of them. 'I don't want you to cheat yourselves.'

The whole thing was Dottie's fault. All week long, we'd worked mornings – scouring shower stalls, waxing floors, distributing laundry packages to the vacant rooms. By midweek, Dottie had brought in her record player and we'd done our cleaning to her soul albums. We both like the duets best: Sam and Dave, Marvin and Tammi, Ike and Tina. Our favourite was 'Mockingbird.' From our respective cleaning areas, we called the lyrics into the empty hallways – called out to each other – our voices echoing off the cinderblock walls.

> *Mock-*
> *Yeah!*
> *-ing-*
> *Yeah!*
> *-bird!*
> *Yeah!*
> *Yeah!*
> *Yeah!*

In the afternoons, exhausted and sweaty from work, we showered on separate floors, then met each other down in the lounge where we ate and watched TV and played Dottie's favourite card game, Chinese rummy. I was good at it almost immediately. After the first couple of games, we were even-steven.

Throughout the week, Dottie brought me treats: day-olds and Kentucky Fried, hot fudge sundaes melting from the ride across town. She waved away whatever money I held in front of her. 'You don't owe me anything,' she always insisted. 'This was my idea.' She left each evening at dusk. She had to get home to her fish, she said. I'd lie awake in that strange, darkening dormitory, sometimes singing to myself both sides of those soul duets, sometimes reminding myself who I really was: fat Dolores, mother killer, the girl who deserved nothing but shit.

Our party on the last day before the other girls arrived was Dottie's idea, too. She wanted, she said, to celebrate the fact that she'd finished her work a whole day ahead of schedule, thanks to me. She wanted to celebrate our friendship. Besides the cake, she bought a bottle of vodka and four pounds of pistachio nuts, gift-wrapped in a cardboard box. The side of the box said 'Two Size D Flanges.' We started at noon, cracking those nuts with our teeth and drinking Tang-and-vodkas, giggling and trying to guess what a flange was.

We sang and danced to Dottie's records and by midafternoon we were drunk enough to be the singers themselves – the twirling, jiving Temptations, the lovelorn Shirelles. Dottie dropped to her knees as Little Anthony, was up again and strutting as James Brown. When she put on a Supremes record, she insisted we were Flo and Mary, the two nice ones. For scrawny Diana Ross, Dottie stuck a mop into her utility bucket and we snapped our fingers and danced around it, singing that we heard a symphony.

'You can tell that show-off Diana is a real bitch in her personal life,' Dottie declared between tracks. 'And a slob, too.'

Without premeditation, I yanked the needle off the turntable, hunched up my shoulders, and became Ed Sullivan. 'Diana Ross has been fired from our really big shew,' I announced. 'She's been replaced by America's newest singing sensation, Dolores Price!'

I lifted my foot and sent the utility bucket clanging across the room, the mop clattering to the floor. Then I dropped the record-player arm onto the opening of Aretha Franklin's 'Respect' and began a full-out performance. I threw my whole body into it – threw into it, too, my anger, my sense of outrage, all the power of two hundred fifty pounds.

Dottie sat back on the bed, struck dumb at first by what I was feeling, then hooting and shouting the choruses along with me.

> R-E-S-P-E-C-T
> *Find out what it means to me!*

We'd played the song over and over, raising our fists and

shouting about respect until we were both hoarse, until we were both somehow avenged.

Now Kippy's mother's eyes bounced from my unsnapped pants to the knife I'd stuck diagonally into the remaining half of the birthday cake. The father wore high-water flare pants and orange socks. Kippy had shiny chipmunk cheeks. What right did *they* have to judge *me?*

Her father put down two suitcases and walked through the awkwardness, offering me his hand. 'I'm Joe Strednicki . . . heh heh . . . I'm an electrician.' That hand felt solid and sandpapery. I held on to it longer then I should have.

'I took this side of the room if it's all right with you,' I said. 'But I can switch if you want. It makes no difference. Really.' For some reason, I kept saying it to Kippy's mother.

'So wait a minute,' Kippy said. She was shaking her head. 'There's a definite mistake here. There's a mix-up somewhere because—'

'You got mail already,' I interrupted. 'A letter from Dante. Your boyfriend. I'll get it for you.'

Kippy took the letter absentmindedly without noticing the red fingerprints on the envelope. 'Open it! Go ahead!' Dottie had kept teasing me at one point during our party, waving the letter near my face. The red pistachio-nut dye wouldn't erase away. In my wastebasket were five inches' worth of shells I'd meant to dump. All day long I'd been wrestling with my first hangover and passing gas more foul than I'd thought possible.

Kippy sat rigidly on the edge of the mattress I'd chosen for her. Her mother's smile blinked on and off as if it had a short circuit – something Mr. Strednicki might be required to fix.

I pushed the top flap back over the birthday cake box, sinking the knife in deeper, and got up off the bed. 'So I guess I'll let you get unpacked. Be back in a little while. Nice to meet you.'

'Is it your birthday?' Mrs. Strednicki asked vaguely. Come to think of it, she had that chipmunky look, too.

'Not really,' I said. 'Well, sort of.'

Mr and Mrs Strednicki smiled and nodded approvingly, as if what I'd just said made perfect sense.

From the end bathroom stall, adjacent to mine and Kippy's room, I listened to their family argument. It was both a sound and a vibration through the cinder block. '. . . Hard-earned money,' I heard her father say. And from Kippy, *"Not with that hippopotamus!"*

I was glad I'd brought the cake with me. Detaching a blue sugar rose, I placed it in my mouth, on my tongue, then pushed up, crushing it against the roof of my mouth. It was so sweet, it burned.

At five p.m. Rochelle, the dorm president that Dottie hated, led the eight of us freshmen girls downstairs to the lounge, where she passed out Styrofoam cups and poured us each two inches of Boone's Farm apple wine. We watched and waited while she lit herself a Cigarillo, sipped her wine, and flipped apathetically through her paperwork. Dottie had made her sound more beautiful than she was. A willowy redhead, she kept her eyelids at permanent half-mast indifference. It was as if Robert Mitchum had mated with an Irish setter and this bitch was the result.

Rochelle said her job was to tell us about useful things they didn't print in the Merton College catalog. Such as which professors were assholes and which boys' dorms to stay away from. Such as how to outsmart the fire inspector when he checked our room for hot plates.

None of the other freshmen had sat anywhere near me. I sloshed the wine around in my cup and realized I was going to be as powerless and invisible to these girls as I'd been to the girls in my high school. 'So, why don't you just all say who you are and tell a little about yourself,' I heard Rochelle say.

They started at the opposite end of the room. Bambi, Kippy, Tammy: each girl up front had a cute and sunny personality to match her Walt Disney cartoon name. Each seemed thrilled to have landed at cruddy Merton.

The girls nearest me were plainer, frumpier. Someone named

Veronica had a noticeable twitch. She said she was enrolled in the honors programme and took her studies seriously. Naomi, frail and nervous as a parakeet, said she'd been at Woodstock over the summer and the experience had woken her up. Then she veered on to the subjects of Vietnam and civil rights and the mercury content in swordfish. Kippy and Bambi exchanged uncomfortable looks. Rochelle rolled her eyes and interrupted. 'And last but not least?'

I had been chewing on the edge of my cup, dreading my turn. The squeak of my teeth on the Styrofoam was the loudest sound in the room. Everyone waited. 'Oh, me?' I finally said. 'Dolores.'

'And?'

What was I supposed to tell them? That I'd been stupid enough to arrive a week earlier than the rest of them? That I'd been raped at thirteen?

'I'm wicked glad to be here,' I mumbled to the coffee table.

It occurred to me as Rochelle read dormitory rules from her clipboard that you could tell a lot more about people from watching their behaviour with Styrofoam cups than you could by what they told you. Kippy had stopped taking notes and was poking holes into the side of hers with her pencil point. Naomi dismantled her cup into small chips. I had gnawed mine into one long spiral.

'And a word to the wise,' Rochelle said. 'Don't get involved with any of the guys in Culinary Arts. You have to be horny and a jerk just to get into that program. It's a prerequisite.' Kippy and Tammy widened their eyes at each other and giggled. 'Their whole dorm is on academic probation this semester. You'll see them at supper tonight. They're putting on a barbecue for our dorm. Don't say I didn't warn you. And then, of course, there's ten-ton Dottie.'

My breathing stopped. At the mention of weight, several girls glanced instinctively toward me, then immediately away.

'Dottie,' Rochelle continued, 'our famous lezzie cleaning woman.'

Kippy looked lost. 'Famous what?' she asked.

'Lezzie,' Rochelle repeated. 'As in lesbian. As in girl loves girl.'

'Oh, ick,' Kippy said. 'Don't make me chuck my cookies.'

The drunken night before came pounding back. In the midst of the vodka and confusion and singing – right after my performance of 'Respect' – Dottie had stood up, orbited close to me, and kissed me on the lips. A single kiss, followed by laughter. At the time it had struck me as odd and silly and then I had dismissed it. Now it scared me – not so much the kiss itself, but what someone like Rochelle or Kippy might make of it. The gas from all those pistachio nuts rumbled inside me and mixed itself up with a fear of each one of them in that room. I wanted to be anywhere else in the world but on that frigging frayed sofa.

'I'm sick,' I said. 'Can I go?'

'Just a sec,' Rochelle said. 'Are there any questions?'

'I have one,' Kippy said.

'Uh-huh?'

'Well, never mind. I'll talk to you after the meeting's over.'

'It *is* over,' Rochelle said.

Kippy's mother had hung the Indian-print curtains before she left. A breeze from outside billowed them, the cloth rolling in toward me like surf. That entire week, it hadn't once occurred to me to open the windows.

Kippy's high-school yearbook was on the bed. In her picture, she had longer hair and a warm smile.

Junior Red Cross Volunteer I, II; Majorettes II, III, IV; Class Secretary III . . . Pastime: Talking during study hall. Weakness: Juicy Fruit gum. Quote: 'Today is the first day of the rest of your life.'

She had unpacked a framed picture of a dark-haired boy and put it on her bureau. I found the same picture in the yearbook;

sure enough, it was Dante. *'Saint Dante.' Pastimes: Milk and Cookies, praying for sinners. Quote: I cried because I had no shoes. Then I met a man who had no feet.'*

I got off the bed and walked over to Kippy's bureau for a better look. His bushy eyebrows were crimped up in a sad, sympathetic way. There was a struggle in his eyes.

When Kippy got back to our room, she banged shut her suitcases and shoved them under her bed. I could tell Rochelle had vetoed her escape.

'Your parents seem nice,' I said. 'You look like your mother.' She slammed cosmetics and perfume bottles on to the shelf above her bed. Her fingers tweezed nervously at a knot in the speaker wire of her stereo. She jumped from chore to chore without accomplishing anything.

She had loved me in my letters, I wanted to remind her – had trusted me with volunteered intimacies. It was my fat that made her hate me.

I walked over to her bureau and picked up her boyfriend's picture. 'Dante's cute,' I said. 'If you don't mind my asking, whatever happened between the two of you?'

That's when she finally looked at me.

'You wrote that he was pressuring you, remember? I was just wondering, well . . . Not that it's any of my business.'

She walked over, took the picture, and slammed his face down against the bureau top. 'I wrote *nothing* to you!' she said. 'Understand?'

Down the hall, two girls whooped back-from-vacation hellos.

'I didn't write a *thing* to you, okay? I wrote to someone else. Someone you *said* you were. Okay?'

I lit myself a Salem, the match shaking in my hand. Pistachio-nut gas bubbled up from my insides. 'Well, can I help it if I have a gland problem?' I said. 'It's something I was born with. Go ahead and shoot me.'

She was the first to look away.

*

At the picnic supper I took tiny spoonfuls of the various salads, arranging them like small islands against the white space of the heavy china plate. It was an act of good faith for Kippy's sake: I would lose weight and be normal for her. But Kippy didn't notice. She and Bambi were busy trying to distance themselves from me. I had shadowed them from the dorm to the food line.

The barbecue was an oil drum cut in half and covered with wire. Sauce-slopped chicken pieces sizzled between us Hooten girls and the boys from Culinary Arts. The barbecue guy was soap-opera handsome, with his straight white teeth and wilty chef's hat. He wore a red bandanna around his neck and smiled from behind a veil of blue barbecue smoke.

'This one wants you,' he told Kippy, spearing her a dripping chicken breast. He pushed it off the fork and on to her plate. If you could believe his name tag, his name was Eric. 'Where you girls from?' he asked. A plump chicken leg hovered above Bambi's plate.

'Edison, New Jersey.'

'Stoughton, Massachusetts.'

Eric licked his greasy finger. 'Oh, yeah? Well, where's that at?'

'It's near Boston,' Bambi said.

'Boston? I hear they're a bunch of old farts up in Boston. I hear they ban everything.'

Kippy laughed so hard, someone might have been tickling her.

'Not everything,' Bambi said.

'She's a wiseass,' he told Kippy. The three of them laughed. He turned to me. 'Which one?' he said, nodding businesslike at the chicken pieces. I couldn't decide. The other two were escaping down the line. I pointed to the ugliest, most shriveled leg.

When I turned to look for them, I saw Kippy and Bambi sitting across the lawn on a stone bench. Both were bent over the plates in their laps, laughing at something. Me. I didn't know where else to go.

I stood waiting for them to push over, but they didn't. There was no place to sit but the ground. I lowered myself partway down and let myself fall the rest of the way. I hadn't meant to grunt. The chicken leg rolled off my plate and on to the lawn. I could feel the two of them stop eating to watch. I could hear them listening to my heavy breathing.

Their conversation turned from boys to hair. I wanted to tell them about Ruth's peppermint shampoo, to point out that Ruth had thought my hair was beautiful. Why hadn't my fat mattered to Larry and Ruth?

After dessert, the Culinary Arts boys began pulling off their floppy chef's hats, unbuttoning their white jackets. Two of them spit watermelon seeds at each other, looking around to see which girls were watching. A Frisbee sailed across the lawn.

Some of the Hooten girls got coaxed on to boys' shoulders and a kind of wrestling contest began. The girls laughed unsurely, grabbing each other's wrists and pushing with half-hearted swipes. Below them, the boys slammed into each other, more in earnest.

'Come on, New Jersey,' someone said. That barbecue guy, that Eric. He knelt down on the ground next to me, close enough so that I smelled cooked meat. Kippy giggled and refused, then climbed up on to his shoulders. They rose, swaying, and galloped toward the others.

'I couldn't decide between you or the fat one,' I heard him say. Kippy's laugh was a shriek.

Joined together, they made a kind of centaur – half bastard, half bitch. Dottie would have laughed out loud at that. She wasn't due back to work for two more days. I could make her hate Kippy; I knew just the kind of thing to say. Rochelle had said that thing about Dottie just because she was fat. They needed some excuse to hate her. That stupid kiss had meant nothing. That kiss was nothing at all.

Kippy hooked one arm around Eric's neck and began to fight the girl opposite her like she meant it, pulling hair and whacking at her ear. Below her, Eric whooped encouragement.

He hooked his leg around the other boy's, toppling the duo.

Eric and Kippy ambled in circles, fanning out the hesitant competition. Neither saw the burly boy coming at them from the side. He had served Jell-O mold slices in the buffet line – delicately, I remembered. Now he lowered his head like a bull and charged.

When they collided, Eric faltered slightly but maintained his upright position. Kippy went flying backward, landing with a thud on her shoulder. 'Oh, God!' she screamed. 'It hurts! It Jesus fucking hurts!'

A circle of people blocked my view. I tried to get up and go to her, but no matter which way I attempted to raise myself, I seemed anchored to the ground. Kippy's voice rose up over everything. 'Oh my God! Oh my God!' She kept yelling her pain until it became a sort of chant.

Rochelle took charge. Dispensing her physical-therapist's wisdom, she prodded and poked, then decided Kippy needed to go to Wayland Hospital's emergency room. By the time they got her off the ground and into the back of somebody's station wagon, it was dusk. I thought of phoning her parents. Or Dante at his Lutheran school. Instead, I sat and smoked.

After everyone else had gone inside, a man in a Buildings and Grounds truck arrived and hissed water onto the barbecue coals. He collapsed the buffet tables (one blunt, efficient whack to each leg), loaded them into the truck, and drove them away. Mosquitoes were out and biting.

I managed to get on to my hands and knees and over to the stone bench. By the third try I was standing, puffing, my heart jackhammering. I walked unsteadily on pins-and-needles feet.

In the room again, I locked the door. My mumbling to myself turned into a silent conversation to Dante's picture. 'Look out for her,' I told him. 'I wouldn't trust her farther than I could throw her.' Saying it made me think of the way she'd looked flying backwards, mid-fall. I felt giddy.

I wanted Dante to talk back.

She'd read his letter without expression, then put it in a

paisley box in her dresser. Second drawer. I walked over to it.
Hesitated. Slid it out of the envelope.

> *. . . goes back to the time when my mother found out about
> my father and made me promise her that I would never be
> a WOMANIZER like him. But now I wish we made love
> like you wanted us to, Kathy. Maybe God doesn't even
> think it's wrong, who knows? I don't know anything
> anymore. I'm sorry I made you cry that night at the Ridge
> when I refused. I wanted to so badly but I was confused. I
> love you more than I can take.*

The letter shook between my hands. Instantly, I loved him –
for his confusion, for the promise he'd made to his mother. It
was *Dante* who'd resisted, *Kippy* who had wanted them to play
with fire.

I was playing with fire myself. What if I didn't hear her
coming? How could I explain his framed picture in bed with
me, the letter in my lap? I kept begging myself to get up and put
everything back.

I needn't have worried. When they got back, somewhere after
ten, you could her them from as far away as the parking lot – a
big fanfare with Kippy in the middle. I lay in bed in the dark
with my eyes clenched shut and a blanket over my head.

The door banged open and the light snapped on. There were
at least three or four of them, guys and girls both, everyone
whispering. Rochelle's voice was still in charge. 'Thanks so
much, you guys,' Kippy kept saying sweetly. Someone
whispered a wisecrack I couldn't hear. The others laughed
through their noses. People left.

It wasn't fair. Being fat was a handicap, too, but people ran
the fuck the other way. Or shit their nasty wisecracks all over
you. Or both. I *could* have been born with a gland problem for
all any of them knew. She had climbed up on to his shoulders
of her own free will. If you played with fire, you were going to
get burned.

The quiet was so absolute, neither of us might have existed. Someone might rush in, snap on the light, and find our room as empty as July.

The clock from downtown struck once. Kippy began to whimper. I counted my heartbeats past two hundred, daring myself to speak.

'Are you in pain?' I finally said.

She kept me waiting. Then a bedside lamp snapped on and Kippy was squinting at her clock. 'My first day at college,' she said. 'Shit!'

I grabbed for my Salems before the light went out.

'Does it hurt?' I asked again. 'If there's anything I can do—'

She put the light on again. 'I fractured my collarbone,' she said. 'They gave me something for the pain at the hospital. I'm supposed to wait another two hours before I take the next one. Can I have one of your cigarettes?'

I struggled out of bed, put it to her mouth, and lit it.

'Menthol,' she said. 'Ick.'

'There's a machine in the basement. I can get you some regular ones tomorrow. Or if you want, I could go down and get them now.' I sat on the edge of the bed waiting for her to decide.

'A broken collarbone,' she repeated. 'I have to wear this asshole Ace bandage thing for at least three weeks.'

She had been warned about those Culinary Arts idiots. What did she expect? 'Why don't you just take that other pill now? Where are they? I'll get you some water.'

'Maybe I should,' she said. 'They're in a little envelope in my purse. Thanks.'

I recognized the pills, the same kind Grandma fed me the weekend of Ma's death. She put two in her mouth and took the glass of water.

'It'll be okay,' I said. 'Really.'

She swallowed hard. 'Oh, right. Like I'm supposed to believe anything *you* tell me!' She handed me back the glass. 'You seemed so nice in those letters. And funny, too. I thought you were going to be so cool. Then I get here and you're . . .'

'I'm the same person,' I said. 'I wrote the letters.'

'Bullshit you're the same person. Just because you have a gland problem or whatever, it doesn't give you the right to pretend to be something you're not. Is the truth too much to ask from someone who's going to be your roommate? Ow! Shit! My shoulder!'

I turned off the light. 'I thought you'd like me better if you didn't know what I looked like,' I said. She didn't answer. 'And you *did*, right?'

I could tell she was looking over at me, staring at me in the dark.

'Kippy?'

'What?'

'I don't have a gland problem. I'm just fat. And I—' I was about to confess I'd opened Dante's letter, then stopped short of it.

'And you what?'

'And my mother died this summer.'

The room was quiet for the next several seconds. 'How?' she said.

'In an accident.'

'Well, I'm sorry,' she said. '*If* it's true.'

I lay there in the dark, aching, crying in silence. When I was finally close to sleep, she spoke again. 'Dolores, guess what? The pain's not there.' Her voice sounded calm and foggy. 'Oh, by the way – you know what you asked me this afternoon?'

'What do you mean?' I said.

'About Dante? About him pressuring me? We *did* make love. Just before he left for school. Out at this place called the Ridge.'

I didn't say anything.

'It was so beautiful,' she said. 'It was unreal.'

Chapter 14

Kippy's broken collarbone provided the inroad I needed. I was allowed to become her loyal, devoted servant, carrying her tray at supper, buying her textbooks, doing her laundry, rapping on Rochelle's door whenever Kippy needed to borrow the heating pad. She had forgotten to pack her soap dish; I gave her mine. 'Mucus green, Dee?' she said. (By the second week, she'd started calling me Dee instead of Dolores.) I went back to the bookstore and bought her a shell-pink one like she'd left in New Jersey. Her medication made her thirsty. I'd wave away the change she offered whenever I returned from the basement soda machine with her Orange Crushes. 'Oh, go on – it's on me!' I'd insist, pushing away her quarters, trying as best I could to swallow back the panting and huffing that climbing those flights of stairs left me with. Instinct told me to hurry on these errands. If I gave her enough time, she might move out.

That first week, I went to more of Kippy's classes than my own, collecting semester schedules and first impressions. I reported back in the wisecracking way she had liked about my summer letters. For a role model, I used Juliet's old nurse in *Romeo and Juliet:* a good-hearted fussbudget, a woman who spoke her piece but knew her place.

In junior year at Easterly High School, Mrs. Bronstein had made us read *Romeo and Juliet,* then see *West Side Story,* her favourite movie, for comparison. Sharks and Jets, Montagues and Capulets. The class had laughed at the singing parts – people interrupting the crises of their lives to belt out a tune. At the end of the film, Mrs Bronstein snapped on the classroom lights. 'Well, what did you think?' she asked, hopefully.

I had sometimes loved Mrs. Bronstein for her efforts, could have volunteered just the sort of response that would have thrilled her. None of us spoke. Mrs. Bronstein watched us and waited. Finally, Stormy LaTerra raised her hand and said she thought George Chakiris had a cute ass. Mrs. Bronstein left the room in tears and the kid from audiovisual played the movie in reverse for us: Maria leaping backward away from Tony's slumped body, Tony undying, the Sharks jerking their knives back out of him. Maybe you *could* come back to life after you'd been dead to it. Or pick a new person to become – just shuck you old self, let who you used to be die a quiet death. It was funny how my high-school education was turning out to be more useful after the fact than while they were putting me through it.

I cast Eric from Culinary Arts as Kippy's Romeo. Kippy liked it when I called him that. He appeared at our door – off and on at first, then on a kind of schedule, sipping his Miller High Lifes, pacing, slowing for his own reflection each time he passed our mirror. In the name of Kippy's honor, Eric had fixed the assailant who had sent her flying and broken her collarbone by flattening his tires and signing him up for memberships in three different record clubs.

Eric nodded acknowledgement to me but never spoke. His arrival was my cue to wait three minutes, then go. The waiting was Kippy's idea. 'It's not like we're – you know – animals or anything,' she told me. Grabbing my Salems and some miscellaneous magazine, I always went to the same place – the bathroom stall closest to the wall and adjacent to our room. He usually stayed for two or three beers' worth of time. Kippy's moans and giggles sometimes made their way through the cinder block. There was an occasional shriek of pain as well. 'My shoulder! You're leaning on my shoulder!'

By the first of October, Kippy had gotten seven letters from Dante at Lutheran college. Since Eric, she had put Dante's

picture in her sweater drawer and written him back only once.
'Would you mail this for me?' she'd asked, affixing a stamp and
sighing. I'd mailed it, all right: mailed it into the storm drain
outside Hooten Hall. It wasn't that I *hated* her, exactly; she just
didn't deserve someone as sensitive as Dante.

Which is why I began stealing his letters, instead of waiting
and reading them after she opened them.

Passing the mail slots at mealtime and going to and from the
soda machine for her Orange Crushes, I'd pluck the now-
familiar beige envelopes with their clipper-ship insignia from
Kippy's pigeonhole and slide them into my fatigue-jacket
pocket. I read and reread them while I sat on the hard toilet
seat, waiting for Eric and Kippy to finish fucking. Poor Dante.
Lutheran college wasn't going well. Even his tissue-paper
stationery was fragile. *'Sometimes I think I may be going crazy
. . . sexual thoughts right in the middle of Tuesday-night prayer
service . . .'* I began to fret over the deterioration of his
penmanship – the way the words slanted first one way and then
the other, sometimes in the same line. *'. . . That manager's-
training offer back at my old job . . . an important question to
ask you at Thanksgiving . . . would NEVER do to my wife what
my father did to my mother.'* That handwriting swayed like the
beach grass on Fisherman's Cove, those banks below Mrs.
Masicotte's mansion. I hadn't thought of that spot in years. I
was struck suddenly with where I was. Where I wasn't.
Wayland, Pennsylvania: the farthest from the ocean I'd ever
been.

Whenever I was sure Eric had left, I'd return to our room to
cluck at Kippy like Old Nurse and throw away the Miller
empties. I wasn't actually *stealing* the letters, I told myself. I was
withholding them for the good of someone whose suffering I
felt I understood – committing a federal offense only in some
narrower sense. 'Everything's relative,' Mr. Pucci used to be
fond of reminding me. 'Look at the *big* picture.'

Dottie's mop handle rested against her shoulder, riflelike, her fist white from the grip. I was halfway upstairs with a piece of lemon-meringue pie and a glass of milk for Kippy. For three weeks I had managed to nod covertly at Dottie and pretend I didn't hear her calling me from the opposite end of the corridor. Pretend we had no history.

'You ain't supposed to bring dishes out of the dining room,' she said. 'That's the rule.'

'It's for my roommate. Her collarbone is throbbing. Don't worry – I'll make sure I bring them back at suppertime. I won't forget.'

'I'm supposed to report anyone I see with dining-room property.' She walked down the stairs toward me.

I flinched as she reached out to me and pulled a loose thread from my sweatshirt. 'What's the matter?' she said.

'Nothing's the matter,' I said. 'Nothing at all.'

Three girls from the dorm had said hello to me that day. Being Kippy's errand girl had given me a kind of authority through the corridors. I was making headway. Talking to Dottie was suicide.

'Are you mad at me or something?' Pink blotches blossomed on her cheeks; her eyes squinted as she waited for my answer.

'Me? No. Why should I be mad?'

'I don't know. That's what I'm trying to find out.'

That kiss: weird and unreal, delivered drunk.

'I better get this food up to Kippy now,' I said. 'She missed breakfast and when she takes her medication on an empty—'

'Dolores?'

'Phew, I sure have been busy. Those teachers assign reading like their class is the only one you've got.'

The truth was, all the books I'd bought sat like a small untouched monument on my desk. The felt-tipped yellow Hi-lighter pens I'd purchased the first day of classes still had all their sharp corners.

'So how do you like that roommate of yours – that Krippy or Crappy?'

'Kippy? She's supernice. We get along great.' I glanced down at the meringue pie quivering in my hand. 'She broke her collarbone the first night, see, so I've been helping her out with stuff.'

'I hate her guts,' Dottie said.

My eyes kept jumping to the fire door. Any second, someone was liable to come out and catch us. 'You don't even know her,' I said.

'I know she makes fun of you behind your back.'

The pie plate went heavy in my hand. 'No, she doesn't,' I said. 'Why? What did she say?'

'I go on break at two-thirty. I could meet you down in the utility room.'

'Oh, gee, I can't because—'

The fire door banged open. Veronica walked down the stairs past us.

'You're waitin' on her hand and foot and then she goes and says that about you. It's sickening.'

'Maybe she was talking about someone else,' I said. 'Or maybe—'

Dottie shook her head. 'Oh, it was about you, all right. That twat.'

I wasn't any ten-ton lezzie if *that's* what Kippy had said. I wasn't anything. Fat girls didn't *have* to be anything!

Back in the room, I handed Kippy her pie and milk. She held out a quarter and smiled. 'Dee, I don't feel like milk right now. Could you do me a big favor and get me an Orange Crush?'

'I'm busy,' I said. 'Get it yourself.'

I didn't *mean* to stop going to my eight o'clock history class. I didn't have anything personal against Dr. Lu; it wasn't her fault she limped. But before I could take my shower, I had to wait until the whole dorm was asleep – until the only thing I could hear was the hum of the hallway lights. Two a.m. Three-thirty. Nobody was going to accuse me of staring at them. Or see me naked, either. I was nobody's freak!

In the middle of the night, the dorm was mine again, just like that first week. I'd undo my bathrobe and step into those cumulus clouds of steam, into water so hot and forceful, I imagined it purifying me, liquefying my fat and sending it swirling down the drain. Life seemed nearest to acceptable at four a.m. – relaxation such a well-deserved reward that I began not to have the heart to set the alarm on myself for early-morning class. I'd wake up groggy, long after the kitchen had stopped serving breakfast, and thank God for Pop-Tarts. Most of the other girls were midway through their classes.

On TV, in the downstairs lounge, a woman from Rhode Island named Hattie became the 'Jeopardy' champion. (For some reason, I liked holding on to that iron staple in the wall while I watched.) I promised myself I'd start going to my 12:30 biology class as soon as Hattie lost, only she kept faking everybody out – coming back from the dead on the strength of her Daily Doubles. I was planning to drop Introduction to Biology anyway. It wasn't as if euglenas and paramecia were going to change my life. And where else but stupid Merton College would they hire an art-history teacher that laughed like Jethro from 'The Beverly Hillbillies'? Every third slide he'd put in upside down or backwards, then laugh that laugh. It made me a nervous wreck just listening for it. How could you take notes from someone like that? I didn't see cutting his class as entirely my fault.

Kippy had begun borrowing my yellow Hi-lighters without even *asking* first. Why didn't she just colour in every page yellow? *Squeak squeak* all afternoon long while I chewed the inside of my cheek and tried to nap. Broken collarbone my fat ass. She was such a hypocrite. 'Dear Dante,' I felt like writing. 'You don't know me, but I'm telling you this in friendship . . .'

By mid-October, the dean of women had sent two while-you-were-out phone messages asking me to call her back about my 'attendance issue.' I balled up the notes and threw them into Kippy's Snoopy wastebasket. Did Dean What's-Her-Face have to wait until three a.m. for *her* shower? Tiptoe around a cleaning lady's schedule?

I had just started a bag of dried apricots one afternoon when someone knocked at our door. 'Kippy's at class,' I yelled out.

'I don't want her. I want you. Dolores.'

It wasn't Dottie, that much I knew. I slid my snack under the pillow and pushed myself off the mattress.

Marcia, a round, motherly senior, stood smiling at me. She'd risen from her chair during dinner one night to inform us she was an Avon representative and would be happy to order us whatever we needed.

'Hi,' she said. 'Mind if I take a moment of your time?' She had a wide, shiny forehead. She wedged herself inside before I could answer.

'Dolores,' she began, 'as recording secretary for Hooten and the head of the Sunshine Committee—'

'Plus you're the Avon lady,' I said.

Her laugh was fake. 'Righty-o, but that's not the reason for my visit today. How are things going?'

'Fine,' I said. 'Super.'

'Super,' she repeated. 'Now one of my jobs as recording secretary is to take attendance at house meetings. We've had four so far and my records say you haven't shown up once.' Her smile bordered on squinting.

'I could use some perfume,' I said. 'Sign me up for ten dollars' worth of whatever. I'm not really fussy. Our own Avon lady. Wow.'

'Is there any reason in particular?' she asked.

'I'm just no good at picking out stuff. What's that kind *you're* wearing? Order me a bottle of that.'

'Any reason why you haven't been coming to the meetings, I mean?'

'Oh, well . . . I get these migraines.' I pinched the skin between my eyebrows and made a face like the woman on the Anacin commercial.

'So are you and—' she stopped and checked her records. 'Are you and Katherine getting along? Is it roomie problems?'

I shook my head.

'Homesick?'

You could show a drive-in movie on that forehead of hers, I thought. 'Kippy and I get along fine,' I said. 'Why? Did *she* say something to you?'

'Oh, good golly, no. We were just wondering, the other officers and me. If there's a problem, we want to know about it. My first semester, I was so homesick, I used to upchuck before class.'

I had called Grandma only once on the pay phone. She'd been on her way to bingo. Ruth and Larry never even answered their phone.

'Everything's really great,' I said. I smiled hard enough to see my cheeks in my peripheral vision. '*Really super.*'

'Terrific!' she said. 'Then we'll see you tonight at the meeting after supper. It's important you're there because we're discussing the big Halloween party. Can I pencil you in for a committee?'

'Well,' I said, 'as long as my migraines cooperate.' I made a fist and tapped my head for emphasis. Migraines had always made Mr. Pucci back off, but Marcia acted as though she'd never heard of them.

'Fantabulous!' she said. 'See you then. And I'll put your cologne order in, immediately if not sooner. Do you need any sachet?'

'I guess I'm all set on that,' I said. 'Thanks.'

'You're entirely welcome.'

Pushy bitch.

That night I skipped downstairs supper and ate the rest of my apricots and a package of Mallomars. But just as I dozed in the quiet of the deserted floor, Marcia's voice boomed from the PA box in the hallway. 'Dolores Price! Dolores Price! We're holding up the meeting for you. We need you downstairs to make it one hundred percent perfect attendance.'

I unlocked the door and spoke to the box. 'My head is *pounding*,' I said in a quivery voice. 'I don't think I can make it.'

'I can't hear you, but I'm clicking off now,' she said. The cheeriness dropped suddenly out of her tone. 'Get down here *quick!*'

The meeting had already begun by the time I sat down at the outskirts, on the piano bench. From up front, Marcia looked up from her reading of the minutes and gave me a wink. The truth was, I sat as far away from other people as they sat away from me. The closest person to me was little Naomi, the girl who had been to Woodstock and made a speech that first day. I watched her tap her knuckles against her knees. Her skin was pale and scaly, her chewed-up fingernails rimmed with dried blood.

As Marcia had promised, the key item on Rochelle's agenda was the upcoming Hooten Hall Halloween party. She said she was against a costume-party theme. Hadn't last semester's luau made them the laughingstock of the campus? She, for one, was tired of the guys from Delta Chi making pigs-on-a-spit jokes every time they passed Hooten on their way to class.

After some discussion, Marcia took the floor. She said that since it was a Halloween party, she, personally, felt costumes would be cute, though she was happy to go along with whatever we gals decided democratically.

In the spirit of cooperation, with Marcia beaming proudly at us, we voted in costumes (Rochelle rolled her eyes but abstained), keg beer, vodka punch, and a $2.50 cover charge for girls from other dorms.

Rochelle invited new business.

'Right here!' Naomi called, loud enough to make me jump. She rushed to the front of the room.

'For those of you who don't know me, my name is Naomi, okay? And I feel it's real important for our dorm to take a stand on Cambodia.'

She hopped nervously from one side of the room to the other. There couldn't have been much more than eighty pounds inside those bib overalls.

'I've drafted this petition' – she waved a clipboard at us – 'and if we all sign it, then it's a start. See, we need to get organized. If hundreds of thousands of college kids across the country unite, then how can even a cocksucker like Nixon not hear us?'

'Excuse me,' Marcia said, smiling her Avon lady smile at Naomi. 'You have a perfect right to your opinion, but, personally, I don't think it's necessary to refer to the President of the United States as . . . as . . .'

'Nixon *himself* is the obscenity,' Naomi snapped back. 'Anyway, that's not the point. The point is My Lai.'

I wasn't unsympathetic to her argument. Those My Lai pictures in *Life* magazine had made my stomach heave. My mother's Tricia Nixon essay was what had gotten me stuck at this cruddy school in the first place.

Naomi's petition passed unsigned from girl to girl as she spoke. Kippy's hands didn't even touch the clipboard. Up front Naomi hopscotched from one world problem to another. Private conversations broke out around the lounge. They were treating her like a joke.

'Well,' Rochelle finally interrupted, 'we apologize if Merton isn't radical enough for you, but some of us have studying to do.'

'Okay, okay,' Naomi nodded. 'I just want to say one more thing, okay? I was at Woodstock this summer. That was re-*al*-ity, you guys! We owe it to our generation to get *political!*'

Rochelle wielded her gavel and declared the meeting over. Someone handed Naomi's clipboard back to her. No one had thought to pass it to me.

'Just a second! Just a second!' Naomi protested. She ran from one exiting girl to the next. 'Why aren't there more names on this thing? Innocent women and children, you guys! Wake the fuck *up!*'

She and I were the last two people left in the room, slumped at opposite ends.

'Let me see that thing,' I said.

Counting Naomi's, mine was the fourth signature.

'Do you get it?' she asked. 'I just don't get it.'

Her eyes were wet and jumpy. The best I could manage was a shrug.

That night, Kippy and some others were playing rummy in our room. I was lying in bed on my side, watching the wall.

Bambi came in without knocking, her face bloodless. She was clutching an album jacket. 'Something awful has happened, you guys,' she said. 'Something really horrible. Paul McCartney is dead.'

'No sir,' Kippy said.

'It was just on the radio. He's been dead for months.' She thrust the *Abbey Road* album at us. 'Look! His eyes are closed and he's barefoot. It's all symbolic. George is the gravedigger. John Lennon is God.'

Other Hooten girls entered, asking if we'd heard. Mine and Kippy's room was becoming some sort of headquarters. Was it an assassination? No, a disease, someone said. A tropical disease he had had for over a year. The other Beatles were in mourning and couldn't be reached.

Marcia said he probably caught it down in India when they were studying with that greasy old maharishi. She said she'd read someplace that in India people just squatted down and pooped right in the street.

There were girls on the beds, girls on the floor. Someone listening to a different radio station said if you played the *White Album* backwards, it said, 'Turn me on, dead man.' Kippy put the record on her turntable and spun with her finger. People moved closer to the eerie gibberish.

They were treating death like some kind of game. I wished all of *their* mothers dead.

'This is bullshit!' I said.

They turned and looked.

'It's all just some stupid practical joke the radio is playing. Can't you tell that? Real death isn't fun, it's painful. She was right tonight – what she said about Vietnam. Naomi. About poor women and children.'

The record on the turntable spun in silence. Nobody spoke.

Then the door opened again, allowing in a wedge of hallway light.

'Phone,' Veronica said.

Kippy sighed. 'Is it Eric? Tell him I'm too upset to talk.'

'It's for her.' Veronica pointed at me.

The hallway made me squint. If it was that busybody dean of women, I'd hang up in her face.

'I was wondering,' Dottie said, 'if you'd like to come eat supper next Saturday. And see my fish.'

'Next Saturday? I can't.'

'I'm making pork. And this string-bean casserole. You make it with cream of mushroom soup and a can of onion rings. You put the onion rings on top. Like a crust. I'm not sure what I'm having for dessert yet.'

'I can't go,' I repeated. 'I'll be studying all that weekend.'

'I thought they were having that Halloween-party thing. You won't be able to study with a party going on. It'll be quieter over here.'

'Well, thanks, but—'

'*Please*. My brother's not going to be here. He's got National Guard that weekend. If you don't like pork, we can have something else.'

Rochelle walked past. If any of them knew she had called me . . .

'Maybe some other time,' I whispered. 'I'll have to go now. See you.'

'When?'

'When what?'

'You said some other time. So, when?'

'I'm not sure. It's hard to say.'

'He's going to be gone that whole weekend. I already bought some of the stuff. You can't freeze pork, you know. It gets some kind of germ'

'I can't. Honest. I have to go.'

'You know what she said about you?'

I gripped the phone so hard, it hurt. 'What?'

'Well, I was going to tell you on Saturday. It's not something I want to go into over the phone. But believe me, she's no friend of yours.'

Suddenly, I was crying. About my poor attendance in class. About that lecture I'd just given them. It wasn't as if my mother's death was their fault . . . They never once asked *me* to play cards with them. My being at college was one big joke.

'You won't even want to sleep in the same room with her when I tell you. It was really rotten.'

'I can't.'

'That first week you were here was so much fun. I could pick you up in my brother's car. He always leaves it here when he's got National Guard. If you'd rather, we could go out somewheres and eat. Some restaurant. Don't say yes or no. Say maybe.'

I waited.

'Dolores,' she said. 'I love you.'

It scared me. Jack Speight's tickling me up there on that porch.

'I love you so much.'

'I have to go now. See you tomorrow.' Only I wouldn't see her. I'd stay in my room all day long with the doors locked. If she tried to come in, I'd report her.

'Why are you treating me like this? That week was the best week of my life. I really miss dancing with you.'

'Did you hear the news?' I said. 'Paul McCartney is dead.'

'Honest to Christ, Dolores, I keep thinking and thinking about you.' There were some funny popping noises: crying. 'I just meant I love you as a friend, that's all. Don't get the wrong idea. We're so much alike, you and me. Who cares about us couple of fatties?'

I hung up.

The bathroom was empty. I locked myself in the stall, shaking so hard that the toilet seat rattled beneath me.

*

By the time I returned to my room, the others had left. Kippy stood in the dark, playing with the flickering candle flame.

I expected her to be angry, but when I flopped on to my mattress, she came over and sat down next to me, the first time she'd ever done that.

'You were thinking about your mother before, weren't you?' she said. 'Is that what got you so upset?'

I'd kept Ma's flying-leg painting in my closet. I didn't trust Kippy with the subject of my mother.

'You said she died in an accident. Tell me about it.'

'A car accident . . . Well, a truck. I don't really want to—'

'It must be hard,' she sighed. She put her arm around me. 'I feel real close to you tonight, Dee.'

Dottie had lied about her – I was convinced Kippy hadn't said anything terrible at all.

'I'm not really a bad person,' I said. I was thinking of all the letters I'd stolen – how I might reglue the envelopes, return them to her. I could blame it on the post office.

'I know you're not,' she said. 'Can I ask you something?'

'Yes,' I said. 'What?'

'Could you wash us a load of darks tomorrow?'

The next day there was a new letter from Dante, thicker than usual and in a bigger envelope, marked 'Fragile/Do Not Bend.' I stuck it in my laundry basket with Kippy's and my dirty clothes and headed down to the basement. (It was safe to go to the basement at noontime; Dottie always cleaned the third floor then.)

Art Fleming leaned toward the camera and announced the Final Jeopardy category: human anatomy. 'It is the small groove between your nose and your top lip,' he said.

The champion frowned. You could tell she'd bet her wad and didn't know the answer – that they'd be packing her off with a round of applause and a set of Grolier's encyclopedias. I walked over to the set and changed the channel.

On the news, Paul McCartney smirked and held up the front

page of that day's newspaper. Then he pinched himself and told the reporters it still hurt, so he guessed he was still alive. I turned off the TV.

Kippy had promised to give me the laundry money this time but she'd spent all her quarters on soda. Between us we had two loads. I put our dark colors and some detergent into the first washer and started it up.

Dante's envelope sat in the laundry basket amongst the whites. I picked it up and peeled back the flap as carefully as possible.

The Polaroid pictures were in a separate, smaller envelope paper-clipped to the back of his letter – five snapshots of him, standing and sitting, completely naked.

Their starkness immobilized me. His hands were on his hips in one. In another, they reached up behind his neck so that his arms, bent at the elbow, formed wings. His pubic hair, the hair beneath his arms, looked black and blunt against the whiteness of his body – a glowing whiteness, as if he had somehow been lit from within.

The letter explained how he'd locked the door while his roommate was at class and placed the camera on a pile of books on a chair. *'Not making love to you that night was the biggest mistake I've ever made in my life. It's all I can think about. I'm hoping these pictures deepen our commitment to each other. I TRULY TRULY love you.'*

I recalled that altered picture I'd come upon in my seventh-grade religion book at St. Anthony's School – how that surprise dirty picture had both shocked and informed me. Yet there was nothing pornographic about Dante's Polaroids. His face, cut off at the forehead in some of the shots, had the same struggling expression as his graduation portrait – almost a holy look. It was clear from the way he'd posed that he was *offering* his body, requesting – not pushing and ripping like Pig Jack Speight. 'All men are pigs,' I'd said to Ruth that morning. 'No they're not,' she'd replied. In one of the pictures, Dante was seated on the edge of the bed, holding himself down there, offering it, somehow politely.

That struggling face: I thought of another picture – the one hanging in the parlor at Grandma's: Jesus, his sad eyes looking out into your eyes, his sacred heart exposed. *Beseeching:* a word from a prayer I'd once memorized. Dante's face beseeched me.

'You know, you don't have to keep feeding your hard-earned money to big business.'

I reeled around, stuffing the Polaroids into my jacket pocket. Little Naomi was wedged between the wall and the whirring clothes dryer.

She stood up and took a book of matches from her bib overalls. 'Here,' she said. 'I'll show you.' Ripping off a strip of cardboard, she wedged it into the washing machine's coin slot and pushed gently. There was a soft click, a humming sound. Water gushed into the tub.

'Thanks,' I said. She couldn't have seen the pictures from where she'd sat, I told myself.

'Well, we don't have to choose to be victims of General Electric and the power company.'

She sat back down and continued her reading.

I wanted to think. To look again. But I wanted to keep talking.

'Excuse me,' I said. 'You were at Woodstock this summer, right?'

She put down her book. 'Yeah. It was so far-fucking-out. Incredible.'

'Did you by any chance happen to see this couple when you were there? With a little girl about two years old. She has curly, curly Shirley Temple hair. The guy is tall and skinny.'

Naomi laughed. 'That was the thing about Woodstock. You didn't think of people as individuals. We were all this . . . mass entity.'

'Oh,' I said. 'Right.'

She must have seen my disappointment. 'I was two people back from Joni Mitchell in the portable toilet line, though,' she said.

'Joni Mitchell used the public toilets?'

'Well, yeah. See, the whole point was that we're all one, you know? You and me and Joni and your tall, skinny friend: a bunch of equals sharing the same small planet. It was a rush – very political!'

'Yeah,' I said. 'You bet your bippy.'

She looked at me funny, then smiled. 'Hey, you going to be down here for a while? I want to get something up in my room. Don't go anywhere.'

She clomped out the door and up the stairs.

I took out Dante's pictures again. I was closer to him now than Kippy was, though neither of them knew. The photos linked us together, somehow, brought the two of us to some new place. I was at the verge of a mystery I'd held inside me since Jack: how women might love men back, how women could love men's bodies. Ruth had moaned with pleasure that night on the floor with Larry. I thought of Ma, standing naked at her mirror after Daddy had left her – holding her breasts and aching for Daddy. Thought about the foolish way she'd acted around her dates . . .

Naomi returned with a lavender-coloured joint. 'You feel like doing a number?' she asked.

Things sped too fast. I was making a potential friend! Dante was naked in my pocket!

Naomi teased the joint in front of my nose, back and forth like a windshield wiper. 'I think my biology teacher said something about canceling class today, anyway,' I said.

'Come on, then. It's too nice a day to sit in here and watch lint.'

I had never been out behind the dorm before. Past the dumpsters and the kitchen helpers smoking their parking-lot cigarettes, we climbed a long, sloping hill. The copper meadow grass, dead from frost, crackled under our feet. Maple trees were maroon and yolky-colored in the noon sun.

The joint was tighter, more streamlined, than Larry's had been. I imitated Naomi, taking several short, jerky sips, and a buoyancy passed over me so completely, I half suspected a breeze might blow me skimming along the edge of the dead grass.

Naomi leaned back into the straw. The wind flapped her pant legs.

'Paul McCartney came back from the dead,' I said. 'He was on the news just now. It was all a stupid joke.'

'You know the trouble with the Beatles? Capitalism bit them in the heart. They *are* dead, the four of them. The joke's on them.'

'Yeah, well . . .'

'It's a pretty far-out concept, though,' Naomi said. She looked over and smiled.

'Death?'

'Resurrection.' We were both quiet for a second. Then she started talking about socialism.

I wasn't listening. If resurrection were possible, then so was God. God might be someone unpredictable. Dante, maybe, or John Lennon with his freaky ways. Or even someone with an average, forgettable face: a lady customer in pin curls at the superette, that old garlic-breath man on the bus ride down to Merton. God could even be the audiovisual boy at Easterly High School – a person who could flick a button and run your life in reverse . . .

I imagined Dottie unkissing me. Me traveling backward up the interstate in that Greyhound bus . . . Ma jumping back to the safety of her tollbooth. Arthur Music's truck speeding away from us in reverse.

I reached into my pocket and fingered the edges of the secret Polaroids, the answer to that scary riddle: how women might love men, how men might not be bullies. Resurrection: the word made a pretty sound.

Naomi tapped me on the arm. 'Hey!' she said. 'Watch this!'

She lay back on the ground and wrapped her arms around herself, then began rolling down the hill – slowly at first, then faster, then *fast*. At the bottom she rose drunkenly, laughing and calling for me to join her.

'I can't,' I said.

'Bullshit you can't.'

'No, really.'

'Come on!'

Then I was doing it, rolling crookedly toward her applause, whooping and laughing and travelling in a blur. I closed my eyes, amazed and horrified at my own momentum.

We sat at the bottom of the hill, straw-strewn and giggling in the bright sun. 'Are you wrecked?' Naomi asked.

'Probably,' I said. 'Who knows?'

Chapter 15

An aluminum-foil spaceman walked by, two rubber-faced Nixons. Howdy Doody was dancing with Marilyn Monroe.

'There's nothing like the Four Tops to get everybody hopping around like they were colored people,' Marcia sighed. She had strong-armed Veronica and me for the Halloween-dance refreshment committee; Marcia herself was chairman. We stood in the glare of fluorescent lighting and stainless steel, mixing jugs of screwdriver punch and tubs of onion dip. Marcia had assigned Veronica deviled eggs. She stood at the sink, peeling her shells at close range, picking and worrying over each egg as if it were a midterm exam. Naomi was there, too, seated on the counter, watching us work.

'Colored people at milky-white Merton college, Marcia?' she gasped.

Marcia shooed at her with a dish towel. 'Now don't you start that prejudice business with me, Naomi Slosberg. Who owns three Dionne Warwick albums – you or me?'

Naomi was spending Moratorium Weekend at U Penn with 'real people,' but she'd come downstairs to make fun of the party until her ride got there. At Kippy's request, I was spending the weekend in Naomi's vacant room. Eric had bought a nickel bag of marijuana and borrowed a special hookup from someone in his dorm. He and Kippy were planning to get high and make love by strobe light after the party.

'I mean, black, colored. I don't see what people get so huffy about,' Marcia continued. She had called me 'an old party pooper' when I'd shown up in the kitchen without a costume. She was dressed in a Raggedy Ann outfit she'd sewn from a kit. All week long, she'd hunched over the rec-room sewing machine, preparing herself to look adorable. Eric was dressed as the Jolly Green Giant and Kippy was a New York Met. Kippy had confided to me about the strobe light that afternoon as she cut out leaves from a piece of green felt material and stapled them to a pair of Eric's underpants. After supper that evening, I'd had to leave our room while Kippy painted Eric's body green.

'You know, Naomi, this free love and peacenik business of yours is probably just a stage you happen to be passing through.'

Naomi shot her cigarette butt into the big kitchen sink. 'I was a majorette my first year in high school.' She laughed. 'Used to curl my hair in a flip like Marlo Thomas and wear those watch-plaid kilts with the fringe and the giant safety pins. Had a whole closet of them.'

'And if you were smart,' Marcia said, 'you would have had those skirts dry-cleaned and saved them. Styles come back, you know.'

'I saved the safety pins,' Naomi said. 'Use 'em for roach clips.'

'Oh, shush,' Marcia said. 'Why don't you just slide yourself off that counter and transfer some dip into these bowls for us?'

'Marcia,' Naomi sighed. 'People all over the country are trying to stop America the Beautiful from detonating the Third World. And what are the wing nuts at this school doing? Eating onion dip and dancing the fucking shing-a-ling.'

'Now that's enough,' Marcia said. 'You're hurting my virgin ears.'

'Do you even know where Cambodia *is*, Marcia? How many Billie Holiday albums do you own?'

'None,' Marcia said. 'I haven't even heard of the gentleman, Naomi. So I suppose that makes me a terrible person, doesn't it?'

'Billie Holiday?' I said. I saw Mr. Pucci's boyfriend's face, heard that sad, soothing voice that had come out of their jukebox.

'Anyhow, I've just about given up on that shing-a-ling dance,' Marcia said. She was gurgling and blopping vodka over an ice ring studded with frozen cherries. 'Audrey and Rochelle tried to teach me, but they said I was hopeless. My dancing muscles must be mentally retarded.'

I had assumed she was talking to the group of us, but when I looked up, she was saying it specifically to me, smiling her big, hard smile, her teeth wet and yellow against her white-powdered Raggedy Ann face. It was depressing to see how far off the mark from adorable she had landed.

'I'm only putting half of this vodka in the punch,' she whispered to me in confidence, as if we were two mothers putting something over on our children. 'The last thing I want to do is spend all tomorrow morning scraping dried upchuck off the lounge rug with a butter knife.'

She hefted the punch bowl and walked cautiously toward the door. 'Now, Naomi and Dolores, you walk in front of me. I don't want anyone bumping into me and making me spill this. If we have to wet-mop the dance floor, everybody'll be doing the shing-a-ling whether they want to or not!'

Out in the lounge, they were slow-dancing to 'Cherish.'

'Oh, Christ,' Naomi said. 'Do I have to go out there? This song makes me gag.' But she did as Marcia told her.

Kippy and Eric danced by, crotch to crotch. Kippy's baseball hat was turned backward and her cheek rested against Eric's green chest.

Out on the floor, Marcia asked some guy to dance but he refused. Back in the kitchen, Naomi shook her head. 'All this dancing and drinking while Nixon's president. It's hypocritical. What's there to celebrate?'

Marcia put her hands on her wide hips. Inside the cheeriness of her costume, she seemed to have wilted some. 'Well what about Woodstock? They were dancing plenty at your precious Woodstock, weren't they?'

Naomi blinked. 'That was different. That was political. This party is just a motherfucking embarrassment.'

'Now you just watch your language and I mean it,' Marcia said.

'Oh, yeah, your virgin ears,' Naomi laughed. 'That's probably your trouble, Marcia. Virginity.'

A tremor passed over Marcia's face. 'You know, Naomi, I try hard to love a little something about every gal in this dormitory. But you can just go fry ice!'

'Ding-dong,' Naomi said. 'Avon calling.'

'If you are insinuating by that remark that there is something wrong with Avon products, then—'

Three disheveled, tie-dyed strangers appeared at the kitchen doorway, and Marcia's smile blinked back on. 'May I help you?' she said.

'Zach!' Naomi screamed. 'Babe!' She ran to the tallest of the three and gave him an open-mouthed kiss. Then she reached for her duffel bag and led them through the crowd. 'Adios, pod people,' she called back to us.

Marcia rubbed the sides of her hips and readjusted her sailor cap. 'I hate it when a Hooten girl just won't pitch in,' she mumbled.

Suddenly, I realized I'd forgotten to get Naomi's room key. 'Hey, hold on a second,' I yelled out. 'Wait!' I ran into the lounge after them.

The music was shouting. Naomi and her friends were making their way through the crowd. Someone grabbed my wrist. Eric.

'Cut it out!' I said. 'I have to catch her.' Over his shoulder, I saw Naomi's friend's head go out the front door.

'I'm hot for you, baby. Let's you and me have a dance.' He yelled it over the music, for the others' sake. People laughed and hooted.

'Shut up,' I said. 'You're drunk. Let go of me!'

The others closed in. Eric tightened his grip and began a kind of dance around me. I looked to Kippy for help, but she was saying something in Bambi's ear. The two of them laughed and nodded.

> *What you want, baby, I got it*
> *What you need, you know I got it*
> *All I'm askin' is for a little respect–*

There was a smear of green on my arm where he was yanking. 'Stop it!' I shouted. 'Let the fuck go!'

The crowd whooped their encouragement to him and he laughed his beer breath into my face and rubbed up against me. 'I love it when she plays hard to get,' he shouted.

'He's hard and she gets it,' someone shouted back. He pushed closer, danced right up against me. People laughed and yelled. Now that he'd made me visible, I was their target.

'More bounce to the ounce!'

'Suzie Creamcheese!'

> *R-E-S-P-E-C-T!*
> *Find out what it means to me!*

They closed in on us, chanting. Alone, with Dottie, that had been *my* song. He had no right. I never once . . .

Eric let go of my wrists but grabbed my by the hips before I could pull away. He latched his legs around my leg and rocked up and down. The others barked like dogs.

'Dry fuck!'

'Hump time!'

'Give her what she wants!'

> *Sock it to me sock it to me sock it to me sock it to me*

'You pig!' I screamed, then jerked my knee up into him.

Surprise and pain stopped his dancing. Stopped all of them. The music stopped. I did it again.

Eric grunted and fell forward to the floor. His body curled up on itself; he was writhing and grunting.

I parted them with my elbows and my crazy screaming. I ran.

'Wait'll you see my fish,' Dottie said. 'I just got some new neons last night. You know anything about tropical fish?'

'Not really,' I said.

Her brother's station wagon hit a pothole and went into a shimmy that traveled from the front of the car up my legs and throat. I had called her from the pay phone in the all-night study room. She said she could tell it was me calling before she even picked up.

A cardboard air freshener swung back and forth from the radio knob: a topless woman fondling her breasts. After I'd kneed Eric, I'd hidden at the edge of the parking lot, behind the dumpster. Over an hour I must have sat there on that cold ground – shaking, calming down, shaking again. There was an oil spot next to me, wet and bright, with the moon shining in it. And a dime. I rolled the coin between my thumb and finger, considering. Calling her had been the only thing I could think of.

'Moe, Larry, and Curly – that's my three piranhas. I named one of my angelfish after you. The silver one. Dolores. She's a real beauty . . . God, I was so happy when you called. When the phone rang, I knew right away it was you. This is so perfect. My rat's-ass brother's at National Guard until Sunday. This place we're gettin' our supper at has the best fried clams.'

At the party, after the music started up again, Marcia had come outside and walked to the edge of the lawn. She'd called my name three times, pronouncing it like a question.

'Do you like strips or whole bellies?' Dottie asked. 'They got both.'

'What?'

'Clams.'

I turned toward her. The cigarette smoke we'd made swirled around her head. 'I don't really care,' I said.

The restaurant's window was smeared and steamy. She sat at

the counter with her back toward me, her rear hanging over both sides of the stool. Two men in a booth by the window drank coffee and watched her, smiling. In the restaurant light, the green paint Eric had left on my wrists and hands looked gray. 'Get even with that fat cunt—' he'd said when they'd walked him out of the party, each of his arms locked around a friend's shoulder. They stopped only a half dozen cars away from me. 'I'll fix her good,' Eric promised. Then he coughed and spat and let them ease him back inside.

I'd waited and waited, staring up at the pulled shade in Kippy's and my room. Then I'd risked the rear entrance to the dorm, walking up the stairs past half-empty cups of beer and discarded parts of costumes. My heart thumped like the bass from the music downstairs. People were laughing and yelling, far away.

Our floor was vacant. I walked down the long corridor, expecting him to jump out from behind every door I passed. But I had to chance it. Had to get my things and get out of there, get somewhere else.

Our door was wide open.

On the floor in the middle of the room was a mound of my stuff that he'd pulled out of my closet and destroyed. Ripped-up clothes, kicked-in suitcases, pages torn away from the bindings of my books. My mother's flying-leg painting sat at a cockeyed angle on top of the pile – the wooden frame snapped and broken, the canvas split down the middle. If I started crying, I warned myself, I wouldn't be able to stop.

He hadn't touched my bureau. I grabbed my knapsack from the bottom drawer where I kept Dante's stolen letters and pictures. I threw in underwear, toothbrush, and the money Arthur Music had sent me for killing my mother – twenty-five untouched $20 bills, still in their bank envelope.

I looked again at the ruined painting. 'Ma!' I called out loud – a single syllable of pain that scared me. If I gave myself away, he might come back. Might hate me enough to do what Jack had done.

I grabbed Kippy's scissors. Hands shaking, I cut myself a zigzag square of Ma's painting: green tip of the wing against the cool blue sky. I stuffed it into the knapsack and ran like hell, down the corridor, down the stairs, away.

Outside, I ran, walked, ran again to the mailbox at the edge of campus where Dottie had said to go. She was waiting, the motor running, her blinker winking the mailbox on and off. The door swung open. 'Come on,' she said. 'Get in.'

The car filled up with the reassuring smell of grease; the brown bags of clams warmed my lap. 'Sorry it took so long,' Dottie said. 'One of their fryolators is on the blink. I got bellies.' The front windshield steamed up. She flicked a switch and the defrosters roared to life, fluttering the end of her blunt Dutch-boy hair.

She drove down Wayland's main street, slowed, and parked just past the bus depot where I'd arrived that first day. 'Why are you stopping here?' I asked.

'This is where I live. Across the street.' She nudged her head in the direction of a dry-cleaning store. 'Upstairs '

Three dark-skinned people – a woman and two men – were sitting inside the depot. The slamming of our car doors attracted their attention and they looked out. Dottie waved. They waved back.

'That's the DeAndrades,' she said. 'They're Portuguese. Come from some island over there. They keep that store spotless.'

'The guy in the orange shirt is the taxi driver who drove me to Merton the first day I got here,' I said. My voice sounded numb and flat. I hadn't told Dottie anything about what Eric had done.

'Oh yeah, Domingos. The wife's brother. He delivered a baby last winter, right in his taxi. They had his picture in the paper.'

We crossed the street and entered a side door. At the top of the stairs, she unblocked another door and I followed her in. I heard the bubbling before I could see anything. Then Dottie was in the center of the kitchen, her hand still on the pull chain.

'This is so great,' she said. 'You want a beer?'

I shook my head.

'These are my piranhas.' The tank was on the counter, next to a small TV. 'Watch this,' she said.

She opened a tin and sprinkled tiny shrimp into the tank. The piranhas swam to the surface, ate the food in quick, angry jerks. 'Put your finger in there,' Dottie laughed. 'No, don't really. Come on, let's eat while our clams are still warm. For drinks I got Rolling Rock, cream soda, milk, and blackberry brandy.'

'Cream soda.'

'Oh, have a beer. I'm having one.'

'All right.'

'Me and her are just alike, ain't we, Moe?' For a second, I looked for Dottie's brother, then realized she was talking to the fish tank.

We ate the clams and fries right out of the cardboard containers with our fingers. Silently, we slid the food back and forth across the table to each other. Dottie pulled out several interlocked clams and leaned her head back, dropping the clump into her mouth. My fingers were smeared with grease and ketchup. I ate faster and faster. We drank two beers apiece.

She let go a loud beer belch and laughed. 'I got fudge-ripple ice cream for dessert,' she said. 'You want it now or later?'

'Show me your other fish,' I said.

There was a bigger TV in the living room, and heavy green furniture. 'These are my neons,' Dottie said. 'Ain't they cuties?'

They swam in beelines around the tank, nervous dots and dashes of color. Above them was a paint-by-number picture of sailboats. A photograph was stuck in the plastic frame – a snapshot of a baby wearing a vest, a bow tie, a mongoloid's smile. Dottie caught me looking.

'So which one of these neons is your favorite?' she said. 'Pick.'

I looked inside the tank and tried to give an answer. 'I don't know. This one, I guess.' When I looked up again, the snapshot was missing.

'I can't believe you're really here at my house,' Dottie said.

She mounded the ice cream into wooden salad bowls and poured blackberry brandy on top. She left the carton on the table and we dug out seconds with our spoons.

'Dottie?' I said. 'What was that thing that Kippy said? That bad thing you heard her say about me? You said you'd tell me.'

She didn't answer at first. Then she told me to just forget it.

'Was it nothing? Did you make it up?'

'She said if she ever got like you, she'd get a gun and shoot herself.'

My eyes teared over. 'Who did she say it to?'

'Don't think about her. Think about us.'

She got up and turned on the TV, then went over to her piranhas and fed them more shrimp. 'You want another beer?' she asked, her hand on the refrigerator-door handle. 'I got plenty.'

Kippy had just stood there, laughing, watching Eric's rape dance. Had she been in the room with him when he destroyed my things?

'I'm having another one. Here.'

I took the beer.

The news was on. Nixon, the war, the moon.

'Who was that little boy in the picture?' I asked.

'What picture?' she said. 'Nobody you know.'

'Is he a relative or something?'

'You could say that.'

'Your nephew?'

'My kid.'

'You have . . . oh, my God. Where is he?'

'Nowhere. He died.'

She got up and switched the channel. She wouldn't look at me. 'Do you want anything else? You want to listen to the radio or something? There's never anything good on TV on Saturday.'

'Were you married?' I said.

She turned and faced me. 'Don't wreck things, okay? This could be so perfect.'

'What?'

'The fact you're here. The fact you called me.'

'But what did he die of?' I said.

She ignored me, staring at TV. A reporter was standing on a Cape Cod beach with two dead whales behind him. Whales were killing themselves for no reason, or for some reason scientists couldn't understand. Experts were baffled.

'It was better he died,' she said. 'I was fifteen when I had him. He had all these problems I couldn't even pronounce. The state took him.'

'What was his name?' I said.

'Michael. Except I called him Buster.' She turned off her television. Outside, a car door slammed. All over the apartment, the fish tanks percolated.

'I knew right away something was wrong with him. All the time I was pregnant. I didn't know much, but I knew that.'

I lit her one of my cigarettes and passed it over. Her whole face sagged. 'He lived longer than they said he would, though – outsmarted them. They said he'd die when he was about six months old but he was over a year. Fourteen months. Sometimes I used to take the bus and go out to see him. They used to let me hold him.'

I went to the sink and began to rinse the ice-cream bowls. I was thinking about Anthony Jr. – how his death had changed Ma, had changed the three of us. That painting had been the last real part of Ma I had.

Dottie came up behind me and placed her hands on my hips. She rested her chin between my neck and shoulder. 'Hi,' she said. I felt the word against my neck.

I dunked the bowls into the dishpan.

'Did you like the supper?'

'Yes. Thank you. Let me pay you for half.'

'My treat,' she said. She reached around and ran her fingertips up and down my stomach. My hands shook, shimmying the dishwater.

'I love you, Dolores,' she whispered.

I laughed. 'No you don't,'

'Yes I do,'

I swallowed and tried to concentrate on the row of bright windowsill containers: Pine-Sol, Clorox, All, Joy.

She rubbed her belly against my back and buttocks, soft and questioning, nothing like Eric's dancing. Nothing like Jack. Her fingers moved down to my thighs.

'Look, I don't want you to—'

'Yes, you do.'

'No, I don't.'

'Why not?' she said. Her fingers kept moving. 'Two fatties like us. What's the difference? . . . You and me are just alike. I can make you feel so good – I know how to touch you. Where.'

'No, really. You see—'

She turned me around and brought her lips slowly against mine. Her hair smelled of french fries and cigarette smoke. It was such a soft kiss, I let it happen.

'It doesn't matter,' she said. 'Two big fat mamas. Nobody cares.'

She was right. We didn't matter. People hated us anyway.

I kissed her back. Kissed her loneliness and my own fear. Kissed the part of her that had come out as that small, imperfect boy.

Her tongue was inside my mouth. Her fingers pulled at the top of my jeans. She got the snap undone. 'Come on,' she said. 'No one's here. Nobody cares. This will be nice.'

Her bedroom was neat and sparse. The aquarium sat on an end table next to her bed: angelfish gliding through a cube of water. I stared at them over her shoulder while she undressed us, first me and then herself. She pressed her hands against my shoulders and I sat down on the bed. She sat down next to me. The bed creaked from our double weight.

'Do me first,' she said.

She reached over for my hand and guided my knuckles back and forth against her thighs. Undid my fist. Her pubic hair was silky bristle.

She spread her legs. Her fingers moved my fingers up and down, up and down, against the edge of herself. Her hand dropped away and I continued. She lay back on the bed and closed her eyes. It didn't matter. It was just motion, wet and warm, over and over.

She was breathing hard through her nose, her lips pressed together. 'Don't!' she said when I stopped. Then I continued and she swore and bucked, clamping my hand between her legs. Her body shook us both, shook the bed. Relaxed. Shook it again.

I pulled my hand away. It felt numb and oversized, a paw.

She leaned over and kissed my arm, passed her fingers though my hair. Then she got up off the bed and knelt on the floor in front of me, like someone about to pray.

Her fingertips skidded along my legs. Her tongue poked against my knee. 'This is going to feel so nice,' she said. 'So gentle . . .'

It was wrong and dirty – what her hands, her mouth, were doing to me down there. But gentle, too, like she promised – a little silly. Nobody cared.

I let my head flop back over the edge of the bed, let myself fall into the feeling of it. Her fish swam upside down. One was yellow, the other silver. Dolores. They calmed me, gliding past each other in a sort of liquid dance . . . Nobody cared about us. *Why* was it wrong? Why *shouldn't* I feel what I was feeling? . . . The bed and Dottie dropped away. Her touch became Larry's touch. Dante's. I was at peace, afloat and weightless. I was Ruth, blossoming with the pleasure of Larry. The sensations rose and rose within me, a series of sweet explosions that there was no stopping, that I didn't want to stop . . .

Dottie crashed down on to the mattress and wiped her face in the sheets. She fumbled and turned over on to her back so that we were side by side, belly up on the bed.

We lay on our backs, quiet, watching the ceiling. 'Dottie?' I said.

Her fingers skidded against my arm. 'Hmm?'

'The baby's father. Was he somebody you loved?'

She laughed. 'He was one of the guys down at the field where I hung around. They used to let me play football with them sometimes if I let them screw me. Or gave 'em blow jobs. Me and two or three of them would go out in the woods. They were older than me. Always chicken-shit to go by themselves. Used to stand around and watch each other. Tell jokes about me right in the middle of it.'

I wanted her to stop.

'What did I care? I used to laugh at *them*, see? Sometimes I made them buy me a soda or something before I'd do it.' She nuzzled her head against my shoulder. Then she reached up and turned off her lamp. Her body was restless at first, then still. Her breathing turned predictable. We both seemed to rise and fall with every breath she drew.

'We're whales,' I said, out loud.

I waited for her answer but she had none.

In the dark, in the midst of her sleeping, my clear mind revved. 'I'll fix her good,' I heard Eric say again. I pictured him up in our room, yanking Ma's painting out of my closet, ripping it, kicking it with his foot. Over and over he did it; he wouldn't stop.

I couldn't sleep. I couldn't just lie there and listen to her snoring. I held out my hand, the one that had done it to her. It felt numb still. It smelled of her sex. She'd tricked me. Now I was what she was.

In Dottie's kitchen, in the cutlery drawer, I found a serrated knife. Pain would be better than not feeling anything, I thought. Pain would be better than not feeling anything, I thought. Pain would be a relief. I'd lost Ma's painting, I had nowhere to go. If Kippy ever got like me, she'd take a gun and . . .

I held the scalloped blade against my wrist and passed it across. Once, twice – but lightly. The third time, it made a scratch. I saw it more than felt it. The thin red line of blood took me by surprise.

Then I saw something else, something poking out from

behind her toaster. The snapshot she'd hidden. Her little boy, Buster. His smile was sweet and mysterious. I lost my nerve.

I killed her fish instead. Two glug-glugs' worth of Clorox per tank. The deaths were quick. They passed the poisoned water through their gills, then rested on their sides.

Downstairs and across the street, I tapped my fingers and sipped coffee while the Portuguese family held their private conference about what I was proposing. Four-hundred-dollars' worth of Arthur Music's money lay across the counter, like a game of solitaire.

Now the three of them approached me again – jury members with their verdict. 'You could wait until tomorrow and take a bus there, lady. Get a transfer in New York,' the taxi driver said. 'It would be a lot cheaper.'

'I want to leave *right now*,' I said. 'That's the point.'

'It's gonna take us thirteen, fourteen hours. We won't get there till middle of tomorrow afternoon.'

I nodded.

'And that ain't counting any stops either. Or any naps I might need.'

I nodded again.

The other two shook their worried heads, but the driver shrugged and smiled. 'Okay,' he said. 'Let's go.'

He was looking at me, not the money.

Chapter 16

I sat in the dark of the cab's backseat, watching the double necklace of highway lamps we were constantly approaching. The tires whined steadily beneath us. The driver didn't speak.

Stations drifted in and out on the car radio. Gospel, rock, a woman who advocated self-hypnosis. Somewhere near Harrisburg, a minister promised us salvation in a voice so sharp and reliable, it rattled the cab, then went off on a tangent and became static, returning as Spanish music. When the driver made a highway stop near Philadelphia, I had him leave the motor running while I waited inside with the doors locked, the radio on. I didn't want to think about where I'd been or where I was going. I just wanted to stay in the dark like this, to doze and listen.

By dawn we had ridden out of Pennsylvania.

The morning light was weak and gray. Dottie would be waking up soon, discovering what I'd done . . . I hoped Eric was too sore to walk – hoped I'd made him childless.

'So what you going all the way up to Cape Cod for, anyways, lady?' His voice came out of nowhere and made me jump.

I didn't *know* why, exactly, but caught myself looking at the scratch on my wrist. 'It's personal,' I said. 'I'm meeting friends.'

'Whereabouts on the Cape we goin', anyway?'

'What do you mean?'

He reached over and turned off the radio. 'How far up?'

'Oh . . . near the ocean.'

His laugh was insulting. 'Lady, the whole place is near the

ocean. Cape Cod is, you know, *towns*. Ain't you ever been up there?'

'Of course I've been there. Sheesh.'

'Well, where are your friends at?'

'I'm – we haven't decided where we're going to stay yet.'

'Well, how you gonna know where to meet them then?'

'Look, I just forgot the name of the place. It'll come to me. Don't have kittens over it, okay?'

He smiled back at me in his rearview mirror. 'Okay, lady,' he said. 'Take your time. You got about another nine hours to think of it.'

Mist silvered the highway pavement – miles and miles of mirror. I didn't *want* to think.

'My friend told me you delivered a baby in this cab once,' I said.

'Yeah, that's right,' he laughed. 'Don't remind me.'

Pictures of saints decorated his visors. He'd stuck a magnetized plastic Mary to the dashboard and double-looped a set of rosary beads around the rearview mirror. Its tethered crucifix rocked back and forth, back and forth, with the cab's motion. It lulled me to look.

'So I suppose you believe in God, right?' I said.

He braked and looked back suspiciously. 'Of course I believe in God,' he said. 'Geez, what do you think I am? Don't *you*?'

'Yeah, right. God and the Tooth Fairy and Jiminy Cricket.'

He frowned into the mirror and shook a scolding finger. 'You shouldn't talk like that, lady. God takes care of you and me both.'

In the silence, we both lit up cigarettes. He smoked Trues. Dottie had said his name but I couldn't remember it. It was a pattern with me, really, I thought: Dottie's fish, Rita Speight's baby. I killed off whatever people loved. It was entirely possible I'd driven Ma to it, too – better off dead than living with a monster daughter.

'Your good friend God really took great care of my mother,' I said. 'She got killed last summer.'

He looked at me in his rearview mirror; I looked away, out. 'Well,' he said. 'God has his reasons that you and me don't understand. But I'm sorry for you, though. For your suffering.'

'You know all these religious doodads you have hanging up in here? My grandmother has these things all over the place, too. Her whole house is like a shrine. Says her rosary every night – prays her head off. She had two kids: a boy and a girl. One drowned and the other got killed by a truck. God had her go to both their funerals. What do you think of that?'

In the silence, I thought of Grandma's frayed prayer book, limp and soft from constant use, held together with a rubber band. Her turning and turning of the pages had transformed the paper into a kind of delicate cloth.

'In one way, it's sad,' he said. 'But in another way, it ain't. Both her children are probably up in heaven, waitin' for her.'

I rolled down the window and chucked my cigarette butt out, held my face to the cold inrush of air. 'Yeah, sure,' I said. 'Polishing their little halos. Practicing their harp music.'

I closed my eyes and saw, intact, Ma's flying-leg painting – the way it managed to be both airy and powerful. Maybe that picture was Ma's heaven. I stuck my hand inside the knapsack, fingered the swatch of canvas I'd managed to save.

He said something I didn't catch. 'What?'

'I said, would you mind closing the window? I'm freezing to death.' The cab strayed a little over the center line. 'The thing is,' he continued, 'you and me ain't ever been there, right? So neither of us can really say what heaven's like. Or ain't like. 'Cause we ain't dead. See?'

Maybe that was why I was driving up there: to kill myself. Rid the world of Fat Girl Monster.

'I tell you what. I'll say a little prayer for your mother.'

'Don't waste your breath,' I muttered.

'I ain't wasting it. I guess I better say one for you, too.'

I shifted my weight. My legs and bladder ached. I'd been cramped in this cab for five hours. 'You want to pray so much, pray that a gas station shows up soon, will you? I need to go to the bathroom.'

More miles of grimy road went by. 'I been up there once,' he said.

'Where? Heaven?'

'Cape Cod. One summer when I was a kid. I got a cousin lives up there, my cousin Augusto. His mother and my mother came over from the Cape Verde Islands together. Two young girls – didn't know nothin' about nothin'. Can you imagine that? Couldn't even speak the language.'

I would have preferred radio talk. I couldn't have cared less about his stupid family tree . . . If I killed myself, who would they call? Grandma? My father? Dead or alive, I didn't want Daddy anywhere near me.

'Augusto runs a fishing boat out of Provincetown. I tell you, lady, that's *work*, commercial fishing is! I was about fourteen, fifteen that summer I was up there. Pulling nets, pulling lobster pots.'

Everyone at Merton would be talking about me. My blood would be on Eric's hands. On Kippy's too.

He put on his blinker.

'What are you doing?'

'I thought you had to go to the toilet.'

'I do. Where are we?'

'Perth Amboy.'

'Where's that?'

'New Jersey. We're getting' there, lady.'

The ladies' room was bubble-gum pink, littered with used paper towels. I scowled at my reflection in the smeary mirror. 'Fat monster face,' I said. 'Fish killer.'

Sitting in the stall, I looked again at the scratch across my wrist – studied it – then felt down *there*, to where I'd let her touch me and put her mouth. I should have stolen that scallop-edged knife, brought it along with me. I closed my eyes and imagined myself bleeding – collapsing on that sticky pink floor, dying justifiably in the stink of shit and disinfectant . . . She had loved those fish. Had said she loved me. 'Do me first,' she'd said, then come so hard, it shook the bed. Was that love? What was that?

The coffee shop had racks and racks of plump, glossy doughnuts. I'd gone in only for a map but got into the bakery line. After all I'd gone through, didn't I deserve a couple of stupid doughnuts?

'Next?' the counter girl said. Her eyes widened at my fat.

'Large coffee, cream, no sugar. And a dozen doughnuts.'

'What kind?' She snatched a tissue paper and waited.

'Let's see. Ten lemon-filled and . . . uh . . . two cinnamon.'

She shot the doughnuts into a bag and rang up my total.

'Dollar ninety-five,' she said.

'Hold on. Make that *two* large coffees.' I grabbed a newspaper and a map of the northeastern states from the rack. 'Plus these.'

She rolled her eyes at me. I kept wrecking her cash-register math.

When I got back to the cab, he was dozing, head back, mouth open. I had a perfect right to wake him. I wasn't paying Pedro here four hundred dollars to take a siesta.

I stood there holding his coffee and staring at his sleeping head as if it was a piece of sculpture in a museum. I hadn't realized before that he was handsome – hadn't paid any attention to that sort of thing. I imagined myself touching the tips of his feathery eyelashes, his bristly, unshaven cheek. I reached in and placed his coffee on the dashboard. The steam clouded the windshield, the air around his plastic Blessed Virgin.

Back inside the coffee shop, I ignored people's second round of gawking and walked to the empty end of the counter. I'd bought the newspaper hoping for something about those whales I'd seen on TV. The article was buried on an inner page. Humpbacks, they were. Beaching themselves off some place called Wellfleet.

The folded-open road map took up three counter spaces, counting mine. What did I care? I was a paying customer.

Cape Cod began near Plymouth, Massachusetts, and stuck out into the Atlantic Ocean like an old lady's bony finger. We'd studied Plymouth with Mrs. Nelkin, my old teacher from Connecticut, who scared me – we'd made construction-paper Pilgrims' hats and marched around the school. It was the Indians who taught the Pilgrims to plant corn, she'd said, so they could survive. Planted one whole dead fish for every scoop of seed . . . Dottie would have done something with those fish by now. Flushed them down the toilet? Buried them in the backyard? Her big mistake was loving me, the monster. I should have spared the fish. Drunk the Clorox myself.

Buzzards Bay, Barnstable . . . I'd waited and waited for Daddy that afternoon in Mrs. Nelkin's class, but it was Grandma who finally came to pick me up. Anthony Jr.: strangled by his own cord . . . I tried to imagine what Grandma would say if I killed myself – what she'd feel. A mortal sin: that's what she'd call it. For the rest of her life, she'd pray for me, imagine me roasting in hell like a rotisserie chicken at First National. Only I *wouldn't* be in hell. I'd be in dirt, rotting away like Ma, because God was something people made up – a lie people told themselves. I looked inside the bag. Two of the lemon ones were already gone. My mouth burned with sweetness.

I traced my finger out to the tip – Provincetown, where that relative of his lived – then drew back a little and found it: Wellfleet. I folded up the map. Augusto: I knew his cousin's name but not his.

In the newspaper article, a scientist said any number of conditions could be causing them to do it: scrambled sonar, parasites in their inner ears, some primal instinct to seek land. Or some reason nobody really understood – a scientific mystery. There were two pictures, one of that expert and one of three dead whales lying on the shore in a row. The paper said eleven had killed themselves so far.

The snippy woman who'd waited on me came out from behind the counter carrying an English muffin and a Pepsi. She sat down two stools away, sighed to herself, and lit a cigarette. Someone else was at the register.

Outside, my cab driver was up, awake, talking to a gas-station attendant who was filling the tank. I hated the way he called me 'lady,' like I was somebody Grandma's age, but it seemed stupid to introduce myself at this point. We'd travelled together all night. In a way, having those saints in the car was a kind of comfort – no matter what I did or didn't believe.

I caught the waitress looking at him through the window, checking him out. She was skinny and harried-looking, with limp, pinned-back hair – unimportant in every way. But the lie swam in my head. Her believing it became crucial.

'I see my sleepyhead husband's finally awake,' I said, nudging my chin in the direction of the cab. 'That's him out there, the guy in the red jacket. We're going to Cape Cod on our honeymoon. He'll have kittens if don't get out there with his cinnamon doughnuts.'

She looked down at the size of my leg. Then she looked out again.

'You wouldn't think someone like me would end up with someone like him, would you? But it happened. He's a cutie, isn't he? We're very much in love.

She sat there, blank-faced. I had upended everything she knew.

'He prefers me just this way,' I said. 'Says there's more of me to love. And love me he does. Phew!'

I dipped my finger into some lemon filling that had plopped on to the counter, brought it to my mouth, and sucked. She got up off the stool, leaving her cigarette burning in the ashtray, her Pepsi and muffin untouched. 'You have a nice day now,' I said. 'Nice talking to you.'

Outside, the air felt cool and clean. He smiled when he saw me coming. 'Was you the good fairy?' he said. 'Thanks for the coffee.'

'Here's some breakfast, too.' I held open the bag of doughnuts.

'Nah, that's okay.'

'Go ahead. I don't have leprosy or anything. Oh, by the way, my name is Dolores.'

'Well, you're a nice lady, Dolores.' He looked in, chose a cinnamon.

'So what's *your* name, anyway?'

'Who, me? Domingos.' He laughed.

'What's that – Spanish or something?'

'Portuguese. Cape Verde Islands. Remember?'

'Oh, yeah. Right.' Wherever *they* were. In school I had always thought geography was irrelevant.

Back on the highway, I watched the back of his neck. It was the exact same color as the coffee I was sipping. I began another doughnut. If I reached out and touched that neck he'd probably have an accident, drive us right off the side of whatever bridge we were crossing.

'Can I ask you something?' I said.

'Sure.'

'How old are you?'

'Me? Twenty-four.'

'Oh. I thought you were about that.' Halfway across the bridge, traffic slowed, then came to a standstill. 'What bridge is this, anyway?'

'I'll give you a clue,' he said. 'Wooden teeth.'

'Wooden teeth?'

'Father of our country . . . Dollar bill.'

'How old would you say *I* am?' I asked him.

'You? Geez, I don't know.' He looked into his rearview mirror. 'Twenty-six? Twenty-seven? It's hard to tell.'

'Why? Because I'm so fat?'

He didn't laugh. He didn't say a word.

'I *am* twenty-seven,' I lied. 'You're right.'

'You give up?' he said. '*George Washington*. The George Washing Bridge. You ever been over it before?'

'Not that I know of,' I mumbled.

'Well, now you can say you have.'

'Are you married or anything?'

He laughed. 'Me? Nope. I ain't married.'

'Were you ever?'

'I *almost* got married once.'

'What happened?'

'Oh, it's a long story.'

'What does that mean – she dumped you?'

'No. It means I don't want to talk about it.'

'Okay, fine. Excuse me for breathing.' I finished my doughnut, tried a cinnamon.

I imagined us crashing through the chain link, falling to the water below. I shivered from the sensation.

'By the way, I remembered the name of the town I'm going to. It's Wellfleet,' I said. 'That's where my friends are meeting me.'

'I know where that is,' he said. 'That's pretty far up. Hey, that town was on the news last night! I seen it on Huntley-Brinkley. These crazy whales keep heading for shore and killing themselves. Nobody knows why. Except me, that is.'

I held my breath and waited.

'Yeah, I got that whale problem all figured out. It was that guy walking up there on the moon, see? That Neil guy. That astronaut.'

The weekend of Ma's death. Mr. Pucci and me on the couch, sitting numb before the TV.

'"One small step for mankind." He screwed everything up, that guy – even those poor whales.' Then he laughed. 'If you ask me, that is.'

Miles went by. Time.

'New England and East.' 'Welcome to Connecticut.'

My stomach felt nauseous every time he slowed for a toll, tossed a quarter into the exact-change basket. It should have been me, not Ma. Next month would have been her thirty-ninth birthday.

'Old Lyme.' 'Mystic.' 'Fishermen's Cove Next Exit.'

I wondered if Old Lady Masicotte was still alive – still

drinking Rheingold beer and buying boyfriends. I tried to remember her dog's name – that fat, blinking cocker spaniel who loved cookies.

'I used to live near here,' I said. 'When I was little. If you can imagine that: me, *little*.'

'Hey,' he said. 'I was thinking of stopping for a sandwich, maybe – stretching my legs a little. It's almost noon. You want to stop somewheres near here?'

'This is the *last* place in the world I want to stop,' I said. The second-to-last, really. In another hour, we'd be driving past Easterly.

'Okay,' he said. 'You're the boss.'

But it was a *good* memory that returned, full-blown: a prize I'd won in fourth grade for reading more books than any other kid in my class – a glass paperweight. Inside it, a scene: a tiny Swiss girl – Heidi? – waving in front of a cottage. It snowed when you shook it. It had sat, displayed, on Mrs. Rickenbaker's desk for weeks. Everyone in the class had wanted it – even the boys. When I got my award, I'd had to go up on the auditorium stage with Mr. LaRose, our principal, who was crippled. I trembled and looked down at kids and teachers, applauding . . .

His excitement was what woke me.

'So she says, "Hurry! Hurry! Get me there! I can't wait."'

I opened my eyes. 'What? . . . Who?'

'That lady that was having the baby. I just been thinking about her. We get halfway to the hospital and she starts screaming, "Stop! Stop!" I thought she was yellin' for *me* to stop, see, but after it was over, she tells me she was talking to the baby – talkin' to her own pushing. Next thing you know, the cab's up on the sidewalk and I'm saying Hail Marys and there's all this water and blood and I pull the baby – well, you know – right out of her. This beautiful little girl. All three of us crying. 'Cause it was, you know, kind of scary. Doin' that.'

I sat, dazed. Listening.

'But – you know – a *miracle*, too. Me and this lady I ain't ever seen before and this new little baby. This miracle.'

I leaned forward toward him. 'Can I ask you something?'

'Don't ask me nothing about babies,' he laughed. ''Cause that was my only experience.'

'That summer you were staying at Cape Cod? With your relative? Did you ever see a whale?'

'A whale? Nah. I seen a dolphin once, though. Ain't they cousins with whales or something? This little dolphin swam right alongside the boat, keepin' us company for miles. Had a face like he was smiling at you. I kept throwin' him mackerel until Augusto got mad. Told me I was bad for business . . . But anyways, that's my story about delivering the baby. What do you think of *that* story, huh? Remember, you was asking about it before?'

I shifted and closed my eyes again, too tired to fight the drowsiness. 'You woke me up,' I said.

I lay half-awake, half-asleep, listening to the sound.

'Yoo-hoo,' Domingos called. 'Hey, Sleeping Beauty?'

Behind his voice, the thump of water. Smell of ocean.

Fumbling, I sat up and opened my eyes, squinting in the bright sun 'What time is it?'

'It's three-thirty.'

His answer scared me. 'I thought you were going to stop for a sandwich.'

'I did. Two hours ago.'

We were in some parking lot, amidst cars and pickups and looming banks of sand. 'Where are we?'

He laughed. 'Route Six.'

'Where the fuck is Route Six?'

'Take it easy. You had yourself a nice long nap, been sleeping over three hours,' he said. 'Route Six is the Cape road, goes all the way up. Hey, listen! You know those dead whales I told you about? I stopped for gas down in Orleans and a guy told me another one got stuck this morning. Right on this beach here. Come on, let's take a look. I'll help you up the dune.'

I shook my head. 'I'm paying you good money to take me to what-do-you-call-it – Wellfleet. I don't appreciate surprises.'

'That's what I'm telling you – we're _at_ Wellfleet! Come on and see that whale.'

'I don't want to see it,' I insisted. 'Who died and made you boss?'

'Well, I'm just gonna have a look then. A short one. I ain't going to come all the way up here and not see in person what I seen on TV.'

I pulled my arms across my chest. I was the first to look away. 'Fine,' I mumbled. 'Suit yourself. You will anyhow.'

He shut the door. 'Just a quick look, that's all,' he said.

I watched him hustle up and over the sandbank. Each of his steps left a funnel-shaped dent.

An old man on a bicycle drove down the narrow road and parked hastily, hurrying up the path like he was late for an appointment.

A helicopter chugged in the sky: CBS NEWS. It dipped down toward the ocean, its bottom half disappearing behind the steep dune. There was another TV-station van parked in the lot. I lit a cigarette, drew in, held the smoke in my lungs. I thought of Ma's accident on TV that weekend: her wrapped-up body being loaded into an ambulance on a stretcher, on the hour, over and over.

Two middle-aged women appeared at the rise and walked down the path toward me. They stopped at a nearby car and poured sand from their sneakers. 'I don't know, I just can't fathom it,' one of them said. Then she laughed. 'No pun intended.'

After the helicopter flew away, the parking lot took on an eerie quiet. Sand ticked against the cab in the wind. Over the dune, the ocean thumped its rhythm.

The smell of fish and salt was stronger when I opened the car door. I stuck my feet out and got my bearings, lifting myself off the backseat. My legs felt stiff. One foot was asleep.

Climbing the dune was like my dreams: running from Jack

Speight at a plodding, dangerously sluggish pace. When I reached the top, I was out of breath.

Its mass was what threw me first – a black rock ledge of life. My hands fanned out and I fell back against the cold sand. My heart pounded from the climb and the sight of it.

The whale lay surrendered on its belly, its head pointed out to sea. Most of its body sat stuck in shallow, red-clouded water, but the massive black tail reached up on to the beach. Incoming water lapped and channeled around and over it. The larger waves broke against its face.

Seagulls walked the whale's back and rocked in the water around it. Twenty or thirty people – most on the land, some in wet suits in the water – watched and talked and circled. Two men jabbed at its side with an oversize syringe. Electrical wire ran from TV equipment to some humming machine perched in the front seat of a jeep. The ground was strewn with people's stuff.

Domingos saw me and waved, hastening up the dune toward me. Wind whipped his hair and jacket. He looked shaken.

'Why don't they *do* something?' I said. 'Try to push it back in or something?'

'Too big.'

'They could at least try. Instead of everybody standing around gawking. Jesus Christ.'

He shook his head. 'It's dead, Dolores. Died about an hour ago. Some of these people been here all day with it.'

But it *wasn't* dead.

From out in the water came noises: clicks and sighs and heavings – the sounds of despair. The gulls rose off its back and into the air. On shore, the spectators jumped and shouted. The whale's living had taken us all by surprise.

'*Dios mio,*' Domingos whispered to himself. He took me by the hand. 'Come down,' he said. 'Come see.'

I pulled my hand away. 'I don't like this,' I said. 'I want to go.'

Out in the water, it grunted loudly and writhed, then

suddenly mustered the strength to shift itself on to its side. 'Ohh–!' we all said together, as if some miracle was about to happen. Its colossal tail scraped against the wet sand, carrying along a trail of it in its sweep. Its stiff flipper pointed straight up in the air. A miracle: as if that flipper was a wing that could lift it back out to open water. As if its other flipper weren't lying crushed and folded beneath its weight.

It fell back on its belly again, cracking against the water, raising sidewalls of white spray. The huge, muscular tail thudded, up and down against the beach – so thunderous in its suffering that the vibration reached up into my throat.

I clapped my hands over my ears, trying not to hear or feel that thudding. 'I can't . . . Get me out of here!' I screamed.

Domingos was down the bank, halfway between the whale and me. The others stared up at us. He ran back, took my arm, and guided me away, back down the bank toward the cab. He put me inside, sat next to me, whispering comfort, wiping at my tears with the palms of his hands.

The motel we pulled into had a crushed-clamshell parking lot and a dead lawn bordered with rocks painted white. They gave me the room next to the soda machine.

Domingos brought in my knapsack and the doughnut bag and asked if he could use my phone to call his cousin. He had apologized over and over about stopping to see the whale. My behaviour had made him afraid of me.

I sat on the bed, smoking, as he yakked on and on in Spanish or Portuguese, whatever it was – in a happy tone of voice he hadn't used once during our whole trip up. Honeymooners, ha! What a pathetic fucking joke I was.

'Okay, that's all set,' he told me. 'Augusto's wife's already frying up the linguica.'

'What's that?' I said.

'It's sausage,' he said. 'I ain't had any in—'

'Your cousin sounds nice. I'd really love to meet him.'

His face was scared. 'Oh, well—'

'Not now. I meant sometime. Did you think I meant right

now? God, I was just trying to be polite.'

'Oh,' he said. 'Right. And plus you got those friends you're meeting, right?'

'Yeah, right,' I said. 'If they ever find me.'

He laughed, embarrassed, and moved backward toward the door. 'Well,' he said. 'I guess I'll see you then. I enjoyed meetin' you and, you know, talking to you. Sorry about that whale.'

'Yup.' I looked at the wall, not him.

'Thank you very much for those doughnuts you bought. And that coffee.'

'No problem.'

'Don't forget, now, I'm going to say a little prayer for you. "Saint Anne," I'm gonna say, "you help this lady out now 'cause she's a very nice lady."'

'Yup,' I said. 'Thanks.'

'You have a nice vacation now. If that's what this is – a vacation.'

'Don't let the door hit you in the ass on the way out.'

The wall decorations were dusty metal lobsters and faded pictures of ships. The bedspread had cigarette burns. Inside the nightstand drawer were a complimentary pen and three postcards. 'Vacation Dreams Begin at the Coastal Dreams Motel.' I went out to the machine and got a soda. The sun was going down; the sky was orange and pink.

The TV only got two boring stations. I watched the end of some old movie. Golf. I kept changing the station, over and over around the dial, but all I got were those two channels, or snow. I had spent half my life watching TV.

I thought again about the paperweight. I'd had it less than a week when I shook too hard and accidentally sent it flying across my bedroom where it hit the floor and cracked. Leaked, became useless. At the time, it was my biggest tragedy – breaking that paperweight.

The worms go in, the worms go out, the worms play pinochle on your snout – A song Jeanette and I used to sing . . . *And then the pus comes oozing out.* Mrs. Nord would get mad when we sang it and make us stop.

I lit a cigarette and held the tip to the musty bedspread, made a fresh burn . . . I could smash the drinking glass and follow the line of the scratch I'd made, cut deeper. Or use the curtain cord – strangle myself like Anthony Jr. Suddenly I saw my brother's discarded baby furniture, on the pile at the dump that day with Daddy. Felt in my stomach our wild escape away from there, Daddy, in his anger and loss, gunning the pickup truck over ruts and bumps. I'd looked back and watched that shrinking pile of furniture Anthony would never use. Saw again the pile of my ruined belongings that Eric had made. I'd lost the painting. Lost everyone.

I snuffed the smoldering bedspread cloth with my thumb. I was afraid to die in this ugly motel.

When I reached inside the doughnut bag, I found three hundred of the four hundred dollars I'd paid him to take me here. I began to cry: all my life the best people left me – just drove away. I didn't want to die. I didn't want to live, either.

After dark a car pulled into the parking lot.

Not Domingos, like I'd hoped. A man and woman in their thirties.

In the glow of the soda machine I recognized him: the scientist they'd interviewed for that newspaper article. The man with all the theories about whales.

'You want anything?' he called to the woman.

'I don't know. Fresca, I guess. We still have vodka left, right?'

'I think so.'

The cans clunked down. He walked toward her and handed her her soda. 'Oh, man,' he said, 'I'm exhausted.'

She reached behind him and touched the back of his neck, a gesture so natural it filled me with aching. 'Plus you've had zilch for sleep,' she said.

They walked to a room three doors down from mine and went inside.

Postcards, suicide notes.

I lay back on the bed and tried to decide who to send them to. Grandma? Domingos? . . . The one I really wanted to write was Ma's. 'You didn't deserve what happened. I did.' I thought of that photo of Ma and her friend Geneva Sweet – the one on Grandma's stairs. The two of them, happy and young and pretty, their arms locked, forever.

I pushed myself back up and wrote two of the cards against my leg.

Dear Grandma,
  I just couldn't take it anymore. When you remember me, try to think of me as a person, not some big fat mortal sin.

Dear Geneva,
  You've never met me, but I feel almost as if—

They sounded stupid, so I ripped them up. Lay back again. Closed my eyes . . .

In the dream, Jack Speight and Eric and Daddy had me out on the ocean in a rocky boat. It was snowing – thick snow – a blizzard. I'd never seen snow on the water before and wanted to just sit and look, but they kept leaning over, jabbing at my feet with the edges of their oars.

'Cut it out!' I yelled at them. 'Stop it!'

I jumped into the dark, choppy water. Then I was swimming beside a baby dolphin. Fast and smooth, we glided. The snow had stopped. When I looked back, the boat was far away.

The dolphin's face looked familiar. Then he wasn't a dolphin anymore, but a little boy with a dolphin's smile. Dottie's little dead boy. He swam away.

I woke up thirsty. The office was closed and I'd used up all my change. The sink water tasted warm and poisonous. I didn't like touching that slippery drinking glass.

Dear Grandma,
 Tell my so-called father I don't want him at my funeral.
I don't want him anywhere near me . . .

I didn't want to write. I wanted to talk to someone, some person I hadn't failed – someone who would listen. I could walk down to that door, knock, wake up the scientist. 'Excuse me for bothering you. You don't know me, but . . .'

Or I could just go ahead and do it. Stop those nightmares. End it.

I picked up the phone.

The Cape Cod information operator talked to the operator in California, who said there were three of them: Brian Sweet, M.J. Sweet, and Irving Sweet.

'Irving,' I said. 'Get me that one.'

It rang and rang. Her voice sounded far away. 'Wait a second,' she said. 'Tell me again?'

'Bernice's daughter,' I said. 'Bernice, your friend who died. Her daughter.'

I reminded her about her telephone call after the accident, when she'd had Grandma put me on the line so she could tell me how much she wanted to meet me, how the bottom had fallen out of her life when she heard the news. She'd sent flowers to the funeral home – white gardenias – the biggest, most beautiful spray.

'I've saved every one of her letters,' she told me now. 'We wrote on and off all those years. The night I heard about it, I took them out and read every single one. I know one thing – she loved *you* very much.'

She waited for my crying to stop, she told me to take my time. She asked me how I'd been, what I was doing. I was in college now, wasn't I?

I told her it hadn't worked out.

Was I calling from Rhode Island? From my grandmother's?

I said I was calling from Cape Cod.

'Cape Cod?' she said. 'It's cold up there this time of year, isn't it? What in the world are you doing up there in November?'

'Oh, nothing much,' I said. I watched myself in the mirror as I spoke, twisting the ends of my hair with my finger, watching the way my weight sunk the mattress. The crying had slitted my eyes. 'Just trying to think,' I told her.

'Think about what?'

'Oh, lots of things . . . Death, for one. I saw this whale die today. I'm staying at this place where whales keep dying.'

There was a pause on the other end.

'Tell me some more about my mother,' I said.

She talked about Ma and Daddy's wedding, how my parents had been so crazy about each other, how Ma had prayed to get pregnant. She talked on and on.

'Her letters the last couple of years, though – honestly, they just broke my heart. First the divorce, then her breakdown. It seemed like every time she'd get back on her feet . . . she just seemed so vulnerable.'

If I did it, I thought, I'd be free – of myself, of all those Jack Speight nightmares.

'I used to invite her to come out here all the time. For a little vacation. Have a few laughs, you know? – a little R&R.'

The worms come in, the worms go out, the worms play pinochle . . . I sang it more to myself than to her. Her conversation was beginning to bore me.

'Dolores, honey? . . . Is everything okay with you? You're all right, aren't you?'

'I have to go,' I said. 'There's this pinochle game.' I laughed out loud at my joke.

'Honey, does your grandmother know where you are?'

I hung up on her. Rich bitch.

I walked and walked, down the unlit highway, then down the twisting narrow road, dodging headlights, waiting in the brush when I heard cars. The road went on and on, but I didn't mind. I felt energized, ready for anything. Fat girl on a skinny road, I thought. It struck me as hilarious. I knew this was the way. I followed the sound of the ocean.

There were two cars in the parking lot. I climbed the steep dune, stopped at the top. The ocean looked silvery in the moonlight.

The wet air had a stink to it: already she had begun her sweet rot.

Two men stood below, holding hands and watching her. Their dog kept barking at her size. Down the beach, three people sat huddled in front of a driftwood fire, each of them facing her. I sat above, on the crest of the dune, apart and waiting.

Two teenage couples arrived, slamming car doors, laughing and swigging beer as they ran down the dune toward her. Their loud fun sent the other spectators away. The boys climbed up and walked her body, out to the face and back. They bent and sliced their girlfriends souvenirs.

People came and went like that, like Ma's wake. I outlasted all of them – a chaperone for her corpse. I stayed with her all night.

At dawn I stood and looked down the beach as far as I could see. One side, the other, the parking lot behind me. The two of us were all alone.

I walked down the dune toward her.

The tide was further in than it had been the afternoon before; though she hadn't moved, she was deeper into the water. At the ocean's edge, I pulled off my sweatshirt, pulled down my jeans.

The water was no colder than the wind, but my nipples hardened against the sensation at my feet. My fat turned gooseflesh blue. I waded out to my knees, my legs aching, then numbing to it. I went further in, to my waist. The end of my hair was wet. I lifted up and under. Swam.

From the beach, she had looked black, but now, swimming beside her, I saw that her skin was mottled, blotched with darker and lighter grays. I reached out to touch her. She felt firm and muscular against my palm, my shaking blue fingers. Against my lips. The kiss felt soft and coarse. Salty.

I swam underwater to the front of her and resurfaced,

bobbing and treading water. I was weightless.

Her massive head and snout were covered with knobs – ugly, patternless bumps littered with barbed chin stubble, sharp to the touch. Her scarred mouth gaped open, as if she'd died trying to drink her way back to safe, deep water. Her jaw, half above the surface, half below, was lined with thick broom bristle. Her eyes were underwater.

I held my breath and went under, my own eyes open.

The eye stared back at me without seeing. The iris was milky and blank, blurred by seawater. A cataract eye, an eye full of death. I reached out and touched the skin just below it, then touched the hard globe itself.

This was how I could die. This was where.

I fought against myself, my head butting downward toward bottom, arms pushing and flailing to stay under. I drank seawater in thick gulps and swallows, glimpsing the death eye in the midst of my battle.

Then I fought it, angrily. Burst upward, crashing the surface. I coughed and spit, gasping and choking for breath, letting the good air burn my lungs.

I swam to her other side, around the torn and broken flipper. My feet touched bottom. I stumbled and waded back toward the shore, hit again by the full, throbbing cold. My clothes sat in a wet heap by the water's edge. I struggled them back on.

I had reached some kind of end. But hadn't reached it.

I don't know how long I sat there shivering.

From far down the beach, as far down as I could see, it approached. First just something to look at, then something to hear. A jeep.

The wet clothes, the wind, made my shaking uncontrollable.

A man in a tan uniform cut the engine and walked toward me, smiling. He squatted down beside me.

'Hello there,' he said.

'Hello.'

'Would you by any chance be Dolores Price?'

I nodded.

'Some people been looking for you. They been worried.'

He had plump little yellow teeth, like a row of sweet corn.

I told him I was sorry.

'I got a blanket for you if you're cold. You look cold. Are you?'

I nodded again.

'Then let me get that blanket then.'

Back at the jeep, he talked into his radio. 'Okay, she's here,' he said. 'I got her.'

PART THREE

The Flying Leg

Chapter 17

Gracewood Institute, the private mental hospital where I spent the next seven years of my life, faces Bellevue Avenue in Newport, Rhode Island, and turns its back on the Atlantic Ocean. From the well-traveled road, only the glorious granite mansion is visible, but the driveway forks around the main house and leads from either side to the two unassuming brick buildings that house the wards. A twelve-foot Cyclone fence borders the rear of Gracewood. Behind it are wild blueberry bushes, Newport's cliff walk, the cliffs themselves, the sea.

I was an inpatient at Gracewood for the first four years after my encounter with the Wellfleet whale, an outpatient for the next three. I kept no diaries during that time to chronicle the thousands of hours I must have lost to tranquilizers and television, so my recollections are vivid but gap-ridden. I remember fragments of the worst nights: the detached sound of my own shrieking as they held me down for forced injections – those quick jabs of pain when the needle broke through my skin, violated me, like Jack. I recall how I sometimes doled out progress to them, then snatched it back again. (One Saturday morning I capped off a good week by burning the insides of my thighs with a lighted cigarette. Their campaign to get me into the recreation room ended in my playing a game of Monopoly, then biting my hand hard enough to require inside stitches.) Like the whale herself, my memories of Gracewood have become for me a corpse I'm obliged to carry. Sometimes it occupies the passenger's seat in the car during long, quiet drives; sometimes it lies beside me in bed, on nights when I can't sleep, or on nights when I can. The corpse is either benign or dangerous. It has the gift of speech.

'You're a beautiful person, Dolores,' Dr. Shaw told me the very first day I sat across from him, locked in my fat and self-hatred.

'Yeah, right, I'm Miss Universe,' I snapped back. 'I won it in the swimsuit competition.'

He was the beautiful one, with his lion's mane of hair, that white turtleneck set against his tan skin. You could tell he was the outdoorsy, cliff-walker type when he wasn't stuck inside with us wackos. He kept his office window cracked open to the thump of the ocean. Sometimes I'd look down from his green eyes to his thick, ringless fingers to the straw still stuck in the lacings of his Earth shoes. In those early sessions, Dr. Shaw always leaned toward me, recliner to recliner, and smiled. 'If you will only visualize your own beauty,' he promised me that first day, 'you can make it real.'

Dr. Shaw was my third psychotherapist at Gracewood. My first, Dr. Netler, parted his hair just above his ear and plastered the long remaining strands over his bald spot. He had a little potbelly and stuttered so badly, I spent half my time waiting for him to give birth to the syllables he eventually shaped into questions about my father's leaving and my mother's death – questions I refused to answer. During our months and months of getting nowhere together, I drew my power from stubborn silence; Dr. Netler's power came in the form of orders to the exasperated nurses and aides to take away my cigarette privileges, up my dosages, 'safety-coat' me whenever I got out of hand. Another of my Gracewood memories: the sour smell of that straitjacket, the futility of pulling against it.

They thought I might cooperate better with Dr. Pragnesh, an Indian doctor, a woman. She had perpetual garlic breath and called Jack 'Mr. Speight,' as if he was someone we were required to respect.

'What do you think attracted you to Mr. Speight in the first place?' she'd ask in her squashed little accent.

'I have no idea. Why is your hair so greasy all the time?'

'What is all this belligerence for – protection?'

'What's that dot on your forehead for? Target practice?'

It was Geneva Sweet who paid all my bills at the private hospital she'd flown east to select personally for me. Grandma had at first objected to the financial arrangement – this fairy-godmother approach to making me sane – but Geneva had sat down in Grandma's parlor and pointed out that she and Irv were 'comfortable,' that God had never given her a daughter of her own to provide for, that making me well was something she wanted to do for Bernice, God rest her soul.

It was Geneva, too, who had led that Cape Cod shore patrolman to the Wellfleet beach for my belated rescue. After I'd phoned her from the motel and sung 'The worms go in, the worms go out,' she'd fretted and paced, then telephoned Grandma, who, in turn, picked up the receiver and dialed Hooten Hall and the Rhode Island State Police.

'When you said over the phone that you were staying at a town where whales were dying, it was a clue, a long-distance cry for help,' Geneva told me the first time we sat face to face. 'At least that's what *my* therapist told *me*.' She had rich-lady looks: blond-tinted hair pulled back in a knot, icy-pink lipstick and matching nails, moisturized skin. I let her believe she'd rescued me – kept it a secret that I'd tried death before that patrolman ever arrived, that I'd swum down and met that whale eye to eye.

Gracewood put on the dog for rich visitors. When Geneva flew in at Christmastime, I was driven up to the mansion to see her. We sat on tan leather sofas in the festive solarium, Geneva balancing a cup of eggnog on her lap and calling attention to the lovely falling snow, the charming antique ornaments on the tree, and all I should be thankful for.

Grandma visited me back in the ward, every Tuesday afternoon from two to three-thirty. Gracewood was an eleven-dollar cab ride from Easterly. She came by cab, she said, because she didn't want to trouble Mrs. Mumphy's daughter during the week. The real reason was that she had kept my craziness a secret. Poor Grandma: first a daughter in the state hospital, then me at Gracewood. She kept her coat on during visits and held on to her purse strap, her eyes jumping nervously from Mrs. Ropiek's drool to Old Lady DePolito's peculiar attire: flannel pajamas, fur-trimmed nightgown, high-cut sneakers. But Gracewood spared even Grandma the worst of it: the weekend aide who elbowed you hard if you didn't obey him fast enough; Manny the Masturbator; Lillian, who picked her nose and wiped it on the wall, who shit her pants for spite.

'But you're basically happy here?' Geneva asked me when she visited again the following summer, phrasing it both as a question and the answer she wanted me to give. This time we were seated in Gracewood's spacious front yard on iron-lattice lawn chairs while gardeners primped at the color-coordinated petunia beds and the Atlantic rumbled behind us. My hand was still bandaged from the week before, when I'd bitten it. 'Basically you're happy? You feel you're making progress?' My reply was, as always, a snort of contempt, a drag on my cigarette. Geneva hugged me at the end of each visit, a mannequin's embrace that let you know she was nobody's mother.

Dr. Shaw and I began our work together in the winter of 1971. I'll admit it: when I recall Dr. Shaw, it's with an impish memory that may or may not be playing tricks. I remember him as both my fool and my magician: the gullible idiot from whom I withheld information, the powerful wizard who evoked secrets I'd kept even from myself. More often than not, Dr. Shaw's voice is the voice of the corpse.

'How is Dolores Price this beautiful morning?' he asked me at the beginning of our first session.

'She's fine. How's Dr. Quack-Quack?' I answered, blowing a throatful of smoke in the direction of his 'Thank you for not smoking' sign.

'Dr. Quack-Quack? Why am I Dr. Quack-Quack?'

'You're all Dr. Quack-Quacks here. You're all the same.'

'Several of my colleagues might debate you on *that* statement,' he said, smiling.

'What do you mean?'

'Well, let's just say . . . that I'm a bit of a maverick.'

'Which one – Bart or Brett?'

'Excuse me?'

You could tell he was one of those wholesome types that never watched TV. 'Nothing,' I said. 'Just forget it.'

He nodded, closed his eyes, and smiled at the beautiful version of me he claimed he saw. In our earliest sessions, all that shut-eyed smiling of Dr. Shaw's gave me the creeps. But he was so hopped-up on visualization – saw a better me so emphatically – that he made me curious about the Dolores who existed behind his eyelids.

Visualization was how I lost the weight – not all of it, but enough so that people passing me just ignored another fat girl rather than gaping at a freak. 'You've dropped another seven pounds, I see,' Dr. Shaw would say, smiling at my weekly report. 'You know why you're slimming down, don't you?'

'No, why?' It was better to let *him* tell you what you were thinking, rather than wasting time having him correct you.

'Because you're beginning to conceptualize the beautiful person you really are – you're becoming the young woman you deserve to be.'

'Oh,' I said. 'Yeah.'

After six months with Dr. Shaw, I could shove both hands down between my stomach and the waist of my jeans and flap my wrists in the space I'd made; I'm not going to say *that* didn't feel good. But I wasn't visualizing some beauty-contest version of myself. I was seeing mold.

That was how I did it. The cafeteria servers would cut me a square of shepherd's pie, a block of macaroni and cheese, a wedge of cream pie: enough food so that I'd have to heft, not just carry, my tray. Everyone at Gracewood was pale and flabby – exhausted from all that starch and tranq. I'd plunk my meal down at one of the long tables and close my eyes like Dr. Shaw. When I opened them again, I'd picture the top surfaces gone bad. I could make mold take hold of anything in front me: canned fruit cocktail, the surface of soup. It was a skill I got good at. I'd make it sprout in a corner of whatever was on my plate, then network it out, thicken it into a furry blue rug over whatever I was supposed to chew and swallow. 'She's gaggin' again,' Mrs. DePolito would always complain. 'How are we supposed to eat our dinner with her gaggin' all the time?' As if it was attractive to watch *her* eat scrambled eggs without her top teeth. As if *that* was appetizing. I never told Dr. Shaw about the mold. I let him believe he was helping me visualize some beautiful Dolores. After I got to know him, I didn't want to disillusion him. He walked a pretty thin line.

As I began to drop weight, I began, as well, to drop my cattle prod of hostility whenever Dr. Shaw closed his office door. Our first major project was my night at Dottie's apartment. I took him through the particulars, then asked him outright. 'It means I'm gay, right?'

Dr. Shaw made his face a question. 'Tell me again what you were thinking about during the encounter.'

'Do you mean the part about me looking at the fish or the part about Larry and Ruth?'

'I mean, what was going through your mind as she was bringing you to climax? It was starting to feel very good to you and you were thinking about . . .'

'Larry and Ruth. I was thinking about that night when I woke up and they were doing it on the floor at Grandma's. I might have been moaning a little, like Ruth did. I was kind of . . . imagining I was Ruth and that Larry was . . . What are you saying? I'm *not* gay?'

He gave me a speech about how homosexuality was an orientation, not a life-style choice, and that I should 'perhaps consider' whether or not my being angry at Dottie or Mr. Pucci for who they were was an appropriate response.

Dr. Shaw was a big 'perhaps' man; it was one of his favorite words. 'No, Dolores, your patterns as I see them show a clear attraction to men. Perhaps all that food bingeing you and Dottie did temporarily depressed your anger, made you numb. And in that passive state, you . . .'

He was always doing that, too: turning his statements into little fill-in-the-blank quizzes for me.

'I just let her go ahead and do it?'

'That's right. You merely gave yourself permission to dally.'

'Yeah, but I . . .'

'You what?'

'I had . . . I felt . . . you know.'

'Say it. Say the word. You experienced—'

'I don't want to say it.'

'Why not, Dolores?'

'Because I don't *feel* like saying it, okay? Aren't you always telling me to be honest about what I feel?'

'Well, I'm just curious. I hear you using the word 'fuck' all the time. Which is an angry word when you think about it, isn't it? You usually say that word in anger. I guess I'm just wondering why 'fuck' slips out so easily but you can't seem to say the word "orgasm."'

'I can say it. "Orgasm." There. You happy now?'

'I am, yes. Thank you.'

'You're welcome. Sheesh.'

'Anyway, to get back to your question, I'd say no, your orgasm that night doesn't make you a lesbian. Stimulation feels good, even to the clinically depressed. A finger, a tongue. Friction isn't specifically male or female. It's – well, it's just friction.'

He smiled and hitched a strand of his golden hair behind his ear. 'But of course your sexual climax is what energized you, jolted you out of your passivity. And then you felt . . .?'

'Fucked over!' I said. In the silence, I listened to the way I'd just said it as Dr. Shaw watched the discovery on my face.

'Fucked over,' he repeated. 'By whom?'

'By her, I guess. But mostly by him.'

'Who do you mean?'

'Eric! Who else would I mean? What right did that shithead have to make a joke out of me? I kept telling him to stop, but he . . .'

'What? What is it you're thinking?'

'Is that why I killed the fish? To get back at Eric?'

'Is it?'

'Yes.'

'Yes, of course it is.'

I stood up and walked to the window. Watched the distant whitecaps, the slanted, icy drizzle pelt against Building B. Let my tears fall.

I turned back and faced him again. 'Could you stop saying "of course" after everything, please? All this is new to me. All those "of courses" make me feel kind of stupid.'

'Certainly,' he said. 'Of course. Who else fucked you over, Dolores? Over the years, I mean. Make us a list.'

Blood banged inside my head. 'You know who.'

'Tell me.'

'Jack Speight!'

He nodded solemnly. 'Anyone else?'

'You name it. Kids at school, my father, my . . .'

'Who were you going to say just then?'

'Nobody.'

'Are you sure?'

'Positive.'

I'll admit this, too; part of the reason I cooperated with Dr. Shaw at first was because I had a crush on him. On the ward after lights out, I used to visualize myself unlacing those Earth shoes, unbuttoning and unzipping him. Lying in my bed trying not to hear DePolito's gurgly snoring one room down, I'd conjure up his bare chest and let my fingers do the walking. They kept our rooms so hot – not humid heat, the sexy kind, but oven heat – the kind that collapses your sinuses and makes your head ache. It used to rise up at me from the register between my bed and the wall while I lay there quietly, my fingers turning into Dr. Shaw. 'Friction is friction,' I used to reason. 'What the fuck?'

Sometimes I could figure out what Dr. Shaw was up to and deny him. That felt good: when had men with power over me ever made *my* life better?

'Can you name one thing during that whole Cape Cod business that put you at ease?' he asked me at the end of one unproductive session. We'd spent our whole hour on my suicide trip.

'Those lemon doughnuts I bought on the way,' I said. 'They were pretty excellent.'

He sighed and looked up at his ceiling. 'This is work I thought we'd already accomplished. Where did your impulse to overeat come from? What was the pattern there?'

I sighed impatiently, reciting what he wanted like a bratty child. 'I ate because I was angry.'

'So did eating the doughnuts really make you feel good?'

I rolled my eyes. 'No.'

'Then would you please answer my question seriously?'

I knew what he was after: he wanted me to lift up my rotting whale to see if Ma was under it. He was always looking for Ma. 'What was the question again?' I said. 'I forgot what you even asked me.'

'I asked you to identify a moment up there on Cape Cod when you felt at ease. Felt good. Felt freed.'

'Freed?' The word interested me, in spite of myself.

He nodded. 'Freed.'

'In the water, I guess . . . out in the ocean.'

'Ah,' he said. 'Go on.'

'Go on what? I just liked the way it felt out there.'

'What did you like about it?' He leaned closer. I could smell his Listerine.

'Swimming,' I said. 'Feeling weightless. And going underwater. We're over our time, you know. In case you're interested.'

He reached over to his desk and turned the clock to the wall, an act that panicked me. 'Why did you like it underwater, Dolores? What was good about it?'

When what you said excited him, his hair boinged a little. 'How should I know? It was like you just said . . . it freed me or something.'

Dr. Shaw took both my hands in his. 'Let's suppose,' he said, 'that we're at some crucial place right now, right at this second. I want you to visualize it for me. Let's say for example's sake that it has to do with the ocean. With swimming. With our work together. Picture it for us, Dolores. Are we about to break the surface, crash through to the daylight? Or are we about to take the plunge – to go under and explore the depths? Which do you see us doing, right here, right now?'

He waited. He wouldn't look away.

I figured it was safer to give him whatever answer he *wasn't* looking for, but I miscalculated – thought he wanted sunlight and breakthroughs.

'We're going under,' I said.

'You're sure?'

'Yup. We're taking the plunge.'

He closed his eyes and smiled. 'Do you feel what I feel?'

His pleasure made me twitch. 'How should I know? What do you feel?'

'That we're at the beginning of our real work together?'

'The *beginning*? What's all this other stuff been – jumping jacks?'

But sarcasm was a broken tool when Dr. Shaw got hopped up like that. 'Do you know, Dolores, why you felt the urge to swim underwater – why that came first to mind just now when I asked about feeling good?'

'It didn't come first. I thought about the doughnuts first.'

He looked disapproving. 'Well, technically, I mean.'

'The water, your submergence: weren't you perhaps recreating . . .?'

I shrugged.

'The womb?'

'The womb?'

He smiled and nodded. 'Trying, perhaps, to reenter the safety of your mother – to return to the warm, wet protection of the person who hadn't yet failed you.'

'Failed me how?'

'By leaving you those times she was sick? By dying?'

'The womb?'

'It was instinctive.'

'It was?'

'Primal, really. Atavistic.'

He looked so satisfied with me.

'Look, just leave my mother out of it, okay? Besides, it *wasn't* warm. It was fucking freezing. When I got out of the water, I turned blue. I was *crying* it was so cold!'

'Exactly!' he said, slapping the arm of his recliner. 'Why does a baby cry at birth?' Now he was up and pacing.

'I don't know. Because the doctor smacks it?'

'The baby cries because of the drop in temperature. From ninety-eight point six to room temp, a good twenty-five degrees colder. It's a shock. The shock of becoming! The chill of the life force. On a symbolic level, we could say you were midwifing yourself out in that water, couldn't we?'

I shrugged my fake indifference. 'You're the boss,' I said.

'I'm *not* the boss. *You're* the boss. The incredible thing we just learned here is that you didn't begin your recovery here at Gracewood. You began it that morning out there in the ocean – long before I entered the picture. I'm just along with you for the ride.'

'For the swim, you mean.'

Dr. Shaw's infrequent laughter was an alarming snort of cheer that distorted his handsome face, turned him into Francis the Talking Mule. 'For the swim,' he repeated with a hearty guffaw. 'Yes, that's right. The swim! Let's close now, Dolores. There are some calls I want to make – there's a doctor on the West Coast I want very much to talk to. I think we've covered some valuable ground here today. I think we've found some real directions. Don't you?'

'Perhaps,' I said. He didn't get the joke.

The next day he told me he was going to take his cue from me and reparent me – start from scratch because of all the inadvertent damage my real parents had done. 'Together,' he said, closing his eyes to visualize it, 'together, we are going to rewind your childhood and record over it.' He was always doing that: making my life seem like electronic equipment.

'Look, I told you before. Whatever this has to do with my mother, I'd just as soon we keep her out of it,' I said. 'My mother was a *saint!*'

He cocked his head to the side, slightly. 'A saint?'

One of the things I'd withheld from him was Ma's flying-leg painting. That lost picture was the closest I came to believing in anything like heaven – in some kind of world that was calm and right. I didn't want him going anywhere near my mother.

'She's dead, okay?' I said. 'Just leave her alone.'

'In my opinion, it's a mistake to keep playing hide-and-seek with this, Dolores. It's counterproductive.'

'Last time you said *I* was the boss. What was that happy horseshit about?'

He sighed and nodded. 'All right,' he said, 'all right, I'll try as best I can to respect your ground rules until you're ready to step over them yourself. Now I want you to go back to your room and relax. Tomorrow we're going on a rather amazing trip together.'

'Yeah, well, if it's Mystic Seaport again, forget it. I spent that whole last field trip bored out of my skull.'

'It's not the seaport, no. But it *will* be one of the most mystic experiences of your life. That much I promise you. Tomorrow *I* become your surrogate mother. You and I are going back to the womb.'

'Maybe *you* are,' I said. 'Send me a postcard.'

He leaned toward me, close enough so that our knees

touched. 'I know it sounds a bit unconventional, Dolores, but I spent most of yesterday afternoon on the phone with a doctor in California who's had very good results with this approach. And I've spent half this morning battling the Freudians at this staid institution to gain permission . . . well, that's not the point. The point is that I believe what I'm proposing can really help you. But if you have misgivings – if you don't trust me enough to let me take you to where I think we need to go – then stop me now. Let me know right away and we'll travel a different path.'

He waited, his eyes pleading in some eerily familiar way. His face looked flushed with fever. 'Okay, okay,' I said. 'Fine. Don't have a bird over it.'

His excitement that session – the aroma of his mouthwash, the kiss of his knees as we sat recliner to recliner – made me catch a kind of fever, too. But in the dark of my room that night, I wasn't exactly thinking of Dr. Shaw as my mother. It suddenly occurred to me why his expression – that look in his eyes – had seemed familiar. It was that same vulnerable, pleading look of Dante's in the Polaroid pictures. (Another of my secrets.) Dr. Shaw had spent all yesterday afternoon, half that morning, on *my* case, on *me*. I lay awake, transferring his head to Dante's body . . . I must have been groaning when I came because Evelyn, the night supervisor, was there with her flashlight in my face before I was even through.

'What happened?' she asked.

'Oh, nothing. I just had a dream. About my mother.'

I smiled hard at her. Under the blanket I was still bucking.

You had to give Dr. Shaw credit for enthusiasm. The next night at the pool in Building B he almost killed himself on my behalf.

He came for me in the ward just before lights out, like it was a date (that really rattled old DePolito!), and drove us to the other end of the grounds. I had to unlock and open all the gymnasium doors with Dr. Shaw's keys while he lugged a big reel-to-reel tape recorder and a jumble of extension cords.

He told me his plan as we sat at the pool's edge. I was going to start over pretty much as a fetus, he said, and grow up all over again, this time getting my life right. It might take six months; it might take six years. The process would be unpredictable; the rhythm would be more or less up to me.

As he spoke, I dipped my finger in the water and traced my initial on the pool apron. I kept doing it. By the time he was through, all the *D*'s I'd made had become a puddle.

'Any questions?' Dr. Shaw asked.

I stared at the shiny water in front of us, scared of whatever might emerge. 'Nope,' I said.

'All right then. Let's go.'

He hypnotized me first. 'You are on an elevator, traveling down to the level of your subconscious,' he said. 'I'll call out the floors and when I get to the basement, you'll quietly slip off your clothes and get into the water.'

We were somewhere around the fourth floor when I told him to hold it. 'Can't we just do this with my clothes *on?*' I asked.

At Gracewood, nakedness wasn't such a big deal. You were always seeing somebody's ugly body or vice versa. Still, parading my flab and broken capillaries in front of Dr. Shaw wasn't exactly the same as having DePolito or Mrs. Ropiek check me out.

Dr. Shaw gave me one of his disappointed looks. 'Do you not understand this, after all we've gone over? What are you, Dolores?'

'I'm a fetus.'

'And what's this?' His arm extended out to the pool.

'The womb.'

'And who am I?'

I was too embarrassed to look him in the face. 'My mother,' I said.

'Right. Mother, womb, fetus. Do you trust me?'

I looked out at the still water. 'Do you trust me?' he repeated. I nodded.

'And does a fetus have an aversion to her own body? Does a fetus have any expectations whatsoever?'

I shook my head.

'Does a fetus wear clothes?'

I shook it again.

'Our elevator has reached the basement floor, an environment of trust. Take your clothes off, please.'

I eased bare-assed into the shallow end and waded out.

The bathwater temperature matched Dr. Shaw's tone of voice. When I was over my head, I closed my eyes and began floating.

It sort of half worked, for a while. I didn't seem to be in quite the same dingy pool with the missing wall tiles where they forced us to do calisthenics every Wednesday and Saturday morning. With my ears under water, with Dr. Shaw's voice blurring away, I *did* mislay my expectations. Fell back. Felt fetal.

It was his enthusiasm that wrecked it. 'Ah, I'm quickening,' he called down to me. 'My baby must be testing her little arm buds.' I would have preferred him to keep quiet. I was under two hundred pounds by then, but not that much under. My arms were still twin hams, not 'little buds.'

'I wonder what my baby is thinking at this moment,' he called, rubbing his stomach with his hands. What I was thinking about was whether or not his being my mother was going to wreck my nightly friction ritual.

'There's something very special about the bond between a mother and her baby,' Dr. Shaw called out over the water. All this stuff about mothers made me think suddenly of Grandma. I imagined her walking in on Dr. Shaw and me. 'It's not what you think, Grandma,' I'd explain. 'I'm a fetus. He's Ma.' I knew just how she'd react: her jaw would unhinge itself; she'd clutch that purse of hers. Getting caught by Grandma made me slosh the water.

'My baby is very active this evening,' Dr. Shaw called down. 'She's flailing inside me.'

He'd flail, too, if she was *his* grandmother. Now I was strictly myself again: fat Dolores floating in chlorine.

'Perhaps I'll play some music to soothe my baby.' That was where the tape recorder came in. I cocked my head out of the water and watched as he snaked out the extension cords, plugging one into another until the wires reached across the room to an outlet.

'Maybe some Dvořák. Or Mozart, perhaps.'

Ma called this 'hotsy-totsy' music. Her own tastes ran more to the Ink Spots and Teresa Brewer.

'Music soothes the savage breast,' Dr. Shaw announced, then crouched to make the last of his electrical connections.

I was trying to visualize savage breasts when I both heard and saw the sizzle. Dr. Shaw was down on his knees, twitching and jerking. Then he curled up on himself and was still.

I got out and ran dripping past the arc and crackle of the extension cord that had landed in the puddle I'd made on the side of the pool. If he was dead, I'd killed him.

I wrapped my sweatshirt and jeans around my wrist and gave the cord a yank that sent it flying out of the socket. Then I inched over to him, still dripping, my hands clamped to the sides of my face. 'Dr. Shaw? Dr. Shaw!' I turned his name into a scream.

Down on all fours, I slapped his face. Hesitantly at first – more of a tap than a slap. Then harder. Then hard enough to sting, to bring him back to life.

He blinked.

'Are you all right?' I asked.

He stared at me as if trying to recall who I was, then reached for my hand. I hoisted him up and led him over to the cement bleachers.

The pool water quivered before us. We sat holding hands, me wet and naked still. Shivering passed between us like electricity.

Chapter 18

Dr. Shaw was the first parent who hadn't left me.

Or, rather, the first parent who had left me and then come back from the dead. His near electrocution opened up the floodgates and made him, truly, my mother. From the recliner in his office, I guided him around my parents' troubled marriage. From the edge of the pool, he guided me – swimsuited, after that first session – through my prenatal and toddler stages. 'My little guppy,' he nicknamed me affectionately as I swam beneath his proud gaze. He saw me daily.

Early and middle childhood were my easiest phases. After a while, I asked Dr. Shaw to come down into the water with me. He declined my request the first several times, then one day gave in to my pleading. Seeing Dr. Shaw in his baggy plaid bathing suit wasn't the thrill it would have been earlier. I *had* come to regard him in a maternal way. We chatted and treaded water or glided together in underwater silence, swimming the length of the pool like mother and daughter sea creatures: a seal and her pup, a whale and her calf. I was happy.

'Tomorrow is your tenth birthday, Dolores,' Dr. Shaw announced one evening as we breaststroked side by side. 'My little girl is growing up. What do you say we take a trip to the store tomorrow and you can pick yourself a birthday present to celebrate your progress?'

'Excuse me,' I said, 'but is this going to be an *imaginary* trip – one of those symbolic jobs?'

He laughed his mulish laugh. 'A real trip! A real present!'

'Suits me, Mommy.' I said.

In the toy department the next day, the clerk, a middle-aged woman wearing a scowl and a smile button, watched suspiciously from her register as I pranced from aisle to aisle, ruling out Barbies and board games and the ant farm Dr. Shaw was pushing. Then I saw what I wanted.

'An Etch-a-Sketch?' Dr. Shaw laughed. 'Okay. Why not?' He reached in his billfold and handed me a ten-dollar bill.

'Who gets the change?' the clerk asked. 'You or . . . your fella?'

'Oh, he's not my boyfriend,' I said. 'He's my mother.'

Her hand tightened into a fist around the money. 'Dolores—' Dr. Shaw began.

'Oh, it's all right. See, I'm kind of wacked out. He's really my shrink but . . .' I could tell I was the only one of the three of us who wasn't having a bird. 'Oh, just forget it,' I told her. 'It's a long story. You don't look like the kind of person who would get it, anyway.'

I began twisting the Etch-a-Sketch knobs during the drive back to Gracewood, even before I'd gotten the thing out of its cardboard packaging. 'You know, Dolores,' Dr. Shaw began, 'in the greater arena, in the world outside the hospital—'

'I know, I know,' I said, cutting him off. I was too busy watching the Etch-a-Sketch staircase I was creating with the flicking of thumbs and fingers.

At first, Dr. Shaw saw my Etch-a-Sketching as something deeply and wonderfully symbolic: my attempt to move forward linearly into a new and better life. I'd bring the toy to our office sessions, half listening to him as I twisted the knobs simultaneously; I was perfecting my curves. By the end of the second week, cursive writing had stopped being a challenge and I'd begun a series of seascapes: tropical fish, underwater plants, and mermaids, all bubbling together in harmony.

But Dr. Shaw began to lose patience. 'I'd like you to put that thing down now so we can talk,' he requested on more than one occasion. One time he snatched it away from me and slid it under his recliner so that I'd speak. Another time he noted that the Etch-a-Sketch screen looked suspiciously like a television set to him and wondered aloud if it wasn't some sort of crutch.

'Whatever you say,' I told him, twisting the knobs, not looking up. I enjoyed his disapproval. I was Etch-a-Sketching my way toward adolescence.

In the summer of 1973, I moved into Project Outreach House, Gracewood's halfway home for the half crazy. Six of us lived there, not counting counselors and case aides. Anita, Fred Burden, and Mrs. Shea had jobs out in the 'greater arena'; the other three of us got stuck cooking and grocery shopping and cleaning the house. I'd whiz through dishes and vacuuming each morning and then Etch-a-Sketch in front of the television all afternoon. Dr. Shaw and I were down to three sessions a week: Tuesday morning group, Wednesday morning one-to-one, and our Thursday evening swims. Chronologically, I was twenty-one years old; in the pool, I was twelve, a year away from being raped.

That was the summer Watergate preempted all the afternoon soaps and then *became* a soap itself. At first I was indignant about not getting my daily fix of 'Love Is a Many-Splendored Thing' and 'Search for Tomorrow,' but gradually I got sucked into the pull of those Senate hearings: the play of good guys against bad guys, truth against lies. My favorites were grandfatherly Sam Ervin and Mo Dean, John's wife, whose platinum-tinted bun reminded me of Geneva Sweet's.

My sessions with Dr. Shaw that summer were not going well: he kept wanting to talk about sex and I kept wanting to talk about Watergate. I'd start each hour with rambling speeches about Nixon and Haldeman and liars in general and he'd guide me back to the subjects of menstruation and masturbation and what I was feeling sexually that summer nine years earlier, when Jack and Rita moved into Grandma's third-floor apartment.

One morning I entered Dr. Shaw's office sputtering about

Rose Mary Woods, Nixon's secretary. 'She has some nerve,' I railed, 'expecting the entire country to swallow her bullshit about accidentally erasing those tapes. What's she keeping *his* secrets for?'

Dr. Shaw steepled his fingers and smiled me.

'What?' I said. 'What's so funny?'

'Oh, nothing. It's just that I find your indignation interesting. Ironic, really.'

'What's that supposed to mean?' I was sorry as soon as I'd asked.

'Well, you're very hostile toward Nixon's secretary. You perceive her as dishonest. And yet, whenever we get on the subject of your mother, you swerve in another direction. Blank out your own tape, if you will.'

'I do not.'

'You do, too. You've even set it up as a condition of your therapy – we're not to criticize her. When it comes to the subject of Bernice Price, you're a regular Rose Mary Woods.'

'Fuck you,' I said.

'Uh-oh. There's that angry word. Why are you angry, Dolores?'

'I'm *not* angry. There's a difference between lying to a whole country and having a little respect for the dead.'

'Oh?' he said. 'Tell me about that.'

'Just forget it.'

'No, tell me.'

I stood up. 'Don't give me that know-it-all look of yours. I don't have to listen to any of this.'

'Of course you don't. You're entirely free to—'

One of the most annoying things about Dr. Shaw was the air-controlled closer on his office door. It was impossible to slam your way out of there; the best you ever got was a cushioned hiss.

I considered standing him up at the pool the next evening, but decided against it. Dr. Shaw had ways of getting back at you.

'What about Dolores?' he'd ask during Tuesday group at the outreach house. 'Does anyone have any observations to make about her?' It was always Mrs. DePolito who led off, bulgy-eyed and yipping some accusation or another.

He was already in the water doing crawls when I got there.

'Hello,' he said, swimming over to me as I eased in.

'Hi,' I answered, barely audibly.

'I'd like to apologize for making you angry yesterday.'

I pushed off and turned over, floating on my back. In the quiet, I tried to recall any other time when *he* had apologized to *me*. For over three years it had been the other way around.

He floated up alongside me. 'Ah,' he said. 'This is nice, isn't it?'

'Uh-huh.'

'Do you accept my apology?'

'I guess so.'

'Good. Because even we argue, I love you very much. Do you know that, Dolores? Disagreements don't alter a mother's love for her daughter. Nothing does. Nothing alters that.'

'I know,' I said.

'I love you, Dolores.'

'I love you, too, Mommy.'

We swam for a while without speaking. Then, unexpectedly, he came up from an underwater somersault and said, 'Now that you're menstruating, it's nice, because I can love you as a friend, too – as an equal. Not just as a little girl anymore, someone I always have to protect. We can talk more honestly now. Share womanly things.'

I looked at him but didn't speak. I backstroked a little away.

I recalled what Jeanette Nord had told me long ago about the day she got her period: how her mother had taken her out to lunch to celebrate. Recalled, too, the night I got mine – that night Ma called Daddy a whore and he beat her up for it, slammed open the back door and sent Petey flying away. Sometimes it had seemed like she loved that stupid bird more than she loved me. Or that she couldn't even *notice* me, could only notice Petey. When I came back from my wild bike ride that night, I'd wanted only to hold Ma, to help her, but I'd made it worse. Now I swam beneath the surface, eyes closed, and again saw her face as she noticed the bloodstain on my pink shorts – noticed my period even before I had. My bleeding had made her angry, had made her cry.

When I broke the surface, Dr. Shaw was there beside me. 'You know what I want to talk about?' he said.

'What?'

'I want to talk about Jack.'

'Yeah, well I *don't*.' I swam hard, half the length of the pool away.

'Oh, come on,' he said, treading behind me. 'Don't be such a fuddy-duddy. Admit it. Jack is gorgeous. His body is—'

'Shut up!' I said.

'Look, Dolores, I may be your mother but that doesn't mean I can't look at men and feel certain things.'

'Stop it, will you? Why are you doing this?'

'Because I'm a sexual person.'

I turned and faced her. 'You're a slut,' I said. 'That's what *you* are.'

'I am not.'

'Yes you are.'

'I am not. What makes you say that?'

'Because you are! You called *him* a whore and then . . .'

'Who? Who did I call—'

'Nobody. Just forget it,' I said, plunging down toward the bottom. But the trouble with going underwater was that you had to come back up.

'Why am I a slut, Dolores? Is it because after I got out of the hospital, I dated other men? I don't think that makes me—'

'Who cared about your stupid dates? I told you to just forget it.'

'I don't want to forget it. You can't call someone a slut and then say "just forget it." Was it because of Jack? Because I liked to look at him? Fantasize sometimes?'

I willed myself not to answer.

'Dolores, I had absolutely no way of knowing he was going to—' She reached out for my arm but I yanked it away.

'Bullshit! You're a fucking whore of a liar and I'm sick of it.'

'Why am I a liar? I can't see why—'

'Because I figured it out, that's why! Because I'm not as stupid as you think I am.'

'Figured out what?'

'I know what you two were doing up there while she was at work.'

'While who was?'

'Rita!'

'What were we doing?'

'Don't play innocent with me. I could *hear* you.'

'What were we doing?'

'Dancing. Laughing. *Fucking!* Don't bother denying it. I could hear the bedsprings. You let him fuck you whenever he . . . and then—'

'And then what, Dolores?'

'And then he— My *feet!* He kept touching my *feet* . . . and then he drove me out to those woods and he just . . . those dogs . . . How was I supposed to— I didn't even . . . and it *hurt* and he just kept hurting me and hurting me. I was so scared and he just . . . and *you!*'

My arms, my fists, flew with anger let finally free. I lashed out at her, walloped her, smashed at her with the truth.

'All those things you used to buy me to eat and I'd eat them, sit up there in my room and eat them, swallow the truth, eat your dirty secret. "You're too goddammed fat" that old fuck of a doctor says to me while you sat out there – Get fat! Get fat! Get fat on your lies and I'm sick of it! I'm sick, Mommy! *I'm sick!*' My voice was a moan outside of me. '. . . Try and get rid of me. Make me take that physical and send me off to college the way I was and get rid of me so that you could . . . And then you just *die*, you just die and how am I supposed – well, I hate your fucking *guts!* So what if you died? So what? I'm not keeping your fucking secret anymore! I'm sick·. . . He hurt me, Mommy! He kept hurting me and hurting me, Mommy, and I'm not eating any more of your—'

I saw Dr. Shaw then. Saw him wet and shaken in the Gracewood pool. Blood dripped from his nose. A ribbon of blood floated in the water. He wrapped me in his arms.

I cried against his neck and he hugged me and took my shaking. I don't know how long we rocked there like that, but my sobbing and trembling was gradually overtaken by a profound exhaustion. I felt more tired than I'd ever felt in my life.

'How are you doing?' he whispered, finally. 'Are you okay?'

'When I came here, I was this fat . . . And now—'

'And now what, Dolores?'

'I'm empty.'

He hugged me, cradling my head. 'You're triumphant!' he said.

Chapter 19

In the wake of my self-disclosure about Ma and Jack – during the year or so that followed my discovery – Dr. Shaw and I turned over and studied who my mother really had been: a fragile woman, a victim in many ways – of her mother, her husband. Of herself. She'd been wrong to aid and abet me in the way she had after the rape, to feed her own and my guilt, overindulging and tolerating overindulgence. But I came to realize that she'd done what she'd done out of fear and limited understanding. She'd been neither a saint nor a whore, but a fallible, sexual woman.

'You've made some remarkable strides thus far,' Dr. Shaw told me at the end of our session one clear morning. 'How does that make you feel?'

My answer, a smile, had nothing to do with happiness.

We tackled Daddy next. In those sessions that centred around my father, I began to notice a curious pattern: I'd be talking calmly about Daddy – or sobbing something or whispering it – then suddenly veer off into a memory of Jack.

'There's a connection between the two of them,' I said abruptly one day. 'Isn't there?'

Dr. Shaw leaned forward in his recliner.

'*Isn't* there?'

'That's not my decision,' he said. 'That's your decision.'

For the next several months, he sat and listened as I wove an entire network of those connections, a kind of visualized rope ladder over the gorge of the two people in my life I still feared and hated most: Jack Speight and Tony Price. I told Dr. Shaw about the ladder and he kept leading me to the edge, coaxing me to step out cautiously. 'How much do you weigh now?' he'd ask. 'One-sixty? One sixty-five? The ladder can hold you. Go on.'

Eventually, I reached the other side of the chasm and understood the differences between the two men. I no longer hated Daddy: he had been a shitty father and a shitty husband – a man who'd made bad choices based on lust and coveting and then been too weak either to live with them or undo them. But he had not been a rapist.

In the spring of 1975, Dr. Shaw introduced the idea of outside work. 'It's a mail-order photo-developing company,' he told me. 'You'd be developing people's snapshots from all over the country.'

I was resistant at first, afraid of what was coming: the end of childhood, the end of his mother. 'I'd have to keep going over that bridge,' I reminded him. 'Ride past the exact place where my mother died. Have that pushed in my face, twice a day.'

'We could work through that with hypnosis. I feel it's time for you to engage outwardly. You can't stay on this island forever.'

'You're rushing me,' I said. 'I'm only fifteen years old in the pool. How many kids my age have to work full-time?'

A van drove us from Project Outreach House to the photo lab, two towns over, one street away from the ocean. To my surprise, I only needed to close my eyes and do cleansing breaths over the Newport Bridge for the first week or so.

Giving birth to people's pictures turned out to be therapeutic. Those mail-order customers were all so trusting and vulnerable. They gave you their names and addresses and the moments they most wanted to keep – babies squatting on potty chairs; grandparents slicing through anniversary cakes; half-dressed lovers asleep in bed. On third shift you could go outside during break and listen to the waves – close your eyes and still see all those people's happy times in your head.

Within three months of my employment, I quit smoking, opened a checking account, and petitioned successfully for unlimited shopping privileges. Developing pictures further reduced my craziness – shrunk it down like a tumor. It was a matter of perspective, I began to see. The whole world was crazy; I'd flattered myself by assuming I was a semifinalist. There was a man from South Hero, Vermont, for instance, who liked to photograph his cocker spaniels in military uniforms and lingerie. And a woman from Detroit who took close-ups of bugs crawling over people's faces. Smiling amputees with their wooden body parts in their laps, senior citizens standing on their heads: seeing what people wanted pictures of amazed me. We weren't supposed to mail back the pornographic ones; we were supposed to send a polite little Xeroxed apology. 'We regret that federal law prohibits the distribution of salacious photographs through the United States mail.' But I usually snuck them through. I felt a kind of obligation to those people who trusted me with their asses and erections and opened-up legs. Who was I to criticize someone else's choices? Who was I to judge?

There was this one couple, Mr. and Mrs. J. J. Fickett of Tepid, Missouri, whose rolls of film came across the continent at the end of each month with unswerving regularity. Thirty-five-millimeter prints, a thirty-six-exposure roll, ASA 100. The Ficketts liked to photograph each other in coffins: eighteen shots of Mr. Fickett and eighteen of Mrs. Fickett. The coffin styles and the Ficketts' outfits changed from month to month. One month they'd be lying in a polished ivory casket wearing formal clothes. The next month they'd be stretched out in a plain pine box, dressed for the beach. Here's a curious thing: Mr. Fickett always kept his eyes open and Mrs. Fickett kept hers closed. One month they were both naked, but with their hands crossed discreetly over their private parts (which was okay to develop and send). Mr. Fickett saw fit to enclose an accompanying note. 'To Whom It May Concern: These pictures are for an experiment in living, not private enjoyment. Please forward without judgment. Sincerely, J.J.F.' By then, everyone at the lab knew to save the Ficketts' order for me. I'd begun to feel as if they and I had established something between a business acquaintance and a friendship. To tell the truth, I was a little put off by the stuffy tone of that note.

In December of that year an unanticipated Christmas card from Daddy threw me into a minor panic and I discussed with Dr. Shaw whether or not to send one back. 'Well, how *do* you feel about your father these days?' Dr. Shaw asked. 'Let's start there.'

'What are my choices?'

'I don't see it as a matter of choice. Your feelings are facts. You've come to understand that you loved your mother – love her, still – despite her limitations. You've come to a similar conclusion about your grandmother: she's not perfect but she tries to do her best by you. How about your father? Do you love him?'

'I think . . . I think I pity him.'

'Pity,' he said. 'There's control in that statement. Power. What do you want to do with this power you now have?'

'What do you mean?'

'Well, one of your options would be to contact him, try to re-establish your relationship with him. Or, rather, to establish a different *kind* of relationship. Is that something you'd like to do?'

'No. I don't think so. I wouldn't be able to trust him.'

'What would you like to do, then? Picture it for us.'

I closed my eyes and saw a crowded department store. My father and I and Dr. Shaw were three Christmas shoppers there, strangers to one another, passing randomly without recognition. 'I don't want to send him a card. I just want to let go of him. Can I do that?'

'What do you think? Can you?'

'Yeah,' I said, unable to look at him. 'Sure. Why not?'

All that afternoon and evening I kept stopping and wondering why Dr. Shaw had been one of the shoppers.

My falling-out with Dr. Shaw four months later – my letting go of him – may have been worse for him than me. He was the one with tears in his eyes. 'You're hard on shoes,' my mother used to tell me when I was a little girl. I was hard on mothers, too.

'How are things going at the halfway house?' he asked me at the beginning of what turned out to be our final session.

'I'm definitely thinking of moving out. Those people are crazier than I am. DePolito's driving me nuts.'

'All in good time,' he said. 'Those people help support you.'

'I support myself. They're making me second-shift assistant supervisor at the photo lab. I'm getting thirty-five cents more an hour.'

'That's nice. Congratulations. But what I meant was, they help support you emotionally. They help you cope.'

'I support myself,' I repeated.

'You missed your last appointment. You were angry with me the time before because I accused you of holding back. Then you stood me up.'

'I've been busy,' I said.

'You've been rebellious. A typical teenager.'

'I'm not a teenager. I'm twenty-four.'

'I wasn't speaking about chronological age. You know that.'

'Look, I'm tired of this whole thing,' I said. 'Over four years of this mother-and-daughter stuff. It's starting to seem kinky or something. Embarrassing. Sometimes I don't think it's even helped that much.'

'How much do you weigh, Dolores?'

'One thirty-eight.'

'And that doesn't make you happy?'

'*I* lost the weight. You didn't.'

'I'm not suggesting otherwise. You should take full credit for your accomplishments, which are considerable. That's what I'm trying to say.'

I lit a Doral. I'd started smoking again after my first session with Nadine, my psychic. She was the real reason I was fed up with Dr. Shaw. I was sick of my stupid past; I wanted a line on my future.

'I see you've picked up the habit again.'

'Just for when I'm nervous. These things are like smoking straws.'

He steepled his fingers.

'Anyway, I'm thinking of quitting.'

'It *would* be healthier. The nicotine is addictive. And it doesn't take away your feeling of edginess. It adds to it.'

'Quitting this I mean. Quitting you.'

I savored his stunned reaction. 'I . . . I always thought that was a decision we would come to mutually.'

'I'm in outreach,' I said. 'I don't need your permission.'

'I know that. Does Mrs. Sweet know? Have you written to her yet?'

'I'm going to. I plan on it.'

'I think you owe her that. As a courtesy. And I think *I* owe *you* the benefit of my professional opinion, which is that we still have some crucially important—'

'Guess what?' I said. 'I have a psychic.'

His head tilted questioningly, birdlike. 'A sidekick?'

'Psychic. With a *p*.' His startled look pleased me.

'Male or female?' he asked.

'Her name is Nadine. Why?'

'Why did you go to a psychic?'

'Some of the people at the photo lab went to her. Why does *anyone* go to a psychic? I wanted to find out about my future.'

'You create your own future, Dolores,' he said. The same old blah-blah. I got up and walked to the window. 'Sit down, please,' Dr. Shaw said. 'I'd like some eye contact here.'

'I don't feel like sitting down.'

'Well, *indulge* me then.' He said it in his fed-up, parental voice. I flopped down in the recliner, legs over the side.

'You create your own future, Dolores. I thought you had

come to understand that. You *build* happiness out of insight and good habits.'

'Like flossing my fucking teeth?' I said.

He gave me one of his patient sights. 'I feel a need to clear the air,' he said. 'Let's do a few cleansing breaths together.'

We'd been doing them together since my 'birth' five years earlier. 'No thanks,' I said. 'I'm clean enough.'

'I'm hearing sarcasm again, four-letter words. You haven't been wearing that defensive armor of yours for a long time.'

'Look, I *know* I create my own future, okay? I just went to Nadine's to find out what I was going to come up with.'

He got up, yanked a Kleenex from the box, and began dusting his rubber-tree leaves.

'What happened to eye contact?' I said.

He sat back down, looking at me without saying a word.

'You don't leave your name or anything when you make an appointment. She didn't know me from Adam.'

'And what did she tell you?'

'She told me there had been violence in my childhood. She said it had been very painful to me.'

'That's a highly interpretable remark,' he said. 'Show me a childhood without some sort of violence. Show me a painless childhood.'

'She told me I had undergone enormous physical changes. Now how would she have known that? It's not like I pulled up my sweatshirt and showed her my stretch marks.'

'And what did she say about your future?'

'That happiness was *looking* for me if I was ready to receive it.'

'You *orchestrate* happiness, Dolores – you work at it. You don't catch it as it hurls towards you like a football. If you're going to be your own person, if you're going to support yourself, as you say – and I'm not talking about thirty-five-cent-an-hour raises – then you'll have to stop consulting charlatans.'

'You know what *your* nickname is at the house? Charlatan Heston – the doctor who likes to play God.'

He closed his eyes, but I could tell he wasn't visualizing. 'You frustrate me,' he said. 'This feels like a betrayal.'

'If this is a guilt trip, it won't work. You're not my mother.'

'No?'

'Nadine said I was a born artist. She held my hands and felt real talent in my fingertips, the actual vibration of it. You never even ask to see my work.'

'You never communicated that need. I always assumed your . . . your drawings . . . were something you wanted to pursue on your own. I'd *love* to see your machines.'

'You said to stop bringing them to sessions. You told me I needed to engage outwardly.'

'I didn't know before today how important they were to you, artistically. When can I see them?'

'Your voice sounds fake,' I said. 'You're insulting me.'

'So let me get this straight: would you prefer that I see the drawings or that I not see them?'

'It makes no difference to me is what I'm saying. I'm tired of all this. I'm sick of your voice, no offense. I'm sick of looking at Old Lady DePolito and her bald spot. I want to live in a place where I can have a bedroom-door lock. Where I can be my real age and not have to pretend some man is my mother.'

That's when I saw his tears. 'Well,' he said, 'feelings are facts. How many . . . works have you accumulated?'

'I don't accumulate them. I create them.'

The answer to his question was thirty-six; that's how many finished Etch-a-Sketch works I'd done. I stored them in the attic at the halfway house on a plywood table held up by two sawhorses. The ones I was still working on, I kept under my bed. Whoever was on housekeeping duty knew enough not to vacuum in my room. It was one of the house rules.

After my first couple of months of Etch-a-Sketching – after no one else at the house would even pick it up and fool around with it because I was so much better than everyone – I began to walk to the park and work there. Sometimes people would stand behind the bench where I was creating and watch quietly

– strangers at first, then regulars, people who perked up when they saw me coming. They brought me coffee from the store across the street. Everyone was hushed and respectful while I worked. One woman kept saying she was going to write to the 'Mike Douglas' show about me, that she could just see me Etch-a-Sketching on 'Mike Douglas.'

Sometimes I took requests: Elvis, Jesus, Archie Bunker – people had to supply me with a picture to go on. One day in the park, Al, a regular, put an album cover, Santana's *Abraxus*, next to me on the bench. 'Okay, hot shot, draw this,' he said. I resisted at first, but everyone kept begging me. In the middle of it, it began to look so much like the original that I held my breath. When I finished, Al held out a twenty-dollar bill and I handed over his reproduction. The others clapped and cheered. I bought two more Etch-a-Sketches with the twenty.

At the library I found a book called *The Great Artists* and began Etch-a-Sketching works of art: Degas's ballerinas, Modigliani's stretchy-necked women. Most of the people at the outreach house liked my van Goghs the best; ever since that song 'Starry, Starry Night,' we all kind of thought of Vincent van Gogh as one of us. Fred Burden even bought the album; we played it over and over. Poor, gentle Fred. He used to like to go with me to the park while I worked, but I just couldn't respond to his crush on me, couldn't separate his gentle nature from that incredible acne – the deep pits and crevices that studded his bluish face.

One time when Fred was thumbing through the great-artists book (I'd bring it back to the library every two weeks on the due date, then sign it out again before I left), he saw a picture of van Gogh's painting *Starry Night*. He hadn't realized it was a song *and* a painting, he said. I Etch-a-Sketched it and gave it to him for Christmas.

He cried when he saw it and kept it displayed on a TV tray in the rec room with a gooseneck lamp shining on it. 'So the whole house can enjoy it,' he announced. Then one evening Mrs. DePolito, off on a rampage, picked up *Starry Night* and shook it free. That made Fred cry again, only this time with a steak knife in his hand. 'Let me at her!' he screamed as several of us held him back. 'Let that bitch over here so I can hack her fucking ears off and ram this knife in her fucking gullet!'

That night rocked me badly, rocked all of us. We'd all known Fred as such a harmless soul. They took him away for weeks and took away the regular silverware, too. From then on, for the rest of the time I lived at Project Outreach House, we had to eat with those throwaway plastic picnic utensils – the kind where the fork tines snap somewhere around your fifth bite. It had all started over my artwork. Well, mine and van Gogh's. But Dr. Shaw dismissed it as Fred's Christmas-season depression.

'Nadine felt talent right in my fingertips the second time I ever saw her,' I told Dr. Shaw that last day. '*She* was sensitive to it.'

'The *second* time? How many times have you seen her?'

'Three.'

'And how much does she charge you for a visit?'

'How much are you charging Geneva Sweet for me?'

'Mrs. Sweet is billed by the Institution, not by me personally, as you know. Do you feel this Nadine person is actually helping you?'

'I don't *feel* she is. I *know* she is.'

'More than I've helped you?' His face was flushed. It was the most powerful I'd ever felt with him.

'As *much* as you have.'

'In three visits?'

'Yup.'

He leaned back in his recliner and closed his eyes. ' "Your children are not your children," ' he said. ' "They are the sons and daughters of Life's longing for itself." '

'What's that supposed to mean?' I lit another Doral.

'It's from *The Prophet*. Kahlil Gibran.'

'Yeah, well, if it's supposed to make me feel better . . .'

'It's supposed to make *me* feel better,' he said.

He opened his eyes. 'Dolores,' he said, 'as your therapist, it's my obligation to tell you I feel you're making a mistake. May I say why?'

'Go ahead,' I said. 'Knock yourself out.'

'Because you're not ready. You've come an amazing distance, but we still have some critical issues left to deal with.'

'Such as?'

'Such as your father. Such as your relationships with other people.'

The cigarette quivered in my hand. 'My relationships with other people are *fine*.'

'Yes, you've done very well with that. You're well-liked at the house, and by your coworkers. But you're a healthy young woman, Dolores, and I imagine that at some time in the future, you'll want to become sexually active. And at the moment, you're still vulnerable because—'

I *already* wanted to become sexually active. *Was* active, up to a point – that's how much he knew. I'd tongue-kissed with both Dion and Little Chuck in the chemical room down at the photo lab – had flirted and lured them in there and then yanked their hands away from anything more than what I felt like doing. What was so vulnerable about that?

'So what are you saying? I'm supposed to come running in here and ask your permission or something if some guy and I decide to – ?'

'What I'm saying is that we still have work to do.'

'It's the bicentennial, Dr. Shaw. I want to be independent.'

'I'm trying to teach you how to be.'

'I already *know* how to be. Look, all this talking isn't going to change anything. I've already made up my mind.'

He got up and began dusting those rubber-tree leaves again.

'You just dusted those about two seconds ago,' I pointed out.

He reeled and faced me. 'Well, that's *my* prerogative, isn't it?'

'Okay. Pardon me for breathing,' I said. 'So when should we stop?'

He sat back down in the recliner and closed his eyes again. 'Well, Dolores, I believe we already have.'

'Just like that?' I'd always visualized something more elaborate and ceremonial: a stage or something, people clapping at my accomplishments.

'Apparently you're already out of the nest. So, fly!'

I wished he had said 'swim'; he'd put me in a pool, not a tree. I wished, too, that he would look at me. 'Okay then. Adios.'

'Adios.'

He was so big into eye contact, you'd have thought he'd want a little during the good-byes. I stood there. 'Dr. Shaw?'

'Hmm?' He said it as if he was surprised I was still there – as if I was a calendar page he'd already torn off and thrown away.

'I didn't meant you haven't helped me. You *did* help me. Sometimes I really do think of you as my mother. In a good way, I mean.'

'Good luck,' he said.

I opened the door. Cleared my throat. Waited for him to open his eyes. But Dr. Shaw had already become a corpse. I let myself out.

'Well, what kind of person are you?' Nadine asked me. 'How would you describe yourself?'

I'd gone to her directly from Dr. Shaw's office – gone without an appointment to find out if happiness was a football you caught or something more complicated, something you had to invent.

'What kind of person am I?' I repeated. 'I'm . . . a visual person.'

She nodded her head toward the Etch-a-Sketch in my lap. 'Create yourself a picture then.'

'Of what?'

'Of whatever might make you happy.'

We were in her kitchen, not the office out front, because I'd surprised her, had just rapped on her back window. I'd expected her house to have a phosphorescent, lava-light atmosphere, but she had mother-of-pearl Formica and café curtains with pom-poms. A little girl with rashy cheeks and big eyebrows like Nadine's sat in a playpen by the stove, chewing on an empty Saltines box.

Nadine and I stared down at the blank gray Etch-a-Sketch screen, waiting for me to begin. I started twisting.

At first it was a whale, my Wellfleet whale – only back in the ocean, her open mouth nosing the upper left corner of the screen. But I realized I was making a mistake and turned the picture into a man. A big man. I was committed to whalelike proportions.

Nadine looked puzzled. 'Is it a bear?' she said.

So I covered his head with loops of curly hair and added eyes, a beard, linear eyeglasses – wire rims.

'It's my husband,' I said.

She closed her eyes and smiled.

'Open your eyes, Nadine! Is this him? Is he going to make me happy?'

She blinked and looked at me. 'I told you to draw something that *might* make you happy,' she said. 'Fate doesn't give warranties like Sears Roebuck. That will be thirty-five for today.'

I walked out of there holding the Etch-a-Sketch horizontally in front of me, like a religious offering. I didn't want that picture to erase itself free before I'd memorized it. I got all the way home with it more or less intact.

DePolito was outside on the porch. 'What you got there, Dolores?' she said. 'You got a new one? Let me see.'

I took one last look, then shook like hell.

Chapter 20

It may have been fate that made Eddie Ann Lilipop's rolls of Instamatic shots sail south from Montpelier, Vermont, and land – kerplunk! – at my station at the photo lab. But I took over from there.

Eddie Ann's picture order arrived in the spring of 1976, four rolls' worth of a high-school trip to New York City: teenage girls grouped together and giggling on hotel beds and museum steps, teenage boys flipping their middle fingers out the windows of a coach bus. It was impossible to tell which student was Eddie Ann herself, but I recognized her teacher in the very first picture that slid down the chute.

I *should have* recognized him; Dante's letters and naked Polaroids, now seven years old, sat back at the outreach house, stuck secretly – along with the ragged remnant of Ma's flying-leg painting – in my big Webster's dictionary between the words 'embolden' (to foster boldness in) and 'en brochette' (broiled on a skewer). Tucked inside my knapsack pocket, those photos and that small square of canvas had made it up in the cab ride with me from Pennsylvania to Cape Cod, but I'd left them behind in the motel room that night when I left to meet my whale. Grandma, of all people, had returned them to me – in an unopened UPS box the motel had shipped to the Easterly police, who, in turn, had driven over to Pierce Street in the cruiser. I still visited with the photographs and that swatch sometimes, usually when I needed to look up a word or prop open a window or feel some kind of intimacy with something.

Dante's beseeching look still got to me. Those pictures were one of the few secrets I'd managed to keep from Dr. Shaw.

Eddie Ann had it bad for Dante; her camera had stalked him their whole trip. There were shots of him from the front, the back, both sides – pictures of him eating and snoozing and one of him out in a hotel lobby wearing an undershirt and pajama bottoms, looking fed up. He'd filled out some and cut off his muttonchop sideburns. His straight brown hair was longish in back. Even when I squinted, I couldn't see a wedding ring.

I began to think of Eddie Ann as a sort of kid sister in conspiracy – and of Dante as my future. All of Dr. Shaw's speeches about self-actualizing and taking charge began, suddenly, to take on new meaning. Dante looked nothing like the big, curly-headed man I'd Etch-a-Sketched in Nadine's kitchen, but, I reasoned, any number of things could explain the discrepancy. Maybe Dr. Shaw was right and Nadine *was* a quack. Or maybe predicting a future just wasn't as exact a science as I'd presumed. I made myself an extra set of Eddie Ann's prints and sent her order back to her, minus the pajama-bottom shot, which, I decided in a big-sisterly way, was inappropriate for her to have taken. I worked overtime through May, June, and July, saving for my new life.

None of the operators I called would give out his address, but the Providence Public Library had a whole wall of phone books from around the country. Out of those thousands and thousands of pounds of tissue-paper pagers, I found him. 'Davis, Dante. 177 Bailey St. 229–1951.' In the hush of that library, my own breathing was the loudest sound.

There was a copying machine on the third floor. I intended only to Xerox Dante's telephone-book page as a souvenir, but in the quiet I heard Dr. Shaw challenging me to create my own happiness. I looked around, then ripped out the original. (I tell you, I was *emboldened!*) I dropped a nickel into the copier anyway, then pushed my face to the glass, and felt for the button. The heat from the flash made me feel like I'd done something permanent to myself, something I wouldn't be allowed to undo – that I'd sizzled myself in some way that was both risky and right.

On the bus back to the outreach house, I took out my growing portfolio: the old stolen letters and Polaroids, Eddie Ann's shots of him, that phone-book page, my Xeroxed face. Jack Speight and my father hadn't been vulnerable men and Dr. Shaw had wielded power in a style all his own. But there Dante still sat, naked and confused – someone to love.

In my Xerox self-portrait, the hair around my face, the cracks in my lips, were clear and razor-etched, lines sharper than any Etch-a-Sketch I'd ever made. But the rest of my face had a vaguer, more foggy look, like something religious – a smiling, closed-eyed Shroud of Turin woman, some mysterious saint Grandma might pray to. 'If you want your prayers answered, get up off your knees and do something about them.' That was a poster in the kitchen at the outreach house. Maybe I'd peel it off the wall and sneak it with me when I left.

What had derailed Dante from his Lutheran-school education and made him go north to Vermont? His voice, more baritone than I'd expected, wouldn't say. 'Hello? . . . Who *is* this?' he kept asking. 'Be patient,' I'd answer, but never out loud.

I made up lies about mountain air and back-to-nature to explain to my coworkers at the lab why I'd chosen Montpelier. On my last night at the halfway house, Mrs. DePolito made manicotti and meatballs and hugged me so tightly that I half-wondered if I'd imagined all her meanness. There were crepe-paper streamers and dancing and, at the end, Fred Burden made a speech about me and gave me my going-away present, a twelve-inch black-and-white portable TV they'd all chipped in to buy me. I hugged Fred and whispered that my Etch-a-Sketches up in the attic were his.

In mid-August, Fred and his sister Jolene drove me to the Providence bus station. The bus was late, the humidity a killer, and Fred looked pale as a mushroom. 'Is it scary?' he asked me.

'Is what scary?'

'Doing this. Moving where you'll be all alone.'

For the first time, it occurred to me that, with or without a wedding band, Dante might be married. Or engaged. Until Fred's question, I'd imagined Dante in a sort of Lutheran sleep, lulled into inertia by his subconscious instinct to wait for me. 'Not at all,' I sniffed.

When the bus driver announced we were ready, I squeezed Fred's hand and kissed him on that rocky road of a cheek. It wasn't nearly as awful as I'd imagined: my lips against those ruts and eruptions. When the bus pulled out into the traffic, I waved to Fred, who was crying, and wondered if I hadn't made a crucial mistake, obvious to everyone but me.

I had rented my basement apartment by letter: 177 Bailey Street, Apartment 1-B. The landlady, Mrs. Wing, had described the house's Victorian features but failed to mention anything about its being located at the top of a hill so steep that you practically needed mountain-climber boots. My suitcase and shoulder bag took on weight with every step. The palm of my other hand ached from the handle of my portable TV. I thought about that first day at Merton College, climbing the steps to Hooten Hall. About getting out of the cab and climbing that sand dune at Cape Cod. I set the suitcase down on the sidewalk and sat on it, looking back down at the town. It was dusk; lights were going on all over the place. 'You're a whole different person now, reparented and everything,' I reminded myself. 'Dante's waiting for you. Not that dead whale.'

The key and a note were Scotch-taped to the door. 'Welcome, Miss Price. Please join us upstairs for cocktails at 4:00 tomorrow. Sincerely, M. Wing and C. Massey.' Real smart, I thought to myself: I'd given up a perfectly good life to drink sherry with old ladies.

Apartment 1-B was two dampish, furnished rooms – kitchen and bedroom/sitting room – both illuminated by bare bulbs that stuck out of porcelain necks in the ceiling. The bathroom had a cracked toilet and a shower head closed up in a kind of narrow tin closet. The floor of that shower stall looked cruddy enough to grow a disease.

The closets were roomy; the phone was already connected. An oval window above the kitchen sink looked out to the tenants' parking spaces like a two-foot eyeball.

I unpacked and had my supper: a cigarette and a travel-dented Milky Way I'd bought out of a machine at White River Junction. I set up the TV on the bureau across from the studio bed, hooking a coat-hanger antenna off the back the way Fred had shown me. 'Charlie's Angels' was on: Farrah Fawcett snooping around some crook's hotel room, wearing just a camisole. 'Ten-thirty,' I said out loud. I'd been in Vermont almost three hours without any physical proof that I was living in the same place as Dante. On TV, there was a close-up of a turning doorknob. Farrah sprinted toward the closet, her breasts bobbing.

In the kitchen I pinned a towel up over the eyeball window and boiled water for a cup of instant coffee. Some occupant before me had stuck 'Keep on Truckin'' decals on the cabinets and left, in the refrigerator, a half-empty jar of Maxwell House, three Pabst Blue Ribbons, and an unopened jar of Spanish olives. The oven was thick with grease.

In the cupboard was a single ceramic cup with a Hawaiian hula girl built into the side, Mt. Rushmore style. They'd dug out her chest area and put a wire across and a pair of free-swinging ceramic breasts. 'Shake 'Em, Don't Break 'Em' the cup said. 'Honolulu Lulu's Novelty Shoppe.'

I went back to the bedroom and flopped down on the scratchy daybed. Back home at the photo lab, third shift would be just getting started – doing their address labels, checking their chemical levels. I picked up the phone to call, to just say hi, then hung up. You didn't telephone people if your new life was working out.

You're a dumb asshole for drinking coffee at eleven p.m., I thought to myself. Now you'll be up all night long. I thought I heard my doorknob click – imagined Dante opening it without even knocking, smiling, entering my apartment on the power of his intuition. Did I like that or didn't I? I faded off to sleep trying to decide.

By next morning I was up early, watching tenants' feet pass by my round window: nurse shoes and orthopedic scuffies. Teachers travel in summer, I reminded myself. He was probably visiting family or off somewhere on a religious retreat, praying for a girlfriend who'd love him unconditionally.

I walked out into the crisp, sunny day and down the hill to Montpelier. Red geraniums bloomed in storefront window-boxes; clerks whistled and swept the sidewalks. 'He'll show up,' I told myself. 'This place is Happily Ever After.'

The Grand Union was nearly empty. A row of checkout girls stood at their stations, chatting to one another in their matching red smocks and Farrah Fawcett hairstyles. I bought a bag of low-calorie groceries, a *TV Guide*, and a can of Easy-Off for that mucky stove. At the drugstore, I treated myself to a 'Mount Peculiar' T-shirt and some rubber shower flip-flops. The purchases relaxed me, made me feel like a part of the town, some ordinary shopper.

Just before trudging back up the hill, I spotted a second-story beauty parlour on State Street: Chez Jolie House of Elle. There were two banners in the plate-glass window. 'Walk In's WELCOME!!' and 'Hey LOOK! The FARRAH LOOK!'

In the stylist's chair, I faced myself – drab, pouchy-faced Dolores with long hair the color of dirt. I chose ash blond from the color wheel. My stylist smelled like coconut. Over the snip of her scissors, the whir of her blow dryer, she talked a monologue. She was voting for Ford, not Carter, she said, because at least Ford was used to the job. She'd gotten six Crockpots for bridal-shower presents and had had to give up jogging after her daughter was born because she just kept peeing her pants. 'If Jimmy Carter wants to be president so bad,' she said, 'he should have had those whitish lips of his surgically reduced. Or pigment-tinted at the very least.'

When I left three hours later, I didn't look like Farrah Fawcett, but I didn't look like myself, either; I figured it was a draw. On impulse I turned into a ladies' shop and bought a $25 salmon-colored camisole without once making eye contact with the saleslady. I went back to the drugstore for some pink lipstick and a blow-dryer of my own. At the top of the hill, my panting made me dizzy.

Figuring Mrs. Wing and C. Massey were widow-companions, I dressed in my white oxford blouse and calico skirt. But when I knocked on the door of their main-floor apartment that afternoon, I was surprised to find a bony old man on the other side. He was wearing a blue kimono, pajamas, and those scuffy slippers I'd spied. 'Ah, you must be the new renter,' he said. 'Come in, come in.' His eyes bounced off my Farrah hairdo and landed on the front of my blouse. 'I'm Chadley Massey,' he told my chest.

Inside, chubby little Mrs. Wing sat surrounded by embroidered pillows and Chinese antiques. Her kimono was in blood-and-egg-yolk colors and her hair was a black pageboy wig. 'How wonderful to meet you in person,' she said, smiling. She had white-powdered skin and yellow teeth.

Mrs. Wing assigned me a love seat across from her. It had carved wooden dragons for arms. Roving Eye squeezed in next to me.

I figured talking might quiet my shaky lip. 'Nice decorations,' I said. 'I'm getting a craving for egg rolls just sitting here.'

Mrs. Wing didn't seem to get the joke. She asked me if I was returning to the area or if Montpelier was new to me.

'New,' I said. Mrs. Wing nodded. Without looking over, I could tell old Roving Eye was checking me out.

'So are you two brother and sister or something?' I said.

The two of them shared a laugh. 'Mr. Massey and I are close personal friends,' Mrs. Wing said.

'Live-in,' he added.

'Oh,' I said. 'Different strokes for different folks, right?'

'Different strokes for different folks,' Mrs. Wing repeated, clapping her hands. 'That's delightful. We'll have to write that down in our book, Honeydew.'

Honeydew touched me on the wrist. 'Marguerite and I keep a notebook of the interesting colloquialisms we hear,' he explained.

'I didn't make it up or anything. It's from a song. Sly and the Family Stone.'

Mrs. Wing got up off her sofa. 'Now if I don't write it down, I'll forget it.' Chadley slipped his hand into the space between our legs.

'You sure must love China,' I called to Mrs. Wing across the room.

'Oh, yes. Our passion for Orientalia was what brought Chadley and I together initially. Now what was it . . . "A different stroke for a different sort of folk"?'

'Marguerite and I are compatible in every way,' Chadley said. His knuckles skidded against my thigh. 'As a "for instance," we enjoy sexual intercourse nightly.'

My smile twitched. 'Imagine that,' I said. Mrs. Wing sat back down and Chadley's hand went back to his lap.

'How old would you say we were?' he said. 'Take a guess.'

They both had skin like wrinkled-up paper bags, but I figured it was in my best interest to aim low. 'Uh . . . sixty-three? Sixty-four?'

'Ha! Not even close! I'm seventy-seven and she's eighty-one.'

'Really?' I said. 'You don't look it. What's your secret?'

'I believe I've already mentioned it,' he said, winking. Then an oven buzzer went off in another room and he shuffled out to get us our drinks and snacks.

'So what brings you to Vermont, dear?' Mrs. Wing wanted to know. 'Your letters were written with such a sense of urgency.'

I fed her my line about fresh air and nature.

'Oh, well, you'll have to meet one of our other tenants, then.'

'Really? Who?'

'Mrs. LaGattuta. Lovely woman. She's a nurse. Very active in the Audubon Society.'

'Oh,' I said. 'Birds.'

'And then of course there's Mr. Davis, right across the hall from you. He's a lovely young man, a schoolteacher here in town. Has quite a green thumb, too. He's planted a lovely garden out back with—'

'A teacher, you said? How about his wife or girlfriend? What does she do for a living?'

'Why, *il n'est pas attaché*,' she said, smiling.

'What?'

'He's unattached.'

'Does his share of tomcatting, though,' Chadley called in from the kitchen. 'I hope you like stuffed mushrooms, young lady.'

'They're Chadley's specialty,' Mrs. Wing said. 'He sautées canned crabmeat. Then he crushes Ritz crackers with a rolling pin and . . .'

'Hi-Ho crackers, Marguerite. Hi-ho, hi-ho, it's off to work . . .'

Shut up out there, you little dwarf, I felt like yelling. 'So this teacher guy likes gardening?' I said.

'Oh, yes. He's kept us in vegetables and herbs all summer long. Has the time to spend on it, you know, with his summers free.'

'Has time to entertain a chippy or two every once in a while as well,' Chadley said. 'Overnight, that is.' The ice cubes clinked in our gin and tonics as he hobbled towards us. I'd meant to move nonchalantly to a chair for one while he was in the kitchen, but the information about Dante had distracted me. He sat back down beside me.

'Yes, well,' Mrs. Wing smiled, 'that's fine with us. Chadley and I feel you young people have the right idea with your sexual revolution. Why, I was married to Mr. Wing for forty-three years, God rest his soul, and never once achieved an orgasm. Had never even *considered* clitoral stimulation until I was in my early seventies. Had I, Chadley, dear?'

'But we've made up for lost time, right, Honeydew?' Chadley said.

Yes. Honeydew,' Mrs. Wing beamed. 'This man is a precious gift.'

It occurred to me that Chadley and my grandmother were exactly the same age. If Grandma had ever heard about clitoral stimulation, I was pretty sure she had classified it as a mortal sin and dismissed it. She would die before she called someone 'Honeydew.'

You were supposed to transfer the stuffed mushrooms on to your little Oriental plate with a porcelain-handled spatula. I hadn't planned on any chippies. Chadley watched a mushroom shake on its way to my plate.

'What sort of work do you do, Dolores, dear?' Mrs. Wing asked.

Getting a job was a subject I'd let myself ignore during all my planning and plotting. 'Worry about that once you're settled,' I kept telling myself. But now I *was* settled. 'Well, I've been working at . . . a photography studio,' I said. 'But really, I'm an artist.'

Mrs. Wing's hands flew up in delight. 'How wonderful! What medium do you work in?'

'Etch-a-Sketch.'

Mrs. Wing cocked her head into a question. Chadley's mushroom stood poised in front of his mouth.

'But mostly watercolors,' I added. 'Paint them. Watercolors.'

'Ah, lovely,' Mrs. Wing grinned. 'May we see your work some time?'

'Well, it's pretty personal. I don't expect to make a living at it or anything. I was thinking of filling out an application down at the Grand Union to tide me over.' I *hadn't* been until that second, but it was picturable: me in a red smock, bagging groceries.

I chugged my drink, said no to another, and got up to go. Mrs. Wing was on her feet, too. 'Now, dear, if you can sit down again for a minute, I'll get the lease for you to sign before it slips my mind. You sit, too, Honeydew. They're in the armoire, aren't they?'

'Yes, my love.'

When she left the room, I reached for another mushroom, figuring if my mouth was full, I wouldn't have to talk to Chadley.

His liver-spotted hand landed back on my leg and he started stroking. 'You know,' he said. 'I think the three of us are going to be fast friends. I have a sense for such things.' The hand brushed up and toward my crotch.

I sat there, frozen, that mushroom stuck halfway down my throat.

'And we could have a private friendship as well, you and I,' he whispered. 'I'm very partner oriented, you know. There are things I could teach you.' He leaned over and began to sniff my hair.

'Visualize your solutions!' I heard Dr. Shaw say. 'Picture an answer to the problem. Then make the picture real!'

I stared at that little hors d'oeuvre spatula. I picked it up and held the corner of it against the top of his hand, pressing down a little. It was *my* decision who I wanted touching me. I didn't have to take this kind of shit from Jack Speight *or* his great-grandfather.

His hand paused for a second. Then it began kneading my thigh.

I put more pressure on the spatula, enough so that he flinched. 'Cut it out, you old motherfucker.' I said it softly, met him eye to eye.

This time he stopped for real. 'Let's keep the party friendly, shall we?' he said. 'For Marguerite's sake?'

I let up on the pressure. I'd made a red indentation on his skin.

'Tight-assed bitch,' he mumbled.

'Old fart,' I mumbled back.

'Here we are,' Mrs. Wing said, reentering. 'You sign right here.'

I wavered twice in the middle of my signature. My name on the lease was shaky, but legal.

Back in the basement, I flopped down on the bed and cried until my ribs ached. I *could so* have a normal sex life – as soon as I felt ready for one. 'Sex is something shared between two consenting partners,' I heard Dr. Shaw say. 'What Speight did to you out there in those woods was about violence – not sex. It was about *degrading* you.' That old goat upstairs hadn't known me for five minutes before he'd started grabbing. Of all the nervy, degrading . . . Old motherfucker: he could put that one down in their stupid notebook of colloquial expressions. Honeydew my ass.

A normal sex life: I *was* ready for one. That was why I'd come all this way – why fate had put Eddie Ann's pictures in front of me in the first place. I opened my dictionary and studied Dante's Polaroids. Then I went to my drawer and took out the camisole. The silk material slid coolly against my skin. Did a tight-assed bitch wear one of these? I walked unsteadily towards the mirror.

My face was puffy and pink from the crying. The lingerie hugged the bulge around my middle. There I stood: fat, ugly Dolores with a new Halloween wig of a hairdo. Who did I think I was kidding?

Fred Burden wasn't home at the outreach house when I called. Neither was Mrs. DePolito. 'A bunch of them went bowling together,' an unfamiliar voice said. 'Can I take a message?' I couldn't tell if she was a new case aide or a new crazy person – someone occupying my old bed and eyeing Fred, seeing all those good qualities he had beneath that rocky complexion.

I opened the refrigerator and stared at the food I'd bought in town that morning: cottage cheese, tuna salad, Diet Pepsi, yogurt. Hopeful things. I blushed at my own idiotic hopefulness. I'd been a stupid fool to sign that lease, to give up all I had.

I reached past my purchases and took out the three beers the last tenant had left, opened one and poured it into the hula-girl cup. I sipped my way down the foam, drank, twisted open the second beer.

The hula woman's eyes were closed and she was smiling coyly. I gave her breasts a little swing. Some man was supposed to think he was giving her sexual satisfaction by playing with them; some man, no doubt, had made the cup in the first place. 'Don't let them degrade you like that,' I told her. I drained the cup and turned it on its side, prying with a fork until the wire propped out. I slid off her ceramic breasts. Back at the photo lab, it was *me* who spoke up when they gave the dirty work only to the women. 'Right on, Dolores!' Grace and Lydia would say when I stormed toward the office . . . Now the hula girl had a caved-in chest. Mastectomies. Her shut-eyed smile transformed itself into something else: the smile of someone brave and knowing, someone whose pain had made her wise.

Unlike myself. Who sat in a basement wearing a dumb-ass hairdo and getting woozy on Pabst Blue Ribbons. I got up and paced, feeling that beer slosh in my stomach. I belched so loud it scared me.

I pulled off the camisole and got into my new flip-flops and my paisley muumuu – the one I'd worn since fat days. It wasn't *entirely* true about my not learning from pain. Upstairs, I had stopped him – hadn't just let him degrade me, the way I had with Jack. Or taken my anger out on a tank of innocent fish. I'd hurt him back a little, directly. Visualized a solution to my problem and then made it real. 'Take a chance! Be gutsy!' Ma was always saying after she got out of the crazy hospital. Moving here might have been stupid, but it was gutsy, too. I was standing in my own apartment that I'd rented all by myself. Those were *healthy* things in the refrigerator. I had lost a hundred and twenty-six pounds.

In the kitchen I spotted that can of Easy-Off and got down on my knees. The directions said to wait an hour, to let the 'foaming action' do the work for you. Bu work was what I wanted. I wished I had remembered to buy paper towels. I used a Brillo and the camisole instead, scouring and wiping away the grease of a thousand fatty meals. I only stopped once, to pull my hair back into a sweaty ponytail. Maybe I'd dye it back. Maybe

I wouldn't. Part of me hoped Fred Burden wouldn't call me back. I stepped back to admire the oven's gleam but looked instead at what was in my hand. I'd turned that fancy under-wear into a brown rag.

Outside it was cooler and a breeze dried my sweaty face. I walked clear of the house. Out back I found his garden.

He'd terraced it against a bank at the edge of the woods. The lowest row was a neat line of marigolds, then cucumber vines and summer squash, waxy-looking cabbages, glossy eggplants. The staked tomato plants were heavy with fruit in all stages of ripeness.

If Fred called back, I thought, I might not hear the phone.

A rusty Volkswagen rumbled up the driveway, radio blasting. The brakes made a watery sound.

He got out without turning off the engine and walked around to have a look. Tank top and cutoffs, no shoes. He'd grown a beard since Eddie Ann's picture. I tried to tiptoe past, tried to calm my heart.

'Hey, whoa,' he said. 'Hi.'

'Hi.'

His finger pointed at me. 'New tenant. Basement apartment. Right?'

I nodded. 'I've . . . I've been cleaning the stove.'

'I'm Dante. Live right across the hall from you.'

He seemed less real than his pictures. 'I'm Dolores,' I said.

'Dolores,' he repeated. 'Okay, great. Welcome.'

'I have to go wash up now,' I said. 'I've been cleaning the oven.'

'Right. You just told me that.'

'Oh, I did? Sorry. I . . . I like your garden. At least I assume it's yours, right?' I started toward the house on wobbly legs. Wearing my muumuu, for Christ's sake!

'Hey, whoa. Could you do me a favor? Could you put your foot down on the gas so I can check something back here?' He patted the car's roof. 'Piece-a-shit automobile.'

The driver's-side door was dented in. There was a hibachi on the passenger's seat, a jumble of mail and newspapers on the floor. The radio was playing an oldie, one of my and Jeanette Nord's old 45s.

'Yoo-hoo,' he said. 'Now.'

'Now? The gas?'

'Yeah.'

'Okay.' I pushed my foot against the pedal. The whole car vibrated.

Our day will come
If we just wait awhile . . .

'Once more,' he said.

I made the engine roar. My body shook with its revving, and when it subsided, with the sound of that song – its promises of everlasting love and dreams made magic.

'Okay, fuck it,' he said. 'Thanks.' He reached past my leg and turned off the key. The back yard went quiet.

'Mrs. Wing says you're a teacher,' I said.

'Uh-huh. How about you? Professional oven cleaner?'

'I'm . . . an artist. I'm not that good, though. How about you?'

'I'm not that good either.'

I laughed. 'What do you teach?'

'High-school English. You know, *The Scarlet Letter*, who and whom, where to put the apostrophe. Hey, listen. I'm getting this brainstorm. You want to do some supper after you get cleaned up?'

'Oh, well, actually I have some more stuff to do—'

'Okay, I got it! Take your shower – take your time. I'll go get us some wine. What goes with cheese popcorn, anyway – white or red?'

Nothing charming would come out of my mouth – only my stupid, nervous laugh. 'You decide,' I said.

In the shower stall, my elbows kept whacking against the tin walls, calling up a rumble like thunder. He was real! We had a date! All of it was actually happening!

I began humming something. Quietly first and then I was singing.

Our day will come
If we just wait awhile . . .

It was something I'd never done before: sing in the shower. I sang and sang over the ringing telephone, Fred Burden returning my call. If I answered, I'd regain my life at the halfway house. Or worse, be demoted back to the wards at Gracewood – be fat and crazy again. I stayed under that hissing water until Fred gave up.

We sat at his glass-top kitchen table drinking wine from coffee mugs. Through the clear glass, I saw that my thighs were bigger than his.

'She and her husband were New Deal Democrats,' Dante said. 'Henry Wing. He was pretty high up there in the Roosevelt administration.'

Her nonorgasm years, I thought to myself. Come to think of it, she'd started in late on her *normal* sex life, too.

'She sure loves antiques,' I said.

He sipped his wine and smiled. 'Yeah,' he said, 'and Chadley's her favourite one.'

'Dirty old man,' I mumbled.

'That he is,' he laughed. 'But harmless.'

He is now, I thought.

'By the way, I like your shirt,' he said.

I had put on my jeans and my new 'Mount Peculiar' T-shirt. His looking at it made me self-conscious and I pulled my knees up to my chest and stretched the shirt up over them. I'd bought a large out of habit.

'Get this one,' he said. 'I was going out with this girl last spring who used to come over here? One afternoon, right after she leaves, Chadley shows up at the door – says he'd appreciate my letting him know if we might ever enjoy the pleasure of a third party in our lovemaking.'

'No, sir,' I said.

'I kid you not. "The pleasure of a third party": like something out of the etiquette book.'

'Did Mrs. Wing know about it?'

'Oh, hell, no. This was strictly confidential, he assured me. The randy old bastard.'

He made it sound funny, turned Chadley into a cartoon. Dante was nothing at all like I'd imagined he'd be. Nothing like his old letters. If it wasn't for those eyes, I'd have almost wondered if I'd aimed my new life at the wrong Dante.

'So you're an artist, huh? What kind?'

There was a second where I almost told him the truth. But I was afraid I'd start with Etch-a-Sketching and end up with Dr. Shaw and reparenting and stealing Kippy's letters. Instead, I wove him a lie about watercolors and disillusionment and a guy named Russ, a long-term relationship I'd just decided to move away from. 'And my artwork was part of all that,' I said. 'So I'd just rather not go into it.'

'A clean break,' he said. 'I can respect that.' He took a sip of wine, watching me over the rim of his cup. Then he leaned forward and his smile turned into a long, soft kiss.

Supper was bakery bread and his garden vegetables, raw or just barely cooked. We started with a perfect red tomato, cold from the refrigerator. He sliced it in half and salted both pieces, held out one. My thighs were jiggly from wine and kissing. The tomato tasted sexual.

After we'd done the dishes, he reached up and touched me on the shoulders. 'So,' he said, 'do you want to go to bed with me or shall we keep it at vino and veggies?'

I didn't say anything.

'So anyway, what do *you* think of the New Deal?'

I shrugged.

'So anyway, your phone is ringing.'

'I hear it,' I said.

'We could call it "intercourse," keep it nice and dignified.'

Involuntarily, I cracked a smile. His hand reached down for mine; he glided his fingers back and forth in the spaces between my fingers.

Shared between consenting partners . . . I heard Dr. Shaw say.

'Or we could be very hip, very seventies, and call it "having sex." You know, lots of experimentation and position-switching. Chapter six in the manual.'

'You're embarrassing me.' I laughed.

'Hey, I've got it! Let's just make love. Lights off, candle on the bureau. If you give me a minute, I could probably find my old Roy Orbison album. Ever do it to "Blue Bayou"?'

I shook my head and took a sip of wine. The phone stopped ringing.

'Okay,' I said.

'Okay what?'

'That last choice. I'll take that one.'

'Aha,' he said. 'Very nice. The lady opts for romance.'

In the bedroom, he kept kissing me as he slipped out of his clothes. I was too close, the room too shadowy, for me to study his body the way I would have liked. But when he undressed me – slowly, gently – I was grateful for the semi-darkness. My nakedness was what he was *feeling*, not *seeing*. With the lights on, he might have detected evidence: the stretch marks and puckers of fat whale Dolores, the girl whose body I had and hadn't shed. If he could see me, he might stop.

He guided me down on to his bed and sat next to me. 'Can I ask you something first?' he whispered.

I waited.

'That phone that was ringing? Was that your disillusionment calling you – the guy you moved away from?'

'Yes,' I lied.

He let go of my hand and stroked my cheek with his smooth hand. 'One more question? You on the pill?'

'Yes,' I lied again. I hope he hadn't felt me flinch.

'Okay, then,' he said. 'All systems go.'

My mind floated in and out of what he was doing. I watched the way the flickering reflection from the candle swayed against the wall. Heard his voice speaking the words of his old letters to Kippy. I reached behind his neck, pulled him closer, kissing and kissing him.

He slid his body down the side of me and I felt his lips against my hip bone, his fingers feathering the inside of my leg. His touch was relaxing and exciting both. I closed my eyes and thought: I made this happen. I absolutely deserve the way he's making me feel . . .

His hand reached down and touched my foot.

I bolted up straight in bed. '*Stop it!*' I told him. 'Don't.'

He sat up. 'What?' he said. 'What's the matter?'

The candlelight caught his face, flickered against his worried eyes, he was himself again, not Jack. 'My feet,' I said. 'It's just – I just . . . I don't like anyone touching my feet.' I began to breathe hard. To panic. Then I was crying.

He put his arm around me and waited. My sobbing quieted and the room filled up with music he'd put on: Jim Morrison's doomed voice.

'I'm sorry,' I said. 'I'm just being stupid, I know.'

He took my hand in his. 'Hey, relax. I forgot something, anyway.'

'What?'

'Dessert. Be right back.'

He slipped out of bed and into his jeans. The outside door banged. I reached over and took a gulp of wine. I didn't want to be myself. I wanted those feelings back, the way he'd started to make me feel.

He came back with two small yellow marigolds from his garden. He took his jeans back off and got into bed. Holding both flowers out to me, he twirled them in his fingers so that they spun and blurred.

'Pretty,' I said. 'Where's the dessert?'

He passed the blossoms lightly against my face, then down to my breasts. 'This is it,' he said. 'Marigolds. They're edible.'

'They are? Marigolds?'

He pulled petals from one of the flowers, put them in his mouth, and chewed. Then he plucked some for me and held them to my lips. Hesitantly, I opened my mouth. Their sweet taste surprised me.

'Do you still believe in God?' I said.

The word 'still' hung in the air: I'd blown it – given away my knowing Kippy, his Lutheran-school dilemma, everything.

But then he grinned, oblivious. 'Isn't "Do you believe in God?" a little heavy-duty for our first date? I think you're supposed to hold the line at, "Do you believe in astrology?" or "Do you believe Jim Morrison is still alive?"'

'Oh,' I said. 'Sorry.'

'I don't, though, no – since you asked. Used to. When I was in high school, I thought I wanted to be a minister. Can you believe that one?'

'What made you change your mind?'

'Oh, it's a long story. Basically, I realized it was something I was doing for my mother, not me. Then, let's see . . . lost my virginity, got involved in the antiwar movement for a while, enrolled in a teaching program. Figured it made more sense to save people for the here and now rather than the hereafter, you know?'

I reached for him, questioning. He was and wasn't the boy in the letters. 'How about you?' he asked. 'What do *you* believe in?'

A shiver passed through me. 'Me?' I said. 'I don't know.'

'Not fair keeping secrets. You cold or something? Want a blanket?'

'Whales,' I said. 'That's what I believe in.'

'Whales? You mean like ocean whales?'

I nodded.

He nodded back. 'Yeah,' he said. 'They're cool, aren't they? Sort of mysterious. Come to think of it, I could believe in whales.'

His arm hair felt silky against my fingertips.

'Could you . . .' I began. 'Do you . . . do you think you'd like to try making love again?'

His mouth kissed my mouth, his tongue my tongue. I felt him go hard against my leg. 'It appears I would,' he whispered.

He guided me back down on to the bed and began kissing my

shoulder, my breasts – not kissed, really, but a brushing of his lips against my skin, the kiss of the marigold against my nipples.

He entered me gently, tentatively, waiting. 'Yes?' he asked. I nodded and he began to rock his hips slowly – smooth, sexy figure eights, from side to side. He watched me as he did it. 'Okay?' he said. 'You like?' I kissed him and reached down past the curve of his buttocks, felt for the backs of his legs, pressed my hands against them. He closed his eyes and smiled and drew himself deeper inside of me.

'Oh, yeah, nice,' he whispered. Tears fell from the sides of my eyes, but I was smiling, too. I deserve this, I reminded myself. I'd worked long and hard to feel what he was helping me feel.

He wasn't the boy in the letters. He was. Wasn't. Was. My decision changed with each drawing back, each new thrust . . . I closed my eyes and saw Ruth's and Larry's white bodies against the dark on Grandma's floor – saw them sharing each other. Saw Ruth, her shirt pulled up, her full breasts dripping with milk for Tia. I rose and rose, arching my back, pushing up to meet Dante. His sighs were soft and distant. He could believe in whales.

His movement quickened and I caught his rhythm, matched it, over and over. 'Oh, God,' he said, stopping abruptly. Then he tensed and sighed and I felt that part of him begin to spill and rush into me. Milk, I thought. Men's milk – the milk Larry had let go into Ruth to make Tia, the milk that made Ruth's breasts fill up with milk.

My mind spun, my muscles tightened themselves around him. We bucked and gasped and came together.

Chapter 21

Dante's vacuum cleaner had yards and yards of cord. By plugging it into the outlet just inside my apartment door, I could vacuum three quarters of both our places.

Coins wouldn't stay in his pants pocket. I harvested the quarters from between his couch cushions and used them at the laundromat, marrying our loads. It wasn't that he liked looking disheveled, he said; it was that he hated ironing. I set up the board at my place, in front of my TV. (Dante wouldn't own a television on principle.) Sometimes he'd sneak up from behind and hug me as I ironed. I'd feel his tongue against my neck and hear the sizzle of the hot iron as a single experience. One evening, as I stood ungnarling the pocket flaps on his blue shirt, the steam between us, he told me my ironing was a metaphor – that I was pressing chaos out of his life. 'I've never loved anyone domestic before,' he said. He nicknamed me 'Home Ec.'

They gave me first shift at the Grand Union. Monday through Thursday. Checking out people's groceries proved less interesting than developing their photographs. 'It's a paycheck,' I shrugged when Mrs. Wing asked me about my job. There was a lot of infighting amongst my coworkers, women who hadn't created happiness for themselves the way I had. You were always expected to be on someone or another's side. 'Honest to God, Dante – you can't even keep track of who's not speaking to who.'

'Who's not speaking to *whom*,' he corrected me.

'Well, whatever. I keep my distance.'

We ate our meals in my kitchen and slept in Dante's bed. Each morning, I chose a recipe from his *Vegetarian Epicure* cookbook and each afternoon I trudged back up the hill with the needed ingredients. Dante had been a vegetarian since 1974 when, chewing through a gristly piece of steak, he'd suddenly seen beef for what it was, decaying flesh, and his throat muscles had constricted. Dante called his spitting that mouthful of meat into a napkin an 'epiphany.' When I went to look the word up, his naked pictures – his younger religious self – slid out of the dictionary. For security's sake, I put the photos and the remains of Ma's painting in a shoebox, labelled it 'Insurance Papers,' and stuck it on the top closet shelf.

He'd done nothing less than transform me, I thought. By the time frost zapped the last of his tomato plants out back, I could go a whole weekend without a cigarette, grill sweet-and-sour acorn squash on the hibachi, drive a car, and regulate my orgasms so they'd arrive approximately when I wanted them to. 'A spiritual event in which the essence of a given object is manifested, as in a sudden flash of recognition' is what the dictionary said under 'epiphany.' Each night we spent together seemed like a kind of spiritual event. It was funny, in a way. Dante had stopped believing but started me up again. He was a gift, a nod, finally, from God, whose hand I thought I recognized in this. And if God was up in heaven, then so, maybe, was Ma – wearing those billowy wings and red high-heeled shoes, smiling down on what Dante and I were creating.

Dante kept his home phone number on the school blackboard for any student who needed to use it. Girls called, mostly, with crises involving their friends or boyfriends. They were snippy when they got me instead of him. Two years in a row, the senior class had dedicated the yearbook to him, a fact that Dante said made other teachers jealous. Given the choice, he said, he preferred his students to the bunch of old farts in the teachers' room who could only talk about life insurance, not life.

Just watching Dante type a ditto in his underwear or hearing his soft, reasonable voice with one of those jilted sophomores was enough to fill me up. He corrected his students' papers at the kitchen table, writing page-long reactions in green ink. (Red correction marks, he said, were too stultifying.) Dante's teaching used him up. Each night he'd set his alarm, fall naked into bed, and ask for a back rub.

'Ah . . . you missed your calling,' he said one night.

'What?'

'Your medium. Watercolor. You should work in clay with that touch of yours. What are you stopping for?'

It had slipped my mind that I was supposed to be a frustrated painter. I kneaded his spine bumps and made a mental list of the lies I'd told him: birth control, ex-boyfriend, watercolors. Omissions like Kippy and my breakdown weren't exactly the same as lies, I reasoned. Everyone in the world kept secrets.

The back rubs never failed to bring Dante back to life. Everything we did, every place he touched, he asked first. 'Okay? . . . this? . . . how about here?' A play in two acts, Dante called our lovemaking. Me first and him second was the way we both liked it best, so that I could relax, happy and satisfied, and kiss his eyelids, his mouth, during the in and out, the slow circles his hips made. Sometimes he laughed as he came; sometimes he winced and grabbed handfuls of sheet.

'Wait, stay in!' I'd say sometimes, holding my hand against the small of his back. I was scared of both the truth and the lies. I feared even the name of it: withdrawal.

Sex and love gave me insomnia. After he fell asleep, I'd get up and pace in the dark, convincing myself as I navigated around the silhouettes of furniture that I *wouldn't* lose him – that I'd turned the corner on my old life, on loss. One night during the pacing and nail biting, I tripped over a chair leg – whacked my toe a good one. I got back in bed, ignoring my pain, feeling in the dark for proof he was real: the hair on his chest, his breath against my fingertips, the wet spot we had made.

'Is it broken?' I asked the doctor who looked at my toe two afternoons later.

'Yes, it is.'

'So what do I do now?'

'Nothing.'

Nothing was what I was doing about birth control, too. If you waited and called Planned Parenthood after hours, you didn't have to talk to anybody – you got pretaped advice from some woman's know-it-all voice. 'And of course,' the voice said, 'when you take no precautions, you are making a decision as well.'

My shift at the supermarket ended at three p.m. and Dante was usually finished by four. By October, we'd begun the habit of meeting at the library downtown and hiking the hill together.

One afternoon, waiting for him, I spotted an oversized paperback, *Our Bodies, Ourselves*. It was the black-and-white cover photo that drew me to it. Two happy protestors holding up a sign, 'Women Unite.' One woman was my age, the other seventy or so. That day at the grocery store, there'd been a big fight amongst the cashiers. Tandy, who was getting married that spring, had, in the midst of the battle, uninvited two of the others to be her bridesmaids. 'Bitch!' they shouted at each other from their respective registers. 'Bitch!' All through the first chapter of *Our Bodies, Ourselves*, I kept closing the book and looking at those united women.

I sat back in the chair, missing Grandma. We took turns writing or calling each other every other week, but our letters and conversations were polite and constipated. For Grandma, my bad past was 'water under the bridge' or 'that business a while back.' Listening to us talk, you'd have no indication death or sex or craziness existed. The women in the book hugged each other, played clarinets, made love to their balding boyfriends. I was twenty-five years old, sitting in the Montpelier library waiting for the man I loved and who loved me back – but I was also my obese self pouting up in my bedroom at Grandma's. My six-year-old self in dungarees, riding with my father through the wet blur of a car wash. An eighth grader in Jack Speight's MG, my hair whipping in the wind on the way to that dog pound to be destroyed . . . Except he *hadn't* destroyed me after all. Dante had come along and *un*raped me. There seemed no good way to tell Grandma that. Who was Grandma beyond arthritis and rosary beads, anyway? Who had she been in bed with her husband? 'Women unite!' That idea shook me up.

'Boo,' Dante whispered.

He grabbed my hand and led me toward the door. 'Hold on,' I said. 'I want to check this book out.'

At the circulation desk, he gave me a quick kiss. 'Oh and just for the record,' he said, 'it's "I want to *check out* this book." You don't split your verb phrase.'

On my day off, I read *Our Bodies, Ourselves*, cover to cover. I had no other woman to discuss Dante with, no one to tell me if keeping all my secrets from him was wise or dangerous. I ached for a woman friend.

'Hello?' It was Tandy's fiancé, Rusty; they were living together, same as Dante and me. One time in the store, Rusty had ripped open a bag of M&M's at my register and started shooting them at Tandy while she checked out customers. She thought it was funny. According to another cashier, Tandy had had an abortion.

'Is Tandy there?' I asked. 'This is Dolores. From work.'

'Just a second.'

His hand squashed against the receiver, making a sound like farting.

'She's not here right now,' he said.

'*Dear Grandma*,' I began. The letter came out non-stop.

I'm not sure where to begin this, but I have some news. I'll just come out with it. I'm in love! His name is Dante and he's a high-school teacher here in Montpelier. We don't have any plans yet, but I'm hoping it will come to that. You put up with a lot from me when I was so sad and sick and I wanted you to share my happiness with me, too. We're planning to visit you for Christmas if that's okay. I hope that you'll learn to love him. He's kind to me – and so much fun!

Grandma, how did you and Grandpa fall in love? Were you sure about him when you married him or did you have doubts? When we visit, I'd like to sit down with you and ask you about your life.

I hope these questions don't make you uncomfortable. I wouldn't have written it if I didn't feel strongly about these things. If you would like to answer any of my questions, please write back. Or call me on the phone collect. Being in love with Dante is scary and wonderful. I love you very much.

In the next few weeks, Dante kept picking up *Our Bodies, Ourselves* but it didn't hold his interest.

At work, Tandy and the other cashiers made up; the bridesmaids were reinstated. From their stations, they discussed wedding preparations, calling past me as I straightened up the already-neat rows of Life Savers and tabloids, waiting for customers.

Overdue notices from the library began to appear in the mail, and bills and circulars, but no word from Grandma. One afternoon at work I forgot Grandma's face; when I tried to picture her, all I could see was Mrs. Wing. I kept promising myself I'd return the book as soon as I heard from Grandma. Maybe my letter had gotten lost in the mail, I reasoned. Maybe someone like me had stolen it before it got to her.

'Are we on for Christmas at your grandmother's or not?' Dante asked one morning at breakfast.

'She hasn't let me know yet.'

'Find out, will you? If we're not going, I was thinking it'd be nice to spend the holiday at Sugarbush. Teach you how to ski.'

It took me until late afternoon to dial. Listening to the ringing, I saw Pierce Street, the front foyer, Grandma approaching the telephone. I closed my eyes and willed myself not to hang up.

'Grandma? It's me.'

'Oh, yes,' she said.

There were voices in the background. 'Do you have company or something? I can call back.'

'That's the television,' she said.

'Oh. How are you?'

'As good as someone with my arthritis can expect to be, I suppose.'

'I was wondering . . . if you got a letter I sent you?'

Those television voices. Then, 'I did. Yes.'

'You did?'

'Yes.'

'So, what do you think?'

'What do I think about what?'

'Well, would it be all right for Dante and me to come for Christmas?'

'Of course it would be all right.'

'Okay, great. I've been kind of waiting for you to get back to me.'

'You're my granddaughter, aren't you? Why wouldn't it be all right? I don't want to bother with any tree, though. Haven't put up a Christmas tree since your mother passed on.'

'I can understand that, Grandma. It's not important.'

'Those needles stick in the carpet. They're there all year round, no matter how careful you are. You think you've gotten them all and then in July, there some still are. Sticking like burrs.'

I waited.

'Are you two shacking up?' she said.

'Grandma!'

'Well, I may be old-fashioned, but I'm not a nincompoop. Isn't that your young man who answered the telephone two different times when I called? Said he was a friend of yours or some such?'

'We live in the same house, Grandma, in separate apartments.'

There was a pause. Then she said. 'Well, you're a grown woman now. I suppose if they can do it on "The Young and the Restless" . . .'

'Grandma, do you remember those things I asked about in that letter? Do you think we'd be able to talk about some of them when I see you?'

'It's not an easy thing, you know, planning a holiday dinner. Pies, potatoes. You have to start the turkey first thing in the morning. Do the stuffing the night before, of course.'

'Well, don't worry about that, Grandma. I can help you. Besides, Dante's a vegetarian.

'What's that supposed to mean?'

'He doesn't eat meat. You don't even have to bother with a turkey.'

'I thought you said he was a schoolteacher.'

'He is.'

'Well, am I wrong or are those vegetarian people all hippies and some such? You know, young lady, if you're fooling around with drugs up there after all that other business you've been through, then you'd better think long and hard about what you're doing. You know what happened to poor Art Linkletter's daughter, don't you? Smoked some of that LSD business and took a bad trip – jumped right out the window and killed herself.'

'Grandma, my apartment's in the basement . . . What I was trying to say in that letter is that sometimes I don't feel like I really know you. It's my fault as much as yours. We withhold ourselves from each other.'

'Don't know me? Of course you know me. What's that supposed to mean?'

'It means I don't know things like – well – things like how you and Grandpa fell in love. Or what your life together was like.'

She sighed, disgusted. 'Now I know all this psychology stuff or psychiatry stuff or whatever the dickens you call it – I know it did some good with you. Straightened out what that one upstairs did to you. And your mother's death . . . But your grandfather and I just worked hard all our lives, that's all. People didn't have time back then to stop and worry about things all the time. Pick things apart and such. It's water under the bridge. I've forgotten half of that business.'

'How did you first fall in love?'

'Now, really, Dolores – stop all this badgering. I'm a private person. Why stir up a hornet's nest?'

'Grandma, you can *get* private with me. I'm your flesh and blood.'

She cleared her throat. 'Now, I can give you a wedding if you and this fellow would like. Nothing too fancy, but I have some money put aside.'

'His name is Dante, Grandma.'

'Of course, you'll have to decide whether you want to invite your father or not. That's your business.'

'Grandma, we haven't even discussed anything like marriage.'

'Well, I'm not surprised *he* hasn't. There's an old saying, you know: Why should a man buy a cow when he can get the milk for free?'

'Grandma? Are you happy for me? Are you glad I'm in love?'

'Well of course I'm happy for you. What a thing to ask.'

'Grandma? . . .' I said.

'Excuse me,' she said. 'I'm putting the phone down now to check something.'

When she got back, her voice sounded different – harder. 'I'll say one more thing, Dolores Elizabeth, and then, as far as I'm concerned, the subject is closed. I've buried a husband and two children – a nineteen-year-old son and a daughter who was only thirty-eight. . . .' She paused, cleared her throat twice, and I suddenly realized she was crying. 'If you want to love someone, then go right ahead. I *know* what love feels like; you and this young man didn't invent love. But the Lord Almighty doesn't give out any promises just because you love somebody. Love only gets you so far.'

I listened to the labor of her breathing. 'I'll see you at

Christmas, Grandma. I love you very much, if that's okay?'

'What a thing to ask,' she sputtered. 'Sheesh.'

I hung up and began that night's dinner, Lentil Loaf Supreme. Poor Grandma was wrong: Dante and I *had* invented love – a kind she knew nothing about. If you risked love, it took you wherever you wanted to go. If you repressed it, you ended up unhappy like Grandma. '*Two sixty-two Pierce Street, the house of repression*,' Ma had once said. And Dr. Shaw: '*Repression doesn't make it any easier, Dolores. It just wastes energy.*'

I decided to tell Dante everything that night: my parents, Jack Speight, Kippy's letters, Dr. Shaw. I heard him reacting to the unburdening of my secrets in the same soothing voice he used on the phone with his crisis students, who he didn't even love the way he loved me. *Whom* he didn't love. Objective, not nominative, case. The thought of telling the truth filled me with an enormous, exhausting calm and I left the supper preparations and lay back on the daybed. 'You're triumphant!' I heard Dr. Shaw say, that night at the pool when I'd let out the truth.

When Dante got home, he flung his briefcase so hard against the wall that it flew back at him. 'Tell me something,' he said. 'Am I intense?'

'Uh . . . what do you mean?' I said. It felt like a stranger had barged in.

'Just what I said. Am I intense? You've *heard* of the word before, haven't you? *That* one's in your expansive vocabulary, isn't it?'

There was a vein in his forehead. His whole body leaned toward me, waiting for an answer. I scrapped my planned confession. 'Intense? No, you're not intense. Why?'

'Because my vice principal thinks I am. Asshole Ev. I got my evaluation today – three 'needs improvements.' He says I'm too intense.'

He threw open the refrigerator door and grabbed a beer. Then he went to his own apartment and slammed the door. In another fifteen minutes, he came back for the rest of the six-pack. He pretended I was invisible.

'Do you want a back rub?' I said.

'Nope.'

'Do you feel like talking about it?'

'It's like – their whole philosophy of education at that school is fucked up.' He looked over at me, accusingly.

'It certainly sounds like it is,' I said.

'I mean, Ev Downs has sat on his ass parked in neutral for twenty-five years. I'm the only one at that whole goddamn school the kids can relate to and I'm going to sit there and listen to him make it sound like I've got a *fucking* personality disorder?' He overexaggerated the word 'fucking' – took extra pains with its pronunciation.

'Well,' I said. 'Try to forget it. I made lentil loaf for supper and maybe afterward we can—'

'That's it? "Try to forget it, I made lentil loaf"? Gee, I'm overwhelmed by your loyalty, Dolores. Thanks *so* much for your support.'

'I'm sorry,' I said. 'It's just that, well, you're kind of scaring me and . . . and I don't know what to say.' I began to cry. He watched me, curious, like a scientist.

For the next two nights, I slept alone in my apartment, nursing my nervous stomach with Tums. Then on Thursday a dozen yellow roses arrived for me at work with a card that said, only, 'LOVE/US.' I put the flowers in a coffee can on top of my register. All day long, customers told me they were beautiful. When I'd catch the other cashiers looking at them, they'd jerk their heads away.

That night, Dante wanted sex on the floor, not in the bed. He was rough and urgent; it hurt. But I kept my mouth shut, grateful for his love, no matter how he delivered it.

'Hey, Home Ec,' he asked me later. 'On a scale of one to five, how would you rate me as a lover?' He had walked me over to the mirror and made us look at ourselves. He pawed me while he waited.

'Five and a half,' I said. 'Six, Dante.'

He looked at himself, then closed his eyes and smiled.

In bed that night, I lay awake shaking because I'd come so close to telling him the truth. I'd lose him if I did. Those two nights without him had rocked me back to my senses.

'Home Ec' was the person he loved – not fat, crazy Dolores. Liar, letter thief. Beached whale.

He was his summer self again for a while, gentle and teasing.

'What would I have to do? I don't know anything about being a chaperone,' I told him the night he said he'd volunteered us. A roomful of high-school students was not something I was looking forward to.

'Oh, you know. Patrol the lavatory like a prison matron. Breathalyzer tests at the front entrance. That sort of thing.'

'Come on, Dante. I mean it.'

'Don't sweat it,' he said, kissing me. 'You're eminently qualified.'

The closest thing I had to a fancy dress was my flower-print muumuu. I borrowed Dante's Volkswagen and drove to Burlington to shop. In a way, it was funny, I thought: me finally getting to go to a high-school formal.

I found the dress I wanted in a store run by two elderly sisters. Both wore their eyeglasses suspended on gold chains. The dress was an unpredictable choice for me – risky and overpriced – and it took me a whole afternoon's worth of shopping elsewhere before I finally returned to the store and surrendered to it.

The gauzy material was smoky blue with silver thread running through it; the beadwork sewn into the bodice gave me a gypsyish look. The sisters made me try it on. Size ten fit me better than size twelve.

'Fanny, look at this on her!' one said to the other when I emerged from the dressing room.

Fanny reached down for her glasses. 'Stunning!' she said. 'I use that word all the time with customers. But this time I really mean it.'

'And it falls beautifully on you,' her sister said. 'Twirl.'

I laughed and looked away from the full-length mirror.

'I mean it,' she said. 'Twirl!'

I twirled. Slowly at first, then faster. The gathers of the dress unfolded themselves and the material lifted up and outward – I opened up like a morning glory. '*You're a beautiful young woman*,' Dr. Shaw's voice said. He was finally right.

The sisters both applauded me. The three of us laughed. I wanted Ma.

Back in the dressing room, I lifted the dress up over me, hung it on the hanger, and stopped. Some awareness was hovering on the surface, something that made the giddy feeling keep coming. My mind kept twirling. I reached beneath the elastic of my bra and felt my breasts. They were sensitive to my touch in a way that was both sexy and painful – a new feeling. The knowledge hit me so hard that I slumped to the floor, my shoulder blades skidding along the dressing room wall on the way down.

'We were beginning to wonder if you'd fainted in there,' Fanny joked.

'Guess what?' I said. 'I think I might be pregnant.'

Both women applauded again. Fanny took out her wallet and showed me her grandchildren's pictures. I don't recall the ride back to Montpelier.

The nausea started about a week later. 'We can give you Bendectin for the queasiness,' the doctor at the clinic told me. Instead, I kept nibbling from my perpetual stack of Saltines, swallowing tiny bits of banana I hoped my stomach wouldn't notice. I told Dante a bad stomach flu was going around at the store. At work I tried not to look head-on at the food that passed by my conveyor belt; on break, I opened the window to let out people's cigarette smoke, then sat by the fresh air with my feet up. I'd hidden a bottle of cold duck in my clothes hamper for when I finally broke the news to Dante. By my sixth week, I had already let several deadlines slip by.

On prom night, Dante dressed in his regular school clothes:

Levi's, blue work shirt, brown corduroy jacket, incongruous tie. I made him go sit in his apartment before I took my new dress out of the plastic bag. I was withholding myself from him, like a bride. I hadn't thrown up once that day. The cold duck was in the refrigerator for after the dance.

'Oh, wow,' was what he said when he saw me. I had splurged and bought matching jewelled barettes for my hair and a makeup job at Chez Jolie.

'Am I really beautiful in this dress?' I asked him. Three whole futures rode on his answer.

'On a scale of one to five,' he said, 'I'd give you a six. In the dress or out of it.'

The dance had a theme: 'Time in a Bottle.' Girls began running toward Dante before we'd even crossed the length of the gym. He assigned me to a math teacher named Boomer and his wife Paula and then let students sweep him off to the dance floor.

The decorations were fishnets hung from the basketball hoops and filled with balloons and papier-mâché seashells. In the center of the gym, cordoned off by a three-foot-high picket fence, were a giant cellophane bottle with a wall clock in its stomach and a mermaid propped up in a peacock chair. I recognized the mermaid as one of those life-sized rubber mouth-to-mouth-breathing dummies. The decorators had stripped her of her sweat suit and outfitted her with a paisley bra and a papier-mâché fish tin. Someone had pinned a hibiscus in her stiff nylon hair.

Boomer talked only in monosyllables but Paula made up for him, yelling chitchat over the blare of the band. 'You sure aren't like Dante's last girlfriend,' she shouted.

'What do you mean?'

'Well, I don't know exactly. You just seem more like us – a faculty wife.' Which meant frumpy, I guessed. Dress shields or no dress shields, it was too late to return the dress.

I spent the first hour sitting on a metal folding chair in back of the punch table, collecting students' silent appraisals, a smile stretched across my face like a rubber band. Paula explained her life: how she was different from her three sisters, why she'd bothered to get braces at age thirty-three, the gory details of the C-section that had produced her and Boomer's three-year-old, Ashley. No one seemed to notice how beautiful I looked.

I was surprised at how well-developed the high-school girls were; I hadn't remembered those ripe-fruit bodies when I was dodging everyone at Easterly High. But even at two hundred and forty pounds, high school had been a disembodying experience for me. I'd floated those four years of my life – had looked down at the linoleum and not returned a single stare.

In another couple of months, my pregnancy would shape me like one of Dante's eggplants. *Our Bodies, Ourselves* said some men were turned on by pregnant bodies, but I doubted that. I figured I knew more about the way men reacted to swollen women than that writer did.

The students' filthy language shocked me. One girl done up in banana curls and carrying a parasol called her boyfriend a 'fuckin' douche bag' right as I was passing them their cups of Neptune's Nectar. The foam and the smell of it and the way she talked all made my stomach heave.

Since my life with Dante, I'd stopped swearing as much. Not consciously, really; it had just happened. '*Foul language is part of your armor of defense*,' Dr. Shaw was always fond of pointing out. Dante only swore when he was angry, hurling the words like sharpened spears.

From the dance floor, he managed a wave from time to time. A line of girls kept cutting in on each other to dance with him. I watched him make each dancer laugh and beam. He seemed like a celebrity actor making a guest appearance – someone you could see and admire but not talk to. He kept to the center of the room.

During the band's break, I hooked my chin over his shoulder and collapsed against him. 'Having a good time?' he asked.

'You sure are popular,' I said.

He kissed me on the ear amidst the gaping. 'Dante, don't,' I whispered. 'I feel like I'm under a microscope or something.'

'Well,' he laughed, 'you are.' Then the music started up again and some girl tapped his shoulder.

Back at the punch bowl, I asked Paula what Dante's last girlfriend was like.

She reached inside her dress, fiddling with her bra strap. 'Well, her name was Rafaela – that should tell you something. Had a good idea of herself. At the end-of-the-year banquet last spring, she wore this white jersey dress and you could see her nipples plain as day. I hate when they do that. You're supposed to be too sophisticated to look, so the pressure's on everyone but her. She was *that* type – you know.'

Paula changed the subject to zucchini bread, but by that time I was panicky. Turning to check on Dante, I knocked smack into a passing student carrying three cups. Punch splashed down the front of my new dress.

'Oh, cheese whiz,' Paula said. 'Cold water! It's the best thing for it. It was in "Hints from Heloise" last week. March right into that bathroom before it sets and get some cold water on it, icy as possible.'

The long row of bathroom sinks reminded me of Hooten hall; so did the stares. Two girls were standing in a cloud of cigarette smoke. They each had the same hairstyle: long in back, parted in the middle, bangs hot-combed into curls as tight as playing-card jacks. I wet down the stain, then scratched at it with my fingernails and a wad of sopping paper towels. I recognized one of the smokers.

'Mr. Davis is a fox and a half,' one of them began. I looked up in the mirror at their staring.

'Really,' the other said. 'I wouldn't throw him out of bed.'

'Eddie Ann!' the other shrieked in mock horror. 'Shut your fuckin' mouth, girl.'

'He could have sex with any girl at this school,' she continued. 'He doesn't need to visit the dog pound.'

Her mirror image held my gaze as if we were duelling – as if the one who looked away second would win Dante. I didn't feel

angry; I felt maternal. In another seven months I'd be somebody's mother. Besides, her photo order had landed me here.
Women, unite! I thought.

I walked over to her. 'I want to tell you something,' I said.
'You can consider it a gift.'

Her mouth was smirking but her eyes looked scared. She
blinked.

'High school is like a sickness. Trust me, the fever breaks.
Then you get over it.'

Walking out, I heard their indignant laughter, louder than it
needed to be. 'Some gift!' Eddie Ann shouted. 'What's *her*
fucking problem?'

That night in bed, Dante came and I couldn't. When he fell
asleep, I got up out of bed and crossed the hall to my apartment.
My dress was hanging against the door. You had to go looking
for the stain to find it. I could get married in that dress.

I went back across the hall and climbed into Dante's bed. Our
bed. That Rafaela could could come back into his life
tomorrow. I wanted him and the baby both – permanently.

'Dante,' I said. 'Wake up.'

He squinted into the glare of the bedside light. 'What?' he
said. 'What's the matter?' His eyelids were slits.

'I think I'm pregnant,' I said.

'Come on.' He smiled.

'I'm serious.'

'How?' he said.

I told him I'd been careful about taking the pills. 'Religious'
was the word I used. 'It just happened,' I shrugged.

'Then we have to do something. I don't want any kids.'

I waited before I answered. 'Why not?'

'Because I don't, that's all.'

'That's not a reason.'

'Because they shit their diapers and spill their milk at supper.
I just don't want the *fucking* responsibility.'

I lay on my back, rigid, tears dropping fast down the sides of my face. My mind was revving. I got out of bed to vomit.

When I came out of the bathroom, he was sitting up in bed, arms across his chest, staring at the ceiling.

'But you *love* kids, Dante,' I said. 'You call your students your kids. You act very paternal.' At least I thought he had, up until I'd seen him dancing with all of them.

'They'll probably blow up the planet in another ten years. Having a child is irresponsible. . . . We'd have to buy one of those stroller things. Life-insurance men would start calling up.'

'No they wouldn't.'

'Yes they would. We'd have to push the bureau in front of the bedroom door whenever we wanted to fuck. Couldn't even say the word "fuck" anymore. "Dolores, would you like to go make nice-nice?"'

'We just wouldn't let those things happen.'

'Sure we would. This friend of mine, Nick? Perfectly intelligent mind, philosophy major in college, and now he knows all those dumb-ass Sesame Street puppets by their names – Bert and Bernie or whoever the fuck they are. Acts like they're friends of the family, for Christ's sake.'

'We can't decide anything right now,' I said. 'Let's get some sleep.'

'Yippee, kiddies, it's time for Captain Kangaroo!'

'Okay, okay, I'm tired. I get your point.'

'You get it or you agree with it?'

'I'm tired.'

'Goddamnit, Dolores. Now you've got me all riled up.'

'I'm sorry.'

'I've got to calm down. Let's fuck again.'

'Stop calling it that!' I hadn't meant to scream.

'See?' he said. 'It's happening already!'

After ten minutes of silence, I reached for him.

This time I did come – hard and fast, painfully.

In the silence, afterward, he got out of bed and dressed.

'Dante, where are you going? It's the middle of the night.'

At the door, he pushed me aside. I listened to the Volkswagen go down the hill and across town, keeping track of the sound for well over a mile.

He kept his apartment door closed for a week. When he came home afternoons from school, he played music so loud it vibrated the walls.

I couldn't tell if my vomiting was from being pregnant or being abandoned. 'Your test is positive,' the woman from the clinic had told me over the phone the day I called in for results. 'If that's good news, you should come in for an appointment within the next week. If it isn't, there are options we can discuss, the sooner the better.'

I called in sick the entire week, spending the days crying, throwing up, and wishing I had never written to Grandma about love. I pictured myself living back in Easterly – in the House of Repression – with a small daughter who never saw her father. Having each day to get up and face Grandma, who knew love only got you so far.

Our Bodies, Ourselves said the preferred abortion procedure for someone at my stage was aspiration – that they would vacuum-suction the fetus away from the wall of my uterus. Vacuuming, I thought. I'd be doing Dante's vacuuming.

Later, when the phone rang, I was standing at the mirror, marvelling at how greasy hair could get if you didn't wash it for five days. Everything was like that, I thought. Ready to fall apart the second you looked away.

'It's me,' he said. 'Can I come over? I have something for you.'

I flew around the apartment picking banana peels off the chair arms, whisking Saltine crumbs to the floor. I smeared some blush on to my greenish cheeks. There was nothing I could do about the hair.

He looked handsome and well rested. 'Don't look at me,' I said.

He handed me a sheet of paper. 'Here,' he said. 'For you.'

I stared at his handwriting but couldn't quite manage reading. 'It's a poem,' he said. 'What do you think?'

'I didn't know you wrote poetry.'

'I didn't, until last night. I had this sort of heavy-duty epiphany about how much you needed me and it just came out. It's a love poem.'

It was titled 'Love/Us,' like the card with my roses. It made no sense to me. My name was in it, but I couldn't find the baby. I started to cry.

'You're moved by it,' he said, smiling. 'I thought it was pretty good, too. I think it's publishable.'

'Dante,' I said. 'We have to talk about the future.' But he would only talk about his future as a poet.

'What about the baby?' I said.

He reached behind me and pulled me closer. He shook his head, no.

Chapter 22

'Pregnancy Termination' was what the clinic lady called it. During our ten-minute conversation, she gave me the details: four hours from start to finish, a counselor assigned to me throughout the procedure, $175. Answering her questions, I heard my voice go higher and thinner until it sounded like the high-pitched whine of a mosquito. The woman didn't seem to notice. 'So we'll see you on Saturday afternoon at one,' she said.

Positive the baby was a girl, I couldn't help naming her, and naming her made her real. My alternate plan was to tell Dante I'd miscarried, then go off somewhere, have Vita Marie, and sign the adoption papers. I could make the story foolproof; telling lies to Dante was what I did best.

But the world was full of terrible parents. I saw them at Grand Union all the time, hitting their children on the head, calling them idiots while you stood by in silence, ringing up their bad nutrition. Besides, I was scared to tamper with a nine- or ten-month absence. Rafaela might slip back in through the opening I made. Anyone might.

Maybe Dante would love Vita Marie once he saw her, I thought. Maybe he was only opposed to babies in theory. Maybe subconsciously he *wanted* to be a father. What if the world *didn't* blow itself up in ten years?

But what if he didn't love her? What if her birth caused me to lose him? 'Child-free' he called marriages without babies.

'You'll be in your ninth week by Saturday,' the clinic woman said. 'We don't like to aspirate much after the tenth – it gets complicated. The process we'll use despatches the fetal tissue from the uterine wall by vacuum suction. It passes out of your body through a flexible tube.'

'You're being inflexible,' Dante insisted when I told him I really didn't think I could have the abortion. 'This is the nineteen-seventies, not the Dark Ages. Women have fought long and hard for you to exercise this option – go back and read that precious book of yours.'

I did. But I avoided the chapter on abortion and stuck to the ones on childbearing and parenting instead. I checked out other books on pregnancy, too, but hid them from Dante, in the hamper with the unopened bottle of cold duck. If I hadn't put off that call to the clinic – if I'd acted right away – she would have only been an anonymous little ball of tissue 'no larger than a pearl.' She'd been pearl-sized the day I'd bought my blue-and-silver dress and twirled for those two salesladies. If I drove to Burlington and asked them what I should do, I thought, they'd tell me to keep her. Vita Marie was nine weeks old now, a one-inch baby floating in fluid, with fingers and eye bumps, but no detectable heartbeat.

I wrote my grandmother to tell her we couldn't drive down for Christmas after all. 'But I miss you, Grandma. I really want to see you.' The line filled up with truth as I wrote it and I had to stop and cry.

'I made the appointment,' I told Dante that night. 'I'm having it done the day after Christmas.'

He had stir-fried our supper: bok choy, tofu, and pea pods. Rather than eating, I was separating ingredients back into categories with my fork – the kind of behavior Dr. Shaw called 'passive aggressive.' Dante deserved it, and more, I figured. 'Baby killer!' I thought silently, watching him eat.

'Nick called me today. Wanted to get away, go skiing that weekend. But that's okay. It was tentative. I'll call and tell him I can't.'

'Go,' I told him.

'I should be there with you. I should help you through it.'

'I don't want you there. I'd rather be alone that weekend.'

He reached across the table and took my hand. 'You're doing the right thing,' he said.

'Yeah? Tell *her* that.'

'Who?'

I kept him waiting. 'Nobody,' I finally said.

In my dream that night, Dante helped me deliver her in the backseat of a car. He cut the cord with rusty scissors as strangers looked in, their faces pushed flat against the car windows. Vita Marie was a talking little blond girl. I loved her immediately, but even in my dream, love only got me so far. Before my eyes, she shrank and crusted over until she was a maple-sugar candy. 'Eat her,' Dante urged. I did.

But when I woke and snapped on the night light, he looked handsome and gentle in his sleep. He'd asked about birth control that very first night – made his position clear from the start, no matter what kind of villain I was trying to turn him into. It was *my lies* that got me into this mess, not Dante. But I wouldn't even *be* here without lies. If I wasn't a disillusioned watercolor artist with a Farrah Fawcett hairstyle, then I was myself, Dolores, the person everyone left.

I got out of bed and paced. Back in my apartment, I made two lists:

What I Love About Dante	*What I would love about*
	Vita Marie
1. his hands	??????????
2. his voice	
3. sex	
4. his dedication to his work	
5. he loves me back	
6. he made me someone new	

Seeing it in black pen on a legal pad made it clear. I couldn't leave him, not even for her. As long as he loved me, I was my *new* self: Cinderella, Farrah – living with the guy a whole gymful of girls wanted to dance with. I had a job, monthly bills, a normal sex life. I was weak at the knees with love. I was weak.

Our Bodies, Ourselves said some women found it helpful to bring a friend along for support.

'Hello, Tandy?' I said. 'This is Dolores. From work.'

'Oh, hi.' I heard her exhale her cigarette smoke.

'You're not busy, are you?'

'If this is about switching shifts, I can't.'

'It's not. I was wondering if I could talk to you.'

'About what?'

'Oh, nothing special. Maybe we could go shopping or something.'

'Where?'

'I don't care. Burlington? It's just, well . . . it's always so hectic down at the store, you know? I just thought it would be fun to get together and talk. I bet you and I have a lot in common.'

'I'm eatin' lunch,' she said.

'Oh. I'll let you go then. See you at work.'

'Yup.'

The morning after Christmas, Dante loaded up the Volkswagen and tied his skis to the roof. The day before had been quiet, endless. My presents from him were a pair of cloisonné earrings, a three-inch porcelain whale, and a new love poem he had written.

I had meant to get him a thousand wonderful gifts, but in the midst of all the confusion and resentment, I'd managed only one: a down-filled ski parka, red as blood. It seemed to inflate as he took it out of the box and unfolded it. 'I'm sorry,' I said.

'What are you sorry for? It's great. Are you kidding me? Look, I can still cancel out, stay here.'

I shook my head. 'Don't call me, either. I don't want to have to think about when the phone is going to ring.'

'All right,' he said. 'I'll be home Monday then – early evening, probably. Depending on traffic and weather.'

'If you change your mind or have any doubts about it or anything, then you *should* call me,' I said. 'Don't not call if you think you might want the baby after all.'

'Look,' he said. 'You're not thinking too clearly right now. You have to trust me. We're doing the right thing. It's nobody's fault it happened, but it would be immoral to give life to a random mistake just because—'

'Okay, okay,' I said. 'You don't need to say all this again.'

He pulled me over to him. 'Hey, you know what I've been thinking? That we should get married somewhere on the coast. Maine, maybe. How does this summer sound? June, maybe – or early July.' I watched his chin move up and down with the words.

'I don't know,' I said. 'I don't know anything right now.'

Chadley had flown to Florida to spend Christmas with his daughter's family. All day long, I lay in bed listening to Mrs. Wing's footsteps above my head. I knew if I thought about it long enough, I wouldn't do it.

Her near baldness scared me; I'd never seen her without her black wig. 'I was just about to have a cup of Earl Grey, dear. Come in and join me.'

We drank the tea out on her sun porch. In the late afternoon light, her scalp shone through the white frizzy hair, pink as the inside of a seashell. 'Mrs. Wing?' I said.

She waited for my tears to stop, covering my hands with her hands.

Mrs. Wing squeezed my hand in the waiting room, too. We were the only ones there.

'I thought *I* was pregnant once,' she said. I stared down into my chrome chair arm, watching my warped reflection as she spoke. 'But it turned out to be a false alarm. Mr. Wing always wore a prophylactic. He was meticulous about it. Of course, back then you didn't dare tell people you didn't want children. Everyone just assumed you'd tried and failed.'

The counselor assigned to me wore her hair in a bouncing ponytail. 'It might be better if you wait out here,' she told Mrs. Wing. 'But I'll take good care of her for you.'

The doctor was the woman whose taped voice I'd listened to, the one who'd said not using birth control was a decision to have a baby. I looked at her big chapped hands as she spoke, not at her face. She told me it was best to have her explain the procedure as it was happening, that it took away fear of the unknown. 'Any questions before we start?'

'No,' I said. 'I hate myself for doing this.'

'Do you feel you're not ready to continue?'

'I'm ready to continue. I just wanted you to know I love her very much. Even though I'm doing this to her.'

She just looked at me.

'Go ahead,' I said. 'I'm ready. I *am*.'

'I'm going to insert the speculum now. Would you like to see what it looks like first?'

I shook my head.

'Questions?'

'Will it hurt?'

'You shouldn't feel any pain but there'll be some pressure,' the counselor told me. Her eyes looked sympathetic, but when she wrapped her hands around my fists, they felt as cold as the equipment.

'I'm going to anesthetize your cervix with Novocain now,' the doctor said. I pictured myself screaming and wailing, halting the procedure. But I just lay, my emotions mislaid, and let it happen. I saw Dante high up on his mountain, his shiny red parka against white snow, blue sky. Once, in bed after we'd made love, he told me what he got out of skiing. 'Pure, distilled silence,' he'd said. 'Except for the hushing sound of your skis.' Then he'd touched my arm and made the sound. 'Husshh. Husshh.'

I was up on that slope, watching him fall and unfall through the snow, enjoying the hush.

'Carol has started the aspiration now. This should take about five minutes.' It hummed louder than I wanted it to. It drowned out Dante's skiing. My body itself felt nothing – not even the pressure they'd promised.

Whales made good mothers, I had read. Their babies came out tail first and the mothers nudged them up to the surface for air. They carried stillborns around on their backs until they dissolved back into the ocean. I couldn't tell if I was dreaming or resting. I saw my whale's big dead eye, close up, on the day I'd swum down to it. What did the clinic do with the tissue that went up the tube? Where did Vita Marie end up?

'How you doing?' the counselor asked. 'You feeling strong enough to sit up and rejoin the world?'

The doctor wrote me two prescriptions, one for birth-control pills, the other for tetracycline to prevent infection. I sat out in Mrs. Wing's lavender Cadillac while she had them filled, pressing down on the gray leather upholstery to get through each cramp. 'This is as hard as life gets,' I told myself. 'And you're living through it.' A man walked by wheeling a baby in a stroller. I slumped down in the seat, hid my face from him, and took the next spasm.

When she got back into the car, Mrs. Wing handed me the bag. Inside were the pills and a present, too: a bag of licorice whips. I put one of the ropes in my mouth and chewed, amazed at how good something could taste in the midst of life's being this bad. I chewed and chewed, swallowing back my own sweet licoricy saliva, unable to turn off the undeserved taste.

He got in on schedule at seven o'clock on Monday night, so windburned and healthy-looking that eye contact was impossible. He dropped his soft luggage in the middle of the floor, sat down on the bed, and hugged me tight for over a minute. I hated him.

'How did you make out?' he said, finally.

'All right.'

'Did you have it?'

'Have what? Say it.'

'Did you?'

'Say it.'

'The abortion?'

'Yes.'

He took my chin in his hand and turned my head so that I'd look at him. 'I'm in mourning, too, you know,' he told me. But later he forgot himself, whistling as he unpacked.

We spent New Year's Day napping and playing Scrabble. Dante made us vegetable broth and sourdough bread and got the dirty clothes ready for the Laundromat. 'What's this?' he said. He was holding up the cold duck.

We drank it from the bottle while we sat out in the car, watching our clothes tumble inside. Over the sound of the heater and defrost, the radio counted down the year's top songs.

'Hey, Home Ec?' Dante said. 'Happy 1977.'

'Yeah,' I said. 'You, too.'

He took another swig of wine. 'You know what I was just thinking?'

'What?'

'That we shouldn't wait. That we should get married as soon as possible. What do you think?'

'Why do you call me that, Dante?' I said.

'Call you what?'

'Home Ec?'

He shrugged. 'I don't know, just to tease you. Why?'

'Is that what you and me are all about?'

'Meaning?'

'Me scrubbing your toilet for you. Me keeping you in clean sheets.'

He sighed and took another swig. And another. I went inside to fold the clothes.

When I got back out, the radio was playing Rod Stewart, number one for the past year. *Spread your wings and let me come inside* . . . Dante had finished the bottle.

'*Love* is what you and I are all about,' Dante said.

That was the answer I'd wanted from him, been fishing for. All the way home, I sat and tried to figure out why it wasn't enough.

We set the date for George Washington's Birthday and booked a justice of the peace and back room at the Lobster Pot restaurant downtown. Paula from the high-school dance said sure, she and Boomer would be *thrilled* to stand up for us; she'd even throw in Ashley as flower girl. I decided to wear my blue-and-silver dress and ordered a corsage of yellow roses to cover up that punch stain.

I spent January preparing for the wedding and trying to convince myself I had done the right thing. Sometimes on the worst days, the call-in-sick ones, I let myself pretend that Vita Marie was invincible – that she'd somehow tricked all of us and existed, still, inside of me. An overwhelming pregnant-woman's fatigue took me over, resided in me. Sometimes on my fifteen-minute break at work, I'd fall asleep on the plastic sofa with a lit Merit between my fingers. (I'd gone back to smoking, but only at work.) Walking the hill back home required an effort so total that I'd flop down on the daybed, not waking up until I heard Dante in the kitchen, rattling the pots and pans in a huff, making the supper I'd promised to make.

'You're smoking again,' he said one night in bed. 'Aren't you?'

'I had one cigarette at work today.'

'Well, your hair stinks of it. It's a turnoff.'

Which was just as well; I'd managed to avoid sex since the abortion, except for once. That time, his penis felt like a vacuum cleaner up inside me, looking to suck out life. 'I'm not ready for this,' I'd told him. He said he understood and was willing to be patient, that he would pour all his passion into his poetry and wait for a signal from me. But a few days later he got his first literary magazine rejection slip for 'Love/Us' and started slamming things around the apartment and shaking his head at me. 'Here we lie,' he said that night in bed. 'Monsignor Frustration and Sister Mary Chastity, America's most abnormal fiancés.'

But Dante indulged me in his own way, buying me flowers and herb teas and books I could never quite get myself to read. At the end of January, he sat in the dark with me for eight straight nights, watching 'Roots.'

I ached to tell him how I felt, but how I felt was all tangled up in other babies: my brother Anthony Jr. and Rita Speight's baby and my own fetal self in the pool at Gracewood. . . . Secrets were the way to go with Dante, I was absolutely sure. The one secret I had let him in on – 'Dante, I'm pregnant' – had lost me Vita Marie.

Somewhere during that time, he wrote a new poem, about a woman who shrank her husband and put him in a bird cage. 'What's this supposed to mean?' I asked him.

'It's allegorical. I guess I'm trying to say I feel diminished.'

Not as diminished as Vita Marie, I thought. But to his face, all I said was that he'd promised to be patient with me.

'I *have* been patient,' he said. 'But I'm getting god-damned sick of this pity party every night.'

I put my hands over my wet face. 'I can't help it, Dante. She was growing inside me. I even named her.'

'Named *it*,' he said. 'Not her. It. Why are you doing this to us?'

'I'm sorry. I know I've been awful. I'm going to try to be better.'

He rubbed my back to stop the shaking. When he pulled up my sweatshirt and licked at my nipples, I managed not to scream. Later, between his orgasm and his falling asleep, he murmured, 'You see? You see how good getting on with our life makes you feel?'

'Uh-huh,' I said. 'Get some sleep.'

I had managed not to tell him her name. After that night, I kept my grief a secret, too, focusing as best I could on my new role: bride-to-be.

*

His parents arrived in their Winnebago two mornings before the wedding. Dante and his father hefted our present, a La-Z-Boy recliner, out of the camper and into the middle of our apartment where it sat, parked like a Buick. I avoided sitting in it; it reminded me of the recliner in Dr. Shaw's office where I'd had to sit and tell the truth.

The Davises were a ruddy, meat-and-potatoes couple who wore his'n'hers nylon jackets and gave no clue that their marriage had once been plagued by Mr. Davis's 'womanizing.' Dante looked like his mother, not his father, which somehow relieved me. Mrs. Davis kept smiling at me, flashing her gold bridgework and stretching her shiny vinyl cheeks. She told Dante I was 'an absolute jewel' and reminded him what an excellent judge of character she had always been. Dante's parents called him 'Chipper.'

Geneva Sweet had sent us Lenox dishes and her regrets, so the only wedding guests on my side were Grandma and two of the checkout girls from Grand Union. I'd invited Grandma over the phone, reminding her not to mention anything about Gracewood or my fat days. Despite her initial grumblings about a justice-of-the-peace service not being a true wedding in God's eyes – or hers – she got herself on a Trailways bus in Providence and arrived in town the afternoon before the ceremony.

She looked pale and fragile as she clasped the bus driver's hand and allowed him to lead her down the steps and I wondered for a second if she'd somehow found out about my abortion – if the disclosure had withered her. Easing down into the front seat of Dante's Volkswagen, she said it was the first time she'd ever been to Vermont and now, the first time she'd ever ridden in a soup can.

The trip up had shaken her. To start with, a crazy woman in a filthy coat had sat next to her on the bench during a stopover in Willimantic, Connecticut, and accused Grandma of having, years before, stolen her umbrella. Then, in Springfield, Massachusetts, a slew of colored people had gotten on, all of them wearing those big balloon hairstyles so that she couldn't see a thing around her.

'They're called "naturals," Mrs. Holland.' Dante smiled.

'Hair bigger than your head – you call that natural? Sheesh.'

The young colored man who sat right plop down next to her wore clothing so bright, it gave Grandma a headache. 'I told him right off the bat, I said, "Listen here, if you try to take this purse, I'll put up a fight, no matter how little's in there." 'Course, I probably wouldn't of. The bus driver was a colored, too. Told him that to call his bluff, see?'

Grandma said her seatmate told her he had rechristened himself with the name 'Love' and had founded a new religion based on, of all things, forgiveness – turning the other cheek. Turning the other cheek hadn't helped Grandma, though. He kept talking whether she looked at him or not. She'd had to listen to his malarkey all the way to White River Junction.

Because of her ordeal, Grandma felt justified, she told Dante's parents, in saying yes to the glass of cranberry liqueur they offered her, though she wasn't a drinker and never had been. The alcohol and attention bewitched her. Within half an hour, she was so charmed and spirited that she'd begun to tell stories from her childhood; how her older brother Bill had run away to join the navy and sent her a pet monkey from Madagascar, which had arrived precisely on her birthday, except dead. How a rooster had had it in for her and chased her all the way down to Preston bridge on her way to fourth grade. (Her father later paid the owner seventy-five cents for the pleasure of wringing its neck. They had it for Sunday dinner and it was tough as shoe leather.)

'Your little granny's as cute as a bug in a rug,' Mrs. Davis told me, squeezing my arm.

I sipped the liqueur, too, hoping it would make me as lighthearted as the rest of them. It put me in a slump instead, and I sat and watched Grandma, trying to read from her face if she could ever forgive abortion.

'I think I'm acquiring a taste for the old gal,' Dante whispered about Grandma during the dishes that night. She and Dante's parents were in front of the TV watching 'The Jeffersons.' 'She's got a certain feisty charm for a racist. Not to mention all those great dead-animal stories.'

At ten o'clock, Dante returned to his apartment and his parents went back to their room at the Brown Derby Motel. I was making up the sheets when Grandma came out of the bathroom in her housecoat and slippers and gave me two wedding presents: a cameo locket on a delicate gold chain and two thousand two hundred dollars cash – twenty-two hundred-dollar bills.

'Grandma,' I said. 'We can't accept this much money. And you should *never* have been carrying this cash with you all the way up here.'

She wanted to talk about the locket instead. She suggested I might like to wear it during the ceremony. 'Your grandfather gave it to me on our second wedding anniversary. I can still see the wrapping paper it came in. 'Course, I gave him the rats for spending the money. 'Grouchy Gertie' he used to call me. I was the serious one, you know; he was always full of the dickens.'

I reached over and kissed the soft creases in her cheek. 'It's beautiful,' I said. 'Thank you for coming all this way.'

She shooed away the kiss, a distraction. 'Grouchie Gertie,' she said softly. 'I'd forgotten that.'

Later in the dark, we lay side by side together, not sleeping. 'Grandma,' I said, 'I wish Ma could be alive right now. Here with us. Here for my wedding . . . I never told you this, Grandma, but one of the things I had to work on when I was at the hospital was my feelings about Ma. Her death. And the breakdown she had. And . . . the fact that she and Jack had been . . . before he did what he did to me.'

She reached over and touched my wrist. Neither of us spoke for the next several minutes.

'I was just thinking,' she finally said. 'Maybe that colored fella really *wasn't* such a big kook. The one who sat next to me on the bus. Him and his forgiveness religion . . . I didn't realize you knew about that business that was going on between them, Dolores. Your mother and the one upstairs – Speight . . . I knew, of course. She was never a very good liar around me. One night right in the middle of it, I surprised her at the back door. Sat on a kitchen chair in the dark until she came downstairs. She was on her way up there, see, sneaking up to see him while little Rita was at work. You were fast asleep, of course. "He's a married man," I told her. "You walk out this door, young lady, and I'll never forgive you." That's what I said to her. "I'll never forgive you." I was scared for her, you see. Thought to myself, She'll burn in hell for a month of Sundays because of what she's doing. But she went anyway. Poor thing – couldn't help herself. She always had a certain weakness. Even as a girl – all those asthma attacks . . .'

'Sometimes,' I said, 'sometimes I love Dante so much that it scares me. I feel out of control. Is that normal?'

'Of course it's normal. I was scared skinny when I married Ernest – didn't know what the deuce to expect beyond cooking and keeping a house.'

'Do you think it's wrong that I never told Dante about the hospital or Jack or anything?'

'No,' she said. 'It's for the best. Men scare too easily. And all that business happened a long time ago, anyway. It makes me sad, though.'

'What does?'

'Oh, that Bernice *couldn't* be alive for your wedding . . . That she never heard me say I forgave her.'

She was hesitating in the dark; I could tell she wasn't through yet. 'What is it, Grandma?'

'Well, I can't get that cuckoo bus trip out of my mind, that's all. At one point I got up out of my seat – stood up to get something from the rack overhead – a tangerine, it was. I had packed a tangerine and some Fig Newtons, you see, so my stomach wouldn't be empty when I took my pill. Then we went over a bump and I lost my balance. Went to steady myself and my hand landed in that hair of his. Well, I apologized of course

– it was very embarrassing – my hand disappeared right up to the wrist. He was very nice about it, really. Took out this funny comb he had and said he was just glad I didn't fall . . . But the funny part – the part I was just lying here thinking about – was what that hair felt like.'

'What did it feel like, Grandma?'

'Well, I always imagined their hair would be bristly. You know, steely – like SOS. But it doesn't feel like that at all. I mean, it's stiff, yes. Of course it's stiff. But it's soft, too. That's the part that surprised me. The softness.'

Chapter 23

In spring of 1978, Boomer and Paula put a down payment on a house going up at Granite Acres Estates. 'I get to pick out my own light fixtures and kitchen counter-tops and everything!' Paula told me, loudly enough so that other Grand Union shoppers took notice. 'You guys should come over this weekend! We'll show you our lot!'

That Sunday afternoon Dante and I drove up their makeshift road. Holes and dirt piles covered the hillside, as far as you could look. The finished houses still had their window decals on. 'Look at these cheap-shit things,' Dante said, navigating around the potholes. 'You can see the middle seam where they put the two halves together.'

Boomer and Paula waved to us from the half of their prefab house that had been delivered. It sat bundled in plastic on a flatbed truck.

'Now see, we're going to bisect the basement—' Boomer began.

'Right down the middle!' Paula interrupted. 'Half for my laundry room and the other half for my crafts studio. Now that I have the space, I'm going to take on some students, have a minischool. Just decoupage and macramé at first, but I might branch out later.'

We'd been to Boomer and Paula's apartment once for Friday-night pizza. Their downstairs was an obstacle course of hanging plants in Velveeta-colored macramé holders that Paula had woven. Decoupaged greeting cards and studio portraits of

Ashley covered the walls. Back at our place that evening, I had turned their home – their life – into a cartoon for Dante's entertainment, had even gotten out of bed to imitate Paula's walk. 'Jut Butt,' I nicknamed her. Dante laughed so hard, he couldn't breathe. Then he fell asleep while I sat up in bed, horrified at how vicious I could be toward a woman who'd just fed us.

'We get wall-to-wall shag carpet throughout the whole main floor,' Paula continued. 'It's part of Package B. I'm leaning toward avocado for the color. Boomer bought one of those handyman magazines and guess what was in it? These plans for a bar that would fit just perfectly in the family room! It's got a sink and a brass rail and a knickknack shelf. It even shows you how to upholster your own barstools.'

'Incredible,' Dante said, smiling over at me.

'Just think, you guys! One of these days, you'll be sitting around at our bar, sipping whiskey sours and saying, "Pass the pretzels." Right, Pooh-Bear?'

'That bar is a wet bar,' Boomer said. 'It's got a sink.'

'I already said that, hon. I just told them. You should take that class of mine, Dolores. My own school – pinch me, I can't believe it!'

Ashley pulled at her mother's pant leg and Paula bent down to hear the secret. 'Well, Ashley, maybe next time you'll listen to Mommy about drinking too much pineapple juice. Come on, we'll just have to tinkle behind the car.'

'But I don't have to tinkle. I have to make a stinky.'

Dante turned his smirk to the hillside.

When Paula came back, she thanked God for Wet Wipes and poured us coffee from a thermos. The men had gone off to look at a stump. In the cold air, Paula's talk burst out in white puffs.

'If you were a prude, I couldn't tell you this, Dolores. But between you and me and this whoozie-whatsis,' she said, clicking her wedding ring against the flatbed, 'I was this close to calling up a *marriage counselor*. About Boomer and me. Got as far as circling a number in the yellow pages. But buying this house really woke my Pooh-Bear up out of hibernation. If you catch my drift.'

Ashley sat down on top of her mother's shoes and began humming a pretty song I couldn't quite recognize.

'I mean, he brings those handyman magazines to bed with him and the next thing you know, he's clinging to me like stretch pants. I don't suppose a newlywed like you knows anything yet about dry spells in a marriage, but, phew, happy days are here again! Dolores, I'd be a millionairess if I had stock in the company that makes the cream I use with my D-I-A-F-R-A-M.' She reached down and tapped her knuckles against Ashley's skull. 'Little pitchers have bit ears,' she said.

Suddenly I recalled the name of that tune Ashley was humming: 'Mairsy Doats.' My mother and I had sung it mornings before grade school, when she'd comb the snarls out of my hair. I didn't want Boomer and Paula's life or their prefab house, but I wanted their happiness. I wanted a little girl to sit on my feet and hum. Dante referred to Vita Marie's conception as 'the time we got good and burned.' We were managing sex once a week.

On the way home, Dante said someone ought to gag Paula before poor Boomer went brain dead – that looking down at their foundation felt to him like staring into the abyss.

'Maybe *we* should think about buying a house some day,' I said.

He laughed. 'With what? Our looks?'

'We have that money from my grandmother. I could start saving.'

'Oh, right,' he said. 'With any luck, we can reserve one of those glorified Big Mac containers for our very own – right next to Boomer and Paula. The Mertzes and the Ricardos, happy as pigs in shit.'

The houses we passed on Route 38 were blurs. Dante always speeded up when he was angry. 'Well, anyhow,' I said, 'they seem real happy about it. I guess that's what counts, right?'

'*Really* happy. Adjectives take adverbs – for the millionth time.'

'Really happy,' I repeated.

'Macramé heaven,' he mumbled. 'Shag-rug nirvana.'

But I couldn't shake the idea that a house might make us happier – that settling Dante into a place of our own might even make him want a child. People change, I assured myself. While I was cleaning closets the next day, I found a present Paula had given us the year before, a blown-up snapshot of Dante and me on our wedding day, decoupaged to a rectangle of wood. I'd put it away and forgotten it. Now I tapped a nail into the wall over our bed and hung it up in roughly the same spot where Grandma would have put a crucifix. I *believed* in our marriage – our future together as a family. Pictures didn't lie. We *were* happy.

I had done all the bills and banking from the beginning. 'I'm just not into money – couldn't even tell you which drawer we keep our bankbook in,' Dante was fond of telling people. Now I began clipping coupons and adding what I could from my Grand Union checks to Grandma's wedding money. When I got our savings account to the $4,000 mark, I walked myself down to the bank and made a pinch-faced woman at a desk explain CDs and money markets and mortgage rates – over and over again until sweat formed over her top lip and I finally understood.

I kept my plan a secret from Dante, figuring I'd overwhelm him at some right moment. The more I saved, the bolder I got, throwing out glossy mail-order catalogs before Dante had a chance to see them and place an order. I hand lettered an index-card sign – 'If it's not on sale, we can't afford it' – and taped it to the refrigerator. I Crazy-Glued the soles of my clogs back on rather than buying new ones. 'Sorry,' I told Jehovah's Witnesses and Fuller Brush men. 'Not at this point in time.'

One evening, in the middle of ironing our tablecloth, I committed my most radical act of all. The TV was running a Revlon ad. Just as the commercial was convincing me to try that new makeup – right at the verge of my humming along with the jingle and wishing I looked like the woman in the ad – I walked over to the set and threw the tablecloth over the whole business. The result amazed me. Without the pictures seducing you, TV was just a powerless talking ghost.

Mr. Lamoreaux, the assistant manager at Grand Union, called me into his particleboard office and told me to sit.

I had never liked Mr. Lamoreaux, who whistled 'Hello, Dolly!' through the cracked-open door of the women employees' lounge instead of just yelling at whoever was taking too long on break. That very morning, Mr. Lamoreaux had forced a skinny old shoplifter to empty three tins of Underwood deviled ham spread from his pockets on to my conveyor belt in front of a whole storeful of customers. 'You try living on my pension check, you son of a bitch,' the old man had told Mr. Lamoreaux, just before he cried.

'I'll be blunt,' Mr. Lamoreaux told me. 'We've been watching you.'

I looked away, fingering my cowl-neck sweater. Whatever I was about to be fired for, I figured 'we' must be him and the police.

'For four months in a row now, you've had the most accurate tallies of any girl at this store,' he continued. 'We keep track.'

Being complimented felt the same as being accused. I crossed my leg and fiddled with my clog, prying apart my own repair job.

'We also like the way you conduct yourself out there on the floor. None of this foolish instigating and taking sides.'

'Yeah, well, basically, I'm a wimp.'

'A diplomat,' Mr. Lamoreaux corrected me. 'We think you have the potential to become one of us.' His basset-hound face lifted unnaturally into a smile. 'To start off, we'd like to try you out as head cashier, alternating first and second shift. We could give you a dollar five more an hour but, of course, you'd have to work some nights.'

While he talked about other possible promotions down the line, I did the math in my head. A dollar and five cents times forty hours equaled forty-two dollars a week more toward a house, minus withholding, a figure that offset the prospect of becoming part of any group that included Mr. Lamoreaux. 'So what do you think?' he said.

'I think I'll take it.'

Dear Grandma,

It's Tuesday afternoon. Ordinarily I'd be at work, but I'm getting this root canal done so I'm home taking aspirin with codeine. Last Sunday night I got a toothache you wouldn't believe. I mean, I was in PAIN! But that's not what I'm writing about. I'm writing about the present you sent.

When the UPS man delivered the package and I opened it up, I couldn't help crying. I remember those twisted candlesticks from our old house in Connecticut. I even found candles that smell exactly like the ones Ma used to keep in them. Bayberry. Things weren't always bad between Ma and Daddy. When I was little, I used to sometimes walk into a room and catch them smooching. I haven't talked to Daddy in years and years. Dante thinks both my parents are dead. He just assumed it one time and I never bothered correcting him. In a way, Daddy is dead, I guess. A dead secret – just like what I'm supposed to end up with after two more appointments with Dr. Hoskin. Don't mind me, Grandma. I guess I'm a little goofy from this codeine stuff I'm taking.

I hope you're not taking on too much, trying to clean up that whole big attic by yourself. When Dante and I get down for a visit (probably the end of this month if I can swing it), we'll help you with the heavy boxes. Don't you dare try to move them yourself.

We're doing great up here. We're both real happy and in love. Work is fine, too. I'm doing a pretty good job as head cashier, if I do say so myself. I'm the one who has to rotate the weekly schedule for everyone, so I got the idea to write

*it down in pencil first and post it in case there's problems
or complaints. Everyone really liked that. I bought a Mr.
Coffee at a yard sale (never even used!) and brought it in
for the lounge. Now everyone's bringing in plates of
goodies and plants and posters, stuff like that. It makes it
nicer with people not fighting each other. I used to wear
jeans to work, but lately I've been wearing skirts and dress
pants. The other day I asked my boss, Mr. Lamoreaux, if
we could give out an Employee of the Month award. He's
thinking about it.*

*I put up a shelf in our bedroom for the candlesticks –
drilled the holes and everything myself. I walk over and
touch them twenty times a day. They make me happy.*

Love, Dolores

*P.S. Remember – leave those boxes for when we visit. I
love you, Grandma!*

Dante started the summer of 1979 with a bad bout of
insomnia. I'd wake on and off during the night, cracking open
my eyelids to the sounds of his disgusted sighs and turning
magazine pages. He frowned and twisted as he read under the
little cone of light from his high-intensity lamp, taking the
covers with him. No, he *didn't* want to talk about anything, he
said – what was bothering him wasn't anything he could
verbalize. By then, I had $4,800 in our secret savings account.

'*How* much?' Dante asked, blinking. I hadn't meant to tell
him; I figured it might give him peace of mind and get us both
some sleep.

'Forty-eight hundred. Mim, this lady I know, says it's enough
for a down payment on a house – a smaller one.'

'Mim?'

'Mim Fisk. A real-estate lady. She comes into the store.'

I'd never actually seen Mim Fisk *in* Grand Union. She usually
picked me up out in the parking lot during my lunch hour and
drove me around to possibilities in my price range, houses that

had a lot of character but needed things like a new roof or a plumbing overhaul.

'Mim says a mortgage payment won't be that much more than monthly rent, and plus, we'll keep building equity. Just think of it, honey. We could have a nice big yard for your garden. And a room for you to write your poems in – your own little study instead of you having to drag the typewriter out to the kitchen table all the time.' I skipped the part about the baby's room.

'Equity?' he said.

'Yeah, something to fall back on. Mim explained it to me. Kind of like we're paying rent to ourselves instead of to Mrs. Wing.'

He shook his head. 'I've been thinking of taking an extended leave of absence so I can write full-time,' he said. 'In which case, a house would be out of the question.'

'Dante, be realistic. We couldn't live on just my salary – even if we didn't buy a house.'

'Well, now that you're one of the movers and shakers down at the supermarket, how long could it be before they line you up for a corporate vice president's salary?' He raised his arms into a long sleepless stretch that knocked our wedding photo off the wall and into bed with us. He looked at it and smiled. 'Here we are,' he said. 'Stuck to a board. Shellacked for life.'

I got up, yanked on my bathrobe, and went outside. I walked around and around the house, listening to the crickets and thinking of the things I *should* have said to him. Then I went back in and said them.

'Look, I'm getting sick of your sarcasm all the time.'

'Sarcasm?' He said it sarcastically.

'That shellacked-on-a-board stuff. And my work may not be as important as yours, but people say I'm doing a good job. Yesterday, Shirley brought in a plate of blond brownies and said I'd made it fun for her to come in to work, the first time in twelve years.'

'That reminds me,' Dante said. 'Your Nobel Prize came in the mail today.'

'Last week, when I asked you if you wanted to go to that cookout at Tandy and Rusty's house, you could have just said no. You didn't have to say what you said – be mean about it.'

He sighed. 'What did I say? It's so significant, I've forgotten.'

'You said you'd rather spend the afternoon coughing up blood. How do you think I felt – having to make three-bean salad and drop it off and lie to every one of my friends.'

'*Your* friends?' he said. He pretended to look under the bed.

But early the next morning, he woke me up, patting and stroking me, asking for my patience. 'I'm going through a rough time right now,' he whispered.

But you're on *vacation!* I wanted to scream. Instead, I told him to just forget it. His apology turned into sex and I clung tightly to him, my eyes on the candlestick across the room. When he was through, I burst out crying.

'Hey?' he said. 'What are the tears for?'

'Nothing,' I said. They were for my mother – for what her banged-up face had looked like the night she'd called my father a whore and he'd given her that swollen purple lip, that Chinese eye. I'd been lying there reliving that night during Dante's grunt and thrust.

'Hey, babe,' he whispered. 'You and me.'

He's nothing like Daddy, I told myself. No couple is happy all the time. He's nothing like him at all.

All that next week, Dante drove me to work so he could have the Volkswagen. One afternoon, I walked back up the hill, happily unaware. The thick orange extension cord was what I noticed first, not the harsh sound of the drill someone was running out back. I followed the cord from our kitchen window out to where the noise was painful. What I saw was painful, too. The cord ended at Dante, who was wearing plastic goggles and standing on our stool, armed with a power tool. He was drilling a hole into a shiny green van that still had its price sheet stuck to the window.

'Well,' he said. 'What do you think?'

I said I hoped he had permission to cut into whoever's van it was.

He laughed. 'It's ours, babe. I'm putting in a teardrop window.'

'What do you mean it's ours? Where's our bug?'

'Traded her in. Don't worry. I got this *below*-sale price – super deal. Bought it three days ago but there was some paperwork. Surprise!'

'You bought this thing without even telling me?'

'They install these windows for you at the dealership, but it's a rip-off. I'm saving us a good hundred and a half. You like it?'

I couldn't think of anything to say.

'You and I are going on a belated cross-country honeymoon trip. First three weeks in August.

'Dante, I . . . I can't just pack up and go on a three-week vacation. I only get a *one*-week vacation.'

'All taken care of. I called what's-his-face, your boss. He finally agreed to give you your week with pay, plus two weeks off without pay.'

'You planned my vacation without even asking me?'

'I'm putting shag carpet down on the floor. Boomer's got a remnant left over from their place. All the comforts of home, huh?'

His using the word 'home' was what woke me. I ran into the house.

He'd found which drawer the bankbook was in, all right. The balance said $671.

He came inside. Wearing those safety goggles, he looked like a giant insect. 'I wanted to leave some in there for the trip. The payments are only one fifty-five a month. . . . I figure we can camp out right on the van floor in sleeping bags, save some money. Maybe splurge once or twice and get a motel room.'

He walked over and put his hand on my rear end – cautiously, like he was testing the flatiron. 'Well,' he said. '*Say* something.'

'I thought you were going to write poems all summer. You said that's what you *needed* to do.'

'Travel will feed my writing. I figured you can take the wheel when I want to write.'

'You never even *asked* me!'

His fist whacked down against the mattress; dust specks zoomed around us. 'I thought you'd be excited about it. You think it was easy putting all this together?'

'But a lot of that was money my grandmother gave us.'

'Oh, I get it. Hands off the wedding stash because she's *my* grandmother, not yours? I never realized you were such a fucking materialist before. Little Miss Equity.'

'That's not the point. Making decisions without me is the point.'

'How about Mim whatever the fuck her name is? Doesn't she get her usual vote in this, too? Look, I wanted to surprise you with the honeymoon we never got to have. Not that our marriage needs a jump start or anything. Not that we have room for any more wedded bliss.'

Dear Grandma,

Exciting news! Dante and I decided to use your wedding money to buy a van. We're taking a cross-country trip in August. (I'll buy you a pair of Mickey Mouse ears when we get to Disneyland!) We don't know our exact route yet, but we're either planning to drive down and see you the first part of the trip or the last part. I had to give up my head-cashier position because the trip will take three weeks, but I'll still have a job there when I get back. People are always coming and going at that place, so who knows? I might be head cashier again before too long.

Sorry to hear about Mrs. Mumphy breaking her hip. I sent her a card at the hospital. Maybe you should go on that bus trip anyway. I'm sure there'll be other people you know. Take a risk! That's what Ma always used to say.

I really WASN'T crying the other morning when you called. I had a cold. (It's better now.) I'm very happy.

Love, Dolores

Dante got the carpeting in smoothly enough, but he'd cut too wide a hole for the teardrop window. On and off all one afternoon, I was required to train the garden hose at the error while Dante sat inside the van and studied the leak. Somewhere near dark, he hopped out the back, let loose a string of curses, and kicked a dent into the passenger's-side door.

'You happy now?' he shouted, forcing my hand against the dent. 'You like the feel of that? Well, you can thank all your bitching and moaning for the last several days.'

I prized my hand away. I thought he might hit me.

'That's your tactic, isn't it? Chip away at me little by little? I should jump into this thing and leave you rotting in the driveway – good fucking riddance.'

'Don't say things like that, okay? I *know* the trip will be good for us. It's just that I thought if we bought a house, then . . .'

'You're not going to be satisfied until we're in one of those prefab coffin things over there at Granite Acres. Until we have some tiny little life we can predict right up to the funeral.'

The abortion had been a choice between Dante and Vita. If he left me, I had neither of them. I had my old self back. 'You're right,' I told him. 'I felt a little disappointed at first, but it was just temporary. Don't say that about leaving, okay? I love you, Dante.'

That night he did anal sex on me out in the van. I pressed my face against the new carpet, inhaling the chemical smell and reciting things I'd memorized in school. '*Seven times eight is fifty-six, seven times nine is sixty-three . . . This is the forest primeval, the murmuring pines and the hemlocks . . .*' I winced and waited for it to be over. It was nothing like what Jack did, I told myself. This is my husband, our van. We're two consenting adults.

'Being open to new experiences is what will keep us alive,' he murmured to me afterwards, on the verge of his sleep. 'I could tell you liked that just now, felt the exact second you relaxed and went with it. You *telegraphed* your enjoyment right to me – put me on fire!'

His whispering voice was moist against my ear.

The next day I drove the van for the first time. The ride was smoother than our Volkswagen and the seats were up so high, I felt like I was levitating. The body-shop man said the dent would cost $375 to fix; I told him we needed it done before we left. I walked to the bank and withdrew two hundred more dollars. For Dante, I bought two pairs of shorts, two T-shirts, all seven volumes of the *Mobil Travel Guide*, and a leather-bound journal for his poems. I got myself a new pair of clogs and, at the drugstore, renewed my birth-control prescription.

'Anything else?' the register clerk said.

I slid the tube of first-aid cream across the counter at her. I'd had rectal bleeding that morning.

If you looked quickly at our three-inch stack of cross-country pictures (ten rolls' worth, developed free of charge at the photo lab back in Rhode Island), you'd swear Dante and I had had a wonderful time – that his plan to ignite our marriage like a camp stove had worked.

Most of the shots are of Dante, posed in the lower right half of the picture with Mt. Rushmore or the Wall Drug sign or the Magic Kingdom just over his shoulder. Even when he was in one of his moods, he transformed himself for pictures, breaking into a self-assured, Robert Wagner kind of half smile, so that what got developed was the illusion that he was content. Out of the hundreds of shots, there was one truthful picture: one of me by myself, standing in the hot-springs steam at Yellowstone Park, leaning my arm against a wooden sign that says 'Dangerous Thermal Area' and looking weary and scared. All the other photos Dante took of me were ambushes: one of me getting surprised inside the camp shower, another where I'm sleeping on the van floor with my tongue out, vulnerable as a dead woman. 'Bam! I got you!' Dante would say whenever he took a shot. If I was going to take *his* picture, he'd borrow my hairbrush first.

The photographs don't say how lonely I was, sitting up front, driving the van through whole states while Dante sat cross-legged, snickering at some book, some private joke between him and an author. Or writing out his private thoughts, his black Flair pen squeaking along on the oversized pages of the leather-bound journal. It was thinking about distances that made me so lonely – how Nebraska went on forever one day, how far away I was from Grandma and from Grandma's idea of what my life was like. Looking from a distance at those purple Bighorn Mountains made me wonder about God again: if he was real, if he was too far away to matter. For whole days on that trip, Dante, sitting beside me, was as distant as those mountains.

'You're trapped by your own lies is what it is,' I told myself in the rearview mirror one twilight. 'Gracewood, Kippy, how you got pregnant with Vita Marie – that whole rat's nest of secrets.' We were parked in a supermarket lot someplace in California and Dante was on his way inside for groceries. I watched the automatic doors close behind him. 'You've got all that distance because you've never been honest with him – not once, not since before you even met him.'

He usually slid his journal under the seat when he wasn't writing in it, but this time he'd forgotten to put it away. There it sat, within easy reaching distance. Between the leather covers might be his real thoughts: why he got so angry, why he'd married me, what he felt. I could see him in the store, wheeling his cart. It would be so easy.

I shook with the choice I gave myself: I could be the same girl sitting in that empty classroom back at St. Anthony's School, undoing the clasp on Miss Lilly's pocketbook – the fat, wrecked girl locked in the toilet stall at Hooten Hall, prying the flap off Dante's stolen letters. Or somebody else. Somebody better. The person Dr. Shaw and I had started but never finished.

I looked in at Dante, fourth or fifth back in a line of customers, two thicknesses of plate glass away. I scraped an emery board across my fingernails. Listened to my breathing. Left the journal unread.

Chapter 24

There were miracles on the road.

At a snack bar at the top of Pike's Peak, I asked for real milk, not powdered, for my coffee. The waitress said they couldn't keep real milk on the top of the mountain, that it went bad – something about the altitude.

'Isn't that odd?' a woman said to me. She was at the table next to us, she and her husband. 'About the milk? I ordered the exact same thing a minute ago. I couldn't help overhearing.'

Anyone but me up there on that mountain would have just looked over and seen an ordinary, friendly tourist couple. But it *wasn't* anyone else. It was *me*, looking right directly at my coffin-picture people, Mr. and Mrs. J. J. Fickett from Tepid, Missouri. I even recognized Mrs. Fickett's polka-dot halter top; she'd worn it in one of their series I'd developed. It was a powerful moment for me, one of the most powerful moments of my life if I'd chosen to use it. 'Why, Mr. and Mrs. Fickett,' I could have said. 'Have you been taking any more of your casket pictures lately?' They would have probably run screaming right off the mountain. Of course, I didn't. I didn't say a word, not even to Dante. How could I?

Vita Marie would have passed her first birthday while we were on the road. One early morning, in a campground shower stall, I closed my eyes and saw her, heard her – so vividly, it felt like a visit. She was plain and real and had my eyes: a chubby, brown-haired little thing in red corduroy overalls. I felt the ribbing of the material, smelled her smell. She took a step, then ka-boomed backward to the floor, sitting in her own surprise. I closed my eyes against the spray and leaned to the wall, laughing out loud. Who'd sent me this gift? Ma? God? Vita Marie herself?

On the return route through New Mexico and Arkansas and Tennessee, I only half noticed what was around me; I was more interested in what was ahead. I'd start up our house fund again, I decided, as soon as we paid off the trip bills. Dante and I might have our own home by 1981 or '82, and maybe a baby by the following year. Now that this trip was out of his system. Now that school was starting up again.

Dear Grandma,
    I can't believe I've gotten to see so much of the country. Remember back in high school when I was scared to even leave my bedroom? There's more to tell you about our trip than I can fit on a postcard. We're planning a visit this fall. I'll bring all our pictures! Dante and I are fine and happy. Love, D.

Driving past the 'New England and East' sign, Dante sighed and said he'd be glad to get home over with.

'That's a strange way of putting it,' I said. His jaw locked and his hands tightened around the wheel.

We got back to Montpelier in late afternoon. The down-town streets were steamy and slick from a shower we'd just missed. Even shut up for three weeks, the apartment smelled good to me. I grabbed Dante as he walked in with our suitcases. 'I love you, honey,' I said, squeezing him tight. 'Thank you for our trip.'

'Too bad we're not still on it,' he said.

Afterward, I sat sifting through old mail and newspapers and back-to-school circulars. 'Well,' I said. 'Eight more days for you and two for me and we're back to the grind.'

'Yup,' he said.

Then he snatched the keys to the van and disappeared until midnight.

That was the first hint that Dante was keeping secrets, too. Well, one secret – one big one that was already a whole summer old.

'I guess I better tell you,' he said. I had just come back from shopping for his back-to-school clothes. He was standing next to me, not taking the bag with his two new shirts in it.

'Tell me what?'

'I lost my job.'

'Lost it?' I sat down, the wind knocked out. 'What do you mean?'

'They fired me. In June.'

'In June? . . . Why didn't you . . . What's going on?'

He sat down and put his hands to his face. 'Ev Downs and his vigilante committee. They got me.'

'Dante, I still don't—'

'I said it all along, remember? That he'd get me if he ever got a chance.' With his arm, he smeared the tears across his face. 'I wanted to just drive us away, to protect you from all the gossip – from that fishbowl where you work. But I'm exhausted from keeping it in. It fucked up the whole trip.'

I took his hand and squeezed it to stop my own shaking. 'Okay,' I said. 'Okay.' I was taking deep breaths. 'Gossip about *what?*'

'There's this kid, Sheila, all right? A student in my American lit class two years ago. She was a senior this past year. Used to come around to talk about her problems, that kind of thing. So the last day of school, I'm sitting at my desk correcting exams and she comes into my room. It must have been three-thirty, quarter of four. I thought I was the only one in the building. She said she wanted to talk to me. Boyfriend problems – she was confused. So we went for a ride out to Barre, to the quarry.'

'Just the two of you?'

'I was tired of correcting,' he said. 'I needed to get out of that building. It was just to talk.'

'Then what happened?'

He looked up at me. 'What happened?' he repeated. 'Well, whose version do you want – mine or the PTA cunt who decided to "come forward" a week after the fact about what she saw?' He laughed bitterly. 'Did I say fact just then? I meant fiction.'

I wanted us to be in the van, a thousand miles away from what I was hearing. 'What did she tell them, Dante?'

'Let's just say I'm accused of breaching the sacred trust.'

'Dante, skip the fancy vocabulary and—'

'Kissing her. Feeling her tits. According to this bitch, we had quite a time out there.'

He started to cry. 'I swear to God, Dolores, we were just *out* there. I never so much as touched the tip of her sleeve.'

I thought I could hear the truth in his quivering voice. We were both in tears.

'Hastings and my good buddy Ev called me into school the first week of vacation. Introduced me to the Board of Ed's attorney – this mutant asshole who looked like he just stepped off the set of *Deliverance*. They gave me two choices: a statutory rape charge or clean out my desk.'

'But why didn't you just tell me, Dante? Maybe I could have—'

'Could have what?' he said. 'Overcharged one of my accusers down at the fucking Grand Union? Thrown their canned goods in the bag on top of the tomatoes? You realize what a public hearing would be like? How much fun it would be to see me skewered on the front page of the fucking *Times-Argus*? I didn't tell you because I wanted to protect you from it. And because . . . because I thought you'd believe—' Now his crying came out as weird, strangled gulping. I sat down and hugged him, rocked myself against him. 'We'll fight it,' I said.

'They had me by the balls. I'm gone. I'm out of there.'

'But Dante, they can't just accept someone else's word without letting you defend yourself. What about the girl? Don't they believe *her*?'

'Who, Sheila? Sheila can't tell the difference between wishful thinking and reality. Sheila is officially "confused" about what went on.'

'I'll *help* you fight it, Dante. We'll get a good lawyer and—'

'You want to help?' he said. 'Just stay out of it. Just let it alone – that's how you can help. Take the fucking shirts back and get your goddamned refund. I've already *talked* to a lawyer; he says I might as well hang it up.'

'Why?'

'Just . . . just drop it.'

'But what are you going to do?'

'Take a rest for a while – get my shit together. Then, I don't know – I guess I'll look for another job.'

'Yeah, but that's exactly why you need to clear this up, honey. No school is going to hire you if they think—'

'They won't know about it. That was part of the deal they cut me.'

'What deal?'

'If I left quietly, didn't go to the union or anything, it wouldn't go on my record. No mess, no publicity.'

'But they're forcing you to say it was true!'

'It's the way I want to do it.'

'Dante, you're not thinking clearly. I mean, here you are out of a job and we go off and spend all that money on—'

'Oh, Jesus,' he said. 'You're too much.'

'Well, Dante, what happens if you don't get another job right away? The payments on the van alone are—'

'Do me a favor, will you? Just shut up. Go fuck yourself.'

Dear Grandma,

You mentioned in your last letter that you almost forgot what I look like, so I'm sending you this picture of Dante and me taken on our wedding day. (A friend of ours decoupaged it for us.) Maybe you can put it up on the stair wall with the other family pictures.

I promise we'll get down for a visit sometime before the fall is over, Grandma, but right now we're both so busy! I

*have this nice idea for when we do visit. Why don't you
and I drive down to the beach and take a little walk? It's
pretty down there this time of the year, after all the crowds
clear out. We'd have the whole beach to ourselves. Dante
and I will probably have to come down on a Sunday and
leave that same night because I got a second job
waitressing Friday and Saturday nights at the Lobster Pot
(the place where we got married). They were able to juggle
my schedule at the grocery store so I could swing both. It's
a little hectic, but I don't mind. Whenever I get overtired,
I just concentrate on the house Dante and I are saving for.
One bad thing about being on my feet is that I'm getting
varicose veins. Didn't Ma have them, too?*

*Oh, by the way, did I mention that Dante was taking a
leave of absence from teaching for a little while? He wants
to spend some time writing poetry. (He's very talented.) I
got new curtains for the kitchen – yellow Priscillas. They
look nice, except I hemmed them too short by about an
inch. Oh, well – live with your mistakes, right?*

Love, Dolores

Dante's plan was to get his head together until springtime or
so by writing poetry and reading his way through a list of
classics he'd always meant to get to. He began sending his poems
to magazines with freaky-sounding names. Each rejection slip
they sent him shut him down for days. His reading program
stalled early on when he couldn't get through Montaigne's
Essays, but he refused to leapfrog to the next book.

If I didn't dillydally at the store on Friday afternoons when
my shift was over, I had just enough time to vacuum and pick
up before rushing down to the Lobster Pot in time for my
setups. Dante meant to keep up with the housework, but he was
suffering on and off from writer's block, he said, and couldn't
create a proper internal environment if he had to worry about
Tidy-Bowling the toilet. He said he would have thought
someone who'd been a watercolor artist herself could sym-

pathize about the creative process – that next time around, he'd look for a wife who wasn't anal-retentive. I shut my mouth and cleaned.

'So how was work today?' he always asked me, lying on the bed, stretching from his afternoon nap. He'd begun to be hungry for details about my coworkers, who he called 'the mental midgets.' After a while I withheld news; it felt like I was feeding him their lives.

'Oh, nothing much. How was your day?'

He followed me into the bathroom, peeling a banana. 'Depressing. I was just cranking up on a new poem when some dipshit called, trying to sell us a storage freezer. Writing is a lot like daydreaming, you know? There's a subconscious connection. Once someone intrudes, it's like trying to go back to sleep to finish your dream.' He yawned so wide I saw the chewed-up banana.

At the sink, I scratched at a salad-dressing stain that was still in my waitress uniform. 'I see you didn't get a chance to go to the laundromat after all, huh?'

He watched me with contempt while I climbed into my uniform, towel dabbed at the wet spot, struggled with the back zipper. 'You know what I find depressing?' he said. 'Your love of whatever's perfunctory. Your deep respect for the mundane.'

I told him I was late. He followed me out to the van. When I opened the door, he slammed it shut again.

'Dante, I'm *late*.'

'Oh, excuse me, great important one. May I ask just one quick question? Why is it that every time I talk to you, I get more depressed?'

'I'm sorry, Dante. I'm trying. We'll talk about it.'

'Whoopie,' he scoffed. 'Something to look forward to all evening.'

'Look, you said you didn't want to fight back when they accused you. Okay – I would've if it was me, but I respected your decision. Only now you're always fighting *me* instead. It's just not fair.'

His eyes welled up; he went back in the house. I looked at my watch, got in and started up the van, then cut the motor again.

I sat down on the bed next to him. 'Dante,' I said. 'I know this is hard for you, honest to God. We can talk later, but right now I really have to go. If I'm not there to do setups, then Myrna—'

'So go.'

I kissed his forehead and stood up, straightening myself. 'I feel so ugly in this uniform,' I said. 'Do I look okay?'

He answered without looking. 'You're a vision in blue nylon,' he said. 'A frigging goddess in wedgies.'

In November, Dante cut off his beard and began a daily ritual that included crossword puzzles and word scrambles. I was pretty sure he was into the soaps, too. Sometimes when I'd come home from work, the TV was warm and once I caught him humming the theme song to 'Days of Our Lives.' In spite of his vegetarianism, he won us a free Thanksgiving turkey from the radio station for knowing who recorded the song 'Cool Jerk.' But when I suggested we drive down to Grandma's with it, he said he'd prefer not to spend the holiday 'as traditionally as the fucking Waltons.'

I got in the habit of hand washing whatever I'd worn to work that day and Dante cut down his laundry by wearing the same thing every day: khaki pants, gray sweatshirt, and no underwear. His housework had whittled itself down to just dusting and baking – braided breads and cream-rich desserts that he ate most of himself. He was usually too exhausted to tackle the dishes after supper, so that I had to soap and scour the dried-on batter and stack towers of bowls and pans on to the drainboard while he listened to National Public Radio or played with his Rubik's cube.

One afternoon I got home from work just as he was coming out of the shower. I watched in amazement as he jiggled naked across the room.

'What are you staring at?' he said. My eyes shot away from the overhang around his waist, the puckers in his rear end.

I knew what fat and isolation could do, how they could turn you into a person you hated. 'Nothing,' I said.

'No, what? Tell me.'

'Well,' I said, 'it just looks like you're putting on a little weight, that's all.'

He didn't speak to me for a week.

Dear Grandma,

Thanks for the support stockings you sent me and for the Christmas-shopping $$$. I'm planning to use it for one of those maxi-coats that everyone's wearing now. It gets COLD up here in winter. The stockings really help! A woman I know at work had varicose veins so bad that she had to have an operation. They pull them right out of you and it's real painful, she says. Maybe someday I'll get a job where I can sit down at a desk all day with my shoes off and my feet up. I wish!

We sold our van two weeks ago and bought a used Vega. It's got ripped-up seats but the engine is good. We got $2,100 for the van. The dealer said we could have gotten more if Dante hadn't had an accident – this guy cut right out in front of him but, for some reason, the stupid cop gave Dante the summons. I put the difference ($1,375) in the bank. It's light green. (The Vega, not the bank – ha-ha.) I guess our visit will have to wait until after the holidays, Grandma, because there are a zillion Christmas parties booked at the restaurant and I can't really say no to overtime. January looks like a possibility. When I come down, can we go through the attic and look at some of Ma's and your old things? I'll let you try on my new maxi-coat! I miss you and love you, Grandma. I think about you every day.

Love, Dolores

We rang in 1980 sitting on barstools in Boomer and Paula's living room, but left shortly after midnight, after Dante, drunk on Harvey Wallbangers, told Paula she reminded him of a car horn that had gotten stuck and she told him she'd rather be a car horn than a child molester. Boomer and I got the coats.

Mrs. Wing and Chadley were understanding about the hole Dante punched in our bedroom wall that night. On the ride home from the emergency room, Dante sobbed and told me I was the best thing that ever happened to him and from that point on, he was going to prove it to me. The following afternoon, I took the ornaments off our little fake tree while Dante sat at the kitchen table scrawling his New Year's resolutions with his left hand since his right one was in the cast. The penmanship wobbled diagonally down the page. '1. Think positive. 2. Lose weight. 3. Write at least one new poem a week. 4. Exercise. 5. *Prove* my love to D.'

'What do you think?' he asked me.

'Maybe you put down too many. Why don't you just work on one or two?'

His face hardened against me while he stared. 'Do you *always* have to defeat me?' he said.

'Dante, I—'

He balled up his fist and bounced the paper ball against my face.

'I'm not the one who fired you,' I said. 'Stop it.' He picked the paper ball off the floor and did it again.

'You do that one more time and I'll—'

'You'll what?' he said. He slapped me softly on the face.

He was my father, after all – doing to me what Daddy had done to Ma. I slapped him back, hard as I could.

'Get this straight,' I said. 'I'm not your goddamned whipping girl. Don't you *ever* lay your hand on me like that again!'

By springtime, Dante's energy level suddenly, unexpectedly, increased. He decided to revive both his garden out in the backyard and his reading of great books. He reorganized the kitchen cabinets, waxed the floors, and, with his spare energy, began a daily jogging regimen. A literary magazine called

Zirconia wrote him that they were publishing one of his poems, 'Reawakening.' That night he reached for me in bed. 'Now let's see if we can remember what goes where,' he said.

He was as kind and slow with me as he'd been that first summer and I pushed away all my anger and hurt and distrust because he owed me love. The worst of it's over, I thought, if we can lie together and be this way again. The warm gentleness began to collect itself around his slow fingers and his kisses lost their feeling to that other, better feeling and then I was there, releasing, released.

I reached down and guided him in. He started slowly, easily, and I wrapped my legs around him and hooked my ankles together against his back. He pumped faster and faster; his warm breath was in my face, his eyes open and looking at me. I reached out for his arm. 'Honey?' I said. 'Maybe we better . . . I haven't been renewing my prescription . . .'

'This feels too good to stop,' he said. 'This feels like we're breaking a curse.'

'I know, Dante, but if we don't . . .'

'If we don't . . .' he panted.

'Stop . . .' I muttered. He pulled out, groaning. His penis bounced and jerked against my belly and he laughed and watched his semen ooze and trickle down my side. He kissed my neck and eyelids. He wiped my belly with his frayed gray sweatshirt.

'George if it's a girl and Martha if it's a boy,' he said. 'Jody if it's a hermaphrodite.'

'Don't joke about babies, Dante, okay?'

'I may not be joking,' he said. 'It's one of the things I've been thinking about lately. Babies and work.'

We've outlasted it! I thought. But when I spoke, I was cautious. 'What do you mean?'

'I took this book out of the library: *What Color Is Your Parachute?* It's about career change. How would you like to be married to a social worker?'

I'd wanted him to talk about the babies part. 'What's a hermaprodite?' I said.

'Her*maph*rodite, not her*map*rodite. It's one of life's ambiguities.'

'Oh.'

That weekend I lied and told the Lobster Pot I was sick. By Sunday morning, I felt so frisky and sure we were out of trouble that I decided to go with Dante on his daily jog. I lasted through warm-ups and the downhill swoop out our driveway toward town. But by the first incline, my lungs burned, and a stitch pulled at my side. 'Go on ahead,' I panted. 'I can't make it.' I watched him get smaller and smaller all the way down State Street.

On Monday mornings down at Grand Union, Tandy and I did the magazine racks together. One week that fall, Elvis Presley – dead over three years already – was suddenly on the covers of *People* and all the tabloids. The fat-faced Elvis, Elvis in white and spangles.

'What have they dug up on poor old Porky Pig now?' Tandy said.

I thumbed through the first paragraphs. 'They arrested that doctor who supplied him all his drugs. It says Elvis was a pill addict.'

'Big whoop,' Tandy said.

All that morning, the fruit in aisle one seemed to vibrate with color. The fluorescent light on those shiny Elvis magazine covers made my head hurt. Something felt wrong.

On my lunch break I took copies of those magazines to the lounge. One article said Elvis's pigging out and pills was a kind of suicide, but that no one had read the signs, his calls for help. Two weeks before he died, all the stories agreed, Elvis had swum up from a deep depression and begun a frenzy of racquetball and promises to his fiancée. Some psychiatrist in another article said it was a pattern – that people committed suicide just when their lives started on an upswing and you thought their problems were licked. Suicide required an enormous amount of energy, that doctor said.

'What's the matter?' Tandy asked. 'You're all white.'

'Tell Mr. Lamoreaux I had to go home.'

I ran down Main Street, the very worst pictures flashing in my head: Dante lying in the bathtub in red water, Dante blue and hanging from the closet door. 'Oh, please . . .' I kept saying. 'Please, God.' By the time I reached the top of our hill, I knew every mistake I'd made with him – every single sign I'd missed.

My key kept missing the lock, skidding off the metal. With both hands, I finally got it in and twisted. I ran through the apartment.

They were sitting on the bed watching TV. Dante was eating a hot dog.

'Hey!' he said, choking on a mouthful. 'What are you – ?'

She had long strawberry-blond hair, a roof of bangs that ended just over her big, scared eyes. She was sitting cross-legged, wearing a sweater, Dante's red down vest, underpants, and knee socks. Dante had his shirt off.

'If . . . if you're wondering why I'm eating meat,' he said. 'It's an experiment. *Runner's World* says two or three days before a race you should superproteinize your system.'

I looked from him back to her. 'You're Sheila?'

But she wouldn't answer.

'She's having a hard time at home. She needed to talk, Dolores.'

'With her pants off? How long have you two been doing this here?

Dante closed his eyes. 'To whom are you speaking?' he said.

'Whom schmoom!' I screamed. 'Get her the fuck out of here!'

She hopped toward the door, pulling on her jeans. When I heard the car doors slam, I ran out after them. Dante was backing out of the driveway, his head twisted around; she was staring at me, wide-eyed. I slung fistfuls of driveway gravel at them. The stones clicked and bounced off the windshield.

'Son of a bitch,' I kept screaming. 'You son of a bitch!'

*

For the next few days, whenever the phone rang, I picked it up and slammed it back down again before he had a chance to speak.

But he wouldn't stop trying.

'What do you want?' I finally screamed into the receiver one night. 'Say it fast and then stop bothering me!'

'We have to talk.'

'Bullshit. I don't plan on talking to you for the rest of my life.'

I kept that promise for six days, then located him at his parents' house in New Jersey. There was a long wait before he got to the phone.

'Yes?' he said.

'Uh, it's me,' I said. 'Could you come back? I really need you.'

He didn't answer for a minute. Then he said, 'Look, I've been giving this a lot of thought. Maybe for the time being, we should—'

'I just got a call. My grandmother died. I don't know what to do.'

Chapter 25

Dante drove all night to get back to me. I met him out in the driveway and he squeezed me hard, let up, then tightened his hold again.

We were polite and formal with each other while he drank his coffee and assembled some funeral clothes on a wire hanger.

He carried my overnight bag to the car. 'You must be exhausted,' I said. 'I can drive.'

He touched my shoulder and opened the passenger's-side door for me. 'Let me take care of you, babe. I want to do that.'

All the way down and out of Vermont, he kept reaching over for my hand. His hand felt heavy and numbing. I didn't consciously keep letting go, but I must have, because he kept reaching.

An hour or so into the ride, he turned off the radio. 'Tell me what you're thinking,' he said.

'Oh, nothing much.' What I was thinking was that maybe it was a blessing Vita Marie didn't exist – that if I had allowed her to become a person, I would have failed her. I'd failed both Ma and Grandma – most likely Dante, too, though in ways less obvious. Things always cleared up for me once the person I loved was dead.

'Nothing?'

'I was just thinking what a shitty granddaughter I was to her.'

'How do you mean?'

'I never visited her. She was lonesome.'

He explained to me why my guilt was illogical in a lecture

that lasted past several turnpike exits; it was a lot less comforting than Casey Kasem had been. I asked him if I could turn
the radio back on.

'I know what you need,' he said.

He took his eyes off the road and reached amidst the backseat
clutter for something. With no particular sense of panic, I
watched our car swerve and weave toward the shoulder, a rock
ledge, and then back again. What he was hunting for landed in
my lap: a thick brown book with a grease-stained cover.

'Des-cartes?'

'Day-*cart*. He's French; the *s*'s are silent. What he says is
directly relevant to what you're feeling. It invalidates your guilt.
Read it.'

'I don't want to read it.'

His smile was the one I imagined him using with slow
learners at school. 'Because you'd prefer to flagellate yourself?'

'Because reading in a moving car makes me puke.'

'You wrote or called her every week, Dolores. I must have
heard you tell her a hundred times to take a bus up and see us.'

'Yeah, because I knew she wouldn't *do* it,' I argued. 'I knew
she was scared to travel by herself after that time she came up
for the wedding.' I began to make a case for Grandma's fear,
but lost track of my point and ended up describing that black
man with his dashiki and his religion of forgiveness – how
Grandma's hand had gotten tangled in his hair, how the feeling
had left her with a sense of wonder.

Dante took my hand again. 'Speaking of forgiveness,' he said.
'I'm not saying I deserve it, just that I'm applying. I need you,
babe.'

His words had burned me more times than they'd soothed
me. I cautioned myself not to be taken in by this verbal
Noxzema. 'Why is that, Dante?' I said. 'For as long as we've
been together, all you've done is criticize and correct the way I
pronounce things. Am I your personal dumping ground or
something? Is that what you need me for?'

His smile was patient. 'I was rereading Thoreau last week.

Walden. It's amazing how Henry can remind you of what's sublime and what's—'

'Answer the question,' I said.

'I need you because you're you,' he said. 'With Sheila it was just sex. A conquest – a type of materialism, really. Pleasurable only until the muscle spasm was over, then – boom! – the same quiet desperation. I was a fool to jeopardize what we've built together. Mea culpa.'

'Oh, mea culpa! Mia Farrow!' I made my hand a fist and snatched it away. 'That sounds real fancy, Dante. What about that poor girl? For you it was a muscle spasm. What was it for her?'

'Babe, kids today are nihilists – that's what you're not understanding here. They're not like us. For one thing, they're brain dead politically. Party hardy: nothing beyond that. And I stupidly bought into it. Temporary insanity, Dolores – *temporary*. For Sheila it was an afternoon fuck, something to do instead of watching 'General Hospital.' I doubt she attached anything more to it than that.'

'So that would make *your* guilt illogical, too, just like mine about my grandmother, right? Gee, Dante, this is all pretty convenient.' I rolled down the window and threw his book out.

He braked instinctively, then stepped on the gas again. 'Okay,' he said. 'Okay, I'll allow you the extravagance of that overreaction.'

'Gee, thanks,' I said. 'Babe.'

'Just remember one thing,' he said. '*You* called *me* for help and I came. I'm sitting in this car next to you. I'm here.'

At the funeral home I came face to face with the same smiling, bug-eyed undertaker who had slid along the walls at my mother's wake eleven years before. Seeing him ripped the scab right off Ma's death. Dante and Bug Eyes did the talking; I nodded and signed forms.

Calling hours were that night from seven to nine, her funeral mass the next morning at eleven. 'Would you like me to step forward at the grave site and invite people back to the house after the burial?'

I looked at Dante. 'What do you think?'

He rubbed my arm. 'It's up to you, babe,' he said.

'No, then.'

'The service will be over just before lunchtime,' Bug Eyes said.

'Okay, fine. Whatever you say.'

'Fine. Now, would you like to see the body while you're here? We received it yesterday afternoon. It's been prepared.'

'Do me a favor, will you?' I said. 'Stop talking about my grandmother like she's an order of Kentucky Fried Chicken.'

Bug Eyes told Dante there was absolutely no need to apologize, that death angered loved ones because it made them feel powerless.

Everything was gray in the room where he'd put her: the rug, the wallpaper, the coffin he'd pushed me to select over the phone from Vermont. It looked like Grandma was lying in some cold twilight place. The whole room seemed covered with frost.

The rosary beads they'd twisted and looped around her knotty hands were her everyday amber ones, not the good wine-red ones she took out of their velvet case at Easter and Christmas – the ones Grandma herself would have chosen for this occasion. Mrs. Mumphy and her daughter had gone to Grandma's house to pick out her clothes. She had on the green print dress she'd worn to our wedding. I forced my eyes up to her wax-museum face. Death or the undertaker had relaxed her facial muscles. She was and wasn't Grandma.

During the ride from the funeral parlour to the house on Pierce Street, I pointed lefts and rights without speaking. 'This one,' I told him. 'This gray house.' He eased the car into the alley and I felt my stomach heave.

It was suddenly obvious to me why I'd resisted visiting: Easterly made me, once again, who I had been. Erased all my work at Gracewood and the life I'd made in Vermont. Dante carrying my overnight bag was Daddy carrying my suitcases up the front-porch steps and abandoning me. I walked behind him with the odd sensation that Dante and I were pretend people, Barbie and Ken, and that the real Dolores – the raped fat girl – hadn't gotten away after all. Was watching us from behind the curtain.

'Phone!' Dante said as I pushed the key into the lock. 'Hurry!' He ran toward its ringing. Hesitantly, I stepped inside.

At first I thought burglars had been there.

My steps clattered through the nearly empty downstairs rooms, Dante's telephone voice echoing in the background. The dining-room set was missing, and the mahogany china closet that had taken up half the hallway, and Grandma's cabinet-model TV. Afternoon sun lit up the living room and its two remaining articles of furniture: her overstuffed maroon chair and something new – a waterbed. Disoriented, I sat down on it and waited for the swaying to subside.

In her very last letter, Grandma had mentioned something about a church tag sale and a truck coming to take away some of her old things, but I hadn't pictured this full-scale emptiness. Cars passing by outside vibrated the walls. Dante's steps thundered into the room.

'That was the lawyer,' he said. 'She wants to touch down with us while we're here. I set it up for nine tomorrow morning.'

'If people are coming back here, we'll have to get food ready. Call back and cancel.'

'She says it'll take less than half an hour. We can squeeze it all in. Didn't I see a deli across the street? There must be a bakery around here, right? I don't imagine there'll be a cast of thousands coming.'

He sat down next to me on the bed. We rose and fell, rose and fell, with the shifting water.

'Why did she buy this bed?' I said. 'I don't get it.'

'Maybe it was for her back or something. By the way, I like

this place. Spartan. It's got definite possibilities.'

'It used to be more cluttered,' I said. 'She must have known she was going to die.'

He flopped backward. 'What do we have, about three and a half, four hours before the wake? Maybe I'll take a nap. I'm beat.' He reached up and started massaging the small of my back. 'You okay?'

I looked back at his smile. 'Thank you for helping,' I said. 'Driving me down and everything.'

'You don't have to thank me, babe. I'm your husband.'

'I'm not sleeping with you tonight,' I said.

The massaging stopped. 'Okay, fine. I can be patient. We have all the time in the world. Only I think, if we're going to ever . . .'

'I'll be upstairs,' I said. 'Take your nap.'

Ma's bedroom had blank, bald walls, empty bureau drawers, empty closets. Anger rose in me, filled me up. What harm would it have done to let her stuff wait up here until I was ready to claim it? The emptiness was a betrayal, a slap in the face. 'Goddamnit, Grandma,' I said.

She had left my old room intact. Console television, green plaid bedspread, chair by the window. I'd sat up here for six years, looking angrily out at life and trying to eat away pain. I saw it clearly now: why Ma had fought so hard for me to go to college – had let my awful words bloody her up during those battles about my going off to school. Ma had understood the danger of Grandma's house – how heavy furniture and drapes drawn on the world could absorb a person until she was freakish and mean and trapped. Ma had wanted college to set me free. However badly I'd messed up down in Pennsylvania, going there had launched me, had gotten me away. I saw my mother standing there, steak knife in hand after she'd cut the cord on my TV. Ma, a warrior of love.

I walked over to the bureau. Holding my breath, I pulled out the bottom bureau drawer and removed the folded sheets. 'I love Bernice Holland. Sincerely, Alan Ladd,' it still said. Happy, relieved, I sat down on the bed and cried.

The truth was, Grandma *had* given me enough time to get down here and claim what I wanted. I imagined her struggling down the stairs with those heavy cartons, defying her bad heart because she'd needed to get her business in order. She'd had a *right* to empty rooms. She had loved me the way she could.

I slid the bolt and opened the door to the landing, walking the six stairs to the third-floor apartment. Grandma had kept it locked and vacant since the afternoon Jack and Rita snuck away. Like a graveyard-shift policeman, I checked the knob, then walked back down again.

If Dante was sleeping soundly, I decided, I'd write a note and go to the funeral parlour myself. The people at the wake would be the same white-haired St. Anthony's women who knew what a mess I'd made of myself, who'd sat at Ma's wake and watched me scream Daddy out of my life for good. That funeral-parlour room was the last place I'd seen him. Dante thought my father was dead.

He hadn't fallen asleep. I found him at the bottom of the stairs, studying the photograph of Ma and Geneva, teenagers in their white dresses. 'They're beautiful,' he said. 'Who are they?'

'One of them's my mother.'

He pointed to Geneva and I shook my head. 'Oh, right,' he nodded. 'Now I see the resemblance. You have her beauty.'

'Yeah, sure,' I said.

'You *do*. You just don't see it.' He leaned the back of his head against the wall so that it looked like he was balancing family pictures on each of his shoulders. 'I don't know if you've given it any thought yet, Dolores, but I imagine this house is yours now. Any idea what you're going to do with it?'

'Get rid of it,' I said. 'I don't want it.'

'I thought having a house was your dream.'

'Not this house.'

He wrapped an arm around me and kissed my forehead. He'd

touched me more in the past six hours than he had in six months.

'I love you, Dolores,' he whispered, kissing my neck, my ear.

'Then there's my job,' I said. 'Could you please stop doing that?'

He let go and walked up two more stairs, looking at more pictures. 'Here's what I was thinking,' he said. 'Maybe we could start over again down here – this could be exactly the chance we need. I could get another teaching job. There's nothing on my record.'

'What about me?'

He reached down and traced my elbow with his thumb. 'Every grocery store in the world needs clerks, babe.'

I sat on a chair, looking down at Grandma's front door. Late-afternoon sun was coming through the oval of glass, creating an oblong patch of light on the hallway runner. 'Did you marry me because of the abortion?' I said. 'Were you just being noble?'

'I married you because I loved you. *Love* you. Present tense.'

'How can you love me if you think of me as just some stupid checkout girl?'

'You're not stupid. You're . . . unfettered. Want to hear a secret?'

I didn't want to. It might make my own secrets start coming out – make the fat girl throw open her bedroom door and start blurting.

'The truth is,' he continued, 'I envy you sometimes. I wish I could shed some of my own complexity. It's like a heavy weight I carry around, a burden. Your simplicity is . . . well, it's Thoreau-like. Which is why you're so good for me.'

'What's that supposed to mean?'

'You keep me in touch. You keep me honest.'

'You're *not* honest,' I said. 'You told me you hadn't done what they accused you of and I believed you. Then you brought her home and did it with her in our bed. Having nothing on your record is a *lie!*'

He bent his head down against his knees and rubbed the back

of his neck. Then he straightened up again and lifted our
wedding picture off the wall. He looked at it while he spoke.
'Believe me, Dolores, you're not accusing me of anything I
haven't accused myself of. If anything, you're being easier on
me than I'm being on myself.'

'Yeah, right,' I said.

He came up to where I was sitting and squeezed next to me
on the stair. He closed his eyes and kissed the picture. 'Love/Us,'
he said.

He sat there and watched me cry.

I didn't want to touch what was in the refrigerator; the perish-
ables were too close to Grandma, food she would have bought
only days ago. While Dante was out running – 'blowing off
negative energy' as he put it – I heated up canned food in the
old, familiar pans. All my Vermont letters to her were in the
phone-book drawer, held together by a rubber band. I kept
looking up from my handwriting – the Cinderella accounts I'd
given her of my marriage – afraid I'd see her watching me from
the doorway, peeking at me the way she used to after the rape.
If there *was* some sort of all-knowing afterlife, then Grandma
knew by now that those letters were lies, that Dante and I had
nothing like the life I'd invented for her. For myself. In a way, I
deserved Dante's dishonesty. Dolores Price: the biggest fat liar
on earth.

'I feel a hundred per cent better,' Dante said when he burst back
inside in a swirl of cool air. His face was flushed and healthy,
covered with a glaze of sweat. He looked almost trustworthy.

We stood up each time pairs and trios of churchwomen struggled
up from the casket kneeler and hobbled over to shake our hands.

'Honestly, she looked so good at bingo two weeks ago. When
I picked up the paper that morning and read it . . .'

'This fella of yours is a doll, ain't he? My husband's people
were from Vermont. Rutland.'

They sat in their chairs, visiting with each other, occasionally smiling at Dante and me. They spoke loudly for the ones who were hard of hearing. No one said anything mean. No one gave me away.

Near the end, I looked away from a whispered conversation with Dante and saw, at the coffin, a small man in a belted trench coat. His plaid fedora sat on the kneeler next to him while he prayed. Then he made the sign of the cross and walked over towards us.

Dante and I stood up. 'I'm Dante Davis and this is my wife, Dolores,' Dante said, extending his hand. 'We appreciate your coming. Dolores is Mrs. Holland's granddaughter.'

'Dolores?' the man said. 'How are you?'

He'd shrunk some and had given up wearing the toupee. It was his worried brown eyes I recognized. 'Oh, my God,' I said. 'Mr. Pucci!'

I hugged him harder than I should have; his bones felt as light as a bird's.

He examined me at arm's length. 'You look wonderful,' he said.

I brushed away the idea. 'How's school?'

'Oh, it's still there,' he said smiling. 'I'm sorry about your grandmother. I'll miss her Christmas card this year.'

'What Christmas card?'

'Oh, she sent me one faithfully every year since you graduated. Kept me posted on your various activities.' He smiled at Dante. 'Vermont's a beautiful state. A friend of mine and I drive up for the foliage every year.'

'Gary?' I said. 'Do you and Gary still live together?' Mr. Pucci blushed and nodded.

His lover's face came back to me – and their apartment – the guilty way Mr. Pucci had looked that afternoon I'd gone over without calling.

'Yes. Well . . .' Mr. Pucci shook Dante's hand and told me again how sorry he was.

I watched his exit into the foyer. 'Former teacher?' Dante asked.

'Excuse me,' I said.

Bug Eyes was holding open the door for him. 'Mr. Pucci, wait!' I said. 'I'll walk you to the car.'

We talked for five minutes about nothing. It was the sound of his car engine that scared me enough to begin.

'I'm sorry if I embarrassed you in there about Gary just now.'

'No, no – don't be silly.'

'He was so sweet to me that day I showed up at your apartment. God, what nerve of me to barge over there like that. He played me Billie Holiday records before you got there. Do you still have your jukebox?'

He nodded.

'Mr. Pucci? The thing is – through this whole wake, I've been sitting in there watching Grandma on one side of the room and her church friends on the other side, wanting to apologize to someone. Except I couldn't. Dante doesn't even know about – What I'm trying to say is, it means a lot to me that you came tonight. And that you were my friend – my *pal* – when I was so messed up. I'm just so sorry that—'

'Let me ask you something, pal,' he said. 'Where were you the afternoon President Kennedy got shot?'

'Uh . . . I was at St. Anthony's. Miss Lilly stopped a spelling test to tell us.'

'And I was at my mother's kitchen table with my cousin Dominick when it happened. Eating lunch – pasta e fagioli.'

I stood there looking at him, waiting for it to make sense.

'And where were you when you saw Neil Armstrong land on the moon?'

'You know where. With you, sitting on the couch at Grandma's. It was the night after Ma got killed. You brought me an African violet.'

'That's right,' he said. 'That's exactly right. So whenever anyone mentions the Kennedy assassination, I think of my cousin Dominick. And whenever anyone talks about that moon landing, I think of you. You and I are locked together for life, kiddo. It's fate; not a damn thing either of us can do about it. Apology accepted.'

Then he drove away.

Dante slept that night on the water bed. Upstairs in Grandma's room, I closed the door and got into my nightgown. Popes and saints covered the walls. The statues of Jesus and John the Baptist seemed to stare back.

In her top dresser drawer were a small vial of holy water, handkerchiefs, nitroglycerin for her heart. In the back I found an envelope with childhood pictures of me. No pictures from my fat days – Grandma hadn't wanted evidence either. Her good red rosary beads were in their velvet case.

Without warning, a moment I'd shared with Grandma came back so powerfully and unexpectedly that it hurt me behind the eyes. It was right after she'd found out about the rape. Ma was at work and I was home from school. The shades were drawn against the sun. Grandma put on the table light and said she wanted to show me something about her rosary beads, her special ones. 'They've got a little secret,' she said. 'I use it when things are bad.' She slid up the back of the hollow metal crucifix and brought my hand up to it. When she tipped the cross, a tiny, rust-colored nugget fell out and into my palm.

'What is it?' I asked.

'A pebble from the road Jesus walked when they crucified Him. You just put it between your fingers and play with it – roll it back and forth, like this. Makes you feel better. I'll leave the beads here for you for a couple of days. In case you want to say the rosary or feel the pebble. On account of that business – what he did to you.'

I'd gone out of my way not to pick them up. Then, a few days later, they were gone again. My memory always insisted that Grandma had been remote and unforgiving about me and Jack. But there, back again without warning, was that moment.

I listened for Dante, then got up and locked the door anyway. I sat back on the bed and, with my fingernail, pushed open the back of the crucifix. It was there – that pebble, the hard red nugget.

'The estate should take about nine months to get through probate,' the lawyer said. 'It's pretty cut-and-dried. Your wife is sole heir.' She was someone I remembered from high school, Penny something, a popular kid. Now she had a hyphenated name and a puffed-out baseball glove of a face. There was a baby in a frame on her desk. She had no recognition that I was the fat girl at the back table in her English class. 'The Pierce Street property and a smallish bank account. That's basically it.'

'How small is smallish?' Dante laughed.

The night before I'd dreamt I was swimming in ocean water as warm as a bath. Grandma, Ma, Vita Marie, and me. The water was jade green. Breathing was optional.

'Honey?' Dante said.

'I'm sorry. What?'

'Ms. Marx-Chapman just asked if we were planning to sell the property or occupy it ourselves.'

'You mean the house? Move there?'

'Uh-huh.'

'No. Sell it.'

Dante put his hand on my knee. 'Well,' he smiled. 'It's still up in the air at this point. We haven't made a definite decision just yet.'

'Not totally definite,' I told her. '*Pretty* definite.'

'Let me ask you something, Ms. Marx-Chapman,' he said.

'Please,' she said. 'Penny.'

'Penny. Would it be possible for us to live there at the house temporarily – while it's still hung up in probate?'

'Sure, that can be arranged.' They both took sips of their coffee.

'Good,' Dante said, smiling at me. 'Great.'

Connie's Superette had gas pumps now and called itself Kwik-

Stop Food Xpress. Inside the store, the ceiling sagged the same way and the air still smelled damp and garlicky. Connie had been replaced at the register by a teenage girl in tight jeans and a glitter-front sweater. There was a 'Coffee and Microwave Centre' where the Pysyks and I had roughed each other up that day I'd called Stacia a 'dirty DP.' I recognized Big Boy's whistling before I recognized the rest of him. His hair had turned yellowy gray and he'd grown himself a Grover Cleveland body. Dante ordered a pound each of provolone cheese, boiled ham, and roast beef. (I looked away when Big Boy sliced the beef.) 'Don't forget about the bakery,' I said. 'Old ladies are sugar addicts.'

On the walk back, we passed Roberta's forbidden tattoo parlor. The storefront glass had been painted over with black paint, but the peacock sign – faded and chipped – still hung over the door.

'This woman named Roberta Jaskiewicz used to live there,' I said. 'She gave tattoos and sold hand-painted girlie neckties. One time my grandmother saw me over there and she—'

'Shut up! Shut up! Shut up!' Dante said. He locked his eyes closed and stood frozen on the sidewalk. I waited.

'What?' I said, when he opened his eyes again.

'A poem was just beginning to form itself in my head. The idea was embryonic and now I've lost it. Thanks a lot.'

For Grandma's sake, I tried to stay with the funeral mass, but my mind kept wandering away from Father Duptulski's ritual – drifting in a patternless way. Touches and sounds were what came to me: the bristly feel of Ma's neck after she came home from the state hospital with her close-cropped haircut, the pattern of creaks Grandma's footsteps made on the stairs when she went up to bed nights. The gurgle and hum of that suction machine at the abortion clinic.

'And now, we offer one another a sign of peace, asking God to remember the soul of Thelma, one of His faithfully departed, who has rejoined Him in the Kingdom of Heaven.'

The old ladies' hands came at me from behind. 'Peace be

with you,' we all said, shaking on it, like a deal. 'Peace be with you.'

At the cemetery, a warm Indian-summer breeze blew against my face. The pallbearers – Dante, Mrs. Mumphy's son and sons-in-law, and two old men from the Knights of Columbus – carried Grandma's coffin from the purring hearse to the platform above her grave. Twelve old people had ridden out to the cemetery. I counted them, like Grandma would have done.

When Father Duptulski was through, Bug Eyes stepped forward and cleared his throat. 'Mr. and Mrs. Davis would like to invite everyone back to Mrs. Holland's home at two sixty-two Pierce Street for a luncheon buffet.' For a second, I didn't realize he was talking about Dante and me.

When everyone else headed back to their cars, I stood alone and broke a red carnation off the spray that covered her coffin, kissed it and put it back. The limousine rolled smoothly and slowly over the cemetery grass. I rested my head against Dante's shoulder.

Mrs. Mumphy and three other ladies came back to the house. I sat them in a row on the water bed. 'Thelma never told us she was a hippie,' one of them laughed. 'God rest her soul.'

They murmured amongst themselves out front while Dante and I peeled cold cuts off the stack and arranged them on a plate. 'Get that coffeepot going and put those blueberry squares out on this thing,' I whispered. 'We should have had all this stuff ready. I hate this.'

My plan was to keep him busy out in the kitchen in case one of them started reminiscing about me, exposing my secrets.

'I can't tell you how profound it was – the feeling of my hand inside those gray silk pallbearer's gloves,' he said. His eyes were closed again; he'd stopped working. 'I think I've got to write about it now or I'll lose it.'

'The hell you will,' I hissed. 'You stay here and help.' But he was already headed for the foyer. 'If you ladies will excuse me,' I heard him say.

In that big, bare front room, there was no place to put the plates of food but on the floor. The ladies didn't seem to mind. They fed like sharks. I was right about them loving desserts the best. You didn't ring up people's groceries for years without learning about human nature.

I thought they'd leave after they stopped eating, but they just sat there, taking about people I didn't even know. A plump little woman, Edna, reached past me and took the very last blueberry crumb square, the one I was planning to reward myself with after they left. She bit into it and asked me if Dante and I had any children yet.

'Well, no,' I said.

'Female trouble?'

Nodding seemed like the easiest way out.

'Well, it was probably all that weight you piled on a while back. My sister-in-law was a heavyset woman. Big-boned. She and my poor brother tried and tried. The weight raises the dickens with your female system.' She took pictures of her grandchildren out of her purse and told me their names and ages. 'Now these two are in the Talented and Gifted program at their school,' she said. 'The older one's doing sixth-grade arithmetic and he's only in the third grade.'

'They're cute,' I said, 'in a hamsterish kind of way.'

'Beg your pardon?' she said. The other ladies halted their conversations to listen.

'I said they're cute. By the way, you've got some blueberry stuck on your front tooth.'

At their request, I hoisted them all off the bed and got the coats.

At the sink, I did the dishes and cried at how touchy and mean I'd been to those old ladies. I should have made potato salad. If only Dante had stayed downstairs and done the talking. He'd locked himself in Grandma's bedroom for over an hour. I went up the stairs, hesitated, then knocked.

'Not now,' he called out.

Downstairs there was a thumping on the front porch, the doorbell.

Her faced looked as brown and wrinkled as a walnut shell and the black wig didn't quite fit her skull. 'Remember me?' she said.

'Roberta! Oh my God!'

'Figured I'd wait and pay my respects after all the old biddies left,' she said. 'Holy Christ, look at you.'

I swung the door open wide. An aluminum walker had done the thumping. She hoisted it up the step to the foyer floor. She was wearing a lavender jogging suit and red canvas sneakers.

She clunked her way into the living room, aimed her rear toward Grandma's big chair, and free-fell backwards with a sigh. 'So how you been?' she said. 'Where's the ashtray?'

The walker sat in front of her like a cage. With her shaky hand, she lit a cigarette. I offered to make her a sandwich. 'Well, all right,' she said. 'Just cheese, though. I'm a vegetarian.'

'The baby rat in the can of beef stew, right?'

'That's right!' she said. 'So anyways, I'm sorry about Thelma. Her and I never had much use for each other, but to tell you the truth, I think we admired each other's crust.' Then she told me a dirty joke about a man cursed with a three-foot penis. In that bawdy, open-mouthed laugh, you could hear every cigarette she'd ever smoked.

The provolone sandwiches I made us tasted uncommonly good. 'I'm one, too, now,' I said.

'One what?'

'A vegetarian.'

'Good for you! Meat clogs the blood vessels to your brain. Makes you think better if you don't eat it – I read it some-wheres. So let me give you a piece of advice, Dolores: don't ever get Parkinson's disease. Had the shakes for over four years now – like dancin' all day without a partner.' She laughed at herself, so I laughed, too. 'And these migraines – if I don't eat right, man-oh-boy! You know what I told the doc? I said, "Listen, Moneybucks, I'll get rid of old man Parkinson and you and me can get lovey-dovey." Got any beer to go with these?'

I shook my head. 'I can go across to the store and get some.'

'That's okay. The doc ain't exactly wild about my drinking beer with the pills I'm on. So anyways, about your grandmother – you remember that blizzard last year, the big one?'

I nodded. 'We didn't get it as bad as you did.'

'Yeah, well – she called me on the telephone that night to see if I needed anything. Wouldn't give me the time of day for all these years, then she calls me up during that snow-storm. Says she's just sittin' there watchin' the backyard fill up with snow and she wonders if I need anything.' Roberta laughed. 'Two crusty broads, that's what we both were. That's how we both made it. You got any matches around? My cigarette lighter's runnin' out. All's I'm gettin' is a spark. Yup, she and I both had a tough row to hoe – Thelma and me – but we both shut up and hoed it. Hey, how'd you lose all that weight, anyways? You were a two-ton Tillie for a while there.'

I heard Dante walking above our heads. From the top of the stairs he called to me to please keep it down; he was at a crucial place.

'Who's that?' Roberta asked.

'My husband. Dante.'

'Lighten up, sweetie,' she called up to him. 'Come down and join the party. Life's too short.' She stuffed the rest of her first sandwich into her mouth. Her cheeks bulged out as she chewed and talked. 'Other day, Dial-a-Ride brought a bunch of us down to Kmart. This is funny – listen to this. I was the first one done with my shopping – see, all's I was gettin' was a new oven mitt and some Polident. I go along mostly for the company, you know, just to get out. The doc always tells me, "Roberta, you keep your mobility." He means keep movin' around. You sit around feelin' sorry for yourself and you're dead. Sittin' on your ass can get to be a disease worse than what you got. Where was I?'

'Dial-a-Ride?' I said.

'Oh, yeah, right. So I got my stuff and the girl at the register puts these other things in my bag, too. Little free samples: gum and a comb and a marker pen. So I says to her, "Look, girlie, I got false teeth and I wear a wig." So she fishes back in my bag and takes out the comb and the gum. Left the pen in there. Anyways, I went back to the van, even though I knew it was locked. Figured I'd just wait and have a smoke. You can't smoke inside the van, see? So while I'm waiting there, minding my own business, this car pulls into the handicapped space right next to us – brand-new car, white and clean, and it's got this bumper sticker on it that says, "Life Is a Shit Sandwich." Isn't that stupid? So this guy gets out – good-lookin' fella, in his twenties. I say to him, "Hey, handsome, tell me something." He takes a look at my walker and gets all panicky. "I'm just running in for two seconds," he says. See, he thinks I'm going to yell at him for parking in a handicapped space, but I ain't. I don't give a rat's ass about that, you see. I'd rather walk the extra ten feet than be called handicapped. Where was I?'

She amazed me. 'Life's a shit sandwich,' I said.

'Oh, yeah. Right. So that guy goes runnin' into the store and here's what I did. I fished that free pen out of the bag and marched right over there to that bumper of his. Got myself right down on the ground – and I wrote – just after the "Life's a shit sandwich" part – I wrote, "But only if you're a shithead." 'Course, then I couldn't get myself back up again – had to yell over to a couple of kids at the phone booth to come pick me back up. They got all excited – thought someone had run me over!'

She paused for a drag on her cigarette. 'Life's a shit sandwich my ass. Life's a polka and don't you forget it!' she said.

I felt better than I'd felt in weeks. 'Uh, you were asking before how I lost the weight? . . .' Before I could stop myself, I was explaining about college and Gracewood and my technique of imagining mold. 'You're the first one I ever told all this to,' said. 'Including him.' I pointed up toward the ceiling.

She stared at me without laughing. 'Well,' she said, 'if I was you, I'd tell the whole goddamned world. Write one of them diet books – make yourself a couple million dollars.'

By the time Dante came downstairs, the air was thick with smoke and Roberta and I had each had two of the beers I'd run across to the superette and bought. I was barefoot and sloshing around on the water bed, smoking the third cigarette I'd bummed.

Roberta and Dante took turns sizing each other up. I watched his eyes dart with alarm from her walker to the red sneakers to the ashtray she'd filled. 'I was just tellin' your wife how I got my show at the radio station. I do the Sunday-morning polka hour. So anyways, Dolores, the station manager comes to the phone and I says to him, "Listen, hon, you got all these happy-go-lucky polkas and, in between 'em, that announcer guy sounds like you dug him up at the cemetery or something." So this station manager guy's a real smartass over the phone. He says to me, "Oh, well, why don't you go to broadcast school and then send us an audition tape – show us how it's done." So that's what I did. Called his bluff, except I didn't send a tape. I brought myself down there *live* and made that station manager sit and listen. Comes to find out, I gave him a tattoo once, a tiger lily right on his hairy ass – both of us remembered each other. So now I'm the Polka Princess every Sunday morning from ten to eleven. That was my idea to call myself that: the Polka Princess. Just like, what's her name, Lady Diane over there in England. I tell you, hon, put that microphone in front of me and I throw a *party!*'

When I got back from walking her across the street, Dante was spraying the air with Glade. 'I give up,' he said. 'What was *that?*'

'Roberta Jaskiewicz. The lady who ran the tattoo parlor.'

He held up her lipstick-smeared glass and said he hoped to Christ that whatever she had wasn't contagious.

'Yeah, life's just a big shit sandwich, isn't it, Dante?' I said.

He sighed. 'If you're angry because I didn't help you entertain those old women, I'm sorry, but I couldn't help it. I know it's hard for you to understand, but the poetic impulse is fragile.'

He went out to the kitchen and came back with the packages of uneaten cold cuts and one of Roberta's and my beers.

'You see,' he said, 'it started with the feel of my hand inside the gray pallbearer's glove. That was the inspiration, the inception of the whole thing. It's hard to explain. Intellectually, I was trying to make it an elegy – at least that's what I would have predicted it would become. Except it wasn't *feeling* elegiac. It was feeling . . . well, sexual. Isn't that odd?'

He tilted his head back and dropped whole slices of boiled ham into his mouth, chewing as he talked.

'Then, sitting up there amidst all your grandmother's Catholic trappings, the most intimate thing happened – the force was undeniable . . . Any of those pumpernickel rolls left? . . . You see, I'd been blocked for the first hour or so because I was missing the point. It was the *feel* of the gloves, not their symbolic quality, that interested me. The *sensual* aspect. So finally I said, "Okay, fuck it, Davis. Fuck all these plaster saints looking at you." I let the poem swerve toward the erotic – gave it permission – and I was freed.'

'Freed?'

'Yes! Amidst all those saints and martyrs, with all those dried-up talking vaginas downstairs. The dynamic was incredible. It just overtook me. To the point where, in the middle of the writing, I stood up, pulled down my pants, and masturbated myself to orgasm. It wasn't a choice; it was an act of survival. Hold on a minute. The poem is rough still but I want you to hear it.'

He ran up the stairs and back down again. 'Okay, listen.'

> *The solitary pallbearer shoots his seed,*
> *His liquid sex, into the night air*
> *A trajectory*
> *While icons, saints*
> *Bear their blank-eyed Catholic witness . . .*

'You were doing that while I was down here with Grandma's friends?'

He smiled proudly. 'It's still very rough, I know, but the components are all there. This house is *alive* to me! I feel the most incredible psychic energy here. It's radioactive – poetically.'

'I have to be back day after tomorrow,' I said. 'I'm working days at the store through November.'

That night I locked the door to Grandma's room and lay back on her bed, rolling the rusty pebble between my thumb and finger. I'd found his stain on the rug near the foot of Grandma's bed, had gotten a washcloth and rubbed the spot clean, harder and longer than was necessary.

'Where are we?' I asked, waking up. Dante had insisted on driving. We were parked at a Burger King off the interstate.

'Holyoke, Mass. Could you order? I've got to take a leak.'

'What do you want?'

'I don't know – Whopper with cheese, large fries, vanilla shake.'

I approached the stainless-steel counter reluctantly. Fast-food cashiers had so little patience with the indecisive.

'Welcome to Burger King. We flame-broil not fry. Can I help you?'

A freckly, strawberry-blond teenage girl. Like Sheila, who I'd been thinking about before I'd fallen asleep. I repeated Dante's order and she punched her cash register keys. 'Is that it?'

'Uh . . . and a cup of tea, I guess.'

'Cream and sugar, ma'am?'

'Well, whatever. Okay. Yes, please.'

'Five eighty-five, ma'am.'

It was mid-afternoon, an off hour. There were empty booths all around us. As Dante approached, I saw the path our life was making: one continuous Etch-a-Sketch line, looping back and forth through gray.

He took his hamburger out of the box, bit a large crescent shape out of it, and chewed. I looked away. 'I've been thinking,' he said. 'Our apartment lease is up in less than three months.

What do you say we move down to your grandmother's house.'

'I've been thinking, too,' I said. 'In a way, you raped her.'

'*What?*'

'Your high-school girlfriend. Sheila. You raped her.'

He looked around to see if anyone was listening. Then he put down his Whopper. 'How do you figure that?'

'You took advantage of her.'

'Oh, right,' he laughed. 'When *she* orchestrated the whole thing? Calling me three or four times a day? Walking right into the apartment without even knocking?'

'You're thirty and she's, what, seventeen? You raped her by being almost twice her age.'

He took a sip of his shake, staring at me. 'I hope you know you've got it all wrong,' he said. 'I tried to tell you before. Kids today aren't innocent. If anything, the little cunt raped *us*. My career. You and me. Not that this is the appropriate place to go into any of this.'

I dangled and dangled my tea bag. 'You know what's funny?' I said. 'That I stayed a vegetarian and you didn't.'

'What the fuck does that have to do with anything?'

'At first, I didn't eat meat just to please you. I thought it was what you wanted, so I did it. Now it makes me sick to even *think* about eating it. As a matter of fact, I'm getting this little pukey feeling just watching you with that hamburger. It's like the feeling I used to get at the mental hospital, when I imagined mold growing all over my food. I used to weigh over two hundred and fifty pounds.'

He let go a nervous, bewildered laugh. 'Is this just some random kind of mind fucking or am I supposed to be following your train of thought?'

'The abortion is what made me a true vegetarian,' I said.

'Oh, Jesus.'

'Every bite you take, it's like you're eating *her* up. Which is what we did, in a way, Dante. First we made her, then we ate her up.'

'All right, that's enough,' he said. 'Shut up.'

'Here's something else I never told you: I got raped when I was thirteen,' I said. 'By my grandmother's tenant. He lived upstairs.'

A worker pushed a broom past us. The silence lasted so long that I began to wonder if I'd said it out loud or just thought I had.

'I never painted watercolors, either. It was Etch-a-Sketch pictures I did – copies of masterpieces. I was pretty good at it, actually. But I saw through your eyes that it was tacky, so I shut up about it. Oh, and my father isn't dead. He lives in New Jersey, I think, same as your parents. You just assumed he was dead, so I let you. You and he are a lot alike in some ways. That never even really occurred to me until that New Year's Day you slapped me and then – wham! – it was like, "Dolores, how could you have missed it," you know? But anyway, I used to do the Etch-a-Sketches when I lived at this halfway house after I got out of Gracewood. That was the mental hospital. I was there for years.'

He swallowed hard; he wouldn't look at me.

'When I went into the hospital, I weighed two hundred and sixty-three pounds – a real mess. This is how unhappy I was back then: just before my breakdown, I took this taxi from Pennsylvania to Cape Cod? To be honest with you, I was trying to kill myself. See, I was all confused – I had just had sex with this woman who – well, that's a whole other story. Anyway, on the way there, we stopped at this doughnut place? I sat there in the backseat of that cab and ate eight or nine lemon-filled doughnuts in a row. Crying all the way, but still eating them. That's how bad I was.'

He looked at me, a quick, scared glimpse. 'Stop it!' he said. I couldn't stop. I felt wonderful – as free as Ma's flying leg.

'You see, Dante, people don't fall so neatly into the categories you put them in – heroes and villains, unfettered and – what? – fettered? In some ways, Dante, *you're* the one who's uncomplicated.'

'Look, if this is some sort of sick joke you're—'

'My roommate at college was Kippy Strednicki.'

'*What?*'

'Kippy. Your old girlfriend from high school. I used to steal the letters you sent her, then lock myself in the bathroom and read them.'

He sat there, staring and blinking, dumb-faced as Gomer Pyle.

'That was when you were going to be a Lutheran minister. Remember? I was so surprised that first night we met in the driveway at Mrs. Wing's. Well, not surprised we *met*; I planned out that whole part. I mean I was surprised when you said you didn't believe in God anymore. You seemed so religious in those letters – the way you used to torture over whether or not you and Kippy should do it before you got married. Excuse me, I'm sorry. I don't mean to smile. But do you see what I mean? About Sheila? People don't know anything when they're seventeen or eighteen years old. Back then you thought God was in heaven getting ready to hurl a thunderbolt at you if you and Kippy had sex. It's funny, in a way, isn't it? Funny peculiar, I mean. How you were so uptight and moral back then – the boy who promised his mother he wouldn't be a womaniser. Remember that? You just shouldn't make promises you don't intend to keep, Dante. Love, honor, and cherish. Ha!'

He wouldn't stop blinking up at the ceiling. 'We've been married almost four years and in all that time . . . ? You *knew* Kippy?'

'Remember the time you sent her those Polaroid pictures you took of yourself, naked? On your bed in your dorm room out there in Minnesota?'

He curled his fist around his uneaten order of french fries and squeezed. His face turned a kind of purple color. 'What . . . what was she doing? Passing them around so everyone could have a good laugh?'

'It wasn't like that. She never even got them. I didn't think she deserved you, so I kept them from her. Thought I was protecting you.'

I looked around us. The restaurant was starting to fill up.

'I used to steal your letters before she got back from her twelve o'clock class. See, they put the mail out at lunchtime and I always got it first because I never went to my classes. I only lasted one semester. Well, less than that. The funny thing was, whenever I looked at those pictures – all the time I was at the hospital and everything – all I could ever see was this poor, sensitive, vulnerable boy. That's who I thought I was marrying down at the Lobster Pot – someone vulnerable like me. That's who I kept waiting for to show up. I just had this incredible blind spot. I was like Helen Keller when it came to you.'

He slammed his uneaten food into the bag and twisted the neck. 'Shut the fuck up,' he said. 'Don't say one more fucking word.'

'It wasn't until last night that I put the whole thing together. That foolish whatever-it-is, that epic thing you're writing – that's what finally helped me figure it out. Freed me, like you put it.'

'Freed you to do what? Crack up in the middle of Burger King?'

'To see what I should have seen before. I kept waiting for you to turn back into the person you were in your letters and in those pictures. I guess you were right – I *was* pretty stupid, at least in that way. I mean, letting all those high school girls stroke your ego and calling it teaching. Wanting us to move to Rhode Island so you could stay in the house all day and jerk off in front of my grandmother's holy statues. Even way back then. Even posing yourself for those Polaroid pictures. It's *all* been masturbating, hasn't it, Dante?'

'I can't believe . . . those pictures . . . You *violated* me!'

'Oh, I know I did. Don't get me wrong. I'm not saying I'm proud I stole your letters. I've always felt awful about doing that. See, that's what you don't get about Sheila: how you *violated* her with your "pleasant muscle spasm" business. I mean, what it amounted to was you just jerking off into her. And me, too. Which is why you didn't even want to *consider* having a baby. Right? You're like that guy in the myth – the one who fell in love with his own reflection? What's his name, Dante? You know all that kind of stuff. But anyway, this is what it feels like to get violated. What you're feeling now. It's awful, isn't it? I mean, it makes you feel so *powerless*.'

For a second I thought he was going to hit me. But I couldn't stop. I'd propelled myself in some way that felt both scary and right.

'Those pictures of you are back at our apartment in a shoe box marked "Important Papers" or something. In the bedroom closet, top shelf. You can have them back now if you want. I'm through with them. Oh, but I *do* want something else in there. A painting. Well, part of a painting, actually. This little zigzaggy square of canvas. It's something my mother—'

His fist sent our food and packaging flying. 'Why are you fucking with my head like this?' he shouted. The couple next to us looked over, openmouthed.

'I'm *not* fucking with your head,' I said. 'I've been doing it all these years, but now I'm not anymore. You see, I thought keeping secrets was the only way I could get you. Keep you. All these years, I kept *wanting* to tell you the truth. It just wouldn't come out. It was just like Dr. Shaw warned me. He was my shrink at Gracewood. He told me when I quit that I still had issues left to—'

'You cunt!' he screamed.

'Hey,' someone yelled over. 'You want to watch your language?'

'You want your jaw wired?' Dante shot back.

The manager scurried over to our booth, a paunchy man with wide sideburns and a paper hat. In my nervousness, he struck me funny. 'Hi, folks,' he said.

I smiled. 'Hello.'

'Anything I can help you with here? Anything I can get you?'

Dante turned to him. 'Yeah, you can get out of my way, asswipe.' He stood up and shoved the manager back against a booth.

Out in the parking lot, he opened and slammed the car door shut five or six times, then got in and sped away. We all watched him through the plate glass.

I helped the manager back on to his feet, straightened his hat for him. 'As a matter of fact,' I said, 'you *can* get me something.'

'What's that, ma'am?'

'A ride to Rhode Island?'

Chapter 26

Our lawyers handled the division of property in a single long-distance phone call. 'Yup,' I kept saying. 'Whatever.' Dante got the Vega, the La-Z-Boy, our air conditioner, and the TV; I got a shipping carton addressed in Dante's handwriting to 'Dolores Davis, Certified Lunatic.' Inside were my wadded-up clothes, Ma and Daddy's candlestick holder, my Grand Union Employee of the Month plaque, and that box marked "Insurance Papers." He'd taken his polaroids out but sent back the swatch of Ma's painting: green wingtip against blue sky. I got that back. That was home.

He'd put all my shoes in a plastic garbage bag, mistakenly including a pair of his own: brown wingtips coated with dust. With fanfare and satisfaction, I chucked them in the trash. Then, early next morning, listening to the rumble of the garbage truck on the other end of Pierce Street, I panicked and got out of bed – retrieved Dante's shoes from the can, in my bare feet.

Roberta said divorcing Dante was the right thing to do – that life was too short – but that I was stupid not to have held out for the Vega.

'That car was just a piece of junk,' I said. 'There were rust holes you could put your hand through. The engine sounded like it had emphysema.'

'That ain't the point,' she said, rapping the legs of her walker against the kitchen floor. 'The point is *wheels*. It moved, didn't it?'

She hated the thought of the Parkinson's disease grounding

her and fought against it. She'd probably made the owner of Easterly Taxi a millionaire in the two years since the disease had gotten bad, she joked. She told me I needed to get out more, too. 'Engage outwardly,' Dr. Shaw was always telling me. Sometimes Roberta's and Dr. Shaw's advice were remarkably similar.

That first Friday night I got back to Easterly, Roberta and I took a cab to China Paradise for supper to celebrate my independence – she and I in the backseat and her aluminum walker riding up front with the driver. 'Here you go, Teddy, you goddamned robber,' she laughed as she handed up her money. 'Listen to my show on Sunday and I'll dedicatecha a polka. Now get my boyfriend out of the front seat for me, will ya?'

After we ate, we crossed the street to a Mel Brooks film festival at the Wayfarer Movie Cafe. Roberta had never heard of Mel Brooks before, but her big laugh was full-out and contagious; between her and Mel Brooks, the whole room was whooping it up. Here I am, I thought, sitting in the dark with strangers, laughing out loud at cowboys farting around a campfire. My whole life has flopped and I can still do this. Roberta's eyeglasses and walker glinted in the movie-screen light. I reached over and touched her arm.

In those days after I moved back, I raked and bagged leaves, washed storm windows, shampooed rugs, took five-mile afternoon walks. I had the remains of Ma's painting framed at a fancy art shop for $45 and hung it on the stairway wall where my and Dante's wedding picture had been. A nice place: in late afternoon, the sun coming through the front door window cast a ray, a kind of spotlight, right on it.

In November, I got a part-time job at Buchbinder's Gift and Novelty Shop. Mr and Mrs. Buchbinder were Holocaust survivors, a scowling, gray-haired couple with thick accents that required me to make them repeat whatever they'd just asked. All day long, they heckled-and-jeckled each other and pointed out nitpicky little places I'd missed while dusting. That was my job: dusting and watching out for shoplifters and 'stupit-heads' that might break something. They'd hired me for the holiday season, the day after Ronald Reagan was elected president.

'Did you vote for the peanut man or the ecduh?' Mr. Buchbinder asked me during my job interview.

'I'm sorry? The what?'

'The ecduh. The ecduh: thet schmuck from Hollywood.'

'Oh. Well, actually, I didn't get a chance to vote.'

'Smut thinkin',' he said. 'You're hired.'

Joe Wisniewski over at the Pulaski Hall says to remindjas there's a meetin' this Tuesday night at seven. They're electin' officers, so getcha dupkas over there, fellas, if you know what's good for ya. Now here's Walt Skiba and the Vice Versa Band with 'Perk-Up Polka.'

During the week, Roberta wore her jogging suit, but she liked to dress up for our Friday-night China Paradise-and-a-movie outings. 'Deck out' she called it. She wore a shiny rayon pantsuit and made her face up with orangy lipstick and iridescent eye shadow. Her twitching hand sometimes gave her a crooked, clownish line or a lavender-dusted eyebrow. I was forever wanting to reach over my vegetarian lo mein and straighten that awful wig.

It never occurred to Roberta to lower her voice in public or to check that she'd buttoned her blouse buttons correctly. 'They probably recognize my voice,' she'd tell me whenever I made note that people were staring. 'Must be polka fans.'

Roberta rejected most of my attempts to be her nurse. No, she *wouldn't* give up smoking, no matter what the doctor or I said. No, she *wouldn't* let me cook her meals for her; the migraines and dizzy spells had nothing to do with her forgetting to eat once in a while. The only reason she let me do her laundry was because she had a hard time getting quarters into the slots down at the Laundromat. She blamed the slots, not her shaking hands. I told her I'd be glad to walk over and help with her bath and makeup. She said she'd appreciate it if she was an invalid, which she wasn't.

I did manage to convince her to buy some curtains and let me strip the black paint off her front window. Sometimes she'd wave to me from across the street while we talked to each other on the phone. This was the signal I devised: one ring if it was an emergency, two rings if she wanted company. She was forever mixing up the two, causing me to barrel over there, breathless, taking her by surprise. 'Loosen up,' she'd say, sitting in a cloud of cigarette smoke. 'Life's too short.'

The Buchbinders nagged me to smile more at customers and to watch more closely the ones with big coat pockets; they were reluctant to teach me the register. It was my energy level that won them over. When I wasn't up front vacuuming or dusting the merchandise, I was out in back assembling gift boxes or consolidating the stock. At the end of January inventory, Mr. Buchbinder finally smiled. He told me I could have a 15 per cent discount on anything in the store. I was the first girl, he said, who'd gone three months without breaking anything.

That was Walt Wojciechowski and his Accordiotones with 'Who Stole the Kishka?' Now, Eddie Woodka down at the newsstand says he wants me to say hello to him over the air, so hiya, Eddie. How they hangin'?

One Sunday morning while I was folding Roberta's laundry and listening to her program, a record ended and there was silence. I waited, frozen, her warm bedsheets in my hands. A bunch of public-service announcements. The same polka she'd played before. The same recorded announcements again.

Then she was back on. 'You miss me, folks?' she asked her listeners. 'I had to go in the back room and stir the golumpkes.' But the cheeriness in her voice was fake; behind it I heard fear.

It took her until midweek to finally admit to me what had

happened: she'd gotten dizzy and passed out while her engineer was downstairs in the foyer talking to his girlfriend. She'd come to in a heap on the floor with the chair flipped over on to her.

A fat medical manual in the library suggested fresh fruits and vegetables, supplements of B vitamins. She ate them like a cranky child. I began riding the cab with her to the station – pressing the controls and switches she pointed at with her jumping finger, sometimes guessing wrong. She insisted she could still do it all herself – that she was just letting me come along because she thought I should get out and have some fun instead of staying home with the laundry. I drew the line at working her cigarette lighter and looked away while she fumbled and swore, trying to bring the spark to life as happy accordion music turned on reel-to-reel tape behind her.

Next half hour's brought to you by Dropo's Funeral Home. They're real nice people, the Dropos. They take their work serious. Next song goes out to Pete and Bunny Biziewski, honeymoonin' forty-three years tomorrow – ooh, Pete, your achin' kielbasa!

In February of 1982, the Rhode Island probate court declared me the official owner of Grandma's house, and the following month, the State of Vermont sent me a registered letter saying they would dissolve my marriage if I signed the enclosed papers. Dante's smooth signature was already all over them.

Roberta and I went that night to China Paradise to celebrate my freedom, but halfway through my Island Passion drink, I turned gloomy. 'Dissolve,' I mumbled. 'Throw four years of your life in a glass of water and watch it fizz away like Alka-Seltzer.'

Roberta was picking something out of her teeth; she brushed away my remark with a flap of her wrist. 'I say good riddance to that stick-in-the-mud. Life's too short. What are you going to do with the money?'

Between the settlement check and Grandma's savings

account, I had gotten $3,100. 'I don't know,' I said. 'I was thinking of getting one of those VCR things. Or maybe one of those big-screen TVs. I shouldn't have let him have my old black-and-white set. I got that for a present before I even *knew* Dante.'

'You're a dumb bunny if you waste your bundle on that kind of junk. What you need is a car. Wheels.'

'I should just call up his parents' house and have them tell him I want that television back,' I said. I couldn't really tell which percentage of me wanted the TV back and which just wanted to see him again, to hear his voice. Sometimes, half-asleep in bed, I still reached over for him. I wondered if I hadn't made up some of that selfishness of his. It wouldn't have been the first time I'd lied to myself. To say nothing of all the lies I'd told him.

'What you *should* do is start car shoppin',' Roberta said.

I sipped the last of the drink just as my second one arrived at the table. 'Why? So I can spend the rest of my life being your chauffeur?'

The Wayfarer was showing *Body Heat* that night. Woozy from rum, I sat sulking in the dark, watching William Hurt and Kathleen Turner enjoy all that sweaty sex. He'd been so good with me in bed at the beginning, so interested in what pleased me. I looked around at the silhouettes of other movie watchers, wondering how many of them had made love that week, how many of them would go home that night and make some more of it. Roberta slumped toward my shoulder, snoring, her mouth wide open.

Dante's father sounded groggy on the phone when I called that night. He said they hadn't heard from Dante in a month or so – not since he started law school – but that he'd give him my message about the TV.

I held off making a decision about the $3,100 and got a second part-time job instead, weekend mornings at Gutwax's Bakery. The busier, the better, I reasoned.

'What's good today?' people would ask me.

'Everything!' I'd answer and mean it. Sometimes customers would time it just right, buy up muffins and doughnuts and breads that were still warm. 'Ahh,' they'd sigh, feeling the warmth, the freshness, right through their bags.

Mrs. Gutwax loved her baked goods, her customers, her son Ronnie, and me. She told me she swung her feet out of bed and on to the floor each morning at 3.00 a.m. in the belief that the whole world would work right if people just tried being an inch and a half nicer to each other. She had loved her husband until the day he died, she told me, and she *still* loved him, nine years later. What she wanted more than anything in the whole wide world – what she prayed for every night – was that her Ronnie would find a good wife that loved him and took good care of him. Sometimes in her dreams, she said, she played with future grandchildren.

The second weekend I worked there, I suggested she brush our flaky crescent rolls with egg yolk and call them croissants instead. We sold out by mid-morning. 'You're a genius!' Mrs. Gutwax said. 'I'll have to just see that you don't get away.'

'I don't believe in marriage, Mrs. Gutwax, if that's what that means.' You could be as blunt as you wanted with Mrs. Gutwax and know she'd keep loving you anyway.

'Sure you believe in it,' she told me.

'No, I don't. I was married almost four years. It was a big disaster.'

'He just wasn't the right one.'

Ronnie Gutwax baked for his mother. He didn't talk much but went around the back room smiling at everything he made, moving with a kind of plodding consistency that I began to regard as slow-motion choreography.

Whenever he caught me watching, we both blushed. At thirty-three, he was flabby and three-quarters bald. His main passion was the Boston Red Sox, his most prized possessions the thick scrapbooks on the team he'd kept since his childhood when his father took him regularly to Fenway Park. 'He's not retarded,' Mrs. Gutwax whispered one afternoon while Ronnie was out in back at the dumpster. 'He's just a little slow. But he's sweet as sugar, Dolores, as sweet as his father was. Sweeter.'

I made my decision: a big-screen TV and one of those satellite dishes that pulled in hundreds of stations. I arranged to have it installed on the weekend Roberta was scheduled for tests at the hospital in Providence. It took three men a whole morning to get it bolted to Grandma's roof and rotating. Drivers and pedestrians on Pierce Street kept stopping to stare.

I was lying back on the water bed, watching 'The Dukes of Hazzard' – Beau and Luke Duke as big as a drive-in movie! – when the phone rang. Twice. Roberta's signal she wanted to talk. Or, *lecture*, more likely. I ignored it. It rang twice again. I'm sick of that mobility speech of hers, I told myself. I had a perfect right to spend my divorce money any way I saw fit. Who had suffered through a life with Dante: her or me?

The phone rang once.

I turned down the volume and waited. If it was a *real* emergency, she'd call back. Out front, the walker thumped against the porch door.

'What the hell is that astronaut think on the roof?' she said.

'Just watch this,' I said, aiming the remote control at the screen. I flashed past 'Hollywood Squares,' otters swimming in a nature show, 'Hawaii Five-O' in Spanish. The screen took up half of one wall.

'How much did you waste on this junk?' Roberta said.

'Look! "The Patty Duke Show"! I haven't seen this since high school. They're identical cousins, see. One's an egg-head and the other—'

'Get this thing out of here! Get yourself that car!' Her whole face was contorted. Spit flew from her mouth as she yelled.

'Shut up,' I said. 'Just get out of my house! Just leave me alone!'

She fell from the very top porch step. Her face was skinned and bleeding, her skinny legs splayed both on and off the stairs beneath her. She lost consciousness just before the ambulance got there.

The Buchbinders huddled shoulder to shoulder and asked me if anything was wrong. 'Not a thing,' I said. 'Why?'

'Because this whole store hez dust,' Mr. Buchbinder said. 'Because the rug needs vicuuming.'

'And she's pale,' Mrs. Buchbinder reminded him. 'Don't forget about the pale part.'

I'd stayed up half the night before, watching my big TV and thinking endlessly about Roberta's fall – how I might just as well have placed my hands on her back and shoved. How, if she had died, it would have been me who'd killed her. In the sixteen days she'd been in the hospital, I'd sent her two twenty-dollar bouquets but hadn't gotten up the guts to visit her. As the Buchbinders stood there waiting for their explanation, a lie about terminal illness – a brain tumor growing inside my head – created itself. But I chased it away again. The Buchbinders were worriers; I was pretty sure they loved me whether I did the vacuuming or not. 'Nothing's the matter,' I said. 'Really.'

All that afternoon, I dusted begrudgingly, haphazardly. Whenever customers walked to the counter, I ignored them – made them wait for Mr. or Mrs. Buchbinder to take their money and bag their crap. Life was such a pointless joke. The Buchbinders had survived a death camp only to end up in this claustrophobic little hole-in-the-wall, selling rubber vomit and stuffed Smurfs and 'Fuck the Ayatollah' license plates. No wonder I felt like quitting. What was the point?

Just before closing time, I backed into a display of 'Who Shot J.R.' commemorative plates, sending them clattering and smashing to the floor with a sound as ugly as Roberta's fall.

'Thet's it, Dolores!' Mrs. Buchbinder shouted. 'I'm fid up.'

'So am I!' I yelled back. 'You two are the sorriest people I know!'

'You're fired! You don't work here. I don't even know your face.'

'Nice way to treat a person who's got a brain tumor!' I screamed.

I celebrated my freedom from the Buchbinders by buying a microwave oven and two goldfish, whom I named William Hurt and Kathleen Turner. I visited them in short bursts whenever I rushed away from the big-screen TV to microwave myself a snack. I noticed this coincidence: that if I spread my palm a half-inch or so from either the TV screen or the microwave, I could feel a low-grade static. I wondered vaguely if radiation molecules weren't bouncing off at me, if I wasn't poisoning myself slowly with all that television and speed-cooked food. I'd bought the goldfish impulsively, remembering a container of food flakes but not a bowl. They lived in Grandma's kitchen sink, swimming contentedly enough so that, for a while, I half convinced myself I could love something without damaging it. Except I didn't love them. I loved Roberta. Worried about her. Wondered if she hated me now. Her radio station replaced her with some oldies-but-goodies disc jockey canned out in Hollywood. I hadn't seen her in over a month; the hospital told me she'd been transferred to the Sunny Windows Convalescent Home.

'*Sure* I'd like you to work full-time!' Mrs. Gutwax said, hugging me. 'That makes you more like one of the family.' I let her misread whatever she wanted to, look out whatever sunny window she pleased.

All the next week Mrs. Gutwax – Bea, she wanted me to start calling her – hummed and smiled and invented a million errands that required her to put on her coat and leave me and her sweet son alone together.

One afternoon Ronnie stopped working and walked over to me while I was frosting an anniversary cake. He smiled his gummy smile and blushed.

'What?' I said. 'What is it, Ronnie?'

'Who do you like better on the Red Sox? Jim Rice or Dewey Evans?'

'I don't know.' I shrugged. 'Who do you like?'

'Rice,' he said.

'Oh.'

'My mother says I should kiss you. Can I?'

I put down the icing knife and looked at him. Nodded. He rested his floury hands against my cheeks and closed his eyes. He took a deep breath as if he were about to take a dive underwater.

I analyzed the kiss objectively as it was going on – firm and fleshy, neither a pleasant experience nor an unpleasant one.

He smiled when it was over. I smiled back. 'Do you mind if I do it again?'

'Ronnie,' I said. 'I'm in no position to – I don't have any . . . Well, all right. Go ahead.'

This time I kissed him back. I wasn't kissing Ronnie, exactly. I was kissing the smell of cinnamon-raisin bread in the oven, and that warm room with its creaky floorboards, and Mrs. Gutwax's dreams of grandchildren. Kissing him to show myself I could be tender – loving – no matter how I'd mistreated poor Roberta. Then I was kissing Dante, rubbing *Dante*'s thigh. The kissing was as much a lie as my brain tumor . . . as much of a lie as my marriage had been. We kissed and kissed until Ronnie got an erection.

Mrs. Gutwax still hadn't come back by the end of my shift. I wrote my resignation on an overring slip and left it in the register. I didn't answer the ringing telephone for three days. Whenever it started up, I lay back on the water bed and aimed my remote control box. 'The Twilight Zone.' 'Three's Company.' Johnny Carson. 'M*A*S*H.' I absorbed myself in whatever was in front of me.

At the end of the summer I got a letter from a woman I didn't know, a Jacqueline Price, my father's third wife. 'PLEASE FORWARD' it said on the envelope, addressed to me by way of Grandma. She was writing, she said, because she thought I had a right to know my father had died the week before, after a six-month illness. When he'd gone into the hospital in February for an operation, they'd found so much cancer that they'd closed him right up again. It was *his* choice not to get ahold of me until after the funeral, she explained. *His* wish to be cremated, to leave what he had to her children by a previous marriage. 'He was a loving man,' she wrote.

'Battlestar Galactica.' Roller derby. 'Joanie Loves Chachi.' 'Bewitched.'

What was the scariest of all was the absence of grief – the way all day long his death kept slipping my mind in the midst of the shows I watched. 'Can I just let go of him?' I had asked Dr. Shaw one time during therapy. I *had* let go. And now his death showed me the emptiness of my choice. 'He was a loving man,' his third wife wrote. Had she turned him into one? Had he been one all along? Who, exactly, had I missed? Sitting in front of the big TV, I had to close my eyes to picture Daddy, and when I *did* see him, he was sitting at the edge of our new pool on Bobolink Drive, laughing at something I'd said, some joke we shared. I cried then, and at first I thought that was a good sign: those tears made me human, made me a loving person after all. But that was a lie. The tears weren't for him; they were for myself – the unsuspecting girl swimming laps and thinking her father would stay forever, would be there as long as she needed him. I turned off the TV and sat in the uncomfortable quiet. 'Daddy?' I said.

On 'Good Morning America' the next morning, the new Miss America demonstrated how to make sour-cream-and-banana pancakes. I copied down the steps and walked over to the superette for ingredients. They puffed up beautifully, exactly like the TV pancakes. I sat down at the kitchen table, poured syrup, cut my first bite. William and Kathleen swam circles in the sink. I'd let the dishes pile up since they'd arrived. I got up, left the pancakes uneaten, and went back to my TV.

I kept the television going for the next two weeks, afraid that if I shut it off, it wouldn't come back on again. I slept on the water bed instead of upstairs – in nervous naps and near comas, startling awake to 'As the World Turns,' 'That's Incredible,' 'Dr. Who.' My lack of energy fascinated me. I'd sit for hours, trying to convince myself to take a bath or pull up the shades. I felt like those people I'd seen on 'Donahue' – the ones who floated above their own bodies in operating rooms, trying to decide whether to stay or go.

'I'm fine, Mrs. Buchbinder, really . . .' I lied into the receiver, scanning the empty potato-chip bags and soda cans the way she might have. I was down to my last hundred dollars. The goldfish water in the sink began to tint. My banana pancakes still sat on the kitchen table, sprouting whiskers of mold. *Real* mold, not the kind I'd imagined at Gracewood when I'd lost all my weight. I was gaining again – unbuttoning the top button of my jeans, staying all day in my muumuu. Obesity had been part of my pattern of repression, Dr. Shaw taught me. Except now I was getting fat without repressing a thing. What was I repressing? The fact that I couldn't even hold a job? That an old woman had depended on me and I'd practically shoved her down the stairs?

I took the phone off the hook and threw mail away unopened. I began to look at daytime as an invasion of my privacy. The superette closed at 10.00 p.m., so I food-shopped at the convenience store over on River Street. That neon-lit store never failed to surprise me when it emerged like a mirage from the middle-of-the-night darkness. The clerk, a chubby red-haired man, never saw me floating toward him. Lulled, I suppose, by the hum of his various coolers and freezers, he'd startle and fling his dirty magazines beneath the counter each time I entered the store. He stood at attention while I browsed, then rang up my purchases – onion dip, Milky Ways, Ruffles, Pepsi. I watched him count change into a hand I willed not to shake. Though we never spoke, I began to suspect he had a crush on me, that he was courting me in his own shy way, enclosing little gifts in my paper bag – sale leaflets, matches, complimentary contest-entry blanks. One week he started including with my purchases pairs of cardboard glasses with red cellophane lenses. 'SEE THE GILL WOMAN IN BLOOD-THIRSTY 3-D' each said along the sidepiece. 'WATCH YOUR LOCAL LISTINGS.' In what seemed like no time, I had collected half a dozen pairs. I began to wear them around the house, day and night. I imagined myself glowing radioactively from the inside out. I liked the way the glasses turned my vision infrared.

Lights came on across the street at Roberta's. I put the phone back on the hook. Kept my ear cocked for the honking of taxis. None came. She kept the curtains closed – curtains I'd sewn for her, shut, now, against me. I wanted to call her – to offer an apology. Offer help . . . To ask *her* for help, the way I had that long-ago night when I'd walked across the street barefoot, knocked on her side door, and told her I'd been raped. 'The fat girl's coming back again,' I wanted to tell her now. 'I think she may get me.' But I didn't call. Couldn't.

The Gill Woman turned up two Friday nights later on Channel 38 but the 3-D effects were disappointing. The Gill Woman herself, a large-breasted woman in a scaly wet suit and a 1950s hairdo, was part mermaid and part shark. A hurricane had disoriented her. She was being studied by scientists who had captured her but misunderstood her intentions. They kept her chained underwater in a pool and swam down daily to prod her with long poles, then marvelled and cringed at what I saw as her perfectly justifiable anger.

There was a knock on the front door. Roberta.

I figured I'd let her in if she wanted to come in – I wasn't that much of a cold fish – but I wasn't going to listen to one syllable about the way I was running my life. Not one word about TV or mobility.

Except it wasn't Roberta. It was Dante.

With my black-and-white TV. And some woman. A girl, really – someone barely in her twenties. 'I tried to call several times,' he said, 'but the line was always busy. We were driving through. You wanted this?'

I stood there, wishing I wasn't wearing the 3-D glasses or the frayed Disneyland sweatshirt I'd bought on our cross-country trip. My hair was pulled back in an oily ponytail; my legs were hairy. 'Well, thanks,' I said, when he put the set down just inside the foyer. 'See you.' I started to close the door on them.

'Janice really has to use the bathroom.'

His calling her by name somehow gave me permission to look. She had a frizzy triangular hairstyle and reddish-black lipstick. She wore a T-shirt with the word 'innuendo' stretched across her junior-high-school breasts and a pair of those stretchy Lycra pants I had seen reborn women, former fatties, modelling on 'Richard Simmons' that same morning. 'Top of the stairs,' I said.

Dante looked past me and at the screen. 'Holy shit, look at the size of that thing,' he said. He walked inside.

He was wearing a ragg-wool sweater and matching ragg-wool socks. He seemed to have gotten more handsome.

'I hear you're going to law school,' I said.

'Yes, I am.'

'And I see you got yourself a perm.'

'Janice did it. She's a cosmetologist.'

'How old is she, anyway?'

He smiled patiently. 'I don't really think that's a fair question.'

'Oh, sorry. By the way, you packed a pair of your shoes in one of those boxes you sent me. By mistake. Wingtips.'

'Oh, right,' he said. 'I was looking for those. I could use them.'

'Yeah, I bet. Lawyer shoes. They're in the kitchen. I'll get them.'

'No,' he said. 'Stay and watch your program. I'll get them.'

'They're on the floor in the closet. Way in back, I think.'

It wasn't until he was out there that I remembered the moldy pancakes, the goldfish in the sink, the stacks of unwashed dishes that sat balanced all over the counter and kitchen chairs. I closed my eyes tight to clamp off the tears.

Upstairs the toilet flushed and then I heard her footsteps.

'Oh, wow,' she said. '3-D?' I handed her a pair of glasses.

There was some clatter in the kitchen. A commercial came on. 'Watch out for Dante,' I said. 'He bites.'

She looked over at me, her reaction concealed behind the red cellophane lenses.

Dante came back out, each hand curled inside a shoe. His face looked pale, 'Come on, babe,' he said to her. 'Let's go.'

'Wait a sec. I just want to see if the sharks get this chick.'

'I *said* let's get going.'

She took off the glasses. 'Okay,' she shrugged. 'No biggie.'

As she was getting in the car, Dante turned unexpectedly and walked up the porch steps. 'This whole house smells of body odor and dead fish,' he said. 'Wash those dishes in there! Get yourself under control!'

'Mind your own business,' I shouted. 'Fuck off!'

I watched him drive away in their apple-green Le Car – hers, I figured. Across the street, Roberta was at the window, watching, too.

He'd wrapped my TV in an air-pillow bunting. I sat back down, absentmindedly popping the tiny balloons with my fingernail and watching the Gill Woman ooze blood from where they'd torn her.

I looked up 'innuendo' in the dictionary. 'A hint or insinuation, usually derogatory,' it said. I thought his 'dead fish' remark was some kind of sarcastic comment about *The Gill Woman*. But when I went out into the kitchen, I saw what he'd really meant. William and Kathleen were floating at the top of the sink, dead from their own muck.

Roberta had lost weight. There was a pink scar on her forehead and dried egg yolk on the collar of her sweatshirt jacket.

'Don't stare at me like that! I'm *not* crazy!' I shouted.

'Of course you're not. But we'll both be crazy unless you get us the hell out of here! Now can I come inside before January gets here and my ass freezes and falls off?'

I started with the pancakes and cleaned all night, scouring, scraping, vacuuming, bathing. 'I'm so sorry,' I told the fish when I finally got the courage to flush them down the toilet. 'Honest to God, this is all my fault.' In the morning, I snuck behind the superette with my black-and-white portable and threw it in their dumpster. Then I called the satellite-dish company. They balked at a full refund, but I shouted them up to 75 per cent.

The car we bought – a gas-guzzling '67 Biscayne – had a steering wheel that shimmied wildly at speeds over thirty-five and an oil leak that tattooed the road wherever you parked. But it had, as well, a tape player and trunk big enough to hold Roberta's collapsible wheelchair. 'This Car's Climbed Pike's Peak!' a peeling bumper sticker claimed.

I found the unlabeled tapes one afternoon while searching for the seat-adjustment lever. The three of them, eight-tracks, were stuffed underneath the driver's seat amidst the beer bottles and rolling papers and fast-food Styrofoam, stacked in an odd-shaped gray box that said 'Keep in a cool, dry place.' I had saved the classified ad, but when I called to ask the former owner if he meant to give me the tapes, too, all I got was that recorded operator – the one who tells you in her chilly voice that the person you wanted has disconnected and gotten away.

I shoved one of the tapes in later that week, during one of Roberta's and my morning drives. I'd expected country music – the man who'd sold me the car had worn cowboy boots. But I knew immediately what they were. Nor was I surprised. They had followed me all my life.

'Whales,' I said.

Roberta lit a cigarette. 'Humpbacks,' she nodded. 'Heard 'em in person once. The Canuck beat the shit out of me, then took me on a ferry trip to Nova Scotia to say he was sorry.' She chuckled softly. 'Went on that trip with two black eyes,' she said. 'Looked just like a raccoon.'

We drove until I'd played each tape through twice, until our heads were filled with the laments of humpbacks. 'Whatya suppose they're doin', Dolores?' Roberta asked. 'Singin' or cryin'?'

She moved into the house the next day.

It wasn't until November of the following year – she'd had a good couple of months – that we attempted the trip up. We hadn't planned it; we just kept driving one sunny morning until Route One turned into Interstate 95, and then there was the 'Welcome to Maine' sign. We got to Canada – Campobello Island – by mid-afternoon.

'Them humpbacks?' an old man at the dock said. 'Nope. They head due south come September, early October. Missed 'em by a couple of months.'

The drive back was long and hard. Our plans had been so spontaneous that we hadn't thought about Roberta's medication until halfway up there.

'We just got too ambitious, that's all,' I said. 'You're all right. We can still have adventures – as long as we pace ourselves.'

But Roberta was snoring by then. I was talking to the rearview mirror.

Chapter 27

In September of 1984, the roof fell in.

By then I was back at Buchbinder's as assistant manager, selling Cabbage Patch dolls and porcelain Michael Jackson figurines as fast as we could stock them. It was my idea to have the store wired for a stereo system and turn us into a Ticketron outlet. Mr. Buchbinder shrugged and put up with the thumping beat. Customers were clogging the aisles. 'Smut girl,' he shouted over the music one afternoon, squeezing my arm. 'You belonk in cullege.'

The roof fell in figuratively, not literally. Literally, it was the ceiling that gave way. My English 101 teacher down at Ocean Point Community College was the one who finally taught me the difference between 'literal' and 'figurative' – a simple concept, once you were ready for someone's explanation. English 101 was the first class I took. Though I kept pushing Mr. Buchbinder's tuition money back at him, it kept showing up in my coat pocket at the end of the work day.

He seemed to want my college education as bad as Ma had.

'Well, how was it?' Roberta asked me after my first night class.

'I'm quitting. That's how it was.'

She took the nail polish from the drawer and sat down in the chair next to me. I shook the bottle and uncapped it. 'Why?'

'Hot pink, hot pink,' I said. 'I'm sick of this color.'

'Why you quittin' after one night?'

'Because I hate it. I'm not cut out for it. First we had to sit around in a circle and tell people about ourselves.'

'What kind of stuff?'

'Jerky stuff. Like where we'd like to travel and why we were taking the class – what we hoped to get out of it. I was the last one he called on and by that time my whole throat was paralyzed.'

'Maybe you're right,' Roberta said. She was looking at her toes, flexing them. 'Next time I'll get red. Paint 'em up like a hooker.'

'. . . So I started to tell them about our trip to Canada and how we always mean to get back there and never do. But then I stopped halfway through. Everyone was looking at me funny.'

'First-night jitters,' Roberta said.

I put her foot in my lap and dipped the toenail brush. It always amazed me: the way she could let me touch her feet without screaming, the way anyone could.

'The teacher wants us to call him by his first name – as if he's our friend instead of someone who could flunk us.'

'You know what I would've said if I was there? I would've told 'em, "You name the place and I'll go there."'

I sucked my teeth. 'There's this punk-rock woman in the class with her head shaved up the back. Six or seven months pregnant, minimum. And this guy who's so huge, he couldn't even fit in the desks. He sat on the floor during the whole class. All I could think of was when I was so fat in high school. It was depressing.'

'You're going to let one fat guy chase you away?'

'He wasn't fat. Huge like a giant, I mean. I bet he's almost seven feet tall. The punk-rock woman said she's taking the class because she wants to write this science-fiction screenplay where astronauts get lost in space and by the time they get back, there's been a nuclear war. And everyone's primitive again and worshiping statues of Boy George . . . People are killing each other for meat and Boy George is god.'

Roberta threw her head back and laughed.

'I haven't done homework in over fifteen years and this

woman's writing a *screenplay*. She paints her toenails *black*'

'Black?' Roberta said. She looked down at her own feet, considering.

'Takes her shoes off during class, puts her feet all over the furniture. Had this bumper sticker stuck to the back of her jean jacket. "Is your washroom breeding Bolsheviks?" Whatever that means.'

Roberta's laugh turned into a cough. The brush wobbled. I put her foot back down on the floor and got her a glass of water.

'The stupid textbook cost me twenty-four ninety-five. If I keep taking courses at this rate, I'll be forty-two before I even graduate.'

'How old will you be by then if you *don't* graduate?'

'Easy for you to sit there and make jokes,' I snapped. '*You* didn't have to sit for an hour and fifteen minutes having to go to the bathroom. We have this essay due next week. "Write about an everyday task you perform and your emotional attachment to that task." What am I supposed to do – put down how wonderful it feels to make toast for breakfast? What a bang I get out of painting your toenails pink?'

Roberta didn't say anything. I could feel, rather than see, her smile. I lifted her foot off my lap and started up the stairs.

'Hey, I got three painted toenails and seven regular ones.'

'Yeah, well, life's a shit sandwich,' I said. 'Deal with it.'

The ceiling fell that night. Well, the next morning, actually – somewhere around three a.m. It sounded like guns at first. Caught in that place between dreams and waking, I thought, Oh my God! Someone's downstairs shooting Roberta! Then there was dust up my nose, more gunshot blasts, her voice yelling up the stairwell.

'Get me the hell out of here before I get clobbered!'

I put the stairway light on just in time to see another plaster chunk let go. It smashed on the floor near the bed, scattering in a thousand directions. I ducked-and-covered and ran in to get her up off the bed. Another slab fell. I felt like a soldier at war.

There were six home-repair companies listed in the phone book. From the hallway phone, I pleaded my case to wives and answering machines. Whenever they put me on hold, I eyed the exposed wooden slats where the plaster had let go, a kind of ceiling skeleton.

Mike of Mike's Home Repair gave free estimates. 'Nine hundred fifty dollars,' he said.

Roberta banged her walker against the floor. 'Jesus H. Christ! Why don't you just shove a gun in her ribs?'

'Okay, eight seventy-five, but no finish work. Take it or leave it.'

'Leave it!' Roberta shouted, at the exact second I mumbled, 'Take it.' She was the one he heard.

The guy from Superior Homes wanted $1,050. He told me he'd noticed on the way in that I needed a new roof, too – that if roofs had alarm systems, mine would be ringing.

'A new roof? How much would that cost?'

'El dinero grande.'

'How much in American money?' I said.

'Big bucks. I got this cousin who—'

'Aw, get outa here,' Roberta shouted.

Later that afternoon, she supervised while I stood on the top rung of the swaying stepladder and pulled out the sagging plaster chunks that threatened to fall next. We decided we'd live awhile with the holes.

It was Roberta's idea to approach Johnny Wu, the owner of China Paradise, about part-time jobs.

I sat across from her at the restaurant, stirring my vegetarian egg-drop soup and rolling my eyes. 'Look,' I said. 'I already have a job and go to night school. I don't have the time.'

'You can make the time,' she said. 'What you can't make is enough money for a new ceiling.' When Johnny passed by our table, she grabbed him by the tail of his tropical shirt. For someone with Parkinson's disease, she could manage a pretty quick snatch.

'You Chinese guys are smart cookies,' she told him. 'What's your slowest night of the week here?'

'Monday,' Johnny said. 'Why?'

'Because my brain's working overtime, that's why. Have a seat.' Her idea was for Johnny to declare every Monday 'Polish Night,' hiring her as the master of ceremonies and me as the disc jockey. 'You could give Polacks a ten-percent discount – check their driver's license if you didn't believe them. Half this town would turn out – especially if they heard *I* was here. Believe you me, we could throw a party!'

Johnny kept smiling and shaking his head no. 'This *Chinese* restaurant. Would ruin the . . .'

'. . . the ambience,' I said. My teacher had used that word in class that week; I'd looked it up.

'Okay then,' Roberta said, 'how about this? Her and me running a weekend delivery service for you.'

'What do you mean?'

'I mean people call in an order and we drive it out to them.'

'Roberta—' I said.

It was like I wasn't at the table. 'See, I'm a people-watcher, Johnny Boy. And every week I come in here and watch the same thing. People out there by the register, rushing in for their takeout in their sloppy clothes, afraid they're going to see someone they know. Or if their food ain't ready yet, they sit in them squashy little chairs by the coatrack, trying not to touch knees with the person sitting next to them. Home delivery. You're throwing away a goldmine. Ain't he, Dolores?'

Without waiting for my answer, Johnny reached in back of him and drew up a vacant chair. 'Keep going,' he said.

We worked Friday and Saturday nights till eleven, Sundays till six. Johnny got us a desk and a separate phone line and paid for the auto-body people to yank out the Biscayne's backseat and install a warming box. We paid for the CB radio ourselves; it helped us save on gas. Roberta said dispatching made her feel like she was back in show business. For her CB handle, she resurrected her old radio name.

'Polka Princess to Sweet'n'Sour. Got your ears on? Over.'

The jargon embarrassed me but she wouldn't answer if I just said, 'What do you want, Roberta?' and I couldn't afford stubbornness. The Biscayne was getting nine miles to the gallon.

'Ten-four, Princess. What gives? Over.'

'If y'ain't been out to Hillcrest yet, come back to Paradise for a pupu and an Eight Immortals Crossin' the Sea. Over.'

'I hear you, Princess. Over.'

'Now we can certainly understand the step-by-step process of your storm-window-washing system,' Roy told one of my classmates. By about the third class, it got easier to call him by his first name. He was sitting Indian-style on top of his desk, reading excerpts from some of the class's 'problem' papers. 'You see, the exposition is clear. But as yet, there's no emotional quality invested in this piece. There's no *feeling* there – none that I can detect, at any rate.'

The student handbook mentioned partial refunds for early withdrawals; I decided I'd quit as soon as we got to our eight forty-five break, hopefully before he got to my paper. But when the others got up and headed for the snack bar, the punk-rock woman – Allyson, her name was – said, 'Hey, feel this.'

'Excuse me?' I said.

'Quick. You'll miss it.' She lifted up her sweatshirt and put my hand on her belly. Something bulged out, poking me.

'Oh my God,' I said.

'First three months she had me puking my guts out. Now she's into gymnastics.'

'She?'

'Yeah, I'm ninety-nine percent positive. I'm naming her Isis. Like it?'

'Isis? Yeah, it's pretty.'

'My boyfriend's in a band. Wants to name her Cacophony, but I said uh-uh. "I'll name the ones I carry, and you name the

ones you carry," I told him.' A bump moved across her big belly
– a foot, clearly.

After break, Roy read aloud what he said were the two best
papers in class. The first one was mine. I'd written about
painting Roberta's toenails after all – about how holding down
those foot tremors in my hand as I worked gave me some sort
of power over her disease. In Roy's voice, the idea didn't sound
quite so stupid. The other paper belonged to the huge guy who
sat on the floor during class. 'My whole life used to throb like a
headache.' That was the first sentence. It told about how he
cured middle-of-the-night insomnia by tiptoeing into his son's
room and watching him sleep – how he regulated his own
breathing to his son's, how the son would kill him if he knew.

'Let's have a hand for Dolores and Thayer,' Roy suggested.
The applause rattled my heart. I couldn't look up, so I looked
over at Thayer.

He was hard to figure, sitting back there in his own outskirts,
those sequoia legs bent up at the knee. I snuck peeks for the rest
of that class and the next one, gradually noticing things about
him other than his size. His hair, for instance: a mopful of blond
curls so tight you could stack coins in them. His beard was
reddish brown. Going in and out of the classroom, he had to
duck to miss whacking his head. His step had a bounce; those
curls rose and fell as he walked.

'Thayer?' I said.

We were in the corridor on our way out to the parking lot.
Hearing his name spoken seemed to alarm him. 'I just wanted
to say I really liked your paper. The one Roy read last time.'

'Sounded pretty ridiculous next to yours,' he said. But his
face made me glad I'd risked the compliment.

'Can I tell you something? You should try sitting closer to the
rest of us. You miss a lot by sitting apart like that. It sets up
barriers.'

'How do *you* know?'

Heat rose to my face. 'I *don't* know. I just think it must. This
is my car.'

'You're really good at description,' he said. 'When Roy read your paper, I could practically feel her foot in my own lap.'

'You could?'

'Yeah. Which was a real turn-on because I have this foot fetish.'

I unlocked the Biscayne, got in, locked it again. He was talking at me through the glass. The trouble with those little squirt cans of Mace was that you had to rummage in your purse for them while the pervert waited. I rolled the window down a millimetre or two instead. 'What?'

'I said maybe you'd like to go out for a coffee sometime?'

I told him I was pretty busy.

'That was just a joke, you know. About me having a foot fetish. Actually I think feet are kind of ugly.'

'Oh.'

'I was just trying to be witty. Happens when I get nervous. Sorry.'

'How old is your kid?'

'How did you know I had a kid?'

'Your paper? You said you watch your kid sleep?'

'Oh, yeah, right. Thirteen – pain-in-the-butt age. Not that he wasn't always one. I notice you don't wear any wedding ring.'

I shoved my hands in my jacket pockets.

'I'm divorced,' he said. 'If you're wondering.'

I rolled my window down some more. 'The reason I know you miss a lot when you sit apart in class is because I used to do that. When I was in high school. At a table . . . Because I was fat.'

His laugh was one edgy note.

'Not that *you're* fat,' I said. 'You're big-boned. I was . . . well, I was obese. But anyway, I really liked your paper.'

I sat in the Biscayne with the motor racing and watched him walk away. My hands were sweaty on the steering wheel; I wasn't sure why I sat there and stared instead of just reaching down and getting out of neutral. He unlocked a van and got in; the whole vehicle leaned toward his weight.

He waved as he drove past me. 'Existential Drywall,' the van said. 'Responsible Work for Authentic Individuals.'

It would surprise you – the number of people who crave Chinese food on Christmas Eve. Roberta had had dizzy spells that day, so I was running the takeout service myself. Mr. Pucci's order was one of the last to come in – the Dinner for Four Special. I was nervous driving over there.

'Merry Christmas, Mr. Pucci,' I said. My tote box was brimming with brown bags. I shifted a little and almost dropped his entire order.

'Is that *Dolores*?' he said. 'Oh, my God, you're the *last* person – do you have time to come in for a drink?'

'Oh, well, not really. I don't want your stuff to get cold. Half a glass, maybe.'

The dining-room was set like something in a magazine. Men were talking and laughing down in the sunken living room. I followed Mr. Pucci out to the kitchen.

For a couple of quiet seconds, we just smiled and took each other in. 'How long have you been working at the restaurant?' he asked.

The cup of cider he gave me was warm and freckled with cinnamon. I told him about my divorce, night school, Roberta. 'Well,' I laughed, 'here's to the man on the moon.'

His eyes teared over and he shook his head. He looked older, old. 'To old friends,' he said.

One of the men called up, 'The smell of that food is torturing us, Fabio. When do we eat?'

I drained my cup. 'Is that Gary? I'd like to say hi to him,' I said. 'Wish him happy holidays.'

'Well – he's been sick. The flu.' I watched a nerve jump in his face. 'But all right. Come on. Sure.'

I nodded and smiled as he introduced me to his company – handsome Jordan Marsh – catalog men come to life in their beautiful cable sweaters and creased pants. The room was sweet with cologne.

'And you remember Gary?' Mr. Pucci said.

I struggled to control my face, to force my muscles to act normal. There was a quilt over his legs. He had become a skeleton.

He squinted up at me, 'Who is it, Fabio?'

'It's Dolores Price, honey. She was a student of mine.'

He stared without recognition.

'I barged in on you once,' I said. 'You two were going on a picnic. You gave me some cookies and played Billie Holiday on your jukebox.' I suddenly noticed the jukebox, pointed to it. 'There it is,' I said.

His shaking was wilder than Roberta's. 'Now I remember,' he said. 'The big fat girl.'

Mr. Pucci laughed and blushed. 'I'm sorry,' he said. 'He's not himself.'

Roberta was up when I got home. I flopped down on the water bed next to her and stared up at that collapsed ceiling. 'Now I wish we'd gotten a tree after all,' I said. 'No matter what it looks like in here.'

'I know what you need,' she said. 'You need your Christmas present.'

She opened hers from me first: a Chippendales calendar we'd sold down at Buchbinder's. We thumbed through the months, choosing our favorites, giggling together at the sexy men.

My present from her was wrapped in red foil and had cascades of curled white ribbon. 'It's so beautiful, I hate to open it,' I said.

'Red and white,' she said. 'Polack colors.'

Inside the box was a satin Chinese robe – orange blossoms falling on peacock blue.

'What the hell you crying for?' she said. 'Come on, now.'

I took it out of the box and it fell to its full length. 'It's just so beautiful. You rat! We agreed not to spend more than ten dollars apiece. Now I feel even cruddier.'

'Oh, go on,' she said. 'Johnny down at the restaurant got it for me from New York. Half-price.'

The robe slid coolly against my skin; we both stroked it.

I told her about Mr. Pucci's lover.

'If it's that stuff, it's catching, ain't it? The teacher must have it, too.'

'I feel scared,' I said.

'I'm sure you can't pick it up just by walking into their house.'

'Not scared of that. I'm just scared it's there – that it exists. I can't stop seeing him. He looked like a concentration-camp man.'

We held hands, tight.

'Roberta?' I said.

'Hmm?'

'Nothing. I'm just . . . I'm just glad you're here.'

Thayer Kitchen did the ceiling job for three and a quarter during our January semester break, moonlighting for a week's worth of evenings. Sometimes I'd watch from the doorway as he hammered and hefted Sheetrock or clunked around on his steel-spring stilts, whistling along with his Bog Seger and Springsteen tapes. During his break, he set the stove timer for fifteen minutes and flopped back on a kitchen chair. I sat with him, but he did most of the talking.

'You see, it's tricky enough now that he's gettin' hair under his arms and I'm noticing crusty underwear when I do the laundry. But him being half black on top of it makes it a little tougher. Hard on the kid, you know? Lately he's gone heavy-duty into his ethnic thing. Hangs out at the Y with the bros. Gets pissed off if I forget and call him Arthur instead of Jemal. Or Chilly J, I should say. That's his rapping name.'

'What about his mother? Isn't she around here?'

'Claudia? Lives down in D.C. He stays there for part of the summer – August, usually – but he hates it. Claims all the McDonald's in Washington water down their milkshakes, but I think he gets lonesome. Claudia's got a killer work schedule, so it's pretty much him and the VCR . . . I mean, we drive each other nuts, him and me, but we're tight. Chilly J. My man.'

'I'm divorced, too,' I said.

'Kids?'

I shook my head.

'Yeah, well, he must have been a big doofus.'

'Who?'

'The guy who let *you* get away.'

The comment took me off guard. It was several seconds before I heard the droning of the stove timer.

'You got a crush on that big drink of water who's fixing the ceiling, don't you?' Roberta said that night. She'd caught me humming 'Against the Wind' while I helped her into her pj's.

'Don't be ridiculous,' I said. 'What makes you think that?'

'Because all week you've been walking around here in a daze.'

'Paint fumes,' I said.

At the start of spring semester, I reduced my hours down at the store and signed up for two courses, Psychology 112 and Herstory: A Feminist Look at the Past. 'I don't really want to major in business, Mr. Buchbinder, so it's not fair to keep letting you pay for my courses,' I said, pushing back his second envelope of money.

'Don't force her if she doesn't want it,' Mrs. Buchbinder said.

'You keep out of this, Ida,' he scolded. 'This is business between the girl and me.'

I smiled at the word 'girl.' I was thirty-three.

Allyson was in my Herstory class, too. By then she had broken up with her boyfriend, thrown her Boy George screenplay into the wood stove, and given birth to Shiva, a ten-pound baby boy. I visited them one afternoon with a present, one of those snuggle sacks that lets the baby sleep against your chest while you carry on with your life. It cost $39.99, a splurge, but it was the only thing I felt like giving her. Allyson and I read the instructions and she tried it just before I left. 'Whoa, it feels primal,' she said. 'Third World or something.'

The only man in the Herstory class dropped out after the second week. Some nights, class turned into a kind of group-therapy seminar, though, personally, I kept my mouth shut. The more my classmates shared their stories and raised each other's consciousness, the more horrified I became with the marriage Dante and I had put together. I looked up 'existentialism' in the library. If I had the theory right, I was just as much to blame for my bad marriage as Dante had been. Roberta's your family, I told myself. She's all you need. Yours is an authentic life.

Thayer was taking word processing on Tuesday and Thursday nights. Sometimes we sat together in one of the student-lounge booths, but whenever he started talking about new movies or restaurants he'd heard about, I broke in with complaints about my busy schedule.

One evening I spoke out in class. I hadn't meant to; those women just drew me in. 'I think . . .' I said, 'I think . . . the secret is to just settle for the shape your life takes.' My voice hesitated a little but I kept talking; everyone seemed interested. 'Instead of, you know, always waiting and wishing for what *might* make you happy.'

'What might make you happy?' my professor asked.

The rest of the class took over. 'Prince Charming,' someone sighed.

'Small thighs.'

'My boyfriend finding my G spot.'

Allyson hooked her bare feet around the chair in front of her. 'Prince Charming locating my G spot between my thin thighs.'

All around me, women laughed and nodded.

'No thanks, Thayer, really,' I said.

'Any reason in particular?'

'I'm just not seeing anyone.' If he expected something in return because of the ceiling job, that was his problem, not mine. He should be existential about it.

All of which would have been fine if Allyson hadn't brought

Shiva to class one Tuesday night. She'd decorated the snuggle sack with studs and punk-rock buttons. I couldn't tell if the safety pins were decorative or practical. 'Psst,' she said. 'I've got cramps. Can you take him?'

The baby warmed the front of me. Watching that little vulnerable gap in his skull collapse and expand with each breath was a kind of hypnosis. The professor's voice blurred away.

'Why don't I just hold him for you until after the break,' I whispered to Allyson when she got back.

Thayer was in the lounge, eating a bowl of chilli. 'Well,' he said, smiling at the snuggle sack, 'I see you've become a marsupial.' He got me a soda and, when he returned, bent down and brushed his lips against the baby's head in the exact spot I couldn't stop watching. Allyson was at the jukebox, dancing wildly by herself.

The following week, my Herstory professor assigned me a research paper called 'The Biological Clocks of Baby Boomers: A Dilemma for the Eighties Feminist.' Well, 'assign' was the wrong word; I *chose* the topic from her list of possibilities.

In the library, I read article after article, stared at one downward-sloping graph after another once you hit age thirty-five. Down at the store, Mr. Buchbinder started featuring two new lines of clocks, cuckoo and digital. Allyson began wearing a series of see-through watches strapped to her arms, their inner workings exposed like X rays. The whole world seemed to be counting down my remaining childbearing time. Or at least I was. In the student lounge, I'd sometimes catch myself staring over at Thayer, sitting in the same booth where he always sat, directly beneath the big wall clock. But I told him no thanks to whatever he suggested: bowling, the stock-car races, a home-cooked meal.

'It's my size, isn't it?' he said.

'Of course it isn't. I just . . . I just don't have the time.'

Gary, Mr. Pucci's lover, died in March. I hadn't known his last name and I'd forgotten that he was a travel agent. Since the holidays I'd been watching the obituaries for their address.

I wasn't prepared to have it strike me with the force it did. The article mentioned his relatives, an award from the Chamber of Commerce, a 'lengthy illness.' Nothing about Mr. Pucci.

I told myself I was too busy to visit Mr. Pucci: two jobs, a research paper, midterms on their way. That 'pal' stuff he'd said at Grandma's wake – about us being connected by the moon walk – it was just his way of being nice. Comforting me.

But that was it: he'd comforted me.

I couldn't sleep. I tiptoed downstairs, hoping to regulate my breathing to Roberta's. But her snoring sounded like a chain saw. Back in bed, I told myself how rewarding it was to finally have a neat, predictable life, give or take a ceiling cave-in. Being in your mid-thirties brought benefits, I reminded myself. You began to *appreciate* tidiness, smallness, things in their place. This is the shape your life has taken, I said. Be existential. Go to sleep.

For the next three nights, I drove through Easterly's sleeping neighborhoods, burning up gas and listening to my humpback tapes. Each night, Mr. Pucci's upstairs light was on: a single rectangle of pain.

The weekend before my research paper was due, I sat at the kitchen table, index cards fanned out in front of me. Outside, the snow was coming down in fat chunky flakes. The doorbell rang. Roberta was off at jai alai.

'You Dolores?' the boy said. He was lanky and handsome, with smooth coffee skin. He had a sweatshirt hood pulled over his head and something menacing in the bag under his arm.

'My husband always shovels our walks for us,' I said. 'As a matter of fact, he's putting on his boots right now.' I pointed back inside the empty house.

From behind the bushes, a voice said, 'She's bluffing. Get going.'

It wasn't a weapon in the bag – or a snow shovel either; it was a boom box. Suddenly, Aretha Franklin was singing 'Freeway of Love' and Thayer was up on the porch. They began a father-and-son break dance.

The boy – I couldn't remember his name – whirled and spun and managed gymnastic flips all over the snow porch without slipping once. Thayer was a disaster, grunting and repeating – over and over – a single graceless maneuver. A miscalculation with one of his clompy workboots sent three of the railing spindles flying off the porch and into the snow.

'Hey!' I protested.

At the end of the song, the boy clicked off the tape and began snapping his fingers.

> *The name's Jemal*
> *And I'm the best*
> *I got fine ladies*
> *Hangin' off my chest*

'How old are you – twelve?' I said. 'Give me a break.'

Thayer had been staring at his son's hand, trying to get his own finger-snapping to catch up. 'Yeah, get to the point, doofus,' he said. He was still panting hard.

> *This here's Thayer*
> *He's sayin' a prayer*
> *You'll be his lady*
> *The deal ain't shady . . .*

'My term paper is due on Tuesday and . . .'

> *My man here's cool*
> *He ain't no fool*
> *Think about you all day*
> *Make him drool*

'All right,' I said. 'Once. I'll come for dinner once. *After* I get this paper written. And don't forget I'm a vegetarian.'

Thayer smiled goofily and snapped his fingers at me. 'Ain't she sweet? She don't eat meat.'

Jemal shook his head. 'He got it bad for you, mama. He a mess.'

I started closing the door. 'I'm not your mother,' I said, attempting a scowl. 'Fix the porch before you go.'

Back at the table, I couldn't stop smiling at my index cards.

I scared Mr. Pucci when I rang his doorbell in the middle of the night. I could read fear in his face – then recognition, curiosity.

'Dolores?' he said.

'I'm sorry it's so late,' I said. 'I brought you this.'

He reached out and took the African violet, staring and staring at it, turning it in his hands. Then the leaves and blossoms trembled. When he cried, I folded him up in my arms.

During the first of our night rides together, Mr. Pucci and I were mostly quiet. I turned the steering wheel with my left hand and held his hand with my right. We played the whale tapes, over and over. They soothed him, he said.

By the end of the second week, we had established a routine that either of us could trigger with a single telephone ring. He waited for me out on his front porch in a lawn chair, bundled up against the cold in his trench coat and tweed cap. The red dot of his burning cigarette was the first thing I'd see. 'Hi, pal,' he'd say. Then he'd close the door as quietly as he could and we'd be off.

Eventually he started talking – not about the way Gary died but about his beautiful singing voice, the loving way he had with plants, his knowledge of travel. I kept going over to his house, driving Mr. Pucci around in the dark, learning who he'd lost.

In the eighteen years they'd been together, he said, they'd split up only once – in 1982, the year they'd both turned fifty. The separation had lasted just long enough to bring the unknown virus home. Later, they'd worried about the disease,

Mr. Pucci said – but for their friends with wilder life-styles, not for themselves. They hadn't detected anything for over a year, until Gary's hacking cough refused to go away. 'It's amazing, though, Dolores,' he said. 'The more ugly his condition got, the more beautiful he became to me.'

I was afraid to ask Mr. Pucci about his own health, his own future. I didn't talk much at all. I listened. Listening to his life with Gary was like taking lessons in love.

For my dinner at Thayer's I wore my black blouse, black pants, and my blue Chinese robe. That afternoon I'd had my hair highlighted.

'Have fun on your big date, Blondie,' Roberta said.

'It's not a big date. It's a meal. And by the way, this hair wasn't my idea. The stylist talked me into it.'

'My mistake. Watch out for them paint fumes.'

I'd made him and his son chocolate-chip cookies. I got into the Biscayne and put the plate on the passenger's seat. Halfway there I looked at myself in the rearview mirror. You're driving toward a mistake, I started to tell myself. Dante seemed sweet at first, too. Dante drove a van. Learn from your mistakes! But my hair distracted me. It *had* come out nice. I looked pretty good – for me.

They lived in a duplex just past the caution light on Route Three. 'If you get as far as a car graveyard,' he'd said, 'you've missed us.'

I inched and spun the Biscayne's wheels up the steep dirt driveway he'd warned me about, dipping and lurching over the frozen ruts of mud. At the crest, I picked up a little speed, then braked hard just in time to avoid running over a turkey that ran in front of the car. The plate of cookies flew to the floor.

Just drive away, I advised myself. Instead, I picked up the cookies, brushed them off, and got out. That's when the turkey started chasing me – across the front yard and up the steps. It cornered me on the porch, lunging and pecking. I threw cookies at it and yelled for Thayer.

He came out in wet hair and a bathrobe, laughing.

'Get this goddamned thing away from me,' I said. It took another lunge; I beaned it on the head with a chocolate chip.

'Some vegetarian,' Thayer laughed. 'She won't hurt you. Will you, Barbara? Besides, you're early.'

'I am not. You said six.'

'I said six thirty. But that's okay.'

'You said six. I *know* you said six.'

He picked a cookie off the porch floor and bit into it. 'Not bad,' he said. 'A little stingy on the nuts.' He scooped up the turkey in one arm and held the door open with the other.

'Jemal's over at his friend's house in case you're wondering,' he called in from the bedroom while he dressed. 'This way, I can put all my *Playboy* moves on you in private.'

'Ha-ha,' I said.

From my seat on the couch, I surveyed the way he lived: stacks of paint cans, stacks of newspapers, an open bag of carmel popcorn on the television. A calico cat strolled into the room and stepped daintily into the litter box, staring at me while it squatted.

'Have any trouble getting here?' Thayer yelled in over the whir of his blow-dryer.

'No,' I called back. Already, my black pants were covered in cat fur. This is what your life would be like, I told myself. Clutter. Can't-win vacuuming. Always having to dump the litter box. 'Not until I ran into your Welcome Wagon lady, that is.'

'Who, Barbara? She's not ours. Just visits, wanders down from the farm up the road.'

The cat jumped into my lap, circled, flopped down. I scratched its throat and let the purring massage my fingers. The pants were already a lost cause.

Dinner was stir-fired tofu and vegetables over linguine and a bottle of red wine. Our conversation had gaps.

'So did you get your eyes tested?' I asked him. During break the week before he'd told me how he was having trouble reading the screen in his word-processing class.

'Yeah. I need bifocals. I didn't order any, though. The girl holding up the mirror was snapping her gum. I just kept trying on all these frames and getting more and more confused. It's weird, you know? One minute you're this cool young guy with a Camaro and your whole life ahead of you. The next you're some old farsighted fart sitting across from an 'optical consultant' who's young enough to be your daughter. How's the food?'

'Delicious,' I said. It was.

'You were probably expecting Spaghetti-O's, right? You'd love getting involved with me, no kidding. I'm full of surprises. Even marinated this tofu stuff in, uh . . . hold on a second.'

He lumbered into the kitchen in his stocking feet, then reappeared. 'Tahini sauce. So it won't taste so much like Styrofoam.'

'My ex-husband was a stir-fryer,' I said. 'Drove a van, too.'

'What kind?'

'Ford.'

'Mine's a Volkswagen. How tall was he?'

'How tall? Five ten and a half, five eleven. Why?'

'Well, all these coincidences. Just wanted to make sure we weren't the same person, you know?'

He washed the dishes and I dried. He beat me at Trivial Pursuit. At the car, I let him kiss me. Once.

After our second dinner together, we took a long walk on the dark back roads near his house and he volunteered his past. He'd met his ex-wife, he said, at her dorm in the early seventies when he was working for a contractor, doing a rewiring job. 'I was fresh out of Dogpatch and she was three years older. Introduced me to politics, dope, all that good stuff. I got so into the whole thing, I kind of forgot who my parents were until after we eloped. They wrote me back they just couldn't recognize a black daughter-in-law or a half-black grandson that got started out of holy wedlock. We were embarrassments, see. How long were you married?'

'Four years.'

'I was married nine and a half. If I wasn't an existentialist, it would be real tempting to keep blaming our divorce on my parents. Or the times. Reaganomics.'

'Reaganomics?'

'Here's what she wrote in the letter she left. She wrote, "It's not that I don't love you, but that I've somehow outgrown you. My life here has become pot-bound and it's just such an outrageously opportune time for black women with MBA's." And it was, too, I guess. She makes sixty-five thou a year. Got Jemal all financed for college. "Pot-bound." Like she was a spider plant or something.'

'It must have been hard when she left. What did you do?'

'Let's see. First thing I did was whack the shit out of the bathroom wall with a crowbar. Then I Sheetrocked it back up again before Jemal saw it. Memorized the pancake recipe by heart. Learned to iron. Jemal was in parochial school then. Used to get notes from the nuns about his sloppy uniforms . . . After a while we hit our stride, though, old Chilly J and me. Got us some therapy. And we both convinced Claud to drop her custody thing. That's about the time I started going to night school and became an existentialist. Life's absurd. Live authentically. Stop whining. Bam! I got *into* it.'

'It must be hard, though, raising him by yourself.'

'Sometimes. Right now we got this running battle about him getting braces. He tells me blacks just don't wear them – says I'm trying to turn him into a "straight-tooth vanilla wafer."'

'I went to parochial school,' I said.

'And you were fat.'

'And I was fat.'

'And what else?'

The night was moonless and cold. A clean cold, no wind. 'I got raped when I was thirteen years old,' I said.

He put his arm around me and waited, didn't speak.

I started with the night Jack Speight tickled my feet and took him through Ma's death, Gracewood, Dante, my life with

Roberta. I ended with my aching over Mr. Pucci and my aching for a baby.

At the car, at three a.m., I said, 'So now you know enough to go running in the opposite direction.'

He told me not to flatter myself, that I didn't scare him half as much as I thought I did. He asked when we could see each other again.

'Why?'

'Because the other day I kicked over a whole gallon of latex semi-gloss thinking about you. I'm lonely.'

'You've memorized your ex-wife's farewell letter,' I said.

'What letter?' he said. 'What ex-wife?'

Mr. Pucci began to talk about the AIDS, the way death had taken over Gary's life, their life together. By then he had begun inviting me in for herb tea and some of whatever I'd baked for him. His teakettle was the kind that seeped silent steam. Curling-edged snapshots of the two of them were taped all over the kitchen cabinets.

'Is it any easier now that it's over?' I asked.

He looked at me a moment, considering the question. 'It *isn't* over,' he said. 'I still need him so badly – a hundred times a day. The other day I was looking for something in the bedroom closet and got an unexpected whiff of him from one of his sweaters . . .' His face crumpled up but he fought off crying. 'The pain is almost physical, sometimes. I missed him so much that day that it gave me a bloody nose – just started bleeding for no reason. Hadn't had one of those since I was a kid.'

I took his hand, tracing a vein, my fingers warm from the teacup. 'Maybe it'll be better once you get back to work,' I said. 'You're good at what you do – all those screwed-up kids.'

He smiled. 'I'm not sure I can keep doing it – pump them up with my messages of hope. My belief in their promising futures . . . One night near the end – it was worse at night, for some reason – I got up to check on him. He wasn't in bed and I got so scared. And then I noticed the floor was cold, the whole house was. The back door was open and I found him in the yard. Walking in circles around the car . . . And I put my arm around him and led him back inside. "What the hell were you doing out there?" I said. "Don't do that to me ever again." I was angry at him; I mean, we lived in fear of his getting a cold or . . . He just sat in the chair, couldn't stop shivering, even with the blanket around him. He'd been out there in his bare feet, so susceptible, for God knows how long . . . And he looked up and said, clear as day, he said, "Nighttime is when it feeds on me, Fab. Listen. You can hear it." '

He cried then. Hard, strangled barks and snorts of pain, his face against the table, his arms a frame around his head.

When he was quieter, I walked down into the living room and over to their jukebox. My finger ran down the choices and I thought about how love was always the thing that did that – smashed into you, left you raw. The deeper you loved, the deeper it hurt.

> . . . *puttin' rain in my eyes*
> *tears in my dreams*
> *and rocks in my heart*

The music made him look up. He stared at her singing. 'Billie Holiday,' he said. 'AIDS wouldn't have surprised her, Dolores. "Typical," she would have said, "Par for the course." '

That was when I got the strength. 'Do you have it?'

He didn't answer until the end of the song. Then he smiled. 'I'm HIV positive.'

'That means . . . ?'

'It means it's in me, waiting. Deciding if it wants to bloom.'

The third date with Thayer was my idea. I had a plan. We had arranged it after class on Thursday. The long winter had cracked that day and a warm breeze had blown all afternoon. People were in shirtsleeves, tossing each other Frisbees in the mud. 'I'd like to bring you to the beach on Saturday,' I said. 'I'll get takeout from the restaurant and we can take a long walk. Pick you up around noon.'

'Orchestrating the whole thing, eh?' he laughed. 'I got a date with Arthur Fiedler.'

But by Saturday, the weather was cold again. Wind blasted along the shore, flinging prickly sand against our faces. The surf sounded mean; the beach was unwalkable.

I'd parked squarely in the middle of the empty thousand-car parking lot. The food out of the warming box was lukewarm. 'You know this song they're playing?' Thayer asked, nudging his chin toward the radio.

'It sounds familiar,' I said.

' "Life in the Fast Lane." The Eagles.' He sang along a little.

'Yeah. What about it?'

'First time I heard it, I couldn't get what they were saying. Thought they were singing "Flies in the Vaseline."'

I didn't smile.

'Yup, that's us. Life in the fast lane . . . So anyway, you seem a little off today. Something the matter?'

Looking straight ahead, I made my proposal. Waited.

'Well,' I said finally, 'I can see by your silence that I've made an idiot of myself.' I started the car.

'Hold on a second, will you? Shut this thing off. I just didn't see it coming, that's all. I've got to think about it.'

I cut the engine. 'All right,' I said. I got out of the car and walked the perimeter of the parking lot. Walked it a second time, faster. I got back in the car.

I knew what his answer was from the way he'd consolidated the takeout containers and put all our mess back in the foil bags. 'Just do me a favor and forget I mentioned it,' I said. 'Just block it out.'

'The thing is,' he said. 'I spent half a year trying to get you to go out with me and then – pow! – just like that, you want me to help you make a baby. I'm not sure you realize how hard it is, raising a kid by yourself. Sure it *sounds* romantic, but . . .'

'Oh, bullshit!' I said. 'This isn't some impulsive whim.' I started the car again, gave the engine a few revs.

'I mean . . . lend you my sperm? Takes a little getting used to.'

'Just forget it. Really. I'll take you home.'

'What's in it for me?' he said.

'I don't know. Free sex. You want popcorn afterward? A bank check?'

'Don't be a wiseass,' he said. 'I've got a right to ask about it. Then there's Jemal to consider. I mean, do I tell him about this or not? He'd have a brother or sister out there. Half, anyway.'

'No he won't. It was a bad idea. Just forget it.'

'See, I like the idea of giving you something you want so bad. And the sex part – that's got its appeal, too. But I don't know. I'm not sure I could do it.'

'No one's asking you to.'

'You've got to admit, it's pretty heavy-duty – fathering a kid you're not going to raise.'

'I just wish I kept my mouth shut.'

He turned on the radio, tapped his fingers against the seat, turned the radio off again. 'Okay, here's what I'll do. I'll think about it for a week. If you promise to think about something, too.'

'What?'

'Having a baby the regular way. Getting married.'

'Thanks anyway,' I said. 'It wouldn't work out.'

He brushed his hand against my wet cheek. I wanted so badly not to be crying.

'Why not?'

'It just wouldn't, that's all. It never works out. Don't love me.'

Flying sand scratched against the car. I blew my nose. I had the sensation we were parked there for the rest of our lives, that we'd erode before we drove away.

'You're overheating,' Thayer said.

'I'm perfectly calm. I just wish I hadn't even said anything, because now every time—'

'No, I mean your *car*'s overheating. Your radiator. We better get going.'

'Fine,' I said. 'Go.'

'You're driving,' he said.

Chapter 28

In October of 1985, I turned thirty-four years old and began to lay awake nights, listening, scared. Of falling ceilings, Roberta falling down the stairs, and of the dominoes that were beginning to fall, inevitably, against Mr. Pucci. That past summer, lesions had begun appearing at the corners of his mouth and his AIDS test had finally said it: the virus was full-blown against him.

I wanted Thayer's comfort but wouldn't let him know. 'Look,' I told him when he stopped me in the parking lot at school. 'You were right. It wasn't fair of me to ask.'

'That doesn't mean we can't still see each other.'

'For me it does,' I said. 'It's over.'

Mr. Pucci's sense of balance was the first thing that betrayed him. In November, a fall down the second-floor stairwell at Easterly High landed him in the hospital for six days.

While he was there, a medical transcriptionist recognized his name amidst her pile of work. She told the school board that she sympathized with Mr. Pucci and others like him, no matter what their life-style had brought down on them, but that her responsibility as a mother came first. Like it or not, she argued, he was unclean. For all anyone *really* knew about the disease, he could be infecting her sons – anyone's children – even with the things he touched at school, the air he breathed. She lost her job for having spoken out. Mr. Pucci chose not to fight for his.

'They have no right to treat you this way,' I told him. 'Don't be such a saint.'

But he was already tired, he said, and who knew what his condition would be like in six months? 'Besides, I'm just not a battler, Dolores. Fighting the physical side of it is going to be hard enough.'

He put his and Gary's place on the market but declined my invitation to come live with Roberta and me. One of his New York friends had extended a similar offer, he said, but once the condo was sold, he planned to move back to Massachusetts to be with his sister's family. Those nephews he'd kept displayed in the picture cube on his office desk had grown up and begun families. 'I'm a great-uncle,' he said. 'My sister wants me home.'

That year, I got to know his sister, Annette, and the nephews and their wives, and his circle of gay friends – Steve and Dennis, Ron and Robert (who also had the virus), Lefty from New York. In the hospital solarium, over coffee, over the phone – we formed a network, exchanging news about experimental drugs and observations about how, from week to week, he looked and felt. The gay men all fell in love with Roberta, encouraging her foul mouth and begging her for stories about the tattoo parlour and her stormy love life. 'My fellas' Roberta called them. They brought her perfume, dirty jokebooks, off-the-wall costume jewelry. The attention revived her. Whenever she knew they were coming over to the house, she insisted on getting out of her bathrobe and putting on her wig. 'Make me beautiful for my fellas, now,' she'd say as I applied lipstick to her pouting lips.

The hospital discharged Mr. Pucci on the Friday night before his birthday. Both he and Roberta had had a good week. We drove to his house with a birthday cake and a pot of spaghetti sauce. Lefty was in for the weekend and Annette was there; the party fell together spontaneously. Lefty and I were ordered back to the house for Roberta's old records. Back at Mr. Pucci's, we loaded the jukebox with polka music and Roberta was the Princess again, introducing the tunes, shouting encouragement to Dennis and Ted and Lefty as they pranced and hooted through one wild polka after another, reeling in circles around the sunken living room. Mr. Pucci, Annette, and I sat on the sidelines laughing and clapping.

'Well,' Roberta said, in the car on the way home. 'We had ourselves a party tonight. Didn't we?'

'You were wonderful,' I said.

'I was,' she agreed, cackling softly. 'I still got it in me.'

After several months on the market, the condo still hadn't sold. Mr. Pucci looked more tired and pale to me, and some days, in the middle of a visit, he'd turn weepy or bitter. He was anxious, he said, to pay off some of his hospital bills. He didn't feel right about moving to his sister's until he'd sold his and Gary's home – until that was finished business.

One morning, delayed at the store, I arrived late to take him to his doctor's appointment. I got to the house at the same time as the taxi he'd called. 'You took your own sweet time getting here,' he told me, then walked toward the cab. 'Must be nice to have all the time in the world.'

That evening he apologized, over and over, sobbing into the phone.

'Forget it. It's no big deal. What did the doctor say?'

'I have to go for more tests. He thinks the blurriness might be CMV.'

'The eye infection.'

'Yeah. I might be going blind.'

On the Saturday morning of the real-estate woman's open house, I went to pick him up; I was driving him up to his sister's for the weekend.

'He's somewhere around here,' the agent said. She was fiddling with a huge coffee maker. Pastries and brochures were stacked on the table.

I found him in the bedroom, wet-eyed, clutching a handful of the kitchen cabinet snapshots of him and Gary. Their framed living room poster – Nureyev in mid-leap – was propped up against the bed.

'I'm all right,' he said. 'She just overwhelmed me for a minute, the way she started taking things off the walls and out of the bookshelves. "If they smell gay, they'll think AIDS," she said. "And if they think AIDS, then we're dead."'

'Come on,' I said. 'Let's get out of here.'

'Yeah, okay. Slide this thing under the bed first, will you?'

As I helped him out the front door, the woman's high heels clicked after us. 'I hope I didn't offend you, Fabian,' she said.

'His name is Fabio.'

'Fabio – sorry. These open houses make me a nervous wreck. But business is business; we don't want to turn off Mr. and Mrs. America.'

'That's all right,' he mumbled.

'Hey, hold on a minute. Before you two go . . .' She disappeared around the corner and came back with the insides of the coffee maker – a wide basket mounted on a long metal tube. 'Anyone know what I'm supposed to do with this?'

'I have an idea,' I said. 'Why don't you shove it up your ass?'

We were in the car and onto the turnpike before he broke the silence with a belly laugh.

'What's so funny?' I said.

'*You!* You sounded like your old self back there.'

'Yeah, well, I let her out occasionally. She's on call for the truly deserving.'

He reached for me. 'My pal,' he whispered. 'I love you, Dolores.'

It was the first time I cried in front of him. I was laughing and crying, both – so hard I had to pull over. The two of us, parked crooked in the breakdown lane with the emergency blinker on, laughing and crying like fools. 'I love you, too,' was the first thing I was able to say.

'Oh, man,' Thayer said. 'I love you.'

We were naked together in the water bed. I was rereading *The Old Man and the Sea* for my new class, American Lit, underlining the parts I suspected were symbolic. Thayer was just staring at me, smiling goofily.

'Don't get sentimental,' I said, without looking up from the page. 'You just enjoy the sex.'

'This isn't sex, it's science. We're practically doing it with white lab coats on.'

'You're not a scientist,' I said. 'You're a hurricane at sea.'

'Yeah, well you should talk. Or was that *scientific* groaning?'

It was our third try. Well, our fourth, really, but the second time in August had had more to do with a heat wave and some beers than my monthly ovulation. This was our third crack at procreating.

'You know what let's do?' Thayer said. 'Let's just get married.'

I looked up from my reading. 'You agreed to no strings. That covers chains, too. What time did you say we had to pick them up?'

'Them' was Roberta and Jemal. This was their third bus trip to the jai-alai arena in Newport; Jemal wheeled Roberta's chair and she made his bets. Against all odds, they'd become friends.

'Five-thirty. Chilly's going to call us from the bus station.' He free-fell back down on the water bed and smiled up at his ceiling job.

'God, I do good work,' he said. 'I'd say I'm more of an artist that a drywall man, wouldn't you?'

'A bullshit artist maybe.'

His hand on my breast was as big as a catcher's mitt; his palm was rough and ragged but the touch was gentle.

'So what do you think?' he said.

'What do I think about what?'

'Think any little fishes are swimming upstream and jumpin' in the old gene pool?'

I reached down and jabbed his butt with the corner of my paperback.

'Maybe we should give it another shot. You know, a backup.'

'Thayer,' I said. 'I've read the same paragraph eleven times now. I have a test on this book Wednesday night.'

He rolled to the side of the bed and climbed out. Hopping around on one foot, he pulled on his underwear. 'No shit, you'd love being married to me. We'd have a blast. I'm nothing like D.D.'

Which was short for Dante the Dork. In the three months we'd been procreating, Thayer had tried hard to shrink Dante for me, turn him into a kind of cartoon.

'Yup,' he said, 'that's my best advice. Marry me while you got the chance. I'm a good catch.'

I waved *The Old Man and the Sea* at him. 'Good catches are a mixed blessing,' I said.

'Because, to tell you the truth, this arrangement we got is starting to get a little weird for me. Eating away at my existential soul.'

From the corner of my eye I saw him pull his pants on, yank his T-shirt over his head. I was underlining my book. 'Uh-huh,' I said.

He clapped his hands together. 'Hey, Dolores! I'm serious.'

I looked up. He was.

'I mean, I've been sleeping shitty. I get up in the middle of the night missing you. You know, *needing* you – more than just once a month. More than just for sex . . . And then I start thinking to myself, Well, what if she's just using you? Or what if one of these times it *does* take and we *do* make this kid? Where does that leave me, Dolores? I mean, shit, it boils down to an irresponsible act on my part when you get down to it.'

'But you told me . . . You came over to this house and said—'

'Yeah, but the thing is, I *love* little babies. If we make one, I know I'm going to want to hold it. Play with its little fingers. Be its dad.'

I got off the bed and grabbed my bathrobe. 'Okay, fine,' I said. 'We won't do it anymore.'

'What—? I can't tell you how I feel without you getting pissed off?'

'Of course you can tell me how you feel. I just wish you'd let me know before . . .'

'Why *can't* we just get married and make a baby like everyone else does? What are you so afraid of?'

'I'm not afraid.'

'Then what are you?'

'Look!' I said. 'My father used to beat up my mother! I had a husband who put me through the meat grinder and now one of my best friends has AIDS! I just don't believe in happily-ever-after. It's a crock of shit!'

'I *know* it's a crock of shit. I ain't offering you happily-ever-after. I'm offering you . . . happily-maybe-sometimes-ever-after. Sort of. You know, with warts and shit.'

I clamped by hands over my ears. 'Stop it! My whole life still hurts!' It came out as a scream.

When he spoke, his voice was soft again. 'This wouldn't *be* your marriage to him. This would be *our* marriage – yours and mine.'

'And Jemal and Roberta's,' I said. 'And a baby's. You're not being realistic.'

'So what *is* realistic? Screwing me once a month with the thermometer in your mouth?'

I started making up the bed, snapping the sheets. 'Well, you don't have to worry about that anymore. It was a mistake and now it's over.'

'Meaning what? What's over?'

I didn't answer him.

'Don't I at least get a response? What the hell's happening here?'

I still didn't answer.

'All right,' he said. 'Great. Time for me to rock'n'roll.' His keys twirled around his finger. 'I'll drop Roberta off. Have a good life.'

For the next few weeks, Roberta started at me, sucking angrily at her cigarettes. 'You look like death warmed over,' she said. 'Call him.'

'I don't want to talk to him,' I said. 'Mind your own business.'

Convinced I was pregnant, I bought a home test kit and set it up in the attic, tiptoed up the stairs the next morning with my jar of urine. The results were less reliable during the initial weeks, the box admitted. It was probably a hundred degrees up in that attic. A thousand factors could have made the test negative. That night in a dream, I gave birth to an Amazon daughter and woke up laughing, positive I was pregnant. Then I reached down in the dark and felt it: the blood, sticky between my legs.

'They don't want to discharge him,' Mr. Pucci's sister told me over the phone. 'He's been asking for you.'

'How is he?'

She told me he'd been listless all that week and that the fungus growing inside his mouth made it harder and harder for him to swallow. To her, the coughing sounded deeper, too. 'I know you're busy. Come if you can,' she said.

I bought Mr. Pucci a big, lacy valentine and was on my way. It was my sixth trip to West Springfield in the half year since he'd moved there.

Actually, I *wasn't* that busy anymore. I'd put my college classes on hold and resigned from the takeout delivery business. Allyson and Shiva were living upstairs in the Speights' old apartment. We'd put together an arrangement: instead of paying rent, Allyson helped me with Roberta and let me borrow Shiva when I needed to. I baby-sat on the nights she had classes. He was a placid, smiling little boy. We were trying to keep him television- and sugar-free.

Allyson saw Thayer at school; he kept telling her to say hi to me. 'If it helps,' she said, 'his new girlfriend looks like a ferret.'

'What do you mean "if it helps"? What do I care what she looks like?'

*

I could tell he was dying – knew as soon as I saw him why Annette had called. I tacked the valentine to his corkboard and rearranged his cocoon of blankets. Though the effort was visible, he insisted he wanted to talk.

About me.

'At least see the guy,' he urged. 'Clear the air.'

'Roberta's been bothering you about all this, hasn't she? With all you're going through, you shouldn't have to—'

'Marry the guy,' he said.

'You don't understand. It's not as simple as that.'

'Why isn't it? What's so complicated about it?'

'It's freezing out today. The windchill factor's below zero.'

'I know I'm being pushy, pal . . . I just don't have the luxury of waiting to see how it all comes out.'

'Here,' I said. 'Drink some of your juice. I'm putting the straw to your lips.'

'Don't fight me, Dolores, okay?' he said. 'I'm tired and I have something to say and . . . you're making it harder.' His eyes looked out at nothing as he spoke. The chart said his weight was ninety-three pounds.

People had always amazed him, he began, but they amazed him more since the sickness. For as long as the two of them had been together, he said, Gary's mother had accepted him as her son's lover, had given them her blessing. Then, at the funeral, she'd barely acknowledged him. Later, when she drove to the house to retrieve some personal things, she'd hunted through her son's drawers with plastic bags twist-tied around her wrists.

'. . . And yet,' he whispered. 'The janitor at school – remember him? Mr. Feeney? – he'd openly disapproved of me for nineteen years. One of the nastiest people I knew. Then, when the news about me got out, after I resigned, he started showing up at the front door every Sunday with a coffee milkshake. In his church clothes, with his wife waiting out in the car. People have sent me hate mail, condoms, Xeroxed prayers . . .'

What made him most anxious, he told me, was not the big

questions – the mercilessness of fate, the possibility of heaven. He was too exhausted, he said, to wrestle with those. But he'd become impatient with the way people wasted their lives, squandered their chances like paychecks.

I sat on the bed, massaging his temples, pretending that just the right rubbing might draw out the disease. In the mirror I watched us both – Mr. Pucci, frail and wasted, a talking dead man. And myself with a surgical mask over my mouth, to protect *him* from *me*.

'The irony,' he said, '. . . is that now that I'm this blind man, it's clearer to me now than it's ever been before. What's that line? "Was blind but now I see . . ."' He stopped and put his lips to the plastic straw. Juice went halfway up the shaft, then back down again. He motioned the drink away. 'You accused me of being a saint a while back, pal, but you were wrong. Gary and I were no different. We fought . . . said terrible things to each other. Spent one whole weekend not speaking to each other because of a messed-up phone message. . . . That time we separated was my idea. I thought, well, I'm fifty years old and there might be someone else out there. People waste their happiness – that's what makes me sad. Everyone's so scared to be happy.'

'I know what you mean,' I said.

His eyes opened wider. For a second he seemed to see me. 'No you don't,' he said. 'You mustn't. He keeps wanting to give you his love, a gift out and out, and you dismiss it. Shrug it off because you're afraid.'

'I'm not afraid. It's more like . . .' I watched myself in the mirror above the sink. The mask was suddenly a gag. I listened.

'I'll give you what I learned from all this,' he said. 'Accept what people offer. Drink their milkshakes. Take their love.'

The storage company delivered the jukebox six months after his death, on a sunless afternoon in November 1987. The accompanying note read: 'For my pal.'

At the back of my bedroom closet, on a high shelf, I found

what I'd gone looking for: my old 45s. On the stairway landing on the way back down, I stopped and studied the old familiar faces: Uncle Eddie, Ma and Geneva, Grandma on her wedding day. I stood the longest before the small framed remnant of Ma's flying-leg painting, then reached out to touch it: wingtip and sky. I passed my fingers lightly against the surface.

I filled the jukebox with the old records. Then I plugged it in and sat in the darkening room, bathed in the machine's purple glow.

Thayer came when I called him. He was wearing his new eyeglasses, wire-rim bifocals. Something about the way he looked jarred me. I couldn't stop staring.

'They make me look old, don't they?' he said. 'Be honest.'

'They make you look cute. Play me a song.'

'What should I play?' he said. 'Nothing's marked.'

'Play anything.'

He punched at the keys. Looking both at the glass and through it, we saw ourselves and, beneath ourselves, the player gliding, searching.

'Take love . . .' I said.

'What?'

'Nothing. Hold me.'

With my head against his chest, my eyelids closed against his sweatshirt, I saw him. Recognized him. Part man, part whale.

'I made a picture of you once,' I said. 'Years ago, way before I ever even knew you. Your wire rims and everything.'

'You did?'

'On my Etch-a-Sketch. A psychic told me to draw what would make me happy and I drew you. Memorized you before I shook you free.'

He pressed me closer to him. 'So what's that mean?' he said.

'It means I love you. I'm proposing.'

'Proposing what?'

'You and me. Marriage.'

I looked up, saw the tears in his eyes. 'Okay,' he said. 'Yes.'

Chapter 29

'Have you ever noticed,' Thayer asks me, 'that we always take the same chairs when we're in this office? That we never switch seats?'

I give him a quick nod, a half smile. My arms are strapped around myself, straitjacket style. You're not pregnant, I tell myself. But it's a tactic. If I think I'm pregnant, I won't be; if I think I'm not, I'll be surprised. I'm not sure who I'm trying to fool.

'What color is this, anyway?'

'What?'

'These chairs. The curtains.'

'Oh,' I say. 'Mauve.'

'They just redid the McDonald's out in Warwick this color. And that dentist's office I renovated. Mauve.' This is one of the patterns of our three-year-old marriage: when we're both nervous, I straitjacket myself and Thayer talks about nothing. 'Half the walls I paint these days. It's – what's the word that means something's everywhere?'

'Ubiquitous?'

'Yeah, that's it. Mauve. It's u-frickin'-biquitous.'

'I hate this waiting,' I say. 'I wish he'd get here so we'd know.'

He reaches over, rubs tension out of my shoulder. 'Take it easy,' he says. 'If it happens, it happens. If it doesn't, well . . .'

'I think I read somewhere that it's psychological.'

'What is?'

'The way they use mauve. It's got a numbing quality. Dulls

your resistance or something. So that you'll buy another Big Mac.'

Dr. Bulanhagui's voice is outside the door; then the door opens, closes with a hushing sound against the carpet. He hangs up his sports coat and puts on his white lab coat, pulling at the sleeves. The manila folder he's carrying has our life in it.

He says it as soon as he sits down. 'I'm sorry. The procedure was not successful.'

I don't listen to his explanation of estrogen levels and cell life. Six eggs, six deaths. Everything's mauve: I'm numb.

'Well what about the other ones?' Thayer says. 'Those eggs you froze?' His voice is thin with disappointment. Somewhere during our second year of trying, Thayer caught my obsession.

Dr. Bulanhagui smiles and apologizes. He tells us now isn't the time to make a decision about trying the procedure again. But we've made that decision already, weeks ago. Our savings account made it for us.

Back in the car, we buckle our seat belts at the exact same second, so that I hear only one click, not two. We both look straight ahead.

Thayer starts the engine, then flops his head back against the headrest, blows out air. 'You know what we need?' he says. 'We need a vacation.'

I remind him we can't afford a vacation. We've just taken a four-thousand-dollar medical gamble. Four thousand dollars down the tubes.

'Who gives a shit about the money?' he says. 'You want to try again, we'll try again.'

I shake my head no. 'I just need home,' I say. 'Take me home.'

When we pull into the alley, Jemal stops dribbling. He's wearing shorts I don't recognize – baggy knee-length jobs with dinosaurs in blinding colors. He holds the basketball against his shoulder bone. His look asks the question.

'Nope,' Thayer says.

'Shhheee-it,' Jemal says, stretching out the curse for full use. The ball smashes against the blacktop and flies high over his head, clattering the rain gutter.

Inside there's the smell of coffee. Here's what's on the kitchen counter: a stack of mail, Mrs. Buchbinder's Saran-wrapped kugel, and the Styrofoam head that holds Roberta's wig. Laundry is clicking and tossing in the dryer. The chaos I've been visualizing all week in the hospital evaporates.

Roberta is in the front room, napping on the water bed. The radio is next to her, on the seat of her wheelchair, broadcasting a baseball game. She'll wake up mad she's missed it; late in life, she's become a Red Sox zealot. The cat's sleeping, too, draped across Roberta's hip. Outside, clouds shift and sudden afternoon sun illuminates the cat and half of Roberta's face. On the radio, I hear the crack of the bat, the crowd's roar, the announcer's unchecked joy.

Thayer places my suitcase on the floor next to me and curves his arms into huge, inviting brackets. We stand there, watching Roberta, studying her nap. 'Kind of cute when she's sleeping, isn't she?' he whispers.

In the car on the way there, he's too quiet and respectful; it's creepy. 'Say something!' I command.

'What?'

'Anything.'

'This car has good shock absorbers.'

Against all my protests about duty and finances, Allyson and Jemal are taking shifts with Roberta for the next three days while Thayer and I are on vacation. 'How am I supposed to know what to pack if you won't even tell me where we're going?' I complained the night before.

'Pack everything,' he said. 'Little of this, little of that.'

Thayer turns on the radio news. A poll says the women Americans most respect are Oprah Winfrey, Nancy Reagan, Mother Teresa, and Cher. The royal couple may be separating. In a Florida town, neighbors have firebombed the home of a family down with AIDS.

I know it now, accept it: I'll never give birth. I pull out my

journal from under the bucket seat; I started it at the hospital
six days earlier, as I lay in my hospital bed thinking about my
life and waiting for the fertilized eggs to cleave. I uncap the Bic,
meaning to rail about negatives: unfairness, infertility. But
something different comes out, something I hadn't planned. I
write: *Love is like breathing. You take it in and let it out.*

The highway's dips and rises sway my handwriting across the
page so that the penmanship both is and isn't mine. He was
right – we do need this trip. A shock absorber.

Now there's a string of oldies from the sixties and seventies.
Each song carries faces with it – Ma, Dante, Dottie, the Pysyk
twins – and I think how strange it is I've ended up with this life,
this six-foot-eight-inch husband and his mystery trip. Interstate
95 can lead anywhere. 'Niagara Falls, right?' I say. 'Some corny
honeymoon suite with a hot tub?' But Thayer only smiles.

Traffic up ahead slows, crawls, then stops altogether. The
bald-headed businessman in the lane next to us has air-
conditioning and rolled up windows. His white shirt cuff looks
as crisp and clean as the Communion wafers priests used to
place on my tongue.

'She's Come Undone,' Thayer says, turning up the radio. He
sings along with the record.

> *She didn't know what she was headed for*
> *And when she found what she was headed for . . .*

'Hey, look!' I tell Thayer. The businessman is tuned to the
same station – is singing along, too. You can read his lips.

'Harmony,' Thayer says. 'How 'bout that?' He honks the
horn and the man looks over, laughs. The two of them lip-sync
to each other. Or to me, the person between them.

'*Undone*,' I write in the journal – stare at that word, turn it
over. Jack Speight undid me, then I almost undid myself. But
I've undone some of the bad, too, some of the damage. With
help. With luck and love . . .

We inch closer to the green highway sign, close enough so

that I can squint and read it. 'Cape Cod and East.'

'We're going to the Cape?'

He nods and smiles. 'Certain old broad we know says you always wanted to see a whale in action. I'm taking us on a whale watch.'

He springs for The Seaview Inn – cable TV, stereo radio, a restaurant with twenty-five-dollar entrées. 'Cup of coffee?' I call in to Thayer above the shower's hiss. We've got Mr. Coffees, too – built into our wall.

His head pushes out through the shower fog. 'Nah, keep me up all night. We gotta be on board that boat by eight a.m.'

In bed with his wet curly hair, he aims the remote control at the TV and deadens the set. Gently, he takes off his wire-rim glasses and slips out of his underpants. 'Well,' he says, 'how you doin'?'

My hand finds his. 'A little low. Not wiped out. How are *you* doing?'

'Me? I don't know – ache a little, I guess. It's tough after years of this to just say, "Okay, we give up. We quit."'

'Thanks for this trip.'

He smiles and kisses me. 'Thanks for asking me how I'm doing.' His hand slides under my nightgown, up my leg. 'So what do you think?' he says. 'Red light? Green light?'

'I guess yellow light,' I tell him. 'Proceed with caution.'

He was smart about the coffee. My nerves are jangled; I can't sleep.

I get out of bed and put the TV on low, channel-flipping. I don't really see what's on; I see Ma's puffed-out face the second she cut the cord on my big console TV. She turns toward me – toward my old fat self – with that steak knife in her hand. Ma, in her best and strongest moment.

One of the public TV stations is showing the movie *Woodstock*. Woodstock: old enough to be a late movie!

Back on the bed, Thayer sighs, deep in his sleep. On the

screen, John Sebastian in raggedy tie-dye is singing about a dream.

The cameras pan the crowd and there, for one quick second, I see them, unmistakably. Larry and Ruth and Tia. They've made it. They're there!

In the morning, the sky is dark and we've both overslept. On the rushed ride to the pier, Thayer denies the rain, resists putting on the wipers against the dribble. He's too distracted to listen to what I saw on TV last night. Lightning cuts the sky.

'Look,' I tell him, 'maybe we just shouldn't go. That fancy hotel is plenty. I don't need to see a whale.'

He waits for the thunder to finish. 'We're going,' he says.

Inside the cabin, an hour and a half out into open sea, a hundred of us huddle on benches. The air smells of wet hair and wet sweatshirts and some seasick woman's vomit; hard rain pelts the top of the ocean.

Thayer holds me against him. We've both dressed too lightly; we're freezing. 'Disappointed?' he asks.

'Yeah . . . It's okay.'

The marine biologist clicks on her microphone and offers theories on why we've seen no whales. She says the snack bar will be open during the trip back to port, which will be starting in ten minutes. 'For your convenience, beer and cocktails—'

I feel the rumble of the boat's engines in my legs and stomach. 'The rain stopped,' I tell Thayer. 'I think I'll go out back for a minute.'

'It's cold out there,' he says.

'I'm fidgety. I can't stand just sitting.'

'Want company?'

'No, thanks.'

Up in the lookout, the young crew members in their orange rain ponchos are laughing. Their binoculars rock back and forth against their chests. I can't look at their happy indifference.

But I think this: that whatever prices I've paid, whatever

sorrows I shoulder, well, I have blessings, too. Not just my family now, but the others – the ones who have died: Ma and Grandma, Mr. Pucci, Vita Marie. They're with me still. They're here . . .

Just beyond the boat, the gray ocean turns green. Effervesces – a twenty-foot circle of bubbles.

I'm the closest one to it; the crew doesn't see.

Then the water darkens back to normal and, though it's quiet, something is happening – something private only *I* can feel. I look quickly through the rain-dribbled window for Thayer, but I don't have time to get him. I'm trembling. I can't afford to look away.

She breaches.

Nose first, her grooved body heads straight for the sky. Her muscular tail clears the water, her fins are black wings. The fall back is slower – grace instead of power. She cracks the ocean and, in a white expansion of foam, reenters.

I've seen her, swimming and flying both. I'm soaked in her spray. Christened. I laugh and cry and lick my salty lips.

People run from the cabin now, pushing past me, hooting and aiming their cameras and beer bottles at the afterimage. Thayer's head is above the crowd. He's shouting for me. I'm shouting, too, shoving back against the others toward him.

'Thayer, I saw her!' I yell. 'I saw!'

About the author

I was born in a blue-collar Connecticut town in 1950, the youngest of three children. My mother was a homemaker and my father worked for the local utility company. As a child, I wasn't particularly interested in reading or writing, but I drew constantly. My speciality was comic books and it was in the making of these that I taught myself the rudiments of plot, character and dialogue. Our neighbourhood was ruled mostly by girls: my two older sisters, a household of female cousins down the street, and other assorted characters such as our neighbour, Peggy, who was famous for having branded her own stomach one afternoon by ironing clothes in a midriff blouse, and Kathy, who one summer day hula-hooped non-stop from 7.00 a.m. to 10.00 p.m. It was in this environment, perhaps, that I honed my powers of observation of the opposite gender.

I graduated from the University of Connecticut's School of Education in 1972 and became, in this order, a high school English teacher, a husband, a father, and a fiction writer. I wrote my first short story at the age of thirty, the same summer our first child was born. For reasons I can't fully explain, fatherhood and fiction-writing have gone hand in hand for me ever since. Although I usually write in the first person, I feel quite parental toward my troubled characters. I worry about them and never quite feel in control of their lives.

She's Come Undone began as a short story. I showed fifteen or twenty pages to my mentor, Gladys Swan, who advised me that I had 'a few too many pots on the stove' and I might be trying to tell myself that I wanted to write a novel. I almost abandoned the book a couple of times along the way but kept returning to it because I wanted to find out what was going to happen to that troubled soul I had engendered and then grown to love and worry over. I finished Dolores Price's story nine years after I'd begun it. The character had taken me on a wild roller coaster ride with any number of unexpected dips, swerves, and lurches and I emerged from that long process a little the worse for wear but with a better understanding of women. I owe a great deal to the women who gave me the gift of their feedback along the way, particularly my wife and women in the writers' group of which I'm a member. If the story reads credibly, it's partially because I'm a good listener (and an incessant reviser).

My wife and I have three sons, two cats, two dogs, and innumerable blessings. Currently I am finishing a two-year professorship at my alma mater, the University of Connecticut, and will soon run a series of writing workshops at a local women's prison. My teaching and writing are equally important to me.

I write because I am both hopeful and afraid and because I am the father of children: my own, and the students who are my borrowed children, and the children who are born out of my imagination. I write because I wish to better understand the world and its pain and promise – to get at a more universal truth by bending and stretching the factual truth into something called fiction.

Sometimes voices other than my own talk inside my head and I recognise these as gifts – personal challenges – and I listen and follow. Much like my characters and the books they inhabit, I, too, am a work in progress.

WALLY LAMB